THE PHANTOM
LOVER

and OTHER THRILLING
TALES OF THAILAND

JIM ALGIE

TUTTLE Publishing
Tokyo | Rutland, Vermont | Singapore

Published by Tuttle Publishing, an
imprint of Periplus Editions (HK) Ltd.

www.tuttlepublishing.com

"The Death Kiss of a King Cobra Show"
was originally published in the Bram
Stoker Award-Winning American
anthology *Extremes 2: Fantasy and Horror from the Ends of the Earth* in 2001.

"Wet Nightmares," under the original title
"Fucked Over," was the second prizewinner in the Chiaroscuro webzine's annual
short-fiction contest in 2002. It was
reprinted under the new title in the 2013
anthology *Crime Scene Asia*.

"Flashpoints in Asia" was originally
published in the ezine *Read in the Dark*
and longlisted for a World Fantasy
Award in 2004.

"The Legendary Nobody" was published
in the *Dark Dreams* ezine in 2008.

**Library of Congress Cataloging-in-Publication Data for this title is in
progress.**

ISBN 978-0-8048-4388-1

Distributed by

**North America, Latin America
& Europe**
Tuttle Publishing
364 Innovation Drive
North Clarendon
VT 05759-9436 U.S.A.
Tel: 1 (802) 773-8930
Fax: 1 (802) 773-6993
info@tuttlepublishing.com
www.tuttlepublishing.com

Asia Pacific
Berkeley Books Pte. Ltd.
61 Tai Seng Avenue #02-12
Singapore 534167
Tel: (65) 6280-1330
Fax: (65) 6280-6290
inquiries@periplus.com.sg
www.periplus.com

16 15 14 13
10 9 8 7 6 5 4 3 2 1
1309MP

Printed in Singapore

TUTTLE PUBLISHING® is a
registered trademark of Tuttle
Publishing, a division of Periplus
Editions (HK) Ltd.

CONTENTS

For the ghost of my hell-raising, harness-racing, horn-playing soldier of a non-father: Edward Algie (1928-1992)

SHOUT OUTS

Special thanks to Eric Oey, the president of Tuttle, Terri Jadick my ever-helpful editor, the "product evangelist" Steve Jadick, Gail Tok and Michelle Tan in the marketing department, Greg Lowe, agent and advisor extraordinaire from the Watchman Agency, and the blurb writers John Burdett and Christopher Moore.

Certain stories are dedicated to different allies. Let those stand as tokens of gratitude. I'm also thankful to the Algie brood (Patricia, Richard, Anita and Ryan), Ellen Boonstra, Bee, Ooh Mukdavijit, Penny Pattison, Brian Zelnicker, Michael Hirsch, Bill Hammerton, Ben Hopkins, Liz Smailes, Rich Baker, Evan C. Jones, J.D. Villines, the merry pranksters from Farang Magazine, Susan Alduous, Jim Pollard, Bill Bredesen, Mark Fenn, Veeraporn Nitiprapha, Max Crosbie-Jones, Joe Cummings, Robert Fernhout, Janet Brown and Albert Wen from ThingsAsian Press, John Boyer, Lisa Gorecki, Noel Boivin, Paul Dorsey, Alison Riley, Lisa Swaren, Tom Hilditch, and most of my former band-mates in Jerry Jerry and the Sons of Rhythm Orchestra, The Asexuals and The Uncolas, as well as the editors who purchased some of these tales and the judges who awarded or nominated them for various prizes.

While reporting on the Asian tsunami of 2004, many survivors, volunteers, and relatives of the deceased helped me out with interviews and insights. There is not room to thank everyone. But in particular I would like to single out Reid Ridgeway, Kelly May, Bodhi Garrett, Klaus Duncan Bom, Di Duncan, Dr. Pornthip Rojanasunand and Police Colonel Khemmarin Hassiri, the Chief of Police of Takuapa, who all exuded so much courage, grace, wit and kindness in the midst of a series of pressure-cooker ordeals.

Kudos is also due to my former instructors and literary guides at Concordia University: Professor Veronica Hollinger, Professor Geffen, Professor Michael Butovsky, and Scott Lawrence, my

Creative Writing teacher and a fine short-fiction author in his own right, for all his encouragement, constructive criticisms, and for teaching me more about writing and reading fiction than anyone else ever has.

Last but most I need to thank Umaporn "May" Pandee, without whom life would be little more than the living death of a lovesick heart.

"If a way to the better there be it lies
in taking a full look at the worst."
—Thomas Hardy

"Even the most tortuous creepers around the
hoariest tree are not as crooked as a man's heart."
Sunthorn Phu, *Phra Abhai Mani*

THE DEATH KISS OF A KING COBRA SHOW

For May

Before every snake-handling show started, Yai always rubbed his left thumb, which was permanently numb and partially paralyzed from the bite of a Siamese cobra; he could move it from side to side, but couldn't bend it; and the white scars from the two puncture wounds were still visible.

He looked over at the Thai announcer, who was holding up a big placard with newspaper and magazine stories pasted on it.

With his microphone, he pointed at one of the clippings. "This photo shows a seven-meter-long python who ate a man here on Phuket island, and then the snake exploded," he said.

He pointed at another photograph. "This photo shows a golden flying snake. We have many, many in the jungle here. They are one of five species that can expand its ribs to glide from tree to tree. This snake eats birds and geckos."

Yai got down on his knees in front of the cages holding all the deadly reptiles, put his hands together in a prayer-like gesture, bowed his head, and asked them to forgive him for mistreating them. Still on his knees, Yai remembered the shrine in his parent's home, which had an image of the Buddha sitting and attaining enlightenment while Phaya Nak, the seven-headed Lord of the Serpents, protected him from the elements.

But he couldn't even remember the last time he'd prayed to the Buddha or the Serpent Lord.

Now my temple is in the bar, he thought with a snicker, and I pray to the whiskey god every night.

Yai stood up. Since he'd heard the announcer's routine almost every day for the last six years, he scanned the bleachers for pretty white women. If only he could find a rich foreign wife who wouldn't mind helping to support his parents, then he could finally quit this dangerous job, and maybe even buy a Harley-Davidson. He imagined the envious stares of all the people in his village when he sped down the dirt roads on a Harley with a beautiful blonde on the back.

Out of the forty people in the crowd, there were only a couple of older women. None of them looked very rich, but it was hard to tell with foreigners. He could never work out why they all dressed so badly on holiday, walked around with prawn-colored tans, and didn't show off their gold and money.

During the show he'd play to the older women and see if he could milk them for a few tips.

Over in one corner of the bleachers, three white sailors or Marines, dressed in shorts and tank tops, were talking loudly among themselves and drinking beer. The buzz-saw haircuts on these "Jarheads" gave them away.

Just seeing them brought back the humiliating events of the night before and made him swear he would avenge that dire loss of face.

Yai had been drinking a local tonic and aphrodisiac (fermented rice whiskey mixed with snake bile) in a bar that had a wagon wheel, rimmed and spoked with strings of flashing lights, on the wall. A big sign beside it read: "Welcome U.S. Troops for Cobra Gold 2000." Yai wasn't exactly sure what "Cobra Gold 2000" was, although he assumed it was some kind of joint operation between the Thai and American navies.

A few sailors in muscle-baring T-shirts and Hawaiian shorts sat at a corner table under a huge water buffalo skull that had red light bulbs in its eye sockets. Each of them had a Thai bargirl sitting on his lap. Every time they laughed together, every time one of the men touched or kissed one of the women, Yai's loneliness ached like a phantom limb and made him drink faster.

By his calculations, it would cost him about one-third of his monthly salary to pick up one of these prostitutes for the evening. So he debated whether or not to go to a *suan gai* ("chicken farm") for locals; but no, seeing all those sad-faced "chickens" sitting behind the big window with the one-way glass, so the men could walk right up and window shop for sex, was depressing.

If he hadn't slept with a woman for exactly 387 days now, he could at least talk to one and prove that he was smarter than all these other rich tourists and brawny soldiers. So he looked over at the longhaired woman sitting alone at the bar to his left. She was bathed in a purple fluorescent light that gave her teeth a ghostly sheen when she smiled at the tourist down at the other end of the bar.

A local with a huge golden python wrapped around his neck and chest approached the tourist with a Polaroid camera to see if he wanted to have his photo taken with the snake. On the bar's stereo, the CCR song "Run Through the Jungle" was cranked up so loud that Yai had to yell at the girl.

No matter how politely he asked for her name and where she came from, the woman wouldn't respond or even look at him.

Yai kept smiling at her, kept asking the same polite questions until she finally sneered: "*Mai chawp khon tai* [I don't like Thai people]."

For a few seconds, he thought she was joking and that he was just too drunk to get the joke. But she didn't laugh.

To show her how honest and humble he was, Yai said, "You mean, you don't like poor Thai people like me," and laughed.

When she didn't respond, he repeated the joke three more times, always laughing for a tagline, because he didn't want to be mean about it, he just wanted her to tell him the truth.

Finally, not even looking at him, she repeated, "I don't like Thai people," and smiled at the tourist across the bar.

It was that smile—a deliberate insult—which really set him off. "How can you say that? We are Thai people. That's the problem with all these rich tourists: they make us hate ourselves. And every time you sell your body to one of them, you hate yourself a little bit more. Don't you see that?"

The bargirl gave him a sarcastic smile and walked right past him to sit down beside the tourist.

"Hello," she said to him and smiled. "What your name?" Then she turned back to Yai and yelled the Thai equivalent of "Go fuck your mother."

How dare this stupid whore insult him and his mother like that!

To make him even angrier, the three bargirls sitting with the sailors laughed.

Yai staggered over to where she was, so drunk that he felt like he was on the heaving deck of a ship, and grabbed her by the arm, when the golden python wrapped itself around his neck, strangling him. The serpent then coiled around his mid-section and made his ribs ache.

At least he thought it was the python—until he was lifted off the ground and carried to the doorway of the bar. The man dropped him on his feet and then shoved him through the open door.

Gasping for breath and massaging his throat, Yai turned around to see a big sailor blocking the doorway. He tried to scream an insult that the American was a "reincarnation of a water buffalo" but nothing came out except a gurgling wheeze.

The white hulk took a step towards him. "You don't treat women like that, boy." He folded his arms across his chest to show off his muscles. Behind him, the girls were all laughing now—laughing at Yai.

Crippled by alcohol, he staggered down the crowded street past the Viking Scandinavian Restaurant, an Indian tailor shop, and the Vegas Beer Bar, the loss of dignity stinging and tightening the skin on his face like a sunburn as the girls' laughter echoed in his ears.

Why did the dumb brutes like these guys always get the money and the girls and the opportunities and the fancy clothes, nice cars and expensive whiskey, and all he got was insults and snakebites?

Now, as he watched the Marines sitting in the bleachers, he suspected that it was one of them who'd picked him up and thrown him out of the bar. But it was hard to tell; they all looked the same.

After he'd sobered up this morning, Yai had to admit to himself that he had no right to criticize that prostitute. Was he any better? Wasn't he making a living off tourists and hoping to marry a rich foreigner, too?

But the sailor was a different matter. That guy couldn't speak Thai. He had no idea what Yai had said to the woman, or how she'd insulted him. So what right did he have to interfere in their argument?

The announcer was almost finished his routine now: "Thailand has about half a million cobras. If one bites you then you must have the serum in thirty minutes or you will die sure."

Yai frowned at the sailors for so long that it made him cross-eyed. They thought they were so big and tough, but did they have the guts to get in the snake pit and wrestle with banded kraits and king cobras? Now he was ready to teach them a lesson about who the real tough guy was. So he tightened his green headband, rubbed his numb left thumb, and wiped his sweaty palms on his baggy black sweatpants.

"I would like to introduce to you our snake-handler, Yai, or 'Mister Big' as we call him."

To the tune of a techno track shredding the speakers, Yai ran across the snake pit, did a few cartwheels, a back flip and a head-stand, leapt back on his feet, punched the air and, all the while, never stopped smiling. His nimbleness and playful demeanor erased a decade from his thirty-five years.

The music faded out, the crowd gave him a smattering of applause and he grinned and yelled. "Welcome and thank you everybody. Thank you for coming to my funeral…" he paused to let the joke sink in before waving it off and laughing.

Using a wooden stick with a metal hook on one end, he reached into the cage, pulled out a jumping snake, and put it down in the middle of the circular pit. The meter-long serpent, which had black, red and brown scales, twisted across the floor. Yai put the stick down and walked towards it. Immediately, the snake leapt at him. He veered back as it nipped at his crotch. Yai made a funny face and grabbed his crotch with both hands. He looked over at the older women in the bleachers and smiled. "Sorry, ladies, but my little dragon is snake food now."

But the dumb hags didn't even get the joke. That was the trouble with these white foreigners; they were so boring and serious all the time. Even on holiday they rarely seemed to relax.

The next segment of the show was much more dangerous, so he tied his headband a little tighter until he could feel his pulse throbbing in his forehead. Then he wiped his eyebrows, remembering how a bead of sweat had dripped in his eye, distracting him long enough for a Siamese cobra to bite his thumb.

In the center of the pit, three banded kraits with glossy black skins and yellow bands around them, coiled in circles. All three of the venomous serpents were around two-meters long. In order to smell him, they flicked their tongues out in his direction.

Yai looked over at the Marines; they weren't talking now; nobody in the crowd was.

Satisfied that he had their complete attention, he got down on his knees and crept towards one of the banded kraits. Slowly opening his fingers, Yai moved his right hand toward the right side of the snake's head. Immediately, it stopped moving—a sure sign that it was ready to attack. Using his right hand as a decoy, he moved his left towards the other side of the snake. Sweat ran down his back and tickled his spine as he moved his hand closer and closer to it. With a loud groan, he snatched it up by its head and held the writhing serpent in the air. The crowd applauded.

Then he snatched up another one in his left hand and transferred it to his mouth. He had to bite down on the snake's head just hard enough so that it couldn't get loose, but not so hard as to bite its head off and poison himself.

Both of the banded kraits were furiously whiplashing their tails from side to side as he knelt down again. Hot sweat ran down the crack of his ass, and the sound of his heart thumping was louder than the murmurs of the audience. As he knelt down and stared at the serpent's yellow eyes and black pupils, Yai whispered, "I'm not going to hurt you, my little friend. Not going to hurt you. Not going to…" and snatched up the last snake by its neck.

The audience applauded. Yai stepped out of the snake pit and stood at the foot of the bleachers, holding up a banded krait in each hand, the other one caught in his teeth. Flashbulbs went off and made him blink.

Now that he was closer to them, Yai could see that one of the Americans was the same guy who'd strangled him in that python grip last night. When he saw the snake-handler staring at him, the sailor held up an empty beer can in a huge fist and crumpled it.

The threat, and the sudden flashback of last night with the sailor gloating over his loss of face and the "chickens" laughing, made Yai's lower jaw tremble, his fists clench and, for a few frightening seconds, he thought he was going to bite the snake's head off and crush the other two skulls in his hands.

During the next segment of the show, he pried the jaws of a small Siamese cobra open with a pair of tweezers and put a microscope slide between them. He carried the snake around so that the crowd could snap photos and get close-ups of its jaws and the pool of yellowish venom on the slide.

Then, holding the head in his hand and the tail up in the air, Yai and the announcer showed the crowd how to tell if the snake was male or female. The announcer rubbed its belly, near the tail, and two little penises—each no bigger than a clitoris—popped out on either side.

When the two of them approached the side of the bleachers where the three sailors sat, Yai conceded that he should give them one last chance. They had all been drunk last night. He'd been in the wrong too.

After the snake's twin penises popped out, he looked in their direction and smiled. "You have two?"

The older one with an alcoholic's pitted complexion, a pug nose and bloodshot eyes (the man who had assaulted him the night before) sneered, "No, but mine is a helluva lot bigger."

"Oh my god, you have four," said the snake-handler with a laugh.

A couple of the other jarheads laughed, too, but the older guy spat, "Fuck off, ya lil faggot," reminding him of the cobras that spit venom into the eyes of their prey.

Now this was too much. The reincarnation of a water buffalo had humiliated him last night and now again in front of a crowd of forty people. So Yai figured he had every right to make the sailor lose face, too. As he knelt down beside the cage with the biggest king cobra in it, he picked up a piece of rope, whirled around and threw it in their direction. It landed right in the older guy's lap. He screamed and leapt to his feet, knocking the piece of rope to the ground and kicking it away.

"No snake," Yai yelled to the crowd, "only rope. He is no big man. He no Arnold Schwarzenegger. Him afraid too much."

A few people laughed.

But the sailor started screaming insults at him, most of which he didn't understand, and it took all three of his friends to hold him back from jumping into the snake pit. Finally, after about two minutes of more threats, his friends got him to sit down and shut up.

None of the Thai staff were going to kick him out and nobody in the crowd was going to stand up to him. But if Yai stopped the show and slunk off now, the American would win the battle. His face would be broken into a thousand pieces. He couldn't just walk away. His dignity was at stake. And what else did a poor man from the boondocks have but that?

With the wooden stick he brought out the biggest king cobra: a five-meter-long, black-and-grey monster as thick as the Marine's flexed bicep. As soon as he dropped it on the carpeted floor of the pit it moved away from him in a rapid series of S's.

This male was fresh from the jungle on Phuket. Yai had only done two previous shows with him.

"The king cobra is the world's most poisonous snake," said the announcer over a whistle of feedback through the PA. "One bite from this snake has enough venom to kill a thousand rabbits."

The audience gasped when the serpent raised its hood and reared up into the striking position—a meter off the ground—while hissing and flicking its forked tongue in Yai's direction.

A little girl in the audience sobbed, "Daddy, don't let the ugly snake kill him."

As fast as a Thai kick-boxer, the king cobra lunged at him. Yai veered back, quivering with fear. He took a quick look over at the bleachers to see that the sailor with the bloodshot eyes was now sitting by himself in the front row, just above the snake pit.

What would this drunken idiot do next? Jump into the pit and attack him?

In a dramatic baritone the announcer said, "Ladies and gentlemen, our special attraction, what you wait your whole life to see: 'The Death Kiss of a King Cobra Show.'"

Yai bent down so that his head was at the same height as the serpent's. Only two meters separated them. In order to distract it, he stuck out his left hand in front of the cobra's face, while he slowly crept around to his right. His only real advantage was that snakes have very poor eyesight.

But his concentration was blown; he couldn't stop thinking about the sailor. His fear of the man jumping into the pit and getting both of them killed was so strong that he kept sneaking peeks to make sure he was still sitting in the bleachers.

Except for the flicking of its tongue, the snake was still now and facing towards his left hand.

Now he got down on his knees. Closer he crept, trying to bring his knees down softly so the snake would not feel the vibrations.

Now his face was only six inches above the cobra's head, so he could see the white chevron on its hood. Yai held his breath and puckered his lips, lowering his face inch by inch, when another snake leapt at him.

He turned towards it and lashed out with his right arm—and

that's when the king cobra sunk both of its fangs into his nose.

Yai screamed and clutched his nose, feeling the blood spurt from the wounds and roll down his fingers in hot scarlet streams. As the cobra raised itself up to strike again, Yai rolled to his right and saw the piece of rope he'd thrown at the sailor lying on the ground beside him.

Then he looked up and saw the American standing there, listing to his left with a big gloating grin on his face, while the rest of the audience was abuzz with shock and fear.

Nobody came to help him. Nobody dared to stand up to the sailor.

Already he felt the venom kicking in and clouding over his vision. But he fought it off, got to his feet, grabbed a smaller cobra from its cage, staggered over towards the Marine, pulled the snake back like a bullwhip and lashed him across the face with it. Again and again, Yai flogged him with his live whip, until the venom made him too dizzy to stand and he sank to his knees.

Darkness swallowed him.

When Yai regained consciousness he was laying on his stomach in the jungle. He tried to move his arms, but they were gone. He tried to move his legs, but they were gone, too.

His first horrifying thought was that the sailors had cut off his arms and legs and left him to crawl around the jungle on his belly.

But then he saw a forked tongue dart out of his mouth and realized that he must have died and been reincarnated as a snake. Or had he descended into some Buddhist hell?

While he couldn't hear, he could feel vibrations tingling along his underbelly, which warned him that a predator was nearby.

Quickly Yai slithered towards some tall grasses, went up and over a dead log, and then weaved and twisted his way around a pool of water. The thrill of using his new body made him forget his fear for a little while. But when he stopped the tingling in his underbelly was like having an alarm clock going off inside him.

While his new body was much more agile than his old one, his vision was much fuzzier. So he flicked his tongue out to smell how close his enemies were to him.

Close. Very close.

And there were a lot of them.

But what were they? And what sort of snake was he?

He flicked his tail faster and faster to propel himself, but the ringing in his guts didn't stop. Weaving to and fro he searched for a hole in the ground, a big rock, or a tree that would hide him, but there was nothing except tall grass, twigs, leaves and small stones.

Finally, he slithered into a small clearing and found himself surrounded by hundreds of golden cobras.

Cobra Gold 2000, he thought.

Yet more serpents crawled out of the ground all around him: Asiatic rat snakes, Burmese pythons, paradise tree snakes, banded kraits, red-tailed pit vipers, Oriental whip snakes and even a dog-toothed cat snake.

The golden cobras, which all had bloodshot eyes, slithered in for the kill, biting, paralyzing, and then swallowing the other snakes in gulps.

The vibrations caused by all the hissing and all these jaws snapping shut made Yai feel like he was in an earthquake zone.

So he whipped himself around and tried to retreat, but more golden cobras came out of the tall grass behind him.

He was hemmed in from all sides.

Instead of attacking Yai, they slithered right past him, and into what had become a nest—or an orgy—of writhing reptiles. The sun gleamed off their golden skins as they coiled themselves together into one 15-meter-long body which sprouted seven heads.

Phaya Nak, the Lord of the Serpents.

All the deity's fangs dripped rubies of blood, his eyes were the same color, and his biggest head was crested with the skulls and bones of other snakes. As he reared up into the striking position, raising his seven hoods simultaneously, the day went dark.

Perhaps the Serpent Lord might protect him as he'd protected the Buddha from the rain while he sat under the sacred bodhi tree to attain enlightenment.

"Phaya Nak, Phaya Nak, please protect me," he prayed.

"No, you have become the lowest snake of them all. You're as predatory as that bargirl you insulted and as violent, stupid and drunk as that sailor you attacked," said the Serpent King in a voice that rumbled like thunder.

With that, Phaya Nak's biggest head darted down, snatched him up in fangs the size of stalactites and swallowed him.

Through the sewer-damp darkness, Yai crawled towards a chink of light that fell through a crack in the floorboards that opened into a room where his mother sat in her faded sarong looking so old and forlorn and shrunken that she could have been one of those old monks with magical powers whose bodies never decomposed after they passed away.

She was the one who would be the most saddened by his death. He crawled towards her, ready to press his forehead against the dirt beside her wrinkled feet and beg her forgiveness for the six years he'd been away, showing off for foreigners like he was the big star of all the snake-handlers, not some son of a farmer from a village where his mother still ran the TV off a car battery, but an action hero playing to an audience of rich tourists who gave him a little of the respect and the adulation he craved.

In his new reincarnation his own mother did not recognize him. She picked up her broom and, like a good Buddhist who would never even kill an insect, swept him towards the front door like he was nothing more than a millipede.

When Yai regained consciousness he was laying in the middle of the snake pit, the announcer's blurry face looking down at him, and the bitter taste of the antivenin serum in his mouth. He felt like he'd just been awakened after two hours of sleep, still drunk from the night before.

Through a maze of legs, he saw the sailor rolling around and groaning, "I'm dyin', Kenny, I'm fuckin' dyin.'"

Yai grabbed the announcer's arm, made him explain everything that had happened to the sailor. The American was so big and drunk, he said, that the serum seemed to be having little effect on him. Now there was none left. The ambulance was on its way.

Shaking like he had malaria, hot flashes alternating with bone-piercing chills, Yai wiped the sweat from his forehead with one hand while he daubed at the blood on his nose with a handkerchief. He was thinking about his journey into the spirit world, when he overheard the sailor say to one of his friends: "Just tell mom that I love her, and you tell Linda and Kev to take real good care of her, okay?"

So the sailor was human after all. It was not a coincidence that they had both been thinking about their mothers. That was a sign from the Serpent Lord. Yai had asked him for protection and the god had granted his wish.

Now he had to do something to help the sailor. Otherwise he really would be reincarnated as a snake.

So he told the announcer to explain to his friends that he was going to suck the venom from the sailor's wounds and spit it out. It was a risky move, he knew, because if there were any microscopic cuts in his mouth, then he would get another dose of poison.

Since the sailor was completely unconscious now, and the ambulance was nowhere in sight, his friends agreed.

Kneeling over him, Yai sucked as much as the venom out of the bloody holes in his right arm before spitting it out. Then he tied a bandana around his arm as a tourniquet that would prevent the poison from spreading through his bloodstream too quickly

Another tourist ran over and said that they'd flagged down a taxi. The sailors picked up their friend and carried him towards the pick-up truck, which had a metallic shell on the back and two rows of seats for passengers. Just as they reached the truck, he woke up and flailed around. When they put him down, he staggered over and grabbed Yai by the arm, waving off his friends. To them he said: "This lil prick's mine." To Yai: "Get in the back."

One of his friends tried to climb in the back with them, but the sailor waved him off. "I said, 'He's mine.' Get your ass in the front."

He pushed Yai into the back of the pick-up truck. The snake-handler looked around the small crowd for the announcer, or any of his other friends from the snake farm, but the cowards had all deserted him.

The only thing that eased the tension was that one of his friends told him that Yai had tried to save his life.

That didn't seem to have too much effect on the hulk with the pug nose and bloodshot eyes, though; he was still swearing, groaning, sweating profusely and shivering with the same hot flashes and cold chills that Yai felt.

Did they have time to make it to the hospital, which was more than thirty kilometers away?

The two of them sat on opposite sides, the sailor near the back, so he could prevent Yai from jumping out. A breeze carrying the smell of spongy earth blew in through the open sides of the truck.

As the truck sped off down a two-lane highway hemmed in by plantations of spindly rubber trees, the Marine pointed at him and said, "You sure are one crazy lil son of a bitch, ya know that? What the hell didja think you were doin' back there anyhow?"

Yai returned his glare. "Why you hit me in bar last night?"

"'Cause you slapped that poor girl 'bout five, six times. That's why."

Horrified, Yai looked away. Had he really smacked that bargirl?

"I cannot remember. I was drunk too much. But you don't know what she say me. She speak no good about my mama."

The American shook his head and his jowls flapped. "Doesn't matter. Ya don't hit a woman never. My dad was a Marine for twenty-two years and those are the first things he taught me in life: ya don't kick a man when he's down and ya don't hit a woman never. Them's the rules, Mister Drunk Asshole."

"Why you throw rope on me? Snake bite my face because you."

"'Cause you threw the fuckin' rope at me first. Or don't you remember that either?"

"Only joking, make funny… not serious."

"But it wasn't funny. I mean, Jesus Christ, walkin' around askin' guys if they got four dicks. Like what kinda weirdo faggot shit is that?"

Yai daubed at the wounds on his nose with his headband while plotting his defense should the sailor attack him again. Yai had one hand on the rail above him. If he grabbed the rail with his other hand and swung towards the sailor he could kick him in the face with both feet, which might just send him hurtling out the back of the pick up truck. But with all the bumps on the road and his motor skills intoxicated with venom, it might just be him who went sprawling across the tarmac, shedding skin like a serpent.

The sailor lifted up his blood-spattered T-shirt and wiped some sweat off his face with the bottom of it. "You better pray that we're okay, or you're in mighty big trouble, man."

"I think we okay," said Yai, although he wasn't really sure. If he had absorbed some more venom through a tiny cut in his mouth, it might be poisoning him a bit more slowly than usual. And if he was going to die, then why should he back down from this bully?

The snake-handler looked him square in his bloodshot eyes. "How many people you kill in Marine?"

"Huh? What the hell kinda question is that?"

The sailor squinted at the thick jungle.

Yai figured he was reliving all the murders he'd committed and all the atrocities he'd seen.

Finally, he muttered, "Too many... in El Salvador."

Yai had no idea what El Salvador was. Was it a country or a famous battle? "How many?"

The American looked over at him, sadness and guilt making him look much older and uglier than he really was. "One is too many, okay? One is far too fuckin' many. So ya get drunk and you think that'll make all the demons go away, and for a coupla hours they do, maybe a coupla days, but they always come back see, always."

The sailor was holding the bar above his head with one hand, wiping sweat from his jarhead with the other and rocking from side to side. Over the whine of the wind and the drone of the engine, Yai could barely make out what he was saying. It was almost like he was talking to his conscience. "That's what the ads on TV useta say, 'Join the army, it's not just a career, it's an adventure,' or some shit like that. I don't know, man, finding a mass grave in Guatemala with two hundred women and children hacked to death with machetes, that's not the kind of adventure I signed up for. But I had to do somethin' to get off that poor ol' farm and I wasn't good enough to get a football scholarship." He looked at Yai, blinking his eyes to focus them. "You're a farm boy too, ain'cha? I can spot 'em a mile away. It's 'cause we got a certain way with animals, see? There you are in the snake pit with the most dangerous reptiles in the world, and you're still treatin' 'em with so much love and respect. Fuckin' A that impressed me."

Yai had to get him to calm down and stop moving around so much. "You, I, same same farm boys. Sometimes good, sometimes bad, sometimes drunk and angry too much."

"Yeah, I s'pose we ain't all that different, a coupla violent drunks on the long road to hell. Which don't mean we're ever gonna be buddy buddy or nothin'." The sailor put his elbows on his knees. "Ya know somethin', man, not that I'm one to talk, but you're all fucked up. You gotta get off this island."

"I know. You're fucked up too, Mister Drunk Asshole."

The American slapped his thigh and laughed. It was like one of those barroom scenarios where two drunks could not stop laughing. Each time one stopped the other started, so the chorus continued.

After a minute of delirious laughter, the Thai driver and the other sailors looked through the back window at them with puzzled expressions on their faces.

As the pick-up sped past a Buddhist temple, Yai saw two seven-headed statues of Phaya Nak on opposite sides of the stairway leading up to the main shrine, the green balustrades forming their two serpentine bodies. Sunlight gleamed off their golden heads.

Immediately, Yai put his hands together, bowed his head in prayer, and said to the Serpent Lord: "Thank you for your teaching and letting me return from the spirit world. All I want to do now is retire from the snake show, stop drinking and go back to my village to help my mother with farming. I hope the soldier is okay too and that you won't make me into a snake in my next life."

Yai opened his eyes and saw that the Marine was staring at him. Afraid that he was going to make fun of him, Yai looked back at the jungle where the late afternoon sun peeked between the trees.

"Hey, don't get all embarrassed and shit. It's cool. I believe in

God too, and I respect your religion. But who were ya prayin' to any-how? The Buddha?"

"No, Phaya Nak, the big snake at temple."

"Phaya Nak, huh? Yeah, I gotta remember that name. He's beau-tiful. Ya know somethin', I'd like to get a tattoo of him right around my bicep here, jus' above the skull with the switchblade in its teeth and jus' below Marilyn."

An image of the Serpent Lord underneath a woman whose skirt was billowing out around her? Even thinking about it was blasphe-mous. But if that was what he wanted then he would have to answer to Phaya Nak one day. It wasn't for Yai to intervene.

"But is he some kinda god or what?"

"He is king of all snakes and my teacher."

Another series of chills raced each other up and down the snake-handler's spine, his vision clouded over, and the Serpent Lord ripped his soul from his body again. This time, Yai was a tiny snake wrapped around Phaya Nak's great crested head. Together, they flew across the sky, spearing through castles of cloudbanks at the speed of a jet, before nose-diving towards the earth. For a moment, Yai was over-whelmed by that familiar, double-edged feeling of happy misery (happy to be coming home again, but miserable that he was still broke, unmarried and childless) that he always felt when returning to his village, until he saw the parched and cracked earth. Not a plank or plough of the village where he'd grown up remained. There was no water, no rice paddies, no houses, people or animals. These badlands, which contained the country's biggest dinosaur graveyard, had become a wasteland. The only flashes of color came from the sashes tied around the termite mounds where his mother said the descendants of the Serpent Lord dwelled, and where Yai and his boyhood friends would go out hunting for king cobras which took refuge there during the rainy season.

Scraps of discarded cotton from his mother's loom tied around the barren termite mounds were all that remained of his old life and village.

When the Serpent Lord returned him to his body this time, Yai put his head down in his hands, feeling dizzy. What did Phaya Nak want to teach him now? That returning home was useless?

Of course it was. None of the young people stayed in these villages anymore. They didn't want to lead a backbreaking life of eternal debt as rice farmers. There was no money and no face in that.

Everybody looked down on them as country bumpkins and the government never did anything to help them. All of his brothers and sisters and old friends and classmates had left the village long ago to work as taxi drivers, factory workers and prostitutes in Bangkok.

So if he couldn't return home, and he couldn't work at the Phuket Snake Farm anymore, what was he supposed to do?

Yai stared at the two-lane highway that looked like a long grey serpent, twisting around mountains, flattening out as it slithered past palm oil and rubber tree plantations, winding around ocean view points, making it impossible to tell what was ahead of them or what was behind and, when the golden flying snake came whizzing through the pickup truck, glancing off the sailor's shoulder and making him lose his grip on the handrail as the sudden acceleration of the driver coming out of a switchback sent the American tumbling headfirst onto the tarmac, who could really say if it was just bad luck or an accident or karma, and what did it matter anyway? Yai would always claim, when it happened so cobra-quick that all he, the only eye-witness, could do was make a wild grab for the sailor's T-shirt and wind up snatching the silver cross from his neck and, long after Yai had returned to the Snake Farm, still wearing the cross ("A tribute to my dead American friend," he told the pretty young white tourists) and was doing a new army-style act with the golden flying snake that survived the encounter, he told people that maybe the poor ol' farm boy had thrown himself out the back of the pickup truck or maybe they were both confused by the venom and the antivenin or—and Yai always stuck to his story no matter how drunk he was—that of course he hadn't kick-boxed the American in retaliation for the losses of face in the bar and the snake pit, as one of the sailor's friends had claimed (though he was drunk too and the cops were skeptical that he'd seen much in the side-door mirror). So when the tourists and bargirls and locals had gotten bored of hearing him retell the story, the snake-handler always wound it up with the one thing in his slithery world that he could pin down: "People are a lot like snakes. They're very fast and tricky, and you can never predict how harmless or dangerous they might turn out to be."

FLASHPOINTS
IN ASIA

For Vicki Hazou

G unfire exploded, screams singed the air, and the crowd surged backwards to escape the soldiers' shooting spree.

Kendall ducked down but continued snapping frame after frame, his flash shooting out quicksilver light, even as terrified faces came into sharp focus only to become dark smudges in his viewfinder, even as the fleeing demonstrators jostled him on both sides and someone yelled in his ear, "Go! Go!" and grabbed the shoulder of his army jacket, trying to pull him back.

He shook his arm free and shouted, "Cheers, but I'm workin', mate." Then he gestured with his head. "Off you go."

In a crouch, he crept towards the soldiers. The closer he got to them, the louder the gunfire became. Each shot made him blink. More demonstrators ran past him screaming something in Thai that he couldn't understand. Two other men, their arms draped around a third man's shoulders, dragged him along between them as he wailed and wept.

Further down Bangkok's Ratchadamnoen Avenue, the dark hulk of a tank rumbled towards him. Behind it, flames shot up from a city bus and writhed in the humid breeze. No time to attach his zoom lens; another perfect shot wasted.

Kendall turned back to the soldiers—only twenty or thirty meters in front of him—who were lined up in front of Democracy Monument, its four pillars lit with yellow lights. The gunfire was sporadic now.

Kendall knelt down to take close-ups of the bodies strewn across the road, checking the red digital light meter in the upper right-hand corner of his viewfinder. The shutter snapped as the gears whirred.

Flash. A dead Thai woman staring up at him.

Flash. A bloody hand clutching a mobile phone.

Flash. A teenager's face, his nose pulverized by a bullet.

Flash. A flip-flop lying on its side in a slick of moon-silver blood.

Sitting on his haunches, Kendall looked up to see one of the soldiers running towards him, shouting.

A hand grabbed his wrist and he looked down to see the teenage boy with the bloody face, moaning, "Help me. Help me." Then he looked back at the soldier running towards them.

Kendall had to save his Nikon and film. But he needed at least one good shot of a soldier. So he backed up, knelt down, and…

Flash. In the foreground was the teenager (his nose like a black hole in the middle of his face) lying on the ground with one arm reaching up towards the center of the frame; behind him was the soldier, his gun pointed straight at the camera.

As Kendall ran, he put the lens cap on, looked over his shoulder and saw the soldier bring the butt of his machine-gun down on the boy's head.

The crack of that teenager's skull being split open had pursued him through the rainforests of Sumatra when he was on the trail of some headhunters, across the beaches of Bali (a surfboard under his arm), down the street that ran past the Military Veteran's Hospital in Phnom Penh, and deep into the Burmese jungle, when he was travelling with a band of Karen rebels. And still, some ten years after the mass slaughter of demonstrators protesting against a military junta which had overthrown a democratically elected government, the crack kept echoing in his mind like a rifle shot in a cave as he sat in the little Hainan Chicken and Rice Restoran in Penang, Malaysia, smoking a hand-rolled Drum cigarette and sipping a sweet iced coffee. And the memories of that night, which now seemed more like a black-and-white mirage, kept repeating too, with one exception: he'd never taken a photo of a beautiful and dead young Asian woman looking up at the camera, her eyes half-lidded, her mouth slightly open, tresses of hair caressing her cheeks, as if she'd been murdered in the death-like throes of an orgasm.

So where had that image come from?

Although the shot of the teenager and the soldier had won him the World Press Photo Award, made him a heap of money, and got him a contract with a New York photo agency, he had to wonder if all the waking nightmares were worth it. No matter how many times he tried to deny it, the fact was inescapable; if he hadn't alerted the soldiers with his flashbulb, that teenager might not have died.

He glanced over at the glass case on the counter at the front of the restaurant, where several plucked chickens hung from hooks pierced through their necks. Across Chulia Road was a Chinese shop selling stacks of rattan furniture. Just down from it was Lim White Ant Service & General Pest Exterminators. Between them was an empty shop with a metal grill pulled across the entrance. Behind the grill, a figure clad in a dark purple robe and cowl suddenly appeared. It looked almost like a Muslim woman wearing a burqa. An arm, also clad in dark purple, reached through the grill and beckoned to him, but there didn't seem to be a hand at the end of it. Was she calling for help or warning him to stay away?

By the time a black-and-yellow bus with the words "Bas Sekolah" written on the side had driven across his field of vision, the person was gone.

Kendall reckoned he'd better go and investigate. Maybe there was a story here—his first one in six months.

He slung his camera bag over his shoulder and told the cook and cashier at the counter, "That was the best boiled chicken breast and rice I've ever had in Asia. Would you mind writing down the recipe? My father back in Australia loves making Asian tucker, so

I try to send him a fair few recipes from real chefs." The cook wrote down the recipe, Kendall said, "Cheers," and gave him a little tip.

For a few minutes, he stood on the opposite side of the street, watching the metal grill of the three-floor, Chinese-style shop-house. The windows on the second and third floors were also dark. On the red tiled roof sat a Eurasian black vulture. He'd seen this bird before. But where? It was part of a déjà vu he couldn't quite place.

Kendall didn't like the harsh noonday sunlight, but the bird, with its black feathers, bluish grey head and long hooked beak, was beautiful.

Two young Indian women with nose-rings and brilliant saris came down the street. Kendall smiled at them and said, "G'day, ladies." Neither of them even looked at him… *so I'm the sexual pariah of Malaysia, am I?* He looked down at his dirty army pants, the pockets bulging with rolls of film and lenses, and at his old T-shirt and scarecrow arms… *you're looking like a right dag, Ken. They probably think you're an AIDS patient.*

As he stared at their wide, swiveling hips, his mouth opened a little, but before he could even come up with the foreplay of an erotic daydream, he remembered a photo editor in Hong Kong telling him he should go to India and do a story about all the women being set on fire by their husbands because their dowries weren't big enough. The photo editor had told him these murders were officially listed as "cooking accidents"… *now that's barbecuing Indian style. Throw another bride on the barbie, mate. That's sick, mate. You've really become sick and jaded, haven't you?*

As the gangly photographer walked across the street, the vulture laughed at him. Despite the sweltering heat and laser-like sun, a cold tongue licked his spine. Kendall looked up at the bird, framing the shot and setting the exposure in his mind; it was silent now, almost motionless.

Squinting and keeping well back from the grill for fear that arm without a hand would reach out and grab him, he peered into the shop: it was as black as the eye socket of a skull in there.

"Hello… hello."

And now a little louder: "Hello. D'ya need help?"

He moved closer so his face was just behind the metal grill, but he still couldn't see or hear anything.

Thinking he'd try the back door, Kendall walked down the street past an Indian restaurant with an open shop front (where the customers ate curries with their hands from banana leaves), an old wooden Chinese pharmacy that reeked of medicinal herbs, and a little stand where an Indian man wearing a checked cloth around his waist poured tea from one glass held above his head into another glass held at waist level in order to cool it down. He then repeated the process over and over again, never spilling a drop. Kendall stopped to watch him... *now here's the kind of photos I should be taking, in-flight magazine rubbish. But where's the fun in that?*

The vendor saw him watching. "Hello, my friend. How many feet of tea do you want? It's our joke in Malaysia."

That was the tax added to the cost of being an expat and a foreign correspondent in Asia (possibly anywhere, he imagined); never knowing for certain if the locals were being sincerely friendly or congenially mercenary. To be polite, Kendall laughed along with him and said, "Cheers, but I'm strictly on a beer diet."

Around the corner were three, ten-foot-tall joss sticks with the heads of red, yellow, blue and lime dragons at the bottom, their tails curling up towards the smoking wicks, which perfumed the air with the sweet scent of sandalwood incense. Behind the joss sticks was a Chinese shrine. Sitting on the altar before some monstrous deity were pigs' heads, bottles of Guinness beer, trays of sweets, and bowls of rice with chopsticks and spoons beside them.

Kendall asked an old Chinese man, who had a lumpy face like rice porridge and eyes that had long since lost their luster for life, about the shrine.

The man cast a quick, disapproving gaze over Kendall's old army clothes and mesh T-shirt. He looked back at the altar. "It's for the God of Hell. This is Chinese ghost month."

Now Kendall really had to wonder what he'd seen behind that grill.

"Aw yeah," said the photographer in a nasally voice that sounded like a Brit with a bad cold. "I read something about that. At the beginning of the seventh lunar month the gates of the underworld open and the spirits of the dead come back to earth. So these offerings are for the ghosts?"

"For the God of Hell and his helpers. Tonight will be offerings for ghosts, and puppet shows and Chinese operas for people and ghosts to enjoy. You can only make offerings for spirits at night because that is when they come."

Kendall thanked him and the man asked him for the time.

"Sorry, mate, but I never wear a watch. Nothing sadder than watching the time passing I reckon. That's why I love photos so much. You can freeze time and save the moment for ever."

Kendall looked back at the God of Hell. The details and colors rivaled anything he'd seen in the Tibetan scroll paintings he collected: a bouquet of red, pink and yellow flowers crowned a headdress of fanciful lions and tigers; the deity's malicious face was dark blue; his eyes were yellow; and a long bloody tongue lolled out of his mouth between orange streaks of flame.

This could be the next development in Kendall's career. No more black-and-white images of soldiers and corpses, earthquakes and crime scenes. With this series of photos he'd try to do something more colorful and mystical, something more artistic that would be exhibited in galleries and published in a book. He was sick of photo editors ruining his pictures by cropping them, or choosing the weakest ones and then running them beside an ad for expensive shoes, like they'd done with his series of AIDS patients on their deathbeds in a Buddhist temple in Thailand.

For these new shots he wanted to experiment with a technique called "cross processing." So he loaded the camera with 200 ASA color slide film and pushed it two stops to 800 ASA. Later, he would develop the rolls as if they were regular print film and the result would be sharp, color-saturated images with high contrasts.

As Kendall framed the God of Hell in his viewfinder, an Asian headhunter wearing a necklace of pig's teeth and holding one of his "trophies" aloft slowly formed in front of the camera's eye like a black-and-white photo in a tray of developer, hazy at first, but slowly coming into focus. It was the same shot he'd taken in Sumatra, but now it was moving, now the headhunter was alive and glaring at him with the God of Hell's yellow eyes... *fuckin' hell.*

Kendall pulled the camera away from his eyes and the image disappeared. He stared at the Nikon as if it were haunted, shook it, then looked through the viewfinder again and saw a Cambodian soldier with a ragged uniform and a face full of shrapnel floating above the shrine, waving the stumps of his arms around.

Kendall put the camera back in his bag. He'd never taken a shot like that... *it's combat fatigue, Ken. You've seen too many atrocities. Well, so did Don McCullin. Must be why he called his book of photos* Living with Ghosts. *But I'll call mine* Flashpoints in Asia.

The cell phone in his pocket vibrated. A photo editor in Singapore told him there were more riots on the streets of Jakarta, and his newspaper needed a photographer to go there ASAP. He began giving him a list of shots to take.

Kendall interrupted him. "I don't work like that. I have to keep my compositions loose and my shots spontaneous—and nobody tells me what to shoot. If you'll let me take the pictures I want and give me five-hundred US a day, plus expenses, then I'll go."

The editor sighed and Kendall hung up on him... *silly bugger.*

It was a show of bravado to cover up the fact that he didn't want to shoot any more riots, because it was futile. The same atrocities and uprisings kept repeating again and again. All the work he'd done, and all the risks he'd taken, had been in vain; none of those photos had changed anything.

Or had they?

Since there hadn't been any more military massacres in Thailand after the last crisis, maybe, in some small way, his photos had made a difference. It was hard to say, just as it was hard to admit that he'd lost his nerve and now he was losing the plot completely... *but I'm no piker. I'll be back here tonight to take another shot.*

No matter where Kendall went that afternoon, the old Chinese man with the lumpy face and the grey widow's peak kept shadowing him. Even when he ducked into an old theatre that had separate ticket booths for men and women to catch a Hong Kong action movie called *The Kung-Fu Scholar*, the guy sat down about six seats to his right. Halfway through the movie, off Kendall went to a bar. He'd just ordered a Tiger Beer when the old bloke walked in, pretended not to see him, and sat down at another table.

Later in the afternoon—the light was good now, mellow, soft focus—the photographer walked around an old British fort overlooking the city's seaside, where a cannon scabbed with rust served as a fertility shrine for Chinese women who sat astride it and hurled oranges into the water. Reading the sign about that ritual made him smirk… *you Chinese Sheilas can straddle my cannon whenever you want*.

Someone began laughing. Kendall looked over at the Eurasian black vulture sitting on the fort's wall, beside the old Chinese bugger scowling at him, like he knew what Kendall had been thinking about and disapproved. "Oi! Piss off and stop following me," the photographer yelled.

But rice-porridge face stood there shaking his head sadly. "How can you not remember me, Kendall?"

The photographer turned and strode away, trying to recall who the man was, but he honestly couldn't remember.

By twilight he was back in the Hainan Chicken and Rice Restoran, his gaze shifting between the metal grill of the shop-house across the street, and a couple of young Australian men having a loud, drunken conversation at another table. Kendall was tempted to join them. He could use the company of some countrymen right now to remember who he'd once been, not the washed up, jaded cynic he'd become.

So he rehearsed his opening lines. "Hey there, how ya goin'?" Then he'd point at the cigarettes on their table. "Can I bludge a gasper, mate?" But he didn't use so much of that Aussie slang anymore. Had he been away from home for such a long time that he now had to rehearse lines in order to have a conversation with his own people? And the more he listened to them slagging off Aborigines, "Fuckin'

Abos are all mad piss farts," and going on about Aussie rules football, the less he wanted anything to do with them... *why don't these Okkers go home and shear some sheep? They're the kind of bigots I left home to avoid.*

Across the street he saw that arm robed in dark purple reach through the metal grill and beckon to him, but it was too dark to see if there was a hand or a body attached to it.

It might be a trap, but it might also be a Muslim woman who really needed his help. Ten years ago he'd turned his back on someone in peril; he wasn't going to do it again. Maybe, when he'd finally righted this wrong, he could become his old self again, because he hadn't always been like this... *now what was it I said to that mama-san in Cambodia who offered me a teenage girl's virginity for a hundred bucks?* "Call me a hopeful romantic if you will, but the first time should be for love... and every time after that."

He also had to prove to himself that he could still shoot a potentially dangerous story. If he didn't send some new photos to his agency in New York soon, he was not only going to be out of money, but out of the loop completely.

Peering through the locked grill of that dark shop-house revealed nothing. He couldn't hear any sounds or voices either.

Around the corner, at the shrine to the Taoist God of Hell, there were dozens of supplicants praying and making offerings as candles burned and incense wafted. The lights flickering across the eyes of the pigs' heads gave them a semblance of life. He thought about taking some photos, but remembering what had happened at the shrine this afternoon, he couldn't bring himself to take his camera out.

Behind the dark shop-house was an empty, dirt parking lot rutted with tire tracks. The back door was slightly ajar. He opened it slowly, the rusty hinges complaining, and listened. No voices, no sounds came from within. But in the distance he could hear the trebly music and vocals of a Chinese opera.

Kendall flicked on his cigarette lighter and entered the kitchen.

It was filthy: full of newspaper scraps, empty beer bottles, broken glass, battered cupboards, and a refrigerator with the door open.

He flicked a light switch, but there was no electricity.

Holding the lighter up in front of him, its yellow-crested, blue-bottomed flame wavering, Kendall walked through the kitchen, his army boots crunching broken glass. The lighter was burning his thumb, so he released the switch, and the darkness buried him alive. Listening so hard that he could feel his eyes taking on an Asian slant, trying not to breathe too loudly, Kendall stood there with his heart stammering, sweat trickling down his wrists.

Holding the lighter up in front of him again, he walked down the hall past filthy walls spider-webbed with cracks. The front room, just as garbage strewn as the kitchen, was dimly illuminated by a red light similar to the one he used in his dark room.

Flash. A figure robed and masked in dark purple walking towards him, quicksilver light shooting out of its eye slits.

Flash. The figure pulled the cowl back from its face to reveal the Thai teenager with the pulverised nose, except now he looked like a photographic negative: white eyes and hair, black skin and lips.

Flash. The Sumatran headhunter floated above him, and he, too, looked like a life-size, 3-D negative.

Fear, like a hangman's noose, tightened around Kendall's throat.

Flash. Flash. Flash. Flash.

The teenager in front of him, the old Chinese man with the lumpy face to his right, and the headhunter floating down on his stomach from the ceiling, all closed in on Kendall while he backed up, squinting into the barrage of flashbulbs. A pair of furry hands wrapped themselves around his neck and he turned around, eyes widening in shock as he saw that it was a big, black and white kangaroo, the same one he'd photographed when he was twelve. The 'roo, which was several feet taller than him, reared back on its tail, bringing its huge feet up as another flash turned it into a living X-ray of white bones and jaws, pumping gray lungs, and a black pulsating heart.

The 'roo kicked Kendall in the chest with its big feet and sent him flying across the room. He landed hard on his tailbone first, then his elbows. Wheezing like an asthma-attack victim—he couldn't catch his breath, he was going to choke to death—Kendall finally pushed himself up on his aching elbows and wheezed a few accordion-sounding notes from his lungs... *fuckin' hell.*

In the bombardment of flashes, he saw a lovely young Asian woman borne aloft by the 3-D X-rays of two Eurasian black vultures melded with her feet, their skeletal wings slowly flapping. Tresses of black hair covered her breasts. Rolls of film were wrapped around her waist and thighs. But her face and bare limbs glowed like she was the man on the moon's mistress.

It was the same woman who had haunted him this afternoon, the one whom he now remembered photographing—a Vietnamese sex slave held captive in a Malay brothel... *Xao. Her name is Xao.*

"You exploited me," she said, "and exposed my shame for everyone to see."

Kendall sat up. "But, but... I wanted to help you. I gave you money and I never touched you. Remember? Remember? All I wanted was to help you..."

"Nobody came to help me. And when the owner of the brothel saw your published photos, he was so angry that he beat me to death with the leg of a broken chair." As she spoke, bruises blackened her face and buried her eyes; wounds blossomed across her arms and legs.

"You took my photos, too," said the Chinese man through sneering white lips that revealed black teeth, "when I was dying of AIDS in that temple." Dark lesions opened on his cheeks and forehead like a time-lapse film of flowers blooming. "Xao, my dear, he doesn't care about us."

"I know," she said. "He's a vulture, not a man."

Their cutting laugher wounded him. "You're wrong," he protested. "I do care. It's the world that doesn't care. And how can you expect me to remember every picture I've ever taken?"

"Remove his clothes," she said. "I want him to feel what it's like to be exposed and photographed."

The other three negatives tore Kendall's clothes off, then his underwear, their flashbulb eyes popping constantly. He squirmed and wriggled, but they held him down.

Unwrapping the film stock around her waist, which exposed

more black lacerations and a chair leg wedged in her sex, Xao slowly descended on bony wings fanning out from her beaked feet. She wrapped the rolls of film around Kendall's arms, pinning them to his chest, before pressing her fingers and nails, hot and sharp as tattoo-shop needles, into the images. Now she wrapped more rolls around his face and legs so he looked like a film-strip mummy, branded with a photo gallery of his own images.

Around then, Kendall fainted....

When he woke up he was lying on a dark street surrounded by corpses: corpses with limbs splayed, mouths open, hands empty; they had all died in the middle of some thought, some action, some conversation they would never complete. That was always the saddest part of death, the phone call never made, the thought never articulated, the promise never fulfilled, and now it was all too late.

From the depths of unconsciousness, Kendall swam up to the surface, dizzy and gasping for breath, not ready to believe that he was back in Bangkok and that his camera was still around his neck. He pushed himself up on his elbows and looked around. All he could see were dead bodies and some soldiers standing by Democracy Monument, its four pillars lit with yellow lights.

Further down Ratchadamnoen Avenue, the dark hulk of a tank rumbled towards him. Behind it, flames shot up from a city bus and writhed in the humid breeze

His T-shirt was covered with syrupy blood but it was impossible to tell whether it was his own or some of the victims'. Otherwise, he didn't seem to be injured.

The soldiers were about twenty to thirty meters away. Kendall crawled towards them on his elbows, trying to keep his head down. He checked wrists for pulses. Even though their flesh was still warm, all the people around him were dead. One corpse had a mobile phone still clutched in his hand. Beside his bare feet was a flip-flop overturned in a slick of blood as dark and thick as petrol. Kendall could not remember if he'd taken these photos already or not.

As he crawled closer to the monument he saw that each pillar had a fountain, illuminated by yellow lights, which was crowned with the head of what looked like an elephant with a serpent sticking out of its mouth. Somebody grabbed his wrist and he looked down to see the teenage boy with the bloody face, moaning, "Help me. Help me." Then he looked over at the soldier running towards them.

Kendall had to save his Nikon and film. But he needed at least one good shot of a soldier. So he backed up, knelt down, and... then he remembered the vision he'd just had of winning the World Press Photo Award, and the Chinese God of Hell, and the darkroom where all his negatives had come back to haunt him.

The photographer put the lens cap back on his camera and dragged the boy to his feet. With his arm around the boy's shoulder, and the boy's arm around his waist, he tried to pull him to safety. But the teenager's right leg kept buckling under him and they kept stumbling. Kendall looked over his shoulder. The soldier, his weapon pointed at their backs, was gaining ground quickly. In Thai, he yelled something at them that must've been, "Stop or I'll shoot!" for the boy stopped dead in his tracks and Kendall tripped over him, scraping his knees on the pavement... *good-o, kid, now we're both in the shit.*

Kendall stood up and turned around. The soldier leveled his weapon at Kendall's chest. The barrel's mouth was as black as the eye socket of a skull. The photographer held up both of his hands and said, "*Nak khao farang* [foreign journalist]." The soldier, whose face was in shadows, pointed his gun at the boy's chest. Kendall looked over at the kid. He couldn't be more than fifteen. With the cheap clothes he was wearing and his dark skin, Kendall reckoned he was a rice farmer's son, probably slaving away for twelve hours a day in one of the city's sweatshops.

Off to the right of Democracy Monument, another group of soldiers was approaching them, weapons drawn. After a brief conversation, the soldier grabbed the boy's arm and motioned with his gun for Kendall to leave. If he left now, he knew they'd take the boy off and shoot him; he was an easy target, a casualty who would never make the news. Other foreign correspondents in Bangkok had told him about a previous coup, after which the corpses of civilians were dropped from army helicopters over the mountainous jungle in the Golden Triangle near Burma. That would be this kid's fate, too, if he did not intervene.

Kendall put his arm around the boy's shoulder; the muscles in his back were twitching with fear. The kid put his arm around Kendall's waist. The way he tried to push his face into the hollow beneath the photographer's armpit made him think of a frightened child, seeking his father's protection. And that was a lie that just might work.

In pidgin Thai, Kendall said to the soldier, whose gun was trained on him again. "He my son. My wife Thai lady... his mother. We live Australia."

The soldier barked something at the kid that Kendall didn't understand. The boy replied in a quavering whisper that was equally incomprehensible except for one word: *paw* (father).

Now the soldier looked down at Kendall's camera, motioning for him to hand it over. Kendall took it off and gave it to him. The soldier shot a quick glance over his shoulder at the other troops approaching him. Then he held the camera over his head so they could see it and smashed it on the ground at Kendall's feet. The sight of his old friend's innards spilling out and his glass eye broken on the street deflated him like air seeping from a punctured tire.

With a sneer in his voice, the soldier said, "You go!"

His superiors might well overturn the order, so Kendall quickly dragged the kid towards a side street where they should be safe. That stupid bastard had forgotten to check his pockets. There were four or five rolls of film in them. No prize-winners but a few money-makers. All the best shots had been on that last roll.

With the giddy sense of comic relief that sometimes overcame him in danger zones, when the guns stopped shooting and the mortar shells stopped booming, Kendall began laughing to himself... *I just lost the World Press Photo Award but somehow gained a teenage son and a ghostly wife. Brilliant. Absolutely brilliant.*

As they lurched towards a brightly lit Chinese shrine where pigs' heads and bottles of beer had been laid out on an altar for the God of Hell and his minions, Kendall realized that the Festival of the Hungry Ghosts was on in Thailand, too.

Beside the shrine stood an old Chinese man with a lumpy face like rice porridge. Next to him, sitting atop the altar, poised like a bird of prey about to take flight, was Xao. Seeing them dragged an electric razor up the back of his neck.

This was the man from the AIDS hospice? And the bird was a Vietnamese sex slave from some Malay brothel? But he'd never photographed either of them. So what had he just been seeing? Instead of seeing his life flash before his eyes, as people often reported in near-death experiences, had he just seen his future unspooling in front of him?

Xao and the Chinese man were both smiling at him. Slowly, their teeth darkened and their eyes turned silver.

Shooting glances over his shoulder at the two negatives, Kendall and the boy lurched past the altar like they were in a three-legged race.

Only when they were halfway down the street did he slow their pace. The street was deserted. Orange streetlights gave everything a hellish tint and an eerie calm prevailed. The only motion came from bats circling a streetlight like protons and electrons buzzing around a nucleus.

Kendall checked into a guesthouse and paid for two rooms. He sent the kid upstairs while he sat on a plastic stool in the dark restaurant knocking back a big bottle of Singha Beer.

How quickly that image of the bats circling the orange streetlights had changed into a black and white memory that was an out-of-focus blur in his mind. No amount of concentrating could sharpen that image and give it more substance.

There was nothing supernatural about this dilemma. It was one of the problems he associated with getting older and traveling more: the accumulation of memories, experiences, fantasies, dreams and scenarios he'd shot or glimpsed had formed these montages in his mind, so that a reminiscence of getting kicked in the chest by a kangaroo when he was ten could cut to a wildlife documentary about Eurasian black vultures that faded into a still life of a Vietnamese woman he'd once photographed and fantasized about fucking—her hair reminded him of the vulture's feathers—whose hatred of the Khmer then dissolved into a scene from a Cambodian military hospital where armless soldiers waved their stumps around.

Once, five or six years ago, he'd been on a visa run to Penang and he'd seen the Festival of the Hungry Ghosts: the altars with pigs' heads and bottles of Guinness, the blue-faced, yellow-eyed God of Hell, the stages where Chinese opera troupes and young female singers in hot pants performed at night for both the crowds and the ghosts. That was certain. He could remember those scenes well enough, especially that family standing beside the road burning a heap of gold and silver paper, "Hell Banknotes," paper houses and clothes, mobile phones and luxury sedans made out of cardboard. The father told him these burnt offerings were for the dead to use in the afterlife, and so they wouldn't cause harm to the living.

All these years Kendall had spent working as a freelance photographer in Asia and something still surprised him almost every day. That was the upside of the job. The downside was that he would never really understand any of these cultures, and no matter how proficient he became in Mandarin or Hindi or Thai or Khmer, he'd never really feel at home and never feel like he belonged in any of these countries. He would remain exactly where he was standing then in Malaysia, or sitting by himself now in Bangkok: on the periphery of every scene, wandering through Asian lands and flashpoints where he was one of the white foreigners the Chinese referred to as "long-nosed ghosts," watching scenes like that at the Festival of the Hungry Ghosts: a family kneeling in front of a bonfire praying to gods and goblins he could scarcely comprehend, with no one paying any attention to him at all—except for the staring kid. (In any gathering like that, there was always one kid staring at him with frightened awe like he was a potentially lethal animal in a zoo.)

You're the real ghost, mate, a hungry ghost, never satisfied, always on the move, forever on the outside looking in.

There was only one temporary remedy for that long-standing affliction.

Kendall trudged up the worn, wooden steps of the guesthouse to see how the rice farmer's son was doing.

WET NIGHTMARES

The fat guy grabbed Watermelon's hand, pulled her onto his lap and squeezed her breasts. When he kissed her, she felt like digging her long, sparkly silver fingernails into the soft spot at the bottom of his throat and ripping out his vocal cords—anything to stop him from treating her like she was public property and shoving his tongue down her throat so she almost gagged on the taste of garlic and gin and tonic.

Instead, she pulled her mouth away, giggled and said, "You pay bar, I come your room, okay?"

He shook his head and his bearded jowls flapped.

Pay the fucking bar fine or stop squeezing my tits, she thought.

Watermelon leaned over, kissed him on the cheek, and smiled. In her helium-high voice, she squeaked, "You handsome man."

"No, I am fat ugly man, ja."

She suppressed a laugh: at least he was right about that.

Then she looked over at the stage of the Hot Pussies Go-Go Bar, where nine or ten women were dancing in matching red thongs and bras to a techno song. The flashing lights painted their faces and bodies with shades of pink, blue, orange and green. At the front,

Bird was rubbing her crotch against a silver pole and smiling down at some cute young guy sitting at the bar that ringed the stage.

That greedy bitch had stolen Watermelon's customer last night after she'd been sitting with the guy for two hours. It was only half-way through the month and Bird had been bragging to the other girls that she'd already racked up ten bar fines and eighty-five drinks. Although Watermelon, tiny and fair-skinned, considered herself to be the prettiest girl who worked there, she'd had a dismal month: only two bar fines and fifteen drinks.

As Bird turned around to rub her crack up and down the chrome pole, the German leered at her.

"Don't look at her. She have AIDS." It was the kind of vicious lie she'd been telling lately about any of the girls who made more money than she did, to the point where none of the other go-go dancers wanted anything to do with her.

After four years of working at various go-go bars around Patpong, she couldn't hustle the way she used to. More and more often, when she wasn't dancing, she found herself sitting alone in the corner, thinking of ways she could get enough money to start her own little beauty parlor in Bangkok, bring her daughter back from her parents' village in Chiang Mai province, and find a new husband who had a decent job.

She didn't think that was too much to ask for from life. So why was she stuck here?

To end up as a whore in this life she must've committed some terrible sins in her previous one (probably even killed somebody); that's why she was being punished like this. But as long as she kept doing good deeds when she could, and giving alms to Buddhist monks, then she might be able to improve her bad karma.

With the money she'd already saved up, all she needed was a couple of thousand more dollars, and then she'd have enough to go into business for herself.

The fat guy beside her, now rubbing her pussy through her thong, was going to be her ticket out of here. Looking at his gold Rolex watch, diamond ring and Versace shirt, it was obvious that he was rich. Since he was staying in a fancy hotel, it was also obvious that his expensive clothes and jewelry weren't the fakes that they sold in the Night Bazaar right outside the bar.

Earlier, when he'd taken out his wallet to give her a tip, she'd noticed that it was stuffed with American dollars. Then Watermelon lied and said she was going on a trip to Chiang Mai soon—and was it a good idea to take traveler's checks with her?

"I never use in Thailand. I come here three times every year for ten years now, and I never have problem. Thailand is very safe, ja."

So maybe he had more money and jewelry back in his hotel room. Maybe there was an expensive camera she could steal, or even a video camera. But would he keep the rest of his cash and valuables in the room's safety deposit box?

He'd already given her a one-hundred baht tip and bought her three "Lady Drinks," so he must like her. Now she had to get him to pay the bar fine and take her back to his hotel. Hot Pussies was going to close in half an hour, and she was worried that he might wander off to an after-hours disco and pick up someone else. After another song she'd have to go back on-stage to dance again. Her feet were already sore from shuffling and grinding all night in her high heels, and if she did go back on-stage then Bird or one of the other girls might steal her customer. She couldn't take that chance. She had to get him to pay the bar fine now.

With one hand, Watermelon stroked the lump in his trousers, while she rubbed his right nipple through the silk shirt. His blue eyes closed slightly. She then put her hand inside his shirt and circled the nipple with her fingernail as the lump in his trousers grew. The man's eyes closed a little more and she could feel his heart pumping out of sync with the pounding drums. Squeezing the lump reminded her of milking cows on the family farm. She opened another button, leaned over and rimmed the nipple with her tongue, before taking it between her teeth and sucking on it.

His eyes were closed now, and the lump was wriggling as she put her tongue in his ear and tasted some bitter wax. Then Watermelon moaned, "I so horny. You pay bar for me, okay?"

His eyes opened and there was a dazed smile on his face, like he was awakening from a very pleasant dream. "Ja, I pay bar."

Watermelon smiled, gave him a hug and kissed his prickly cheek. "Thank you."

In the dressing room she changed into a bright pink mini-dress with matching high heels and took all of the perfume, makeup, underwear, tampons, her miniature panda bear, and the capsules she was going to use to drug him, out of her locker, and put them in her Snoopy backpack. In the cracked mirror, she wiped the lipstick smears off her cheeks and chin with a wad of damp toilet paper, put some fresh lipstick on, and then brushed her long, lustrous black hair.

Walking out of the bar behind the fat guy, she stopped near the front of the stage and called out Bird's name. When the other woman turned around, Watermelon gave her the finger, yelled, "Fuck off!" and giggled. As she did it, she imagined that it wasn't only the greedy bitch she was telling to fuck off: it was every customer in the bar, the owner, the *mamasan*, and the entire red-light district of Patpong, too.

IN THE BACK of the taxi with her customer, Watermelon's guilt and nervousness about robbing him gave her an upset stomach.

But how many men had ripped her off?

Even after she'd told them in the go-go bar, or in another after-hours club, that her prices were fixed—for "short time" and "all night"—they still kept cheating her. The younger, better-looking guys were usually the worst: they never wanted to pay or they lied and said they would.

As she looked out the window of the taxi at a little stand selling red-pork-and-egg-noodles soup, she remembered that one cute guy with the spiky blond hair. Among her customers, the manicured bankers and cologne-reeking diplomats, the alcoholic whoremongers and the tattooed backpackers like him, many shared the same fantasy: They were such virile lovers that they could even make a prostitute climax. Watermelon spurred on his fantasy with a series of sighs, cresting on each breath as she moaned, "Oh yeah…oh yeah. You hit my G-spot," like an actress repeating lines in a stage play she'd performed dozens of times, while wondering what she would have to eat afterwards (the sweet green curry or the rice noodles with fish balls?). And which pair of flats would go with the new top she'd bought today?

In the throes of arousal, her customers became such mindless animals that they did not realize she was only engaging them with her body. Her thoughts still ranged freely. So it was a little better than working as a seamstress in that garment factory, following patterns on an industrial-sized sewing machine, amidst a racket that made the fillings in her teeth ache and nullified all thoughts. That job demanded both her body and her mind and it didn't pay nearly as well as working in a bar.

Humping away with short, sharp, repetitive strokes, not even varying the tempo at all, he reminded her of the two bunnies she'd bought for her daughter when they got in to mating mode. "Rabbit" was too young and vain to possibly be a good lover. He was more interested in admiring his tattoos, piercings, and muscles in the mirror beside the heart-shaped bed than he was in pleasing her, the kind of customer she had often overheard boasting to his friends, "I shagged that tart rotten last night." Since few of the men spoke much Thai, they were unaware that the bargirls were constantly ridiculing them. Watermelon repeated his boast about her to her former friend Bird, who was sitting in a man's lap beside the bar. Over top of the throbbing dance music, Bird yelled back, "So you had a really big romance last night?"

Watermelon shouted, "Are you kidding? It was the most well paid two minutes of my life." Her and Bird shrieked with laughter.

Another dancer chimed in with an expression for a premature ejaculator, "He's a sparrow dipping his beak," and that caused another chorus of cackles.

All the jokes she made about her customers were less about

revenge than a need to prove she was more than just an empty mortar to be pounded by a series of blood-engorged pestles. Almost any man could rent her body for the right price, but none would ever possess her mind or heart. That was what she used to think. But the longer she worked in a bar, the less true that had become.

After she took a shower and put on her clothes she politely asked Rabbit for her money.

"I don't pay for it, luv."

"You say me already you will to pay, *na*."

And then there was that smug little smirk of his, like he was so superior to her (she wished she could travel back in time now and return the smirk), followed by: "Nobody likes a whore, dear."

Without even letting her pick up her purse, he grabbed her arm, dragged her out of his hotel room, and slammed the door. For a few minutes she pounded on it and yelled at him to give back her purse until a security guard came up and said the man had accused her of trying to steal his watch. So he had to throw her out of his room.

After a long argument with the guard, who also knocked on the door repeatedly, the "cheap Charlie" opened it just wide enough to throw her red purse, emblazoned with gold hearts, on the floor, so that half of the contents spilled out. Blushing with embarrassment, she quickly shoved the package of condoms and the thong back inside it, then checked her wallet to find that the guy had stolen a thousand baht from her. Not only that, the security guard demanded some money—leaving her with barely enough for cab fare—or he said he'd report her to the police for stealing from one of the hotel's guests.

That was far from her worst experience, though. She forced herself to remember the most terrible encounter because it alleviated her guilt about what she was going to do tonight.

Watermelon couldn't remember if that businessman had been from Japan, or Hong Kong, or Singapore—what did it matter?—but he came into the bar after playing a round of golf and still had his bag and clubs with him.

His sick fantasy was for her to sit on the floor of the "short-time" hotel with her back against the bed and spread her legs and sex apart, so he could use his putter to try and tap a golf ball inside her. But he was far too drunk to realize that it was impossible. After about thirty attempts he shoved the ball inside her, raised the club and his other arm above his head, cheered and yelled, "A hole in one!"

Later, he made her kneel on the bed like a dog while he shoved the thin end of two clubs into her anus and vagina, screwing her with them while masturbating. Naked except for his blue socks and white golf cap, the sadist kept ordering her to look in the big mirror on the wall. "Look! Look in mirror!" It wasn't enough for him to make her lose face like this, she thought, his real excitement depended on Watermelon seeing her shame and his superiority.

In between gasps and stabs of pain, she continued to look down at the pillow and think, "I'm being used as a scapegoat for every woman who's ever rejected this fucking creep. And who wouldn't?"

Because he had a pug-nose like a Pekinese, she decided this client's nickname would be "Dog." So when he growled, "You like? You like?" she replied in Thai, "I'll bet you were born in the Year of the Dog, weren't you?" and giggled. Every time he demanded to know if she liked it she made another joke and giggled.

When his pants and moans became whimpers, he grabbed her by the hair, twisted her head around, and spat gobs of disgusting semen all over her face.

Still panting, Dog said, "You don't laugh at me. Too many women do like this already."

Then he punched her in the face and broke her nose.

She curled up in a fetal position, wiping the blood, semen and tears from her face with a sheet, while he got dressed, shoved a couple of bills into her pussy, and left without saying a word.

Since that shameful evening—six months ago—she'd had trouble looking at her face in the mirror without sneering and telling her reflection: "You're nothing but a stupid, rotten whore. No decent man is ever going to fall in love with you again and want to marry you, because you're so disgusting."

Until tonight, Watermelon had never stolen much from her clients except for some loose bills, a couple of expensive watches, and a few hundred multi-hued lighters. Since she didn't smoke, she super-glued them, in the shape of peacocks, flowers and elephants, to cover the cracks in the walls of the one-room apartment she shared with three other bargirls. But she'd been fucked over too many times; now it was her turn to get even and get out of the business. Besides, this fat and hairy "Gorilla" was rich, so he wouldn't really miss the money and jewelry anyway, and maybe she'd give him a good blow-job first, so he wouldn't feel too cheated when he woke up.

If he woke up.

She'd heard a couple of stories about prostitutes drugging their clients. The men overdosed and the women ended up going to jail for twenty-five or thirty years. Watermelon knew one of those women and had gone to visit her a few times at a horrible prison in Bangkok. She always brought her some food, cigarettes, tampons or medicine and fashion magazines. In part, she knew these were selfish gestures: good deeds to help erase her bad karma.

Even working in a go-go bar had to be heaven compared to being imprisoned in a Thai jail, where the cells were so overcrowded that the prisoners had to take turns sleeping on the floor, and the daily food rations consisted of a small bowl of watery rice, and maybe—if you were lucky—a fish head.

Maybe she shouldn't drug this guy. He'd been quite generous so far and would probably pay her well for sleeping with him tonight.

Then she remembered "Dog" growling at her, "Look! Look in mirror! You like? You like?" and that smirking backpacker with the blond hair throwing her favorite purse on the floor in the hallway.

What if Gorilla was a sadist, too? What if he stole her money and beat her up, or gave her AIDS, or even killed her?

To reassure herself, she felt around in her backpack for the switchblade she carried and stroked the plastic handle.

Then she looked down and saw Gorilla caressing her bare thigh. How long had he been touching her like that for? Why couldn't she feel it?

When she thought about it, over the last four years Watermelon had been groped, kneaded, kissed, licked, bitten, screwed and sodomized so many times that her body was slowly dying and that her heart must look like a withered old rose, turning blacker and getting smaller by the night.

If she didn't get out soon, her body and heart were going to die completely. Or she'd end up knifing one of her customers.

But she also had to quit for the sake of her daughter.

A couple of weeks ago she'd telephoned her parents' house in northern Thailand and her five-year-old had picked up the phone. Listening to Duck babble away in that bright voice of hers–a memory of the heart-shaped wind chimes hanging down from the eaves of a Buddhist temple passed through Watermelon's mind–always made her smile and feel like such a proud mother. It was funny how Duck couldn't pronounce some of the Thai tones properly, so when she wanted to say, "We're a very big family," it sounded like, "We're a very big strawberry." She explained the mistake to Duck and they both laughed. In the hope of inspiring her daughter to be more diligent about studying than she'd been, Watermelon taught her the correct tones for "family" and then made her repeat them a few times until she got them right.

Only about three minutes into their conversation, however, her daughter suddenly asked, "Mom, are you really a prostitute? Is that why you never come home and visit me?"

At first, Watermelon was too stunned to say anything. Then she exploded. "I never taught you that dirty word, and I don't want to ever hear you use it again! Do you understand? I'm a beautician and I have to work in Bangkok to help support you and my parents, younger sisters, and my two lazy brothers who never do anything but get drunk."

Duck began crying.

Watermelon rubbed her forehead while scolding herself for being such a bad mother and a liar.

Just then, the taxi pulled up in front of the Watergate Hotel.

WATERMELON TOOK a hot shower and thought about her plan.

Another go-go dancer had told her that the best way to drug a client was to rub some sedatives into her breasts and nipples. But wouldn't he be able to taste the drug when he licked her boobs? Seeing how drunk and horny he was, maybe not. How many capsules should she use? One? Two? Since the guy was so fat, maybe she should use all three. But would that kill him? (The pharmacist had told her that five of them would knock out a tiger.)

Finally, she decided on two capsules, one for each breast.

Before she rubbed the tranquilizers into them, Watermelon moved her gold necklace around so that the tiny Buddha image was facing her back, like she always did before having sex with a customer. That way, the amulet would still protect her, but the Buddha wouldn't be able to see what she was doing.

For lubrication, she put a few globs of Vaseline inside her sex. Then she wrapped a dry towel around herself like a sarong and walked into the cool, air-conditioned room. At the foot of the bed, she put her backpack on the floor with the open switchblade under it.

Gorilla was lying on top of the covers, holding the remote in his hand and channel surfing with the volume turned down. Except for the little lamp with the white shade beside the bed, and the flickering shadows cast by the TV, the huge room was dark.

She lay down beside him, smiled and giggled. "How are you, honey?"

He stared at the TV. "Drunk and lonely."

"Why lonely? I am here, *na*."

"Ya, you are here for money, but you don't like me. It's okay. I don't like me, too."

"I like you."

"*Quatsch!* Don't speak bullshit! I don't like people speak bullshit." What was he so angry about? Was it just all the gin?

Then it occurred to her that the tranquilizers might be seeping into her bloodstream and she'd be the one who fell asleep or overdosed. If she had murdered someone in a previous life, maybe it was this guy and now he'd come to seek revenge. Drugging herself to death while he watched would be fitting karma.

While Gorilla went on and on about how much he missed, and still loved, his ex-wife, Karla, she looked around the dark room. Over by the balcony were two suitcases, but she couldn't see any cameras or jewelry lying around. So maybe they were in the wardrobe? Or was there a safe in the room?

Sitting on the edge of the bed, pretending to listen, she tried to stroke his hand, but he pushed it away.

Now he told her about his job, working as a medic at a clinic for Burmese refugees alongside the border, and gave her a long lecture about Burmese politics and why she should never go there because tourist dollars helped to support their military regime. With only two days off a month, how was she supposed to go anywhere, except if a customer took her on vacation and paid the bar? And who would ever want to visit some poor, boring country like Burma? The only places she wanted to visit were Singapore, for shopping, Hong Kong, because they had a Disneyland, and America, because everyone looked so rich and beautiful in the TV shows she watched.

Watermelon switched off the lamp and squeaked in her helium-high voice, "You think too much. Don't worry, be happy."

He stroked her hair. "Ja, and you think not enough." For the first time that night he laughed.

With her on top they began kissing. Gorilla pulled the towel up over her ass, cupped her buttocks in his palms and kneaded them. His beard scratched her face. Raising herself up on one hand, Watermelon pulled the towel down over her small breasts so that he could lick them. As he sucked her nipples, greedy as an infant for milk and for love, she felt a surprising affection for him that was maternal, not sexual, because he seemed so helpless and needy. The feeling only lasted for a few seconds—until he bit her nipple and made her wince—but it was still good to know that she could feel something for a man besides anger and bitterness.

The pain evaporated while nervousness crept into her mind. He was really licking and kissing her breasts all over, ensuring that he'd get the full dosage. Would it be enough to kill him? How long would it take before he fell asleep?

He rolled her off of him and kissed her neck while he pushed one, then two, then three, fingers inside her. But since that night with the golfer she'd felt nothing when they penetrated her down there but a series of chills that slithered up from between her legs and settled in her stomach, like when a gynecologist put a cold, metal speculum inside her.

Worried that her body, and Gorilla, were both dying on her, she resorted to one of the tricks she used when sleeping with a really ugly customer: rerunning erotic fantasies from her adolescence. Closing her eyes, Watermelon pretended that it was Johnny Superstar fingering her. She saw the pop singer's effeminate face appear in her mind and silently asked him: "Why do all the men that I'm most attracted to always turn out to be gay?"

Johnny, smiling, said, "I used to be gay, my lovely sweetheart, but you turned me into a normal man and now I want to marry you. I'd also love for us to have a child together and—"

Gorilla crushed that fantasy by climbing on top of her, burying Watermelon under his prickly bulk after she'd only felt a few pangs of heartburn for her lost and silly dreams of teenage love.

Automatically, she moaned and sighed with false passion when she only felt sweaty and claustrophobic. But Gorilla was not like her more aggressive customers who wielded their cocks like killers armed with knives, stabbing her with violence and vengefulness. The German knew that he was too big for her and slowed down. He whispered in her ear, "You are like a fine piece of china, the most beautiful girl I ever touch. I don't want to hurt you in any way."

She wished he hadn't said that because, for the first time that night, he became a real person to her, not a customer, not an animal, but a human being. The drug, combined with all the gin, must have been really kicking in now, because Wilhelm's voice took on a new undercurrent of softness, "Karla, do you still love me?" Some of her customers had requested a "girlfriend experience," but no one had ever asked her to play their ex-wife before.

Acutely aware of the sweat pooling in her stomach and needling at the corners of her closed eyes, Watermelon hesitated. She had not been hard-wired to provide any automatic responses to a request like this. Half-heartedly, she said, "Sure, baby, I always love you."

His sweat, salty as tears, dripped on to her closed lips and eyelids. "You will never leave me again, will you?"

Not daring to open her eyes, but with a little more sympathy, she cooed, "No, never. I always stay with you."

Reassured, he began moving his hips again, but slower, gentler, like a man making love to his wife, seeking an intimacy and a connection above and beyond the merely physical. His consideration penetrated a deeper part of her that few of her customers had ever accessed before. Vignettes from her marriage, beginning at the age of sixteen, to a southern Thai Muslim and livestock trader, flickered across her mind like scenes from a grainy film shown at a Buddhist temple fair. Resplendent in his white fez and striped sarong, Vinai smoked tobacco wrapped in a *nipa* palm leaf. Each time he spilled an ash he licked the tip of his index finger, picked it up and put it in the ashtray. It was a small gesture that had grown larger in time, because she'd never seen anyone else do that and probably never would again. It also said a lot about how neat, gentle, and meticulous he was. Unlike her previous boyfriends, he did not expect her to clean up after him, not even a single cigarette ash. After his daily reading of the Quran, her darkly handsome husband always kissed the cover of the book before putting it back on the shelf. Then he would teach her another expression in Arabic that made both of them laugh. "Trust in Allah, but keep your camel tied up." He also enjoyed teasing her about the more extreme elements of Islam that he did not believe in. "You know, sweetheart, by law I could have four wives, but since you're like ten different women rolled into one, I've already got about eight more than I can handle." Watermelon sat down on his lap and tweaked his nose, "If you even have one other wife I'll cut your dick off with a machete and feed it to the pigs." It was the most offensive thing she could possibly say to a Muslim man, but instead of taking offence, his long, feminine eyelashes, which she thought was his most attractive feature, fluttered as he laughed. "Oh, you're such a country girl with all your passion, intensity, and terrible manners. You've got more spirit than all of those prissy, boring office ladies in Bangkok and Had Yai put together." Watermelon answered a phone call from his brother informing her that Vinai, barely twenty, had been killed in a motorcycle accident while visiting his family down south. According to Muslim tradition, they had to bury the body immediately. She would not have the chance to see him one final time or attend his funeral. That, more than anything else, had continued to haunt her.

How could she have ever explained to him that she'd slept with hundreds of men but only ever made love to him? And that grief can don many disguises indistinguishable from madness and not-giving-a-damn depravity.

Watermelon was making love to Vinai. Wilhelm was making love to Karla. How could two people performing the most intimate of acts be so completely lost to each other? This was not sex so much as a form of psychotherapy and mutual grieving. In that it was preferable to grieving alone.

The ghost of her husband, now inhabiting this man's body, pushed his way deeper into her, conjuring a recurring nightmare…at opposite ends of a bridge made from the stretched umbilical cord of their daughter stood Watermelon and Vinai. They called out to each other but the wind whipped their words away. Holding on to the ropes on each side, Watermelon walked towards her husband, foot over foot, on a swaying ribbon of flesh as slender as a tightrope. Vinai walked towards her. But the more they walked the farther away they got. The wind hurled dead owls and palm leaves at her. Digging grit out of one eye, Watermelon watched as the wind grew arms that picked him up and threw him over the ropes. Limbs flailing, he plummeted into a black pit. She let out an ear-piercing scream. Thinking, perhaps, that she was having an orgasm, Wilhelm quickened his pace and, with their thighs slapping together, they filled each other with the desolation of their lovelorn lives, boiled down into the most primitive elements of bodily secretions and saltwater tears.

Wilhelm lay down beside her, panting heavily and groaning.

"You okay?" she asked.

He put his hand on his heart. Ghostly, blue-white images from the TV flickered across his sweaty face. "I feel terrible pain here," he said and patted his heart. "Maybe I am having heart attack, ja."

Watermelon swallowed noisily and it sounded to her like an admission of guilt. When she looked over at him his eyes were closed and he wasn't moving. She tried to wake him up but couldn't. Oh no! Watermelon grabbed his wrist and felt his pulse beating. But for how much longer?

What should she do? She wasn't a murderess. She didn't want him to die. So maybe she should call security and make up some bullshit story; they wouldn't know she'd drugged him.

Chewing on her long, sparkly silver fingernails, Watermelon thought about her daughter ("Mom, are you really a prostitute?"), and then Dog and his golf clubs ("Look in mirror!").

No, she had to stop being a whore. She had to do it for Duck.

Quickly she got dressed and turned on the lamp beside the bed. Gorilla was snoring. Good.

Watermelon crept over to the two suitcases by the balcony, opened the big one and riffled through the contents: shirts, jeans, socks and underwear. Then she opened the smaller suitcase—and hit the jackpot! It was full of plastic bags containing gold Rolex watches, diamonds, rubies, and sapphires. But her smile went flat when she realized they were probably fakes. Either that or this guy was a robber, too.

Stealing from a thief?

"*Wen gum* [That's karma]," she muttered.

A hand grabbed her by the hair and pulled her head back until it felt like her neck was going to snap. Looking up, she saw a dark beer belly.

"You stupid bitch," he said in a groggy voice. "You think you fool me with this drugging trick? No, I fool you."

Gorilla tried to pull her to her feet, but only tore out a clump of Watermelon's hair. Her scalp on fire, she scurried across the floor on all fours to grab her Snoopy backpack and groped for the switchblade, only to hear it click open behind her. "I have your knife," he said.

Watermelon ran for the door in the dark hallway. Feeling around on the carpet for her high heels, she grabbed one of them and stood up to see the silhouette of a monster lumbering towards her. With her fingers wrapped around the toe of the shoe, she pulled it back over her shoulder, took a step forward, and *smacked* him in the face with the stiletto heel.

"*Sheisser!*"

Watermelon dropped the shoe and tried to whip the door open, but it banged against the chain. Just as she slid the chain off and opened the door, he flicked on the light in the hallway. The sudden flash blinded her. She blinked rapidly and looked over her shoulder. Standing there naked, his beer belly hanging down over his cock, he stared at her with tears seeping from one blue eye and blood weeping from an empty socket. His other eye stared at her from the palm of his hand.

Feeling as stunned as he looked, she stood there, muttering, "I'm sorry, I'm sorry..."

Watermelon ran down the hallway and slammed the button for the elevator.

One of them was on floor 18, the other on 12.

"Hurry up! Hurry up!"

Down the hallway she saw Gorilla, a towel around his waist, lumber out of the room and bellow, "Vake up everybody! Vake up! There is a thief in our hotel!"

Watermelon bolted for the stairway.

Holding the metal railing to propel herself around the corners, her bare feet slapped against the concrete stairs while the numbers of the floors flashed by: 6, 5, 4, 2....

Out of breath, she stopped on the ground floor, her heart drumming against her breast. What if he had caught the elevator and was waiting for her in the lobby with one blue eye in his hand? What if he'd called security? But she couldn't stay here and waiting would only increase the chance of her getting caught.

Wiping the sweat from her forehead, she walked across the cool marble floor of the gleaming lobby, feeling very suspicious in her bare feet. Fortunately, nobody seemed to be around except for the doorman and the front desk clerk. She smiled and politely asked the desk clerk for her ID card; it was a fake, so it didn't matter if he'd written down the name and number. For once, she was grateful for the condescending way he dropped her ID on the counter without so much as a word or even a glance.

Quickly she strode towards the front door, shooting glances over her shoulder at the blinking numbers of an elevator descending (6…5). Up ahead was the doorman, who stared at her bare feet and frowned (4…3). The doorman was dressed in this old-fashioned Siamese costume of bright silk. Earlier, when she'd walked in with her customer, he'd opened the door for them, but he made no effort to do so now.

Just as she put her hand on the door, she looked around to see a young Asian guy walk out of the elevator.

Watermelon exhaled audibly and smiled.

When the taxi was six streets away from the hotel, and she hadn't seen any police pick-up trucks or motorcycles, she figured she was in the clear.

It was sickening to remember how she'd knocked his eye out with her high heel, though. If she didn't make a decent donation to the temple in her village, the Buddha was going to be very, very angry with her.

After she'd visited her daughter and family for a couple of months—Gorilla and the police would've given up looking for her by then—Watermelon knew she'd have to come back to Bangkok to work in another bar. Since her parents could only afford to send her to school for six years, she didn't have many other choices. Obviously, she couldn't go back to Patpong; but some of her room-mates worked at a new go-go bar called Bad Girls in Nana Plaza, so maybe she'd work there and finally meet some rich guy who wanted to marry her.

Watermelon let out a yawn that made her lower jaw tremble and slumped down in the back seat. She could still feel Wilhelm's bulk (or was it all the guilt and disappointment?) pushing down on her chest, along with the deadweight of every customer she'd slept with over the past four years. How many had it been? Two hundred? Three hundred? As many as four hundred? She wasn't sure, but it felt as if she had that invisible Siamese ghoul, who sits on the stomachs of dreamers while they sleep and slowly suffocates them to death, sitting on her chest, right now.

If she kept saving her money, however, and stayed away from drugs and gambling like she'd done so far, then maybe in another year or two she'd be able to set up her own little beauty parlor and bring her daughter to live with her in Bangkok.

Whatever happened, Watermelon swore to herself, and made a promise to Vinai's spirit, that their daughter would never end up as a prostitute.

When the taxi stopped at a red light the driver looked back at her and sharked a grin that made Watermelon shiver and look away. Using a slang term for a one-night stand, he said, "Do you want to go up to heaven? I have a big rocket that'll take us there in a very short time." Even though the driver was at least fifty, he laughed and laughed like a teenager.

Resigned to her bad karma for the next few years, but none too happy about it, Watermelon pushed herself up in the backseat with her elbows and smirked at him in the rearview mirror like Rabbit had once done to her. "How much are you willing to pay, *Mr. Rocket?* So you can go up to heaven and I can go down to hell."

THE LEGENDARY NOBODY

For Jody Penhall
(Based on a true crime story)

H is body melted into dreams rising like smoke from an opium pipe, where his wife tickled his face with her hair. "I love to see my cute little mouse wake up with a smile on his face," she said.

When See Ouey opened his eyes, the only thing tickling his face was a creepy-crawly scampering across his forehead. He swatted the insect away. He spat a curse and sat up in the back of the rickshaw. Every night was the same. No sooner had he drifted off to sleep than insects ruined his rest.

See Ouey sparked a match, the smell of phosphorus wrinkling his nose. As the flame flared, he moved the match across the wooden planks of the rickshaw, crawling with chubby brown cockroaches. He smashed a few of them with one of the rubber sandals he'd cut from a car tire. With every smack, he recalled his mother berating him as a boy, some Buddhist or Taoist saying, "If you kill an insect you'll be stupid for a week."

Smashing them was a futile pursuit anyway; the insects scurried away too quickly. Sweat raining down his chest and forehead, See Ouey breathed a sigh of defeat and put on his sandals.

He stepped down from the rickshaw. As soon as he tried to stand upright, pain shot up his spine and struck his head like a hammer blow. He groaned and massaged his lower back. Pulling rickshaws for three years in Bangkok, and the two decades he'd spent bending over rice fields on the Chinese island of Hainan, made it impossible for him to stand up straight anymore.

Little by little, he thought, I'm bending towards the grave. Soon I'll be crawling around on all fours and all those horrible Thais will be right when they call us Chinese laborers "human animals."

The street was dark, the moon cobwebbed with clouds. The only light came from a single streetlamp near the corner of Chinatown's Yaowarat Road. From the moon's position in the sky, perched above the dragon silhouetted on the shrine's rooftop, he figured it must be around 3 a.m.

Now that he thought about it, See Ouey realized that his mother was right. All the insects he'd killed and eaten had made him this stupid and illiterate. It was the only explanation he could think of for his miserable life and rotten luck. Well, there was that, and the Japanese soldiers and the Thais.

He walked around the rickshaw massaging his lower back. As those aches dulled, the stabs of hunger sharpened. See Ouey wrapped his arms around his stomach. He rocked back and forth. All he'd eaten that day was a bowl of rice porridge salted with fish sauce, and a couple of half-rotten bananas. The meat and produce stalls in the Old Market wouldn't be open for another hour or two but, when he counted the coins in his pocket, all he had was barely enough to cover the rent of the rickshaw. Thinking about his favorite Hainanese dish—boiled chicken breasts, dowsed with soy sauce and the red and green chili peppers Thais called "mouse droppings"—deepened his hunger.

Arms wrapped around his stomach, he paced the street, passing Chinese-style shop-houses with metal grates and a pile of garbage where rats scampered through the debris rattling cans. The stench of rotting pineapples and dog shit burned through his nostrils and tunneled into his brain, unearthing memories he had tried to bury:

See Quey crawled through the mud on his elbows, the explosion of cannonballs rippling the earth under his stomach...he ran across the battlefield, a Buddhist amulet in his mouth to protect him, the smoke thick enough to obscure the bayonet on the end of his rifle…a cannonball exploded in front of him and he bit down on the clay Buddha image, choking as he swallowed it…the commander in his brigade ordered the soldiers to cut the livers out of the corpses of Japanese soldiers and eat them raw. "We must take on the power of our enemies. It's the only way we can defeat them."

Even dog meat, even the soup made of offal, tasted better than those bloody livers. For days after consuming them he had diarrhea and nausea.

That was the image he most often associated with the war: a half-eaten Buddha image sitting in a pile of blood, faeces and chunks of undigested liver from a dead soldier.

But their commander was right. Only two days later they overran the Japanese forces along the coastline of Hainan.

Power was what he needed now: power. It was the only way he could earn enough money to go home and see his wife again.

"Hey! I need a ride home."

He looked over at the man, dressed in trousers with some kind of Western-style hat. He was fat, so he had to be rich, and the man was sweating beer. Slowly he swayed from side to side like rice stalks in a breeze. He'd probably just been to see one of the prostitutes in Green Lantern Lane, which was Bangkok's main red-light district in the 1950s.

See Ouey's prayers to the Black Tiger God at the shrine devoted to him had finally been answered. The god had delivered this man to him at precisely this moment for exactly this purpose. But what should he do now? On the battlefield, he only remembered killing one Japanese soldier, and that was by accident: the Jap had leapt into their trench and fallen on the upright bayonet of See Ouey's rifle— a machete lashed to the barrel with strands of bamboo. The bayonet pierced the Jap's stomach. Eyes and mouth agape, See Ouey looked at the soldier sliding down the bayonet towards him, spewing entrails that smelled like a meat market on a hot day. In the cannonade of shells bursting and gunfire cracking, the enemy soldier could not have heard his apology, "I'm sorry. Please forgive me." The Jap tried to speak. All that came out was a dribble of blood trickling down onto See Ouey's face. Under the soldier's weight, the rifle shook in his hand. He could barely hold it upright. The Jap was almost on top of him now, their eyes locked together in mutual surprise. Then the rifle slipped backwards and the dead Jap landed on him face first—

"Hey! I said I need a ride home."

It was that air of impatience and self-importance the rich exuded that bothered him the most, like their time was always more valuable than his, as if See Ouey had been waiting around all night just to lug them home. The rich were like whiny children with teething pains who needed mothers to smear opium on their gums.

See Ouey wiped the sweat from his forehead. He walked over and asked him, "Where do you want to go?"

The man said, "Surawong. I'll give you twenty-five *satang*."

Ashamed of his ragged blue pyjamas, tiny physique and faltering Thai, See Ouey looked down at the dirt road. "Twenty-five satang...too far."

"Well, that's what I usually pay."

"Too far twenty-five satang. Very late." Dealing with drunks was one of the worst parts of the job. Sometimes they vomited in the back of the rickshaw. Then he'd have to clean it up. Sometimes they refused to pay. Often they berated him for not going fast enough.

"Never mind. I'll go and find another rickshaw Chink." The drunk turned and teetered down the road.

Rickshaw Chink. Rickshaw Chink. Rickshaw Chink. How many times had he been called that in Bangkok? Dozens and dozens. Every time he'd swallowed their insults and his anger. He'd swallowed them, yes, but he'd never digested them. In his stomach a wok steamed and sizzled with rage even stronger than his hunger.

But the anger was also a tonic. His back no longer ached. His stomach cramps disappeared. The battlefield memories dissolved like cannon smoke. Walking back to his rickshaw, See Ouey grabbed the hollowed-out buffalo horn he used to scoop water from the canals and stole up behind the fat man, stealthy as a tiger: the meat of a man or an animal made no difference to the Black Tiger God who now guided him.

See Ouey leapt into the air, bringing down the buffalo horn on the back of the man's neck with all the force he could muster. The horn cracked against bone, sending vibrations running down his arm. The man fell face first onto the dirt road, wriggling as blood gurgled from the wound. The god had taken possession of See Ouey; the buffalo horn was its single fang.

The man mewled as the god opened up wound after wound in his back. With each stab, he heard insults clashing together in his head like cymbals at a Chinese opera: "Rickshaw Chink! Human animals! The Chinks who destroyed the temples! Pussy blood Chinks! Chink! Chink! Chink!"

He could not stab fast enough to pay back every slur.

The front grate of a shop-house clanging open or shut pierced his inner ears. He looked up and down the street. He couldn't see anyone. Not yet. But soon enough the vendors would be bringing their food and fruit carts down the street to the market.

He rolled the dead man over. Without looking at the corpse's face, he ripped open his shirt, buttons popping. The Black Tiger God opened the man's stomach with its fang and tore out the liver with its claws. The liver was still warm as he closed his eyes to take the first bite. Blood flooded his mouth. The first gristly bite went down with a grimace. Immediately, his stomach tightened and tried to expel it. Vomit leapt into his mouth. He clamped his hand over it and forced himself to swallow.

The steel grate of a shop-house opened with a clang that caromed down the street. The Black Tiger God forced the rest of the liver into his mouth, gnawing on the gristle as he tried to saunter, when he wanted to run, back to the rickshaw. Wiping his mouth clean with his hand, he grabbed the rickshaw and pulled it towards the canal.

Down by the waterway, flanked by wooden houseboats with corrugated iron roofs, cocks crowed as the sky faded from black to blue. At least the marshy smell of the water drowned out the taste of blood clogging his throat.

Concrete stairs led down to the canal's edge. Squatting like a duck on the bottom step, he washed his hands and cleaned the horn. Its tip was dented and bloodied with scalp tissue. Then he scooped up water with the horn, gulping down mouthful after mouthful.

See Ouey knew he should throw the murder weapon into the canal, but it was the only memento he had left of his homeland. Lately he'd heard the Thais adopt a Chinese expression "to travel with a pot and a mat" for any trip taken on the cheap, because that was all most of the Chinese immigrants had brought with them to Thailand. Hungry and destitute, See Ouey had pawned his cooking pot and sleeping mat two years ago.

The horn belonged to his first pet, a female water buffalo born in the early morning, so he named her *Seow Fung*, the "Scent of Dawn." Thinking of her, he stroked the horn as if it were the animal's dark hair. As Seow Fung grew bigger, he rode her alongside the rice paddies, past the orchards of dragon fruit, and down by the cliffs that overlooked the South China Sea spangled with sunbeams.

When Seow Fung was only eight, she was dragged away by the floods of the monsoon season with winds that pulled back palm trees like catapults, launching coconuts into the sea. For days on end he searched for her. Beside a stand of bamboo, he found Seow Fung's corpse, bloated with water and blackened by the sun. Flies licked the tears from his face as he knelt in the mud beside her.

Ten years later, when he told that story to his first girlfriend, she said, in the special voice she reserved only for him, a smile on her sun-freckled face, "I know I could find a richer and more handsome husband than you, but I don't think I could ever meet a man with such a heart as soft as tofu."

What would she say now that the Tiger God had forced him to kill a man and eat his liver? Could he ever tell her about the cannibalism that both the Chinese and Japanese soldiers practiced on the battlefield? His stomach clenched. His eyes and throat burned.

Sadness, he thought, was a kind of hunger that worked in reverse. It made him feel as hollowed out as Seow Fung's horn, which he had cut off and kept as a memento of her that also served as a good-luck charm.

See Ouey knew that keeping the murder weapon might be his undoing, but it could also be a talisman that would protect him. In either case, he would not part with the horn.

Across the canal he saw a couple of women wearing sarongs walk down the steps to bathe in the water. He wiped his eyes and trudged back to the rickshaw. Using some banana leaves he found on the ground, he wrapped up the buffalo horn and went to hide it under the backseat. His hand stopped in mid-air. Running across the floor of the rickshaw were trains of ants cannibalizing and carrying off the antennae, the wings and the legs of all the dead cockroaches.

Watching the ants cheered him up. He was not alone. He was not strange. Life fed on death. This was nature's way. The fat man had been one of those cockroaches. He had to die so the Black Tiger God could live.

BY MIDNIGHT MANY rickshaw-pullers gathered at the entrance to Green Lantern Lane, a noisy strip of bars where men caroused with prostitutes and took them upstairs to small rooms, or to one of the Chinese hotels in the neighborhood. Groups of women in short dresses sat outside the bars on wooden benches. The light from all the green lanterns hanging above them made their skin look like rotten meat.

See Ouey had never been inside any of the bars. Before he left on the boat for Thailand, his wife made him promise to remain faithful. So far, he had kept that promise. Yet his eyes kept wandering down over the breasts and thighs of the "chickens" as they passed by with their customers. The prostitutes wore the same heavy make-up as the female characters in a Chinese opera. They rarely looked at any of the rickshaw-pullers, who made filthy remarks about them in Mandarin and Hakka slang. "Look at her! She's got tits the size of pears!" See Ouey laughed along with the men, but he never flung any insults of his own, because it wasn't fair. Most of the women (some still teenagers) understood the lewd jokes. Not many of their customers did. He didn't hate the girls. He hated the men, sneering at them every time they walked by, as the envy, the bitterness and the sexual hunger fermented inside him like rice liquor; the longer it brewed the more potent it became.

Was that it? Or was the fresh liver he'd eaten last night finally stirring some kind of power within him? Something was turning and twisting inside his stomach, something waiting to be born. When, he wondered, had he started thinking with his stomach rather than his mind?

Standing on the perimeter of the group oozing sweat, See Ouey eavesdropped on snippets from half a dozen different conversations... "somebody killed a man in Chinatown last night..." "no suspects, witnesses or arrests yet..." "I hear the police are out in force tonight."

None of this had anything to do with him. He hadn't killed or eaten anyone. It was the Black Tiger God. Still, the events of last night had set him even further apart from the other rickshaw-pullers. They were weak and pathetic. They made jokes about the customers, but they still groveled for business. "Where are you going, sir? I'll give you a good price." See Ouey couldn't be bothered anymore. Three years of groveling had gotten him nowhere. Whatever extra money he brought in from building roads and repairing bicycles he stashed inside the buffalo horn to send to his wife. The Hainanese man who composed the letters See Ouey dictated to her folded the bills inside them. But he hadn't received any replies from his wife in six months. Had she gotten the money? Had she given up on him and found another man?

Tik Lin trudged towards him with the same bow-legged, stoop-shouldered gait that marked all the rickshaw-pullers in Bangkok for life. The sweat on his face gleamed under the streetlight. He had a cigarette rolled from a banana leaf hanging out of his mouth just like those white movie stars in the hand-painted posters outside the cinemas.

Tik Lin was one of the few men from his village who had also survived the Japanese occupation and deserted the army to come to Thailand. At least he had learned how to read and write. He'd become fluent in Thai, too, and liked to joke with his customers that since he was actually a wealthy Thai banker, would they mind pulling him around for a while? Thanks to all his quips, mimicry and funny faces, Tik Lin got a lot of tips. So every night he'd buy a bottle of liquor fermented in herbs and pass it around to all of his friends.

Tik Lin knocked back a shot. Passing the bottle to See Ouey, he arched his left eyebrow and winked with his right eye. "This is better than a rhino's horn for making a man's own horn grow big and strong. Wait till we get back to Hainan. Our wives are going to be sore for a month." Tik Lin laughed loud enough for the other rickshaw-pullers to look in their direction.

See Ouey smiled out of politeness and looked away out of shyness. After knocking back a few more bitter shots, spilling liquor down their chins as they got drunker, See Ouey said, "We haven't heard from our wives for months now. Do you think it has something to do with these communalists?"

"Communists."

See Ouey took another swig of liquid fire. "Right. Communists. But who are they anyway?"

Tik Lin snatched the bottle out of his hand. "Can't you remember anything? We've been through this eighty-seven times already."

It was embarrassing the way he would flare up like a match head and make these crazy exaggerations. See Ouey pulled his straw hat down to cover his eyes and waited for him to calm down. He took another swig from the bottle.

When he was drunk, things he never noticed demanded his attention, like the halo of blue rimming the silver streetlight, while questions he never asked demanded answers he could not find. Why were the insects attracted to the light? Was the darkness too lonely for them? Didn't they know the light would kill them? And how did electricity work anyway?

If he kept drinking he might find those answers. That was always the lie of liquor. His body got heavier, his tongue grew thicker, but his thoughts circled the streetlight like those insects, touching down briefly before flying off again in a different direction.

Tik Lin was showing off by counting his money aloud. Trying not to smile, See Ouey interrupted him so he would have to start again. "What were you saying about those…um, *communalists?*"

Tik Lin glared at him. The streetlight glanced off his eyes. "Let's go through it one more time. According to Professor Tik Lin, communism is supposed to be about equality. In our country that means five percent of the population are equally rich and the other ninety-five percent are equally poor. Got it now? Don't make me repeat it again."

See Ouey lifted up the bottle and took another shot. His tongue and throat were numb. "The communists, the Japanese, the Thais, what difference does it make? Life is one losing battle after another, one hardship after another. I'm so sick of it all I don't even care anymore."

"Look at it this way. Many of our friends and family members aren't even alive now. We're lucky we survived." Tik Lin raised the bottle up in the direction of the moon. "To you, father, mother, big sister, little brother, and all our dead friends from the village. I will always be grateful for your many favors and kindnesses."

Every time he got drunk Tik Lin repeated the same sentimental spiel. See Ouey snatched the bottle out of his hand and drained it. "Most of the time I wish I was dead, too."

"Big brother, I'm not going to indulge your bitterness anymore. I have to go and find a rich customer for one last fare of the night." He staggered towards the other rickshaw-pullers.

Tik Lin was a liar, too. He was actually going to see one of the whores like he did every time he got this drunk. "What a fool…rhino horn…oh, I'm a rich Thai banker…yes, sir…please, sir…thank you, sir," See Ouey muttered to himself. "Go to hell, sir. The Black Tiger God's fang is much stronger than your horn."

See Ouey squatted down on the dirt road, losing his balance and falling over sideways on his right elbow. Cockroaches skittered past him. He stood up and began stomping on them, pretending they were communists, Japanese soldiers and rich customers who'd scorned him.

Slathered in sweat, See Ouey squatted like a duck beside the metal shutters fronting a Chinese herbalist. The smell of herbs seeped from under the shutters. He drained the last drops of liquor from the bottle. Just then, one of the women, wearing a short red dress walked out of the huddle of rickshaw-pullers, arousing stares and a few wisecracks. She returned the insults and laughed.

See Ouey stared at the roundness of her breasts, like Chinese pears ripe for the licking. His mouth opened. As she came closer, her heels scraping the dirt, his eyes moved down to the darkened hollow between her legs, imagining the swallow's nest feathered with fine black hair. When she walked past, his eyes fastened themselves to the mounds of her bottom, near enough so he saw the upside down triangle of her underwear.

His testicles began breathing.

Without wanting to, without even thinking about it, See Ouey stood up and followed her. The lane was dark and narrow. It was flanked by shop-houses. He couldn't stop, couldn't think, couldn't do anything but creep up closer and closer behind her. The young woman's hips held sway over him. They pulled him along like a water buffalo with a rope through its nose.

The Black Tiger God *smashed* her over the head with the empty bottle. She fell to her knees beside a pile of baskets stinking of garbage. Wielding the bottle like a club, he dented the back of her skull three more times. She fell on her face. He grabbed her by the hair and rolled her over on to her back. He knelt down and dropped the bottle. Then the god ripped the front of her dress open and tore off her bra.

She let out a shriek and tried to slap his face. With one hand he pinned her arms. With the other, he grabbed the gold chain around her neck and pulled it tight as a noose. The woman gurgled and wept. Her eyes bulged like a toad as he tightened his stranglehold.

After she stopped struggling, he looked at her bare breasts, massaging them with his palms, before taking the bud of her right nipple into his mouth as he slid her underwear down. Moving on top of her, he pulled the bottoms of his pyjamas down.

She screamed.

"Shut up!" he hissed.

She screamed again.

He smashed the bottle open and stabbed the serrated side into her throat. As the bottle severed her jugular vein a geyser of blood erupted.

The coppery smell and taste gave the Black Tiger God a rush of bloodlust. With his fangs, he tore off her nipple. Using the jagged end of the bottle like a phallus, he pushed it in and out, in and out, the bottle squelching as it sawed back and forth inside her sex.

Down the street a dog barked. Another dog howled.

See Ouey looked up. Then he looked down at the woman, her throat gashed open like a vagina. What happened? Where was he? Who was she? He couldn't remember anything. One minute he was talking to Tik Lin, the next he was kneeling beside this woman, whom somebody had murdered. Why? Why would someone do that?

See Ouey picked up the gold chain and put it in his pocket. With blood drying on his face, he ran down the lane as a pack of street dogs tore at the flesh of the dying woman.

II. Meditations on Death Row

THE CELLS IN THE JAIL reminded See Ouey of the cargo hold in the belly of the boat he and Tik Lin had sailed on to Thailand. The hold was dark and dank, too, poisoned with the eye-watering stench of sweat and urine, rats and roaches scuttling everywhere. In a way, death row was better: no swells or storms to turn his stomach inside out. In another way, it was far worse: See Ouey was astonished to find out that he'd become the biggest mass murderer in Thai history.

"Watch your back, cannibal," one of the guards told him, "because you're going to get eaten alive in here. That's why they nick-named this prison the 'Big Tiger.'"

Wearing leg-irons like all the other inmates, See Ouey sat in a corner of the cell with four other Chinese men, near a hole in the floor for a toilet. He always kept his back against the wall to watch the other convicts.

The only relief from the constant threats and the boredom was playing mahjong with bottle caps. Between games, See Ouey and the other Chinese men passed their days complaining about the prison, the guards, the lousy food, their unfair death-sentences, pulling rick-shaws, the communists, the Japanese soldiers—one complaint after another. The other men had been convicted of murdering the local owner of a Thai fishing trawler who had refused to pay them their wages after four months at sea.

None of them complained as bitterly as See Ouey. He had not killed three men, one woman and four children. The police had made him a scapegoat. All he could remember was the Black Tiger God consuming the fat man and the prostitute, pawning the gold necklace and getting drunk with Tik Lin, who berated him in the back of his rickshaw one night. "I can't believe you sent those letters to your wife warning her about how bad life was here and that she shouldn't come unless she wanted to work on Green Lantern Lane."

"I thought it was better to be honest."

"You're not honest. You're just stupid and naïve. No wonder our wives found other men. I also can't believe you trusted that man to actually send the money to your wife."

"He was my friend. He was from Hainan. So I trusted him."

"He's an opium addict and you can never trust them."

"Is he?"

"Look at him! You could stand him up in a field to scare the birds away."

See Ouey remembered their argument, but he didn't recall kill-ing Tik Lin and eating his liver, like the police said. He also didn't recall murdering the pawnbroker who wrote the letters for him and promised to send the money to his wife. Those killings were not his fault. He was drunk and the Black Tiger God was hungry. That was all.

A rat landed in See Ouey's lap. He leapt to his feet, squealing. Some of the inmates laughed. One of them yelled, "Hey Chink, I thought you were hungry." See Ouey snatched up the rat and bit off its head. He spat the head at the inmate who had yelled at him. He bared his teeth and snarled at the dozen other inmates in his cell. Then he threw the rat on the floor and leapt up and down like a monkey, chattering gibberish, until the guards restrained him.

One of the inmates said, "Better leave him alone. The fucking cannibal is crazy."

See Ouey's ploy paid off. The other inmates, even the guards, thought he was insane. From a distance, they still taunted him in the prison yard, where the death-row convicts were only allowed an hour a day of sunlight, but they wouldn't come near him.

That would prolong his life a little. It would not save him from the executioner. The inmates on death row lived with the constant threat of their sentences being executed without any warning whatsoever. There were no appeals and no reprieves, no chances to contact or meet with their friends and families. The guards came for them late in the afternoon. Within twenty minutes they were dead. One convict in the cell next to him had heard a rumor that he was next and slashed his wrists open. The guards took him to the doctor to stitch up the wounds. Then he was executed.

After two months in prison, See Ouey dreamed of a wandering monk he'd once given food and shelter to in his shack by the orchard of dragon fruit on Hainan. The monk reminded him of an old saying he'd first heard his mother use, "Better to light a candle than to curse the darkness."

That was true. For too long See Ouey had cursed the darkness. Now he would light a candle. The monk had shown him how to meditate. At the back of the cell, lit by a single light bulb protected by wire mesh, See Ouey sat cross-legged, his eyes closed, counting to seven as he slowly inhaled. While exhaling he counted backwards. He acknowledged the voices he heard, the smell of bodily wastes, the memories lighting up then dimming, the stabs of hunger. He acknowledged all of these thoughts and sensations. Then he tried to let them go.

Deep in meditation, his breath rising and falling like the sea, he questioned the nature of his anger. What did these words like "rickshaw Chink" really mean? A rickshaw was made out of wood, tires, an axle, seats, and many other things. It was complicated. It was connected to a lot of different things.

Was See Ouey a Chink? There were millions of people in China, all of them different. It was absurd to call them all by the same name.

See Ouey decided that the noises people made with their mouths meant as little as the wind, or children babbling to themselves. From now on, he would speak only when necessary, choosing his words carefully.

Memories kept disturbing his peace of mind. Tik Lin said, "Did you hear about the empress who had a life-size phallus carved out of jade for her personal use?"

"No, I wonder how much that would cost."

Tik Lin cocked an eyebrow. "New or used?"

A smile spread across See Ouey's face. He'd been unfair to his old friend. Sure, Tik Lin was a loudmouth and a braggart, quick-tempered and obsessed with sex, but he loved to make people laugh. Tik Lin liked to remind him that he was too serious, that he didn't see the funny side of life. And he was right about See Ouey's bad memory, his poor judgment of other people, and his selfish bitterness—

See Ouey jumped up and down on Tik Lin's chest, breaking his ribs, crushing his lungs.

Remembering that murder, he opened his eyes. No, no, no. He massaged his forehead with his hands to wipe away the memories. He concentrated on his breathing again. But he couldn't escape the truth. The Black Tiger God had not done that to Tik Lin. See Ouey had. The Black Tiger God hadn't killed or eaten or raped anyone. See Ouey had done these things. There was no one else to blame. Not the alcohol or the opium, the Japanese or the communists, the poverty or the discrimination.

But the four children? He only remembered throwing the pawn-broker's son against a wall to make him stop crying. He didn't remembering devouring the boy's liver.

How did that happen? The last few days of his freedom returned to him through the murky, fish-bowl haze of a week-long debauch, alternating days of alcohol with ten-pipe sessions in different opium dens. He remembered pawning the gold necklace. He remembered the argument with Tik Lin, but what night was that? The third or fourth night? The fifth?

His legs went numb. He unfolded them and rubbed his calves. The chains around his ankles chafed at all the blisters weeping pus.

He remembered lying in the opium den on the wooden bed, beside one of the hard, square pillows the owners used to discourage customers from staying too long, when the woman he'd killed looked down on him, her red dress in tatters, a mirror covering the breast he'd savaged. The mirror was emblazoned with an image of the Black Tiger God holding a blade in its mouth. But the mirror reflected See Ouey's eyes and teeth. She held up her hands, two more mirrors glued to her palms, like he was an evil spirit she wanted to banish. Each of them reflected the same image of the Black Tiger God but with See Ouey's eyes and mouth. He tried to close his eyes but couldn't. He tried to move his head, but that was impossible too.

See Ouey crawled across a battlefield, shells rippling the mud under his belly. See Ouey wormed his way across the floor of the opium den, broken mirrors made out of teeth cutting his hands, the shards spotted with blood, falling down stairs, the street outside, Tik Lin laughing, the moon another mirror image of See Ouey and the Black Tiger God, the corpse of a water buffalo with only one horn trapped inside a cloud, he ran and stumbled, fell and ran, the crazy plan to turn himself in, he'd get a reward if he showed them the murder weapon and told them about the Black Tiger God, they'd send him back to Hainan, he'd be reunited with his wife and Tik Lin...

Stop! He was panting and sweating now. Bottle caps clicked on the floor. An inmate paced the cell, his leg irons clanking while he muttered and laughed to himself: another man gone mad on death row.

See Ouey closed his eyes. He drew in each breath for seven beats, counting backwards as he exhaled. He couldn't attach himself to these memories anymore. The memories were shackles that chained him to the past. Admitting to his guilt, acknowledging his remorse, was enough.

But there was one last thing he had to do before escaping from the prison. He asked one of the Hainanese inmates to write a letter to his wife for him. While the other prisoners slept in rows, packed together as tightly as matchsticks on the bottom of a box, See Ouey and his friend sat together in a puddle of light the color of urine. The heat was such that his friend could only pen a few characters at a time before the sweat from his wrist began to smudge the words.

Slowly and carefully, See Ouey dictated the letter.

"I suppose I could say I love you, but I'm beyond love now. I suppose I could say that I hate myself for doing all these horrible things, but I'm beyond hatred too. At this point, I am almost beyond everything. My biggest problem was my hunger. I was always starving for food, money, love, respect, affection, revenge and many other things. But the more I consumed the hungrier I became and the emptier I felt. It was like feasting on famine. So I was never satisfied.

"My new hunger is much more substantial. I'm trying to attain what that monk called the 'supra-mundane state.' Do you remember when he stayed with us? He told me about how monks practice something called 'meditations on death' by sitting in front of a corpse. There are two hundred dead men down here crammed into a dozen cells. I'm meditating on their breathing corpses and the death of my physical self, which has nothing to do with my mind or karma."

He thought about signing it, "Your Little Mouse," but that was no longer accurate. After considering it for a moment, he told the other inmate to sign the letter from "Nobody."

For the next few days, weeks, months, eons, See Ouey only stopped meditating to drink a little water. He ate little food, he didn't speak, he refused to leave the cell, and he rarely slept. In his mind he conjured up a candle flame and held it there. The flame grew to the size of a lotus blossom that became Nobody's head. The light burned away his hunger, his desires and the darkness around him, so he finally saw the fate awaiting him. It was incredible. It was beyond anything he could have ever imagined.

When the guards came to take him to the execution chamber, they were astonished to find he was in such a good mood, saying goodbye to all the other prisoners, wishing them well, promising them they would all meet again one day. The two guards handcuffed him. Inhale...exhale. On either side of Nobody, their arms interlinked with his, the guards walked him through death row, past two different doors and into a small room that held little except for filing cabinets, a wooden table and a ceiling fan. Inhale...exhale. They took his fingerprints and checked them against their records.

One of them asked, "Are you See Ouey Sae Ugan?"

"No, he died in prison. I have no name, but you can call me 'Nobody' if you wish."

The guard offered him a final meal.

"Thanks, but I'm on a diet, and frankly the food in here is terrible." Nobody smiled at them.

"Would you like a cigarette?"

"No, thanks." Nobody cocked an eyebrow. "I've heard that tobacco can kill you."

The guards looked at each other. When they saw him smile, all three of them began laughing.

By making these jokes and smiling at them, Nobody wanted to show the guards that he did not bear any malice towards them. It was not their fault they were this ignorant and famished for justice that did not exist. No one knew better than him that there is no such thing as justice. It's another meaningless noise people make with their mouths; it means no more than "Chink" or a birdcall.

The guards took him into another room and made him kneel before a monk with a shaven head, an age-speckled face and a saffron robe. The monk asked him if he wanted a blessing. Nobody smiled and looked up at him. "That's very kind of you, but I met a wandering monk in Hainan who told me that real Buddhism has nothing to do with rituals or blessings. In my own way, I'm a religious man, too."

See Ouey sneered at the monk and snapped, "Don't you dare look at me with that self-righteous smile on your face. You can't kill me. None of you can. Mark my words, I'm coming back to haunt all of you. I'm your bad conscience and I'm your worst goddamn nightmare!"

The guards dragged him to his feet. See Ouey spat on the monk's robes. His eyes darting from the guards back to the monk, he shouted, "All of you are a pack of stupid, vicious dogs. You're thieves, liars and hypocrites. You can all go to hell. When I come back I'm going to kill all your children, your wives, your relatives—"

A guard punched him in the stomach. See Ouey doubled over and fell to his knees. The blow forced him to concentrate on his breathing again. Inhale… exhale. Inhale… exhale.

Even now, so close to the end, and after months of meditation practice, he could not control his ego, his anger and his insatiable appetite for revenge.

The guards pulled him to his feet. Inhale…exhale. Down another corridor, cool cement under his feet, the hospital smell of urine and cleaning fluid, out through another metal door, the sun slitting his eyes. Inhale… exhale. Grass, bushes and flowers.

A yellow butterfly zigzagged across the prison yard. Nobody stopped. He said to the guards, "I didn't ask for a meal or a cigarette, but See Ouey and his old friend Tik Lin used to like chasing butterflies across the fields when they were boys. Just a few seconds, please."

The wandering monk had told him a riddle or parable, "Am I a man who dreamed he was a butterfly? Or a butterfly who dreamed he was a man?"

Nobody decided that he was a butterfly who had only dreamed he was a man. As the butterfly zigzagged across the prison yard, he willed the rest of his consciousness to it. When it flew up and over the wall, clearing the brambles of barbed wire, Nobody smiled.

Short steps, the leg irons rattling. Inhale… exhale. Inhale…

exhale. Another room cool and dark. A big gun bolted to the floor and pointed at a white curtain, behind it a wooden cross in front of sandbags stained with blood. Inhale…exhale. The guards made him sit down on a beam jutting out of the cross. They unlocked the handcuffs. In his hands they placed a single unopened lotus blossom, a yellow candle and three sticks of incense, like he was going to pray at a temple, which was exactly what he wanted to do. To bind his wrists together, the guard used the same sacred white thread that monks use for ritual blessings. Inhale…exhale. Sweat tickled his spine. They raised his hands over his head and roped them to the cross. Around his face they tied a blindfold tight enough to make a vein leap in his forehead.

Nobody stared into the darkness, where the flame of a candle grew into a lotus blossom of light. The face of the reclining Buddha, eyes closed, smiling serenely, looked back at him from the center of the flame. Nobody smiled at the Buddha: smiling at the sad, stupid futility of it all, and smiling because it was far too late for it to do him any good, but Nobody had finally solved the puzzle of life, the riddle of nirvana.

It was a bayonet in a soldier's stomach.

A half-eaten Buddha image in a pool of blood and feces.

A coconut tossed at sea.

A smiling woman with a sun-freckled face.

A train of ants carrying a cockroach antenna.

A newborn buffalo that smelled like the dawn.

It was everything.

And it was nothing at all.

Exhale….

III. Nobody's Monster

TRUE TO HIS LAST words to the monk, See Ouey's rebirth began when the prison's doctor and psychiatrist held a press conference to announce their findings one week after the execution.

"During the autopsy we found no abnormalities in his brain and from the interviews I conducted with him in the prison it is my professional opinion he was not insane. During the time he carried out the attacks he may have been temporarily insane, but that's something we'll never know for sure. At times he did speak in a delusional manner that made me wonder if he was extremely religious or simply a nihilist.

"For the first few months in jail he was mostly cooperative. Even though we had a Chinese interpreter on hand, See Ouey did not speak a lot. I got the impression he had always been a very quiet and shy man. He did express quite a bit of remorse about his heinous deeds, but he always insisted that his crimes were nothing compared to those committed by the Communist Party of China and the Japanese Imperial Army. After he took up Buddhist studies, he refused to speak to us for the last few months of his incarceration.

"In closing, it is my professional duty to add that many doubts linger as to whether he actually committed all the murders he has been accused of."[1]

The doctor's comments sent See Ouey's spirit hurtling around the world on teletype wires that inspired editorials and hundreds of hate mails. "See Ouey wasn't a man. He was a monster." "The doctor is even crazier than the cannibal."

The hostility only made See Ouey's spirit stronger. His legend grew as it passed from eyes to mouths, from mouths to ears. Thai parents warned their children, "Don't stay out late at night or the ghost of See Ouey will come and eat you."

It was the children who began seeing him first, skulking in the shadows as he followed them home, or standing beside a street-light, his head tipped backwards, his jaws opening like a trap door to swallow the insects as they plunged earthwards.

Five years after his execution, the cannibal's preserved corpse became the main attraction in the Songkran Niyomsane Forensic

---

1. *Bangkok World*, July 17, 1958

Museum in Bangkok's Siriraj Hospital.[2]

To this day, hundreds of tourists and locals pass through here on a daily basis to gawk at all the autopsy and crime-scene photos, crudely labeled in English with lines like, "Beer bottle slash throat" and "Knife cut vagina." Lined up on shelves are jars swimming with stillborn fetuses. Some of the infants who died of water on the brain have bloated heads. For the spirits of these kids, the Asian visitors leave offerings of candy and dolls.

In another glass case is a collection of skulls with bullet holes in their temples. The skulls came from unclaimed corpses. Doctors at the hospital used them to study entry and exit wounds to solve the shooting death of King Rama VIII in 1946, a case that has never been resolved.

The museum is air-conditioned to the freezing point of a morgue. As befitting a crypt, visitors speak in funereal whispers.

In one glass case hangs the skeleton of the museum's founder, who wanted his students to be able to study him after he died. But the number of medical students coming here for lessons in forensics and anatomy are minute compared to the tourists and locals for whom the museum feeds a different kind of hunger, when the gravest taboo becomes the penultimate form of pornography as living eyes probe the naked flesh and preserved organs of the deceased.

Out of the three preserved corpses of murderers propped up behind glass in what look like wooden telephone booths, it's See Ouey's who draws the most stares and frowns from visitors. The cadaver is naked, his shriveled genitals on display. The bullet holes in his chest are visible, but the empty eye sockets have been filled in and whitened with paraffin. Ragged stitch marks on the forehead expose how the doctors removed his brain during the autopsy. Some of the teenagers, trying to act tough and look cool in front of their friends, mutter the same curses See Ouey heard in his day like the

---

2. The preserved corpse of See Ouey Sae Ugan remains the centerpiece of the Songkran Niyomsane Forensic Medicine Musuem in Bangkok's Siriraj Hospital. Visiting hours are from 9am-4pm, Mon-Sat. Admission is 40 baht.

"Chinks who destroyed the temples."

As more and more guidebook writers put the museum on maps, See Ouey's legend feeds on the notoriety. Tourists turn the killer's corpse into mega-pixels that shoot through cyber-space to reach inboxes all over the world. One blogger dubbed him the "Jack the Ripper of Southeast Asia."

A woman woke from a nightmare in Madrid, certain See Ouey was lurking in her room with a broken bottle sticking out of his groin.

In Hong Kong, a filmmaker heard stories about him from a friend who visited the museum. At first the director couldn't believe it. They put a serial killer's cadaver on public display? This sounds like something out of the Dark Ages.

His friend said, "All sorts of legends have sprung up around this guy. The security guard told me that if you stare at his corpse for more than thirty seconds he'll visit you in your dreams. Sure enough, later that night when I drifted off to sleep, his brown cadaver walked into my hotel room, wings burst out of his back and he flew around the room like a cockroach."

"Sounds like *The Metamorphosis* by Kafka," the director said, already thinking about makeup and prosthetic wings.

The director searched for information about him on-line, finding several photos from the museum and a black and white image of See Ouey. The killer was an unattractive man with a flat nose and huge nostrils. His hair was cut short like a soldier's. Several of his front teeth were missing but it was the look on his face that made the director lean closer to the screen. See Ouey's lips were twisted into a vicious snarl. An image ghosted through the director's mind of an Asiatic black bear that growled at him from behind the bars of a cage in a Shanghai zoo. That was the look on the killer's face: a cornered animal snarling in self-defense. It was a good juxtaposition. He could use that for the film.

On the Internet there were only a few bytes of information about the killer: the date of his execution in 1958, his career as a soldier in Hainan, his life of poverty as a rickshaw-puller and laborer in Bangkok and different parts of Thailand. Even the exact number of people he killed—possibly five, maybe nine—was open to speculation.

At night, on the balcony of his condo overlooking Victoria Harbour, the director liked to stand by the railing, smoking Cuban cigars and drinking Chablis, while he used the sky as a screen to project all the images in his mind: wounds opening in a man's back like the mouths of hungry infants lapping up the blood.

He could use that, too, but what was the killer's real story? He didn't want to make another lunatic-on-the-loose movie.

In a perverse way, the director could relate to the killer's hunger. He was hungry, too: hungry for respect and success. His last two films had been ignored by viewers and napalmed by critics. One more disaster and he'd be back directing music videos again or spending four hours in the studio trying to light a bottle of shampoo. He needed a hit and the public was always ravenous for more films about serial slayers. But there had to be a bigger picture to See Ouey's story.

The director began typing up all the horrific tales of death and deprivation his relatives from Hainan had told him about the mass exodus to Hong Kong, Malaysia, Thailand, Singapore, Indonesia and America, like the story his grandmother related about how some of the Chinese "snake heads" who charged the immigrants exorbitant sums for their passage, robbed them and threw them to the sharks in the middle of the sea. On her deathbed, suffering from Alzheimer's disease, his grandmother was convinced that the hospital was the cargo hold of a junk. Again and again she pleaded with them in a girl's hysterical voice: "Don't let them throw me to the sharks like they did to my brother. Please, not that, not that, anything but that."

His grandfather had told him another story. "This rich woman disguised herself as a peasant, but the pirates saw all the gold fillings in her teeth. So they ripped out her teeth, one by one, with a pair of pliers, and then they used her mouth, well, let's just say they had their way with her. As a warning to the rest of us, they hung her body from the mast of the junk. By the time we got to Hong Kong, the crows and seagulls had picked her corpse clean. There was nothing left except a skeleton and a few scraps of clothing. I know I should have a lot more happy memories of my childhood, but whenever I start thinking about the past those are the scenes that come to mind first."

It was disturbing to think that the cannibal could've been onboard the same junk as his grandparents. It was much more disturbing to think that, in some strange way, this man's story was emblematic of a generation of millions of Chinese who had fled the ravages of war only to find worse squalor and debasement than they'd left behind. It was a testament to the strength and family ties of these immigrants that the vast majority of them did not sink to the same levels of cruelty as the pirates and See Ouey.

Even those stories were not enough to write a film treatment. He had to find See Ouey.

The director flew to Bangkok. He dropped his bags at the hotel and headed straight for the museum. In front of See Ouey's final resting case he stood, dumbfounded by all the comparisons to notorious murderers. This little shrimp was the "Jack the Ripper of Southeast Asia" and the "Chinese version of Ted Bundy"?

The cannibal's size bolstered the director's conviction that See Ouey had been the worst kind of coward, targeting women and children he could easily overpower. Like a tiger, he'd probably snuck up on them from behind, not even giving them a chance to fight back.

Something else about the museum bothered him too. Why were these killers so famous and no one ever spared a thought for their victims and families? He spoke into his Dictaphone: "This is not going to be another one of those films where the victims are dispatched like pigs in a slaughterhouse. I need a sub-plot... something about a victim's mother and father. The death of their daughter has brought all their marital problems to a head. Maybe she's a prostitute on Green Lantern Lane. The cops are not interested in the case, so the parents have to track down See Ouey on their own. Unless they can find him, their marriage is finished. Maybe there's a sibling in the picture who's going through a nervous breakdown because of the death of their brother or sister."

The director walked around and around the museum but the only information he could find about See Ouey was a clipping the color of nicotine-stained fingers from a local newspaper taped to the side of the upright casket. The black and white photo was the same one he'd seen on the Internet. No longer was the director so certain that See Ouey looked like a cornered animal snarling in self-defense. He may have been mugging for the camera, playing up to his image, even enjoying his newfound infamy.

Could one man be the predator and the prey, the killer and the victim?

A young woman studying forensics translated the clipping into English for him. It told him nothing he didn't already know. As a little girl, she said, her parents had warned her not to stay out late or the Chinaman's ghost would come and eat her.

See Ouey's monstrous legend was intact, but what had happened to the man himself? He was nowhere to be found. Unless the film-maker could bring his main character to life, the movie would be a commercial and critical fiasco.

The director closed his eyes. He imagined See Ouey's spirit wafting across the museum, chill and invisible as the breeze from the air-conditioners, fluttering up the back of his untucked shirt to skitter across his shoulders and whisper in his ear, "Do you see me now? I'm nothing and nobody. A tiny, ugly man who had everything stripped from him: his wife, his farm, his money and all his self-respect and dignity. Everyone treated me like an animal, so that's what I became." The killer spoke in the same Hainanese dialect as the director's grandfather. "When I looked into the flame of that candle for five days straight... when my mind *became* that flame, I saw that I was going to become an immortal legend and I would never die. *That* was my greatest hunger." See Ouey chuckled bitterly. "Not bad for a rickshaw Chink, huh?"

"But why? Why go to those lengths of cannibalism?" the director asked.

"Because I was hungry. Because I had nothing to eat."

In his mind's camera eye, the director saw a boy walking a water buffalo beside a cliff top. The camera tracked behind them, slowly panning across a ruffled sea spangled with sunbeams to focus on the boy stroking the beast's horns. The boy said, "You're the only one who understands me. You know what I want, Seow Fung? More than anything, I want for both of us to live forever."

The director opened his eyes. A smile backlit his face. This was great! It was magic. The anti-hero was directing the film for him.

As his eyes zoomed in on the browned and wrinkled cadaver, he saw the movie as a different breed of *The Metamorphosis*, for the Kafkaesque creature trapped behind glass resembled the exoskeleton of a gigantic cockroach, its wings shorn, antennae clipped: an insect trying to become a man.

That was too mundane for the modern-day mythos of the movie world. Any time he had ever suggested a biopic about this or that celebrity to his producer, he said, "You don't make the film about the real person. You make it about the legend."

So how about this? Wings burst open from the creature's shoulders as antennae shot up from either side of its forehead. Again and again, it cracked its carapace against the glass, trying to escape from its tiny prison.

When the glass shattered, See Ouey flew through the museum in the chaotic fashion of cockroaches, his brown wings beating the air in a blur, his jaws unhinged like a python so he could devour the skeletons, skulls, fetuses and autopsy photos. With each bite he grew bigger and bigger, until he was as large as legend, as huge as myth, as hideous as racist stereotype: a monster whose wings threw shadows across the moon as he carried off children to use their bones for toothpicks at his secret lair deep in Tiger Leaping Gorge.

OBITUARY FOR THE KHAOSAN ROAD OUTLAWS AND IMPOSTORS

For Paul Soulodre and Jon McDonald

"I have no money, no resources, no hope.
I am the happiest man alive."

Henry Miller, *Tropic of Cancer*

Few thrills are as harrowing as breaking the law, but only if you get away with it. Getting caught is the worst comedown.

Crime, as we saw and practiced it in Bangkok, was another kind of extreme sport. Slaloming around the security at Don Mueang International Airport, dodging the plainclothes cops, and tricking the check-in staff, was all part of the fun, and gave us a bigger adrenaline surge than we ever got from skateboarding or smoking crack.

All the most exciting memories of my childhood were dragged along in the adrenaline's undertow, like leaves in a flood: shoplifting comic books and candy bars, throwing eggs at the school windows, letting the air out of the teacher's tires, putting a tack on the chair of the teacher's pet and watching him sit on it, daring, and then double daring, James Strate to spit on the door of our local church.

After he did it, we ran down the block, half-expecting God to strike us down with a thunderbolt. He didn't and this was a lesson we never received in Sunday school.

Then it was on to stealing booze from our fathers' liquor cabinets—only a little from each bottle to mix into a vomit-inducing punch for all the boys to pretend we liked—shoplifting and jerking off to porn mags, sneaking into bars while underage, smoking pot, going to rock concerts, leering at strippers, cheating on girlfriends, speeding and drunk driving.

These were all warm-ups for my biggest test thus far: committing my first international felony. In the life of a criminal this is akin to losing your virginity.

I checked the flight times on the board, half hoping mine had been cancelled or delayed. No such luck, it was right on schedule. I could still ditch the bag and the fake passport and retreat, but from somewhere in the past James Strate said, "Don't chicken out, man. Whatever you do, don't chicken out."

I looked around to see where Mohammad and the customer were. Gone. Disappeared into the clumps of travellers pushing trolleys and pulling suitcases on wheels, hoisting backpacks, giving goodbye kisses and farewell hugs. At least the airport was busy. While I was grateful for the crowds and the anonymity they provided, the human camouflage also made it more difficult to spot all the airport authorities and, we assumed, plainclothes cops sauntering past, pretending they were tourists, or hidden away in a security room with a bank of monitors hooked up to hundreds of CCTV cameras.

I was running a fever of paranoia, spouting sweat from my armpits and my skin felt too tight for my face. Second by second, however, the adrenaline was wearing off and mutating into a deep sense of fear. The fear of arrest, interrogations, a trial and prison sentence, and having to explaining all that to my mom. "Well, I guess it started off innocently enough. James and I were curious about whether God exists…"

Exhausted and yawning, in the line up for the flight to Tokyo, I ran over the details of a passport with my photo in it and another man's identity. Bill Davis from Green Bay, Milwaukee. Born February 12, 1969. Passport issued in Bangkok in '91. Tourist visa. I checked the stamp again. Fine. No overstay.

The passport looked okay too. Hard to tell if it was a fake or stolen or whether a broke backpacker had pawned it off for some fast *baht*. The sign in the alley outside the guesthouse where we lived at the top of Khaosan Road read: "We buy anything, dodgy or not." They also sold fake university degrees, fake international press passes, and fake driver's licenses supposedly issued by the United Nations.

Waiting to check in, the biggest hurdle were the airline employees – young Asian women with the same perfunctory smiles and airs of brusque congeniality, always asking the same questions. Is this your bag? Did you pack it yourself? Why are you going to Tokyo? How long are you staying there?

Their concern was understandable. If one of our "customers" made it through to Japan and was then stopped by customs and sent back to Thailand, the airline was fined a substantial sum of money.

The ringleader of our gang said he had an "inside man" in Thai customs and immigrations who would help us out if we got stopped or arrested, but was he telling the truth? That was the question I put to Mick, another resident in the Ploy Guesthouse and my partner in crime, a young Brit whose forearms were inked with two tattoos of the red devils logo of the Manchester United football club. Mick said, "Mohammad's a petty crim who thinks he's a godfather. Don't trust 'im with the steam off your piss, mate. Not enough d's in dodgy to describe how dodgy that cunt is, d'ya know what I mean?"

The way he threw the c-word around all the time made me cringe. Where I come from that's only hurled as the prelude to a fight.

From time to time, and this was the worrying part, the authorities would pull people out of the line up to check their bags. Before a run, we were not allowed to examine the contents of those suitcases. Mohammad said he'd already checked them. All the customers, he reassured us, were good Muslims who did not drink or do drugs. "It is very safe, my friend," he said with a smile that, because I'd never known anyone from Bangladesh, was impossible to gauge for either sincerity or smarminess. My worst fear was that one of the "customers" had decided to take a kilo of heroin with him and I was left holding the bag.

God, this line up was taking forever. Typical. Some Asian family had been on a shopping holiday to Thailand and were now trying to check in a dozen suitcases without paying anything extra.

As soon as I handed over the passport and ticket, I made a point of distracting the woman behind the counter by smiling and asking, "Excuse me, but is the flight on time today?" to make sure she didn't look over the passport too closely. She nodded. "Oh, that's good. Can I have a window seat, please?"

Excellent. She barely glanced at the photo page. The only question she asked was about my luggage. "No, no check-in bags today." I flashed her another smile and made deliberate eye contact to allay any of her suspicions, even though my stomach was aflutter and my button-down shirt was wallpapered to my back with sweat. "Just one carry-on bag, thanks."

Finally she put the boarding pass on the counter, circling the gate and the boarding time with a pen. No need to listen to that spiel; I was not the one who would be boarding the flight to Tokyo.

I thanked her and made a beeline for the chrome gates. The last leg was always the most excruciating part. It was hard to saunter casually when some instinct for self-preservation kept pushing me from behind, wanting to make me break into a trot, ditch the bag, lose the passport, and jump into a getaway cab.

To the right led to Passport Control. Off to the left was an escalator that ran up to a coffee shop, a restaurant and a bathroom, which was where we did the switch. In the last stall, exactly according to the plan, stood Mohammad and the customer, a light-skinned Afghani no more than thirty. I handed him the duffel bag, gave the passport to Mohammad and I was gone, slipping back into the teeming crowd, coasting along on that last surge of adrenaline, and already counting the money in my head—almost three hundred dollars American for less than three hours of nerve-shredding "work"—before fending off the taxi touts to get a metered ride back to Khaosan Road.

At the end of every airport run, I always thought about James spitting on that church door and the two of us bolting down the street wide-eyed with panic for fear of any Biblical reprisals of hell-fire and brimstone, like our Sunday school teacher had warned us. The setting had changed, and human trafficking was far beyond shoplifting and vandalism, but so many of the old scenes and friends I'd once known kept repeating in my head, like an endless film loop, I wasn't really sure whether I'd changed or not—I still looked the same, my voice sounded pretty much the same—because nobody moves halfway around the world to take up a fly-by-night "job" in the criminal underworld of Bangkok so they can be the same old bore they used to be.

In the end, terminal diseases and accidents excepting, I think most people actually die of boredom. Bored of the world and bored of themselves. That's not how I want to go: trapped in a hometown where an entire life is lived within a boring ten-kilometer radius.

PLOY GUESTHOUSE where Mick and I stayed was at the top of Khaosan Road, across the street from a police station adjacent to a Buddhist temple named after a victorious war against the Burmese. Few of the expats, and even fewer of the travelers staying around Southeast Asia's main drag for backpackers, realized that this was the biggest port of call and safe house for international criminals in the region from the late eighties to the mid-nineties. For anyone who needed to lay low it made a good hideout, because it was easy to blend in with all the travellers. None of the guesthouses required a passport to check in, so anyone could register with a fake name. Rooms went for around three bucks American per night. And the local cops, according to Mick and Mohammad, were so busy doing their own deals and scams that they didn't have any time left to scoop up the smaller fish in a dragnet. Every few months they'd round up nine or ten Africans and Iranians who had overstayed their visas, hold a press conference to show them off and then deport them. But they rarely busted any Caucasians.

After I'd done seven or eight boarding-pass runs and proven myself, Mick began telling me about some of his other cronies on the strip and in our guesthouse, peopled with a floating population of every criminal element. Nobody, except the small-time drug dealers, advertised their "wares" and "business interests," but secrecy was impossible in such a small and stifling world. At one time or another, Mick had worked every crime racket there was. "I'm a bit of an outlaw, me. So are these other gits." According to him, Joe, the Irish guy with the bad teeth, was stealing passports from backpackers and fencing them; Taro and a couple of his Japanese friends were buying arms from the Thai military and reselling them to the Tamil Tigers in Sri Lanka; Beyruce, who was either Iraqi, Iranian or possibly Moroccan, though he told everybody, "I come from the moon," was forging credit cards; Hans had set up a business to launder drug money from Cambodia; a huge Hawaiian man nicknamed "Tiny" was working an insurance scam; Nigel was running Thai prostitutes to Japan; and Omar, the friendly Sudanese guy staying next to me, who claimed to be in IT, was part of a heroin-trafficking network.

Whenever any of the backpackers in the guesthouse asked us what we did, I followed Mick's lead and said, "Import export," which was more or less true. We imported men from India, Pakistan, Bangladesh and Afghanistan and, for a considerable sum of money (only Mohammad knew how much), exported them to Japan where they would work illegally in factories. Because most of them could not speak English, Mick and I, and a constantly rotating crew of other wastrels and travellers who'd run out of money, had to get their boarding passes for them.

The Customs and Immigrations Department ran a low-tech operation in those days. They had no databases. One drug dealer in our guesthouse, who had been deported with a black mark in his passport, glued two of the pages together and came back into the country a week later at a small border crossing with Cambodia.

The boarding-pass scam would not have withstood high-tech scrutiny. How it worked was that we had the same name as the customer, even though the passports were from two different countries. Once we got the boarding pass and handed it to them, they would then board the flight. Mohammad never said how many of the passports we used were fakes. It was hard to tell because they looked like dead-ringers for the real McCoy. In criminal circles, Bangkok used to be referred to as the "false documents capital of the world."

In spite of all the fast-food franchises, trendy cafes and boutique hotels that have moved in over the last decade, Khaosan remains a ribbon of road knotted with cheap restaurants, travel agents, streetside bars and cafes, silverware wholesalers and vendors selling plastic Buddhas, wooden dragons, Chang and Singha Beer T-shirts, velcro-strap sandals, and gaudy oil paintings of water buffalos in rice paddies and old men in conical hats smoking opium pipes: a cultural fantasia for backpackers who did not know the difference.

Back then it was almost impossible to walk the length of the street at night without hearing either The Eagles or CCR, as whatever passed for Western culture in Bangkok at that time was still a distant echo of the commotion caused by American GIs on R 'n' R during the Vietnam War. The music competed with the blare of Hollywood action movies playing in the restaurant-bars of the guesthouses. Each of them had a blackboard outside with the names and times of the films playing that night. Most of the backpackers were either dreadlocked punks or old hippies as hairy as Jesus, and their new disciples wearing fishermen's trousers and tie-dyed shirts. Other than the vendors, waitresses, receptionists, and two deaf mute hookers who worked out of the Hello Bar and Guesthouse (long since replaced by a Boots pharmacy and a boutique hotel), no respectable Thais ever came anywhere near Khaosan Road. In the local news it was routinely described as a slum, or *salum khaosan*, and the scruffy backpackers mocked as "bird shit foreigners" because they looked like crap and fell out of the sky.

Most nights we met at the street-side bar with plastic stools in front of the Happy Home Guesthouse ("the Miserable Hovel is more like it," said Mick), towards the end of the strip by the silverware wholesalers. Mohammad always sat at the head of the table. Mick served as his deputy. I mostly just listened and took notes in my head. Whatever new recruits Mohammad had rounded up asked the same questions over and over again. What happens if I get caught? Will I go to jail? Will I get blacklisted from Thailand?

Looking like a father at the head of the table, Mohammad, with a reassuring smile on his densely bearded faced, would repeat the same spiel to every newcomer. He repeated it so many times that I was starting to believe him. "It is very safe, my friend. I have my contacts inside Thai Customs and Immigration. It is a well-known fact, quite beyond dispute, that this is the most corrupt department in the whole Thai government. That makes it very easy for my workers. If I may quote the right honorable John F. Kennedy, 'We have nothing to fear but fear itself.' Mohammad smiled again. "My workers are not having any problems."

"Piss off. I'm not your worker," said Mick, "and JFK was a womanising scumbag. That arsehole killed Marilyn Monroe."

Oh no, I thought, here goes Mick on another one of his conspiracy-theory tirades. The last one he told me about concerned a group of Jewish bankers conspiring to take over the world's financial system. That, at least, was marginally more credible than any of his alien invasion stories.

Mohammad smiled again. "I admire Mick's feistiness and his opinionated nature, but I fear he is having anger management issues again."

Mick made a masturbatory gesture. He glanced at me and the new recruit, "What's he bangin' on about?" as I waved off a grinning tout selling lighters emblazoned with bare-breasted white women.

Mohammad smiled and ordered another round of beers for the three of us, as well as a banana shake for his tee-totalling self. The waitress, who looked like she was about fourteen but was probably nineteen or twenty, would not even look at him. In her eyes, this hairy, dark-skinned man was beneath contempt. She left his drink on my side of the table. The racist treatment that he was constantly dealt out in Thailand, and all over Southeast Asia, did not seem to bother Mohammad. He was too tough for that. In our runs to the airport, and lulls in the conversation during our almost nightly "business meetings" in front of the guesthouse, watching cockroaches skitter past our sandals and rats forage amongst the piles of garbage waiting to be picked up, he would talk a little about his past. "I am the only male in a family of ten sisters. My father passed away many years ago, so I am supporting the whole family. Grow up amongst eleven women and you soon learn the gift of superhuman patience and tolerance, my friend." As he grinned Mohammad's teeth shone a brilliant white against the dark beard. "You also get to use the bathroom about once every six months."

The only other thing I knew about him was that he used to be the headmaster of a private boys school in Dhaka, or so he claimed, which perhaps explained the overly formal English he spoke and why he treated Mick like an unruly pupil who showed enough promise to be tolerated. Besides the "meetings" and airport runs, the only other time we saw him was on Fridays when, all dressed in white, he went to pray at the mosque near Khaosan Road. His rule was that no customers could fly in or depart on the holiest day for Muslims.

Otherwise, Mohammad drifted through our lives like a phantom, showing up at odd hours. Whether it was midnight or daybreak, he gave us the same smile and greeting, "Good morning, my friend." We didn't know where he lived. We didn't have his phone number. We didn't even know his surname or if in fact Mohammad was his real name.

When Mohammad talked about our "business meetings" and "my customers" and "my workers," he was only being realistic; friendship really didn't enter into it. It was the same shady story with most of the other smugglers, swindlers and scammers we knew on and around Khaosan Road. Everyone was using different aliases and nobody got very close, because it was too dangerous. We all knew the deal. At some point, they might inform on us or we'd inform on them.

On that night, Mick had brought a new mate of his down to see if he could get some work. Another Brit of Mick's age (early thirties), Martin had a shaved head, a pink polo shirt with the collar rolled up and a beer keg for a torso. He introduced himself to me by holding up an enormous fist (all the knuckles crooked and scarred) in front of his face and sniffing it. "Smells like dead women, innit?" He turned to Mick, looking for his approval and only laughed after Mick did. I knew then that I wouldn't have to worry about Martin trying to usurp my role as the third in command, because he was a follower not a leader, a corporal who would never be a commanding officer. To keep the new recruit in his place, I said, "That's strange, 'cause I thought your fist would smell like your boyfriend's bum."

Mick laughed that donkey's bray of his and, just as I'd predicted, Martin parroted him. In their love of "dick contests" these guys were monotonously predictable.

Martin gestured with his shoulder in my direction. "For a Yank he's all right."

"Yves is one of the colonials from Canada," said Mick.

"No, I'm from Quebec, which is a different country, culture, language, etcetera."

Mick looked at Martin, expressing in a mere glance the solidarity of gang members and football hooligans, too weak to stand on their own and always ready to gang up on an outsider. "Don't ask 'im about the Frogs or he gets well uppity," said Mick. "All those poncy snobs ever produced was a few smelly cheeses and some birds with big noses and smelly twats."

Martin said, "Too right."

None of their insults meant anything to me, because my name wasn't Yves and I didn't come from Quebec.

Actually, I didn't care very much for Mick and I liked Martin, his new protégé, even less. At the same time, I couldn't help but envy them and how comfortable they looked with their machismo, how brazenly they flirted with a table of young female travellers sitting next to us, how they walked around flaunting their muscles in beach shorts and singlets sporting the logos of Thai beers, and how few anxieties ever furrowed their foreheads or snuck into their voices.

Next to them, with my long unruly black hair sticking up at all angles like the ruins of a Gothic cathedral, my eyes the color of rainwater, and almost always dressed in black jeans and a long-sleeved black shirt, I must have cut an absurdly melancholic figure. But appearances are revealing.

Mohammad saved his parting shot for when Martin was in the bathroom. "Be very careful, my friends, and watch your backs. I hear there are now four or five other gangs like ours operating around Khaosan Road. Business is going to get cutthroat."

Mick, for once, did not argue. "That's us in trouble with the customs and immigration blokes, 'cause everyone will snitch on everyone else. That's how the big drug traffickers do it. They'll send seven or eight mules through on one night, grass up one of the sad bastards so customs is distracted, and the rest get through no worries. Those lazy sods in customs and immigrations couldn't catch a cold unless someone sneezed on 'em. You know what it says in the papers, lads, 'Police, acting on a tip-off, arrested such a body…'"

I was incredulous. "You mean, the drug gangs turn in their own people?"

"Absolutely." Mick pointed his thumb at Mohammad and sneered. "This dodgy cunt will dob us in first chance he gets."

Mohammad, smiling that Teflon smile, looked at Mick, as a Thai vendor riding a bicycle with a rack of dried squid on the back pedalled past. "What if Yves snitches on both of us?"

They clinked glasses. Mick said, "Fair comment. We dunno nothin' about this arsehole, not even his real name."

It was stupid to think that I could hide behind an alias for very long in this little underworld where you could buy or rent almost anything except trust. Neither of these guys could be trusted and they didn't trust me either. Worst of all, I wasn't sure if I could even trust my own judgements anymore.

THERE WERE ONLY so many action movies we could watch and only so many American hits from the sixties and seventies we could listen to—"Hotel California" by The Eagles had become my most hated song—before we reached the end of Khaosan Road's limited nightlife options and headed for our late night hangout, the Thermae coffee shop and bar on Sukhuvmit Road, a last chance saloon for the dregs of foreign drunks and a meeting point for whoremongers, go-go dancers soliciting business after the other bars closed, freelance hookers and ladyboys (some of the older ones looked like Dr. Frankenstein had been their surgeon). The entrance was in the back, down a concrete tunnel that led past a bathroom where the ladyboys would try to grab the dicks, or pick the pockets, of the men using the urinals. Even that was not the ugliest part of entering the place.

The ugliest part was a big splintered mirror on the wall, half clouded with cigarette smoke, that threw back the most warped and distorted images of everyone who walked in there. Literally and metaphorically, your worst half walked into this pickup joint and, after you left, this image of yourself—cracked, crooked, fogged and faded— followed you out into the daybreak, where the last embarrassment of the night came on the taxi ride home, watching the barefooted, bald-headed monks in their orange robes out collecting alms on the streets, leaving me to wonder if this was my karmic punishment for daring James Strate to spit on that church door back in Grade 5.

If there's a bar-cum-bordello in hell, it must be a dead-ringer for the old Thermae: always packed after the other bars closed, always noisy, smoky, and full of drunken whores cackling like witches and men giving them cockeyed leers and spitting out jibes the sex workers could not understand. "She's gagging for some good English sausage."

On that night, we had just lined up at the bar and I was remembering what Mohammad had said about the other human trafficking gangs moving in on our turf, when I saw Mick wheel around, grab another guy by the hair and smash his forehead into his nose, which snapped with a twig-like crack. Blood spouted from his nostrils like rain from a gargoyle's mouth and his face was twisted in the same grotesque grimace.

Immediately, five of his other friends converged on Mick, who smeared the blood on his hands all over his face like it was tribal war paint. "Any of youse other cunts want some. I'll have all of you lot." Mick hunkered down in a boxer's pose, feinting this way and that, jabbing the air, throwing rights and uppercuts.

For the first time I considered the possibility that Mick was not only psychotic, he was certifiably insane. I think the other guy's friends came to the same conclusion, because they backed off and carried their mate to the bathroom.

Like all the hooligans and rednecks fond of fisticuffs, Mick wanted to hang out and bask in his victory. He wanted all the other blokes and birds in there to have a good look at the victor as he sipped his beer, still wearing the other man's blood on his face and hands. Except that half the guys shooting glances in our direction looked like they were trying to remember our faces so they could administer a future beating.

Finally leaving the bar two beers later, I saw Mick pass by that funhouse mirror which did not reveal your exterior, but functioned in the same way as those hideous portraits by Frances Bacon that turn people inside out so their neuroses and insecurities warp their features. In that psychological mirror, Mick, with his long blond ringlets of hair and face smudged with blood that could have been makeup, was Cinderella when she turned back into a scullery maid after midnight. I'd never seen him in that light before: girlish in his vanity and deluded in his pursuit of fairytale riches as a petty criminal.

In the back of a tuk-tuk rigged with turn signals and flashing disco lights just above our heads, Mick and the driver worked out that they were both Manchester United supporters. So he began teaching the elfin, constantly grinning driver football chants.

How did he do it? Inflict such savage violence, and then, not twenty minutes later, while weaving in and out of traffic on Sukhumvit Road in what was little more than a glorified golf cart, began shouting in unison with the driver, "TITS, FANNY AND UNITED! TITS, FANNY AND UNITED!"

I THOUGHT IT WAS finally time to tell Mohammad that if Mick continued playing the psychotic Cinderella, throwing temper tantrums and drawing attention to himself, he was going to get us all killed or arrested. But the ringleader had either gotten busted or gone underground, because he'd disappeared.

Left to our own vices, Mick and I slept through the sweltering days of the hot season, when the streets were like skillets and the mercury nudged the 40 degree Celsius mark. Up all night, we smoked weed, drank beer and chatted on the roof of the Ploy Guesthouse, which had the best panoramas of Bangkok's most historic district. Both the Temple of the Emerald Buddha, with its fanciful pagodas, and the Golden Mount, with its gilded tower supposedly enshrining a hair of the Buddha, were illuminated until 10 p.m. On a clear night you could see all the way across the river to a neon sign for a massage parlour. It was too far away to make out the flashing pattern on the sign, but Mick said, "It's an enormous fanny opening and closing to lure in punters like insects to a Venus flytrap."

The extravagance of Mick's similes suggested an education that contradicted his own claims. "I've been a guttersnipe and a wide boy, sleeping rough on the streets of Mani since I were a lad." Whereas Martin spoke slowly and wrestled with his words, Mick was quick-witted. Whenever he saw me dressed up in a shirt and tie, ready to do another airport run, he'd remark in that dry way only the English can pull off with such deadpan panache. "Court appearance today, Yves?" If he saw me sitting in the guesthouse restaurant looking at the classified section of the *Bangkok Post*, he'd always make a quip about our lack of employability; he loved cutting me down to his size in that class-conscious way the British have of not letting you get too big for your boots. "Why don't you put this on your CV, mate? From '93 to '95 I worked as junior Paki smuggler at Dodgy Mohammad's Emporium of Illegal Migrant Laborers."

I had to laugh. Dodgy Mohammad's Emporium of Illegal Migrant Laborers? Mick was smarter than he let on, which also made him more dangerous. He would not have been the first expat to embroider his past with all sorts of colorful and fictional yarns. Either that or Manchester produces some of the wittiest and most eloquent football hooligans in the world.

Because of the view and the open-air roof, the guesthouse had become a favorite vantage point for potheads who congregated there every night after dark. Many of them were regulars, who would go up north and do some trekking before coming back to the Ploy, head off to Angkor Wat and Vietnam for a few weeks, then come back to the Ploy for a couple of nights, before catching buses from Khaosan Road to hop ferries bound for the tropical islands in the Gulf of Thailand. The rooftop soirees attracted an odd bunch of travellers, from real adventurers to crooks, conmen and the backpackers who only go to places recommended by Lonely Planet. The most memorable included Kenji, who had just returned from Peru, where he had built his own dugout canoe and sailed it down the Amazon, staying overnight in villages with tribesmen who still hunted with blowpipes and poison darts. Rather than going back to Japan and working twelve-hour days as a "salary man" he had decided to become a travel photographer. Valerie, a widowed, childless bank clerk from Toronto had spent six months meditating in an Indian ashram before deciding that her real vocation was teaching Thai children at Saint Gabriel's Christian School on the nearby Samsen Road. Dave, a chainsaw logger from rural Oregon, had brought his sixteen-year-old son with him to Bangkok. Together they would go out drinking and whoring almost every night, until it became apparent that the father had to pay for sex, but the cute blond son was getting freebies. They stayed in the room beside mine for a few months. Because the walls were made of thin plywood with a screen at the top, it was like having roommates. Every night the father would lock the son in their room and the son would call out, "Hey dad, can I come to Patpong too?" "Nope, 'cause ya don't know how to spot a ladyboy and ya don't know how to wear a dick wrapper."

On the roof, Mick always sat on the edge of the conversational circles as potheads passed joints around and spent long minutes staring slack-jawed at the magical spires of gold and orange. This was Mick's preferred position. In taxis and tuk-tuks he would sit on the opposite side, as far away as possible, and never make eye contact when we spoke. Contrary to his "hard man" image, here was a guy so fearful of friendships and relationships that he had banished himself to the margins of criminal society and the outskirts of every social circle. Why? That was what I had to find out.

When it was just the two of us up there sharing a smoke and sitting on opposite ends of a mat, and he was more stoned than drunk and thus in a more reflective mood than normal, with a little prompting Mick would talk more about his past.

I kept passing him fresh spliffs and a lighter. Polite to a fault (I also found that strange), he'd always say, "Cheers, nice one," before sparking it up. After he'd had a good lungful and was staring up at the black velvet sky studded with stars, as if seeing them for the first time, through eyes polished from the inside with potent Thai weed, I would start shooting questions at him. "So why did you choose crime for a career anyway? It's not the easiest way to make a living."

"You're a right nosy git, you are." He exhaled a vapour trail of pungent smoke. "Dunno really. Bit of a lark, innit? See what you can get away with." He must have had the same proudly sneaky look on his face when he was seven and stealing a few pennies from his mother's purse, or putting a tack on another student's seat for him to sit on, or whatever it is that British kids do to assert their individuality by first rebelling against their parents and teachers.

"But Mick, haven't you heard? Virtue is its own reward."

"Bollocks. Virtue is for folks who don't have the balls to do crimes."

I laughed and laughed and Mick joined in too. It was one of the best things about smoking weed: those spontaneous fits of laughter that burned away the residue of adult bitterness and brought us back to a state of childlike glee and wonderment once again.

"So why did you head-butt that guy in the Thermae?"

He looked back at me with the moon still glinting in his eyes. "I get claustrophobia in bars that are chock-a-block, and I don't like people getting too close to me, d'ya know what I mean? That bloke,

I reckon he was queer, rubbed against me a few times and touched me 'air. I don't like blokes touchin' me. So I nutted him, didn't I? Gave him a 'Glasgow kiss'. That'll learn 'im." Mick was too much of a miserable prick to possess a real laugh or a smile. His "laugh" (if you could call it that) sounded like a donkey's bray and his attempts at a grin were always sideswiped by a sad sneer.

In between binges and waiting for Mohammad to reappear, Mick and Martin had started a sideline career, running Thai women to Japan by pretending to be their boyfriends and claiming they were going on holiday together. Most of the women had been promised lucrative jobs in restaurants and hotels only to find out later, after their passports had been taken from them, that they'd been sold into sex slavery by some shady Thais in cahoots with the Yakuza. They would be forced to sleep with eight or ten men a day for months and months until their huge debt was paid off. The word on Khaosan Road from a couple of the Japanese drug traffickers we knew was that one of these women would turn up dead almost every day, her body left on the doorstep of the Thai embassy in Tokyo.

Mick asked me if I wanted to do some runs. Though I certainly needed the money, I already had enough black marks on my conscience. What we were doing, my conscience had decided, was not crime; it was a kind of philanthropy. We were helping all these men, many of whom were dentists, engineers and professors in their homelands, making a few hundred dollars a month, to sneak into Japan where they could earn thousands of bucks per months as factory workers and send much of it home to their families in Afghanistan, India, Bangladesh and Pakistan.

"Criminal philanthropy" is what I called it.

Mick didn't buy it. "Fucking hell, what are you on about? With your gift for spinning lines of shite, you should be writing adverts or speeches for politicians."

He was too hyperactive to hang around the roof of the guesthouse getting high and laying low every night. Just as he had educated me in the periodic table of criminal elements operating in and around Khaosan Road, he wanted to show me the city's underbelly.

It was all part of his bid to get me on his side so he could take over Mohammad's role. "Between you and me and the gatepost, as it were, it'd be a good job if I was the ringleader. I could do what that Paki does."

I did not point out the obvious—that Mick had no contact network set up to get customers—because my loyalties did not lay with either of them.

Mick preferred the darker and sleazier bars. So Kangaroo, an upstairs club near the Surawongse side of Patpong 1, was his favorite den of promiscuity. The main bar was lit only by red light as dark as menstrual blood. Within thirty seconds of sitting down we were surrounded by a gaggle of four bargirls, offering us beer, sex, marijuana and blowjobs. It was such a hard and fast sell that I was tongue-tied, but Mick was pretty much fluent in Thai by then, so he took the lead, ordering us a couple of beers and a pack of pre-rolled joints that came in a Marlboro package. The one with the weed said her name was Noi. She offered to shake my hand but when I proffered mine she pulled hers away, ran it through her hair and laughed. This was a joke that James Strate and I used to play on each other when we were eight or nine. Another woman, all smiles and wind-chime giggles, sat on Mick's lap. She also shook my hand, asked for my name and said, "Nice to meet you." This was not the neon Babylon and the so-called "sex capital of the world" I had been expecting from a thousand tabloid tales. Thanks to the women's cheerful, typically Thai demeanor it all seemed, for a while anyway, deceptively innocent.

Mick wanted to smoke a spliff, so we had to sit near the front window overlooking the night bazaar. Through the open window drifted the sound of touts outside the bars chatting up the passing tourists, "Take a look, sir, no cover charge," while holding up signs for X-rated shows involving ping-pong balls, razorblades, darts and cigarettes. In front of the go-go bars, the girls kept up their patter, "Hello, welcome. Come inside," while the vendors clustered around the stalls running down the middle of the street kept pimping their fake Levis, fake Polo shirts, fake Rolex watches.

On Patpong, almost everything is fake and almost all the women for rent, most obviously the go-go dancers wearing plastic numbers like price tags, who come off looking like a cross between mannequins in a department store window and factory workers in bikinis as excited by the prospect of sex as by stitching another seam in a garment.

Patpong, and its twisted sister Nana Plaza, is a department store, a sweatshop and a freak show of sex, so crass, kitsch, phoney and obscenely compelling that when Mick said he preferred the bar where the girls swam around in a tank wearing mermaid fins, or dressed up in Supergirl costumes to descend from the ceiling of a club on the back of a motorcycle while screwing each other with a strap-on dildo to the triumphant strains of "We Are the Champions" by Queen, I thought he had to be joking—"taking the piss" as it were, in British fashion—but no, this was Patpong, where the ludicrous is a nightly reality show. "It's brilliant, Yves. This bird comes round with a bottle of tequila in a cowboy holster and you can lick the salt off her tit before taking a shot."

Patpong might have been an uproarious, X-rated sideshow if it wasn't for the presence of all these lonely, desperate men like us out hunting for some love, affection and understanding that we would never find there. As it stood then, and still stands today, all the desperation in the air, both financial and psychosexual, combined with all the pheromones and cheap perfume floating around, have formed an invisible cloud that settles on everything like radiation from a nuclear fallout, making beer taste more bitter and cigarette smoke smell more acrid than usual. It's a hypnotic, toxic cloud that fogs your eyes, dulls your senses, contaminates your memories and turns them into lies: *You know, I think number 47 from Super Pussy actually likes me.*

In the dark back corner of Kangaroo, Mick sparked up the spliff and took a hit. What was he doing? This reeked of a setup, the girls in cahoots with the cops. I kept asking him, "Are you sure this is okay?" and he kept answering, "Safe as houses, mate." In spite of his reassurances, I kept checking the shadows by the dark red bar in case they morphed into policemen.

"Thai stick" (as I knew it) and "Buddha stick" (as Mick called it) is like no other strain of marijuana. One of the local drug dealers who worked out of a reggae bar behind Khaosan Road told me that the secret ingredient used to be that the growers would dust their plants with opium resin, which helps to explain the stupefying and euphoric effects. After a couple of throat-scorching tokes we were doughboys with glazed smiles, happy to be kneaded by these attractive, willowy young women who melted our resistance with back-rubs and neck massages and innuendoes delivered in such a giggly, innocent way, "I no have boyfriend and I horny too much," that they didn't seem like prostitutes at all: not as I had observed the street-walkers back home, desperate drug fiends and teenage runaways who looked more scary than sexy.

Between Noi's come-ons and Mick's badgering, I was caught between a rock of a hard-on and a much softer place.

"Go on then. Kick a goal," said Mick, while making an obscene gesture with his fist. "Don't be a poof. We're *hardened* criminals now"—he winked across the table at me as he said "hardened"—"so let's see some good laddish behavior."

Mick went off to one room with two women. I went off with Noi into another little cubicle whose shabbiness was exposed and ampli-fied by a fluorescent light on the ceiling. (Later I would write in my diary that "it stank like a morgue where all the sexual fantasies of all the men who had passed through here had come to rot and die.") The sheets on the narrow bed were a washed-out grey and the lino-leum was the same shade as the nicotine-yellow stains on my fin-gertips. After about two minutes of pumping away on top of her, the sexpot who seemed so sweet and polite in the bar turned into a sour little shrew. She looked up at me and said with contempt, "Why you take so long? You take long time come, you pay more."

That was the end of that awkward and sordid satire of sex. To make things worse, one of the other bargirls began pounding on the door and shouting, "You take two lady, you take two lady. I suck your cock very good, *na*."

I handed Noi some money. She called me a "cheap Charlie" and demanded more. Not in the mood for any arguments—all I wanted was to flee this shabby cubicle that felt like a crime scene where my self-respect had been murdered—I handed her a few more hundred-baht notes while Miss Congeniality resumed pounding on the door and spewing pidgin English filth.

These were not the slinky and pliant, exotic-looking sex kittens that they were reputed to be or acted like in the bar. These were tough, ill-educated, rice farmer's daughters from the fields and backwoods towns of the country's poorest nether regions.

Seeing through the illusion of all the makeup and titillation did not make me feel any better. Some men, like Mick and Martin, think that all sex is good sex. I don't feel that way. To me, awkward sex with someone I don't know and don't care about is not worth the exertion. And the lukewarm, monetary strain served up so half-heartedly in Bangkok's red-light districts makes a mockery of everything I have ever held sacred about male-female relations.

When Mick returned from his tryst he smiled and leered simultaneously as he sat down across from me in the rear booth by the windows. "I had a Bangkok sandwich… two birds. They were a bit of all right, the ol' in and out and a good hard shagging. How was your bunk up?"

"It was awful, wretched, sordid, sleazy, disgusting, demeaning—did I mention sordid enough times yet? In fact, it was one of the worst experiences of my entire life. Since you brought me here and recommended this place, I'm holding you personally responsible." I pointed my index finger at him. "When I'm talking to you, you look at me. You don't fucking look away or I'll take that as a sign of disrespect and then the payback will be a hundred times worse."

I didn't raise my voice and I didn't start gesturing wildly or rolling my eyes around, because anger never had that sort of tropical gale effect on me. On the contrary, it blew through and whipped around me like a wintry blizzard that put frost in my voice and ice in my eyes. Mick had never seen one of my controlled outbursts before. He was more than capable of defending himself against physical threats, but when the intimidation was mental he didn't have the intellectual resources to cope with them. So he sat there picking the label off his Singha Beer.

"If you ever put me through shit like that again, here's what's going to happen. I'm going to break into your room in the middle of the night when you're sleeping and pour hydrochloric acid all over your face. Then you're gonna be so completely disfigured for life that not even any of these stupid little tarts will ever shag you again. In fact, you'll be permanently blinded and the acid will melt the flesh on your ears so you can't even hear properly. Think your life is shit now? Wait till you get a hydrochloric acid bath. Got it, fuck face?"

Mick continued picking at his beer label. I could barely hear his mumble and I didn't give a shit. "Sorry it didn't work out, mate, but it ain't my fault the fittest birds ain't here tonight."

Quite by accident I had discovered his Achille's heel; any kind of criticism made him shrink like a schoolboy before the headmaster.

Had it not been for Mick rolling another spliff and passing the peace pipe as a pair of middle-aged couples in the standard-issue tourist wear of T-shirts, shorts and sandals sat down across from the empty stage with three chrome poles, we would have kept bickering. To be fair, Mick had gotten in a few good stabs too. "If you keep moaning about this, that and the other like a fucking Brit, Queen Lizzie is going to make you an honorary subject of England. Then you'll really be in the shit."

The tourists were already drunk on local spirits and beer which, spiked with all the sunshine and tropical heat, made them deliriously giddy—easy prey for the bargirls who soon had them smoking pre-rolled joints and buying them drinks. Office workers from Wyoming or Winnipeg or wherever, the tourists were living out their one-night-in-Bangkok fantasy. Soon the women were dancing around the chrome poles with a couple of bargirls in bikinis and the men were dancing in front of the stage with two other prostitutes.

Watching the tourists gyrating was rejuvenating, because they'd become born-again teenagers enjoying a second shot at college high jinks. The alcohol encouraged their exhibitionism and the freedom of being ten thousand miles from the prying eyes of neighbors and professional colleagues emboldened them even more. Perhaps this was the wild youth they wished they'd had.

For many of the barflies and sex tourists on Patpong, who looked like the accountants, computer geeks, and middle managers of the world's office towers, guys so bland and meek that you could not even remember their faces or anything about them a minute after they passed by, this was the red-light district's main attraction: it gave them an instant makeover. All of a sudden, the dullest office nerd had become a Casanova surrounded by beautiful women, and an aging secretary was a go-go dancer encircled by leering men.

"Look at these fat Yank slags," said Mick with a sneer that instantly poisoned my good spirits. He cupped his hands around his mouth and yelled at them: "Get your tits out, love, and get your kits off too."

But the tourists were too lost in the aural sex of the dance music and the mists of marijuana conjuring up the ghosts of their youth to pay him any attention.

This infuriated Mick even more. He started rolling another spliff, added some white powder, sparked it and passed it to one of the men. For a few seconds he almost looked happy when he turned to me and smile-sneered. "Put some heroin in it, didn't I? Let's make a move before they cotton on and throw a right wobbly."

On our way out, I trailed behind Mick so I could ask the tourists for a hit. Then I took a few steps, dropped the joint on the floor, ground it out with my heel, followed him down the stairs, and Mick was none the wiser. Nobody deserved to have their night—maybe their whole vacation—ruined by this malicious prick who had a grudge against the world and took everyone else's happiness as an insult to his own misery.

In the guesthouses and street-side bars of Khaosan Road, the backpackers enjoyed bragging about how they were superior to the package tourists, like these office workers, while the expats thought they were superior to everyone, including the locals. In one crucial respect, all of us foreigners were pretty much the same. Everyone was either running away from something or someone, or trying to find some kind of new life, a new love, or just a life-altering adventure.

The trouble was, Mick and me and Martin were changing identities so often that it was becoming more and more difficult to remember who we weren't supposed to be anyway.

NOT LONG AFTER that, Mohammad reappeared at the door of my guesthouse room at 4 a.m. after Mick and I had only just said our goodbyes for the night, with his usually cheery, "Good morning, my friend," followed by a limp and damp handshake.

Through that forest of black beard, he smiled and, offering no explanation for his disappearance, said, "I have a new job for you this morning." He handed me a passport. I opened it up to the photo page with my picture in it and squinted at the details that squirmed across the page: Nancy Lars Cohen, thirty-four, from Invercargill, New Zealand.

I looked back at Mohammad. "Is this supposed to be a joke, man? A Swedish, Kiwi Jew with a woman's name from a town called Invercargill? Nobody is going to believe this."

Mohammad's smile widened. As always, I had no idea whether he was trying to be reassuring, or laughing at me, or himself, or the absurdity of the situation. "It is very safe, my friend, safe as houses. We have changed the sex on the passport and Asians are not knowing Nancy is a lady's name."

"Oh really? Is that what I should tell my defence attorney?"

I can't even remember if it was his persuasiveness or my lack of funds that made me agree to this suicide mission. By the time we arrived at the airport, as bad luck would have it, there was a lengthy line up for the flight. On an hour's sleep, with a brainpan seared by hashish and eyes fogged, with a tongue thickened and putrefied by beer and cigarettes, standing there under the spray of fluorescent lights with needle-sharp rays was agony. The only thing keeping me awake was working out an explanation for the name Nancy in case one of the female ground crew came past asking questions or the check-in clerk got suspicious.

After spending forty minutes in the queue, I reached the counter with the vase of flowers, luggage tags and the digital scale with red numbers to weigh check-in bags. She gave my passport a cursory glance. Then she began typing up the boarding pass when her greying supervisor walked by and glanced at the passport. He looked me straight in the eye and, clearly not amused, said, "Nancy is a lady's name, *sir*."

I smiled, swallowed a guilty lump in my throat and fell back on the only alibi I'd come up with on an hour's sleep: "Not in New Zealand it isn't. It's like the name Michel in France or the nickname Lek in Thailand. Both men and ladies use it."

He looked at the woman in her red uniform. They exchanged a few tense words in Chinese, before the supervisor pointed to a spot down the counter in no man's land, saying, in the way bureaucrats and figures of authority have of making niceties sound like threats, "Please wait over there, sir."

Oh god, the fucking supervisor—it looked like this was the most exciting thing that had happened to him in months—was now on his walkie-talkie. He was one of these company men whose pride and pleasure stems from being sticklers for enforcing all the rules and regulations. Soon he had a small crowd gathered around the check-in counter, all of them poring over poor Nancy's passport.

I had to rest my elbows on the counter and lean over it because my legs were shaking so much that I thought they were going to give out on me. It was hard to think on my feet when my knees were wobbling that much. My Adam's apple felt like it had doubled in size and I was having trouble swallowing my saliva, never mind all the anxieties that my luck had finally run out and I was soon going to be in police custody and on my way to jail. The police thugs might even set me up with a kilo of heroin.

As yet, no one knew what the penalties would be if we were caught with a false identity trying to board a flight. A fine or a jail term? A warning? Deportation? Would they turn us over to the police? No one knew. Nobody had a clue.

In vain, I searched the crowds milling around for Mohammad

and the customer. But they'd vanished, leaving me holding the bag—and what was in that?—as well as the passport, which was either phoney, stolen, or had been purchased from a broke traveller. I prayed that it was the latter.

The last passengers had now gotten their boarding passes and the final pieces of luggage floated past me on the conveyor belt.

All the while, the supervisor kept sharpening the suspense and tightening the thumbscrews with each glance in my direction and call on his walkie-talkie. These company men and petty bureaucrats—dumped-on their whole lives—love to stick the knife in as deep as they can whenever a violation occurs and protocol permits.

First I had to look at the situation from the supervisor's point of view and analyze what he wanted: an admission of guilt, an apology, a bit of grovelling, and some material for his weekly report. That would appease his need for power and respect. But how far would he go and risk a complaint to his superior? The passport and the visa stamps looked fine. He could not prove anything. How many experts on New Zealand could there be in his company? Sure, he could call someone from a Kiwi airline but, given the Asian tendency to avoid losing face, that was unlikely. So would it be worth his while to accuse me of committing any serious crimes and take that chance? No, it wouldn't. Company men like him get ahead precisely because they don't take any chances. They play by the rules and they don't rock the boat.

Secondly, how would a businessman in my shoes feel, pulled out of a long lineup and made to stand around? Outraged. What would he want? To board that flight and make it to his afternoon meeting.

What did I want? To leave the airport with the passport and not get arrested. It was too risky. They would call ahead to check on "Nancy" at the gate. The customer would get arrested. Mohammad would be pissed. I had to abort the run.

Mick said we were outlaws. I thought we were more like character actors in a psychodrama, improvising as we went along.

The supervisor came back alone with the passport in his hand. Nowhere on his bland face could I see any telltale signs of triumph:

no glint in his eyes, no gloating smile pricking at the corners of his mouth just waiting to get out. That told me they hadn't been able to detect anything wrong with the passport. Other than his suspicions about the name, they had no evidence against me.

It was time to make my push. "Excuse me, sir, but is there some kind of problem here? The flight is leaving in an hour." I tapped the face of my watch with an index finger to make my point.

"There is some question about your name. I'm afraid we can't let you board that flight."

I sighed theatrically. I clasped my hands and wrung them. I forced myself to look back at him. "I have an extremely important business meeting this afternoon in Tokyo. A lot is riding on the outcome of this meeting. Surely you can understand that, can't you?"

He looked away. His self-assurance was gone. "I'm sorry, sir, but..."

"Now you listen to me, *sir*." All it took was that interjection and a clipped tone on the verge of escalating to extremely irate for the entire balance of power to shift in my direction. "I'm going to give you a break, okay? I should report you to one of your superiors right now for this heinous mistake and for costing me money, but I'm not going to do that." The word "superiors" caught his attention. He could no longer meet my eye. "But no, no, I'm in too much of a hurry. So I'm going to book another flight now with a different airline and I'll be taking my business elsewhere in the future." I picked up the passport and put it in my shirt pocket. As a payback for his polite threat earlier, I couldn't resist a parting shot, "Have a nice day, *sir*."

I walked towards the exit, trying not to hurry, trying to look casual, while every step of the way I was expecting a hand to grab my shoulder or a few plainclothes cops to materialize out of the crowd and block my path. That was one of the longest and hardest walks of my life.

As it turned out, that walk lasted for a long, long time. The fear and paranoia kept shadowing me for years, when a car backfired, when a silhouette appeared out of nowhere in a dark street, when I caught somebody staring at me on a street corner, because after that first big scare, when every law-breaker realizes that the odds are, sooner or definitely later, you will get caught, and you will go to jail, and you will lay a terrible burden of disappointment on those you hold dearest, that fear is harder to shake off than your own shadow.

Because it's become your shadow.

At dusk, when I told the story to Mick up on the rooftop of the guesthouse during a psychedelic sunset, when the clouds above the pagodas of the Temple of the Emerald Buddha looked like cotton candy and the bats whirled and whirred in search of supper, all he cared about was my latest false identity. Seeing as "Nancy boy" is the British slang for a homosexual, Mick thought Nancy Lars Cohen was the funniest name he had ever heard. For the rest of his short and miserable life, he would introduce me to people as, "This is me mate, Nancy."

Mick was much less amused when he and the Bangladeshi ring-leader got arrested the following week. According to Mohammad, Mick threw a temper tantrum in the airport and tried to head-butt a security guard, forcing Mohammad to interject and then he got arrested too. According to Mick, "Someone snitched on us 'cause those arseholes at the airport had it all sussed out and they was stood near the check-in counters waiting for me."

I didn't know whom to believe.

This might have been proof of Mohammad's suspicions that there were five or six other human trafficking gangs working out of Khaosan Road and everyone was now informing on everyone else. But Mohammad said he would never snitch on any of the other gangs. Grinning that inscrutable grin of his, he said, "We can all make a nice business."

Nice business? Through all the bullshit, the hassles, the crack-downs and Mick's antics, Mohammad never lost his temper. He never swore, never drank alcohol, never smoked. Even when him and Mick got arrested at the airport and taken to a police station, when he called me at the guesthouse to see if another Bangladeshi friend of his was there, he was so calm that I had no clue as to the severity of the situation.

Mohammad felt no twitches of guilt because he never thought of himself as a criminal, nor as a "criminal philanthropist" either. He was a businessman providing a service. To him, evading the law did not entail any moral considerations at all. He approached it in the same spirit, with the same common sense, as a businessman looking for tax breaks and loopholes in business law that he could exploit.

As Mohammad told it, "I brokered a deal with the police. An associate brought down five thousand dollars American in Thai baht and they allowed us to leave."

That was it? Yes, that was all he had to say on the subject. It was a financial transaction, nothing more, nothing less.

But Mick was more like me—he played it up for all the macho melodrama he could muster. Running his hands through his long curly blond ringlets of hair, gesturing with his beer and cigarette, Mick said, "Bloody hell, the coppers had us bang to rights. I thought, 'That's me done… done and dusted. They'll lock us up and throw away the key, d'ya know what I mean?' This female copper was writing up our names on those pieces of papers they'd stick in front of us for the press conference with all the photographers taking our fucking photos. Next thing we're on the front page of the Thai tabloids and the *Bangkok Post*. No such thing as innocent until proven guilty in this Third World shit-hole. It's a good job that Paki came round with the dosh or we might've been locked away for the next twenty years."

Mick sparked a spliff and held it up as an offering to the portraits of the cowboy outlaws Jesse James and Billy the Kid on the hospital-green walls of his guesthouse room, like the Indian insurance scammer we knew used to do to an icon of Shiva, the Hindu god of destruction and hashish, who once smoked a whole mountain of it, Rajesh said. The rest of Mick's room was tidy and barren, devoid of any clues to his personal interests and any photographic attachments to his past. It was a criminal's room; everything he needed could be packed, flung into the backpack by the bathroom, and he could be on the run again in a few minutes.

Mick used a lighter to open another big bottle of Singha, once the world's sourest beers and one of the only choices in Thailand back then. Before they changed the formula a few years later, it tasted like heartache, the perfect aperitif for all the desperate whore-chasers.

I sat on the other bed across from him, emboldened by the weed and beer. "Hey Mick, have you heard the rumors that Singha contains formaldehyde as a preservative? What if it contains estrogen too? Which may help to explain why you've been acting like such a Nancy boy and drama queen after your arrest."

Mick brayed that donkey's laugh of his, as I knew he would. He didn't respond to compliments or praise. I had tried to strike up a more sentimental rapport with him on a few drunken nights and all he ever said was, "Steady on, son." When he was too drunk he'd get angry and shout, "Don't come the raw prawn with me."

"How could I do that? I don't even know what it means."

"It means taking the piss."

Quite beyond the usual British penchant for "winding people up," Mick loved the abuse. He understood that. But the full extent of his self-loathing did not come out until he cut me in on a heroin score, purchased from the pool hall down the street for a thousand baht per gram, which came in a cut-off plastic straw burned shut on one end.

By that point, in less than two years we had exhausted all of Bangkok's lurid novelties. Mick said the whores and the whoring would get better, but they never did. A couple of those bargirls were so unresponsive they made me feel like a necrophiliac. One had a sales slogan she repeated at the front door when leaving, "Thank you. Please come again," and giggled at the pun. Another working girl had an enormous scar curling up her stomach from a botched Caesarian section. After I got up to find her bathroom in the middle of the night she tackled me and wrestled me to the floor, thinking that I was trying to fuck and flee without paying. In the morning, she wanted to take me to meet her mother so we could decide on the dowry before we got married. To escape her greedy clutches, I had to run through the slums of a shantytown and leap into a tuk-tuk, with her and her sister in hot pursuit.

Two other dancers we picked up from a go-go bar on Soi Cowboy and whisked off to a "short time" motel with curtains around each parking space, mirrors on the ceilings and a contraption in the corner that looked like it belonged in a gynecologist's office. Barely had the curtains opened for the act of lust and she was already moaning, "Ohhh, Mick... Mick," turning a potentially erotic production into a bedroom farce. I had to stop and explain to her, half in Thai and half in English, smiling all the while so she wouldn't lose face, that if we were going to try and pretend we were lovers and actually liked each other we should at least try to remember each other's names. She found that funny, but once we started laughing we couldn't get back in the sex groove again, so, for the remaining hour she serenaded me with treacly pop songs and taught me dirty words in Thai, laughing hysterically each time I mangled the correct tones. I liked Watermelon. She was sweet and pretty and good fun. Already a widow and the mother of a young daughter nicknamed "Duck," at the age of twenty-one she was much more mature than either Mick or me, who were a decade older. But even though we saw each other on and off for a few years, the differences in our cultures, educations, personal histories, and languages were so vast that nothing as puny as an erection, or as flimsy as a few banknotes, could ever bridge them for long.

From time to time, I would see older foreign men sitting with younger Thai women (obviously bargirls: the makeup, clothes, pidgin English and the volume at which they spoke, like everywhere was a bar, gave them away) sitting together in a restaurant, not talking, picking at their food, both of them looking miserable. I've been there. And it's lonelier being with someone you can't talk to than it is being alone.

Mick coined the best expression for sleeping with bargirls that I ever heard. He called them "phantom fucks." "The next morning you wake up with a stonkin' hangover and think, who was that bird? Was it Noi or Nok or Nit? Or was there anybody here at all last night? Maybe I just had a wank and fantasized about her. Phantom fucks. That's all they are is phantom fucks."

We were sick of Bangkok, too, a cultural Sahara with nothing but commercial schlock for movies and concerts. At that point in the early nineties, thanks to double-digit economic growth, there was something like five hundred new cars and a thousand new motorcycles driving onto the streets every day. Trying to go anywhere in a taxi took hours. On every third or fourth street was another construction site for new condos, malls and office monoliths. Around the clock, jackhammers bit into the concrete, steel girders clanged, drills whined and dust devils drifted up noses and down throats, making Bangkok into the world's most polluted megalopolis, as it slowly became what Sulak Sivarasak, the country's most caustic social critic, called "a fourth-rate Western city." But the shiny new surfaces and familiar facades of convenience stores and fast food franchises could not hide the lack of basic amenities like a subway system and proper telephone lines. Mick and I would try booth after booth to call Mohammad for work; either the coins would drop straight through or the machine would swallow them. Even if we found a working telephone those glass booths were like microwave ovens in the tropical heat, so we'd keep the door open, but then the traffic was so loud we couldn't hear what Mohammad was saying. Every conversation became a shouting match and after a few minutes the phone line in his apartment would click off and we'd have to call the operator again who couldn't be bothered to answer half the time.

The heat, the noise, the dirt, the traffic, and the communication breakdowns all became unbearable. Mick said, "Bangkok is hell on earth."

Since we had no money to escape to the beach we retreated to his room for a chemical vacation, where we each had a bed to nod out on after snorting lines of heroin or smoking it—"chasing the dragon"—from strips of tinfoil. "Hard drugs for hardened criminals," said Mick.

But heroin is not hard. It's soft. It's the softest drug in the world and the closest you can come to returning to your mother's womb, floating in those warm tropical waters with never a worry and nary a doubt intruding. We might have been sprawled out on a dirty mattress with the occasional cockroach running over our faces, but it still felt like a lagoon in the Garden of Eden. Scratching my balls and itchy nose had never been so pleasurable. This was better sex than I ever had with bargirls. The drug was warming my blood, massaging my brain, stroking my neck and caressing my shoulders like the most loving of masseuses.

Sometimes we'd have to throw up, but that was no big ordeal either. Any drug that can turn vomiting into a pleasant experience is one you should be very wary of.

Heroin, Mick said, was the only painkiller strong enough to kill his pain, but his anguish came from a much different place than I had ever imagined. In my books he was a kind of modern-day Charles Dickens character, one of those witty street urchins and orphans in *Oliver Twist* and *David Copperfield*. Mick encouraged people to think that. He led us on, dropping all sorts of hard-luck fairytales about "sleeping rough on the streets of Manchester since I were a lad."

Mick had dammed up so many of his feelings and so much of his past behind this hard-man façade that once the dyke was washed away by the flow of opiates coursing through his bloodstream, the confessions came pouring out one after the other. Far from the guttersnipe he had pretended to be, Michael Winston Jenner came from a middle-class family of white-collar workers. His father was a senior clerk for British Rail, his mother was a housewife, and his older brother owned a string of dry-cleaning shops.

Had it not been for a severe case of dyslexia, Mick would have followed his father or brother's example and resigned himself to living his entire life in a ten-kilometer radius. "I couldn't read at all when I was a lad, and I could barely write me own name, but I didn't have the bottle to admit it. So I larked about, played the class clown and refused to do any homework. I was rubbish at maths too. The teachers and other kids called me 'thick' and 'daft as a brush.' So I left school when I was twelve and knocked about with a tough lot, sold weed, nicked motorcycles, shoplifted—a right scallywag I was."

I could only listen to Mick's confessions for so long before I'd have to snort another line and sink back into the womb again, basking in the most beautiful memories that I could not recall ever remembering before. James Strate and I were playing ice hockey on the outdoor rink in our neighborhood. I could see the sun glinting off his skates, hear the slap shots in the crisp air and the puck rebounding off the boards, feel the winter wind numbing and then warming my nose, smell the cups of hot chocolate in the dressing room. Heroin catalyzed a 3-D movie version of my favorite memories, all in Technicolor and surround sound.

When I resurfaced, usually because a cigarette had burned down and singed my fingers, Mick was still doing an inventory of his failures. "I wanted to be a professional footballer, but I didn't have the talent for that either... another crushing defeat."

Brought up in a staunchly Catholic home, this was his form of confession. Not that he expected me to play the priest. Not that he cared about my opinion or craved my forgiveness. For all he knew, I was on the nod and couldn't hear anything he was saying.

On and on he went, only pausing to light another cigarette or drink some more cola. "Got married to a lovely lass from Scotland for two years. Swear to God, I loved her to death I did. But at the end of the day we had a big bust up. Dunno why really. I couldn't give her all the attention and security she wanted and Mary Lou thought my life of crime was out of order, *well* out of order. Can't say I blame her. Who'd want to stay married to a fuck up like me? By then, the only things I could do was fight, steal and sell drugs. How many failures can one sad bastard have before he gives up hope?"

Now that I understood his estrangement from the world a little better, and the deep-rooted sense of failure that drove him, I felt a kind of brotherly love for my partner in crime, because we did have a few failings in common after all. Even if I had the power of speech to tell him that it would have been of no use. He'd only say, "Steady on, son," again. Mick was well past the point when a few kind words from a family member, wife or friend would make any difference. Only he could forgive himself for not living up to his family's and his own expectations.

Mick propped himself up on one elbow and scratched his nose in slow motion. His voice was as thick as honey, "When I make the big score and finally get enough dosh to buy a real business, then I'll leave the crime world, get back in touch with my family and prove to them once and for all that I'm not a daft bugger. But when will that be? Fifteen years of petty crime and bollocks and no pot of gold in sight. If I don't get the big score, I won't settle for second best, d'ya know what I mean? Fuck that. I'll go down with both guns blazing like Jesse James."

He tried to smile, but it was sideswiped by that sad sneer of his.

I only made a couple of confessions of my own when Mick had entered the land of nod, a waking dream state of memories and fantasies as real as movies. "One of the first things I can remember is my father getting drunk and taking a bullwhip to my brother and I, but…" I got choked up and couldn't continue.

Later I started in on another one. "Sometimes I believe what's written in the Bible, 'I am infinite. I contain multitudes.' At other times, I just feel like I'm nothing and no one, a blank, a cipher, a nullity, a non-entity with no real skills or redeeming qualities whatsoever."

Mick hadn't moved. He didn't hear a word. That was fortunate. When I looked at him a little more closely I saw that he'd passed out with his face in an ice cream cone, which had melted and was now smeared all over his cheeks and lips.

True to that vision in the cracked and fogged mirror in the Thermae, with his long curly blond ringlets of hair and pretty-boy features, Mick looked like Cinderella gone to pot and smack.

Nancy and Cinderella. What a sad couple of wastrels and would-be gangsters we'd turned out to be.

This wasn't the "blaze of glory" Mick had promised. It was more like a puddle of artificially sweetened misery.

TO CELEBRATE MY move from Khaosan Road into a proper apartment, outfitted with all the high-tech trimmings and designer attire of my ill-gotten gains, I threw a Christmas party for 1996, except I hadn't factored in that Mick and Martin would bring three different bargirls each, nor had I considered the possibility that all eight of them had been up smoking meth for the past three days, nor that Mick insisted my "Christmas prezzie" was getting a blowjob in the bathroom from one of the go-go girls while the rest of them helped themselves to my opium stash.

And I had definitely not anticipated the possibility that the girls, high on meth and opium, would start stripping their clothes off and screaming along to the new Thai pop hit by Miss Moddy that translated into English as something like "Throw Him to the Dogs" and use that as the soundtrack for a six-woman lesbian sex show in my living room. Nor had I ever imagined I would turn to the two Brits, who both had the collars of their polo shirts rolled up, and say, "I think this is gonna be the best Christmas ever, lads," and they would be too high and wide-eyed with boyish lust at this wet dream come true to do anything except grin.

But the euphoria did not last long before the paranoia set in. Completely naked now, the women were screaming too much as they paired off in a lewd pantomime of male-female copulating— "Oh yeah! Oh yeah! Oh yeah! Ohhhhhhh…"—and the music was way too loud too. The neighbors were going to call the cops and the cops would break down the door to find all these beautiful, stoned women eating each other's pussies and they'd spot that brick of opium a friend had brought me back from Vientiane. Then they'd see that I'd made an opium den on my balcony—and what sort of retarded idea was that anyway?

Before long one of the women had fallen into the balcony window, smashed it, and blood was gushing out of a gash in her leg. She was sobbing, Martin was yelling at her, "Leave it out, love," Mick was yelling at him, "Don't throw a wobbly at her. It's not her fault she's hurt, you fucking cunt," and two of the women started bickering about who knew what, and the other girl kept sobbing and the blood kept gushing even though her friends were trying to wrap toilet paper and then a towel around her leg, and I turned off the music and started screaming at everyone to shut up, but they were too high to care and Mick kept braying like a donkey and laughing at me, "Oi! Look at Nancy givin' it all this," and another surge of paranoia sent me scuttling off to get the brick of opium, but no way could I ever flush that down the toilet, so I tried to hack it into pieces with a meat cleaver but it was too hard and my coordination was too skewed and Mick kept braying and Noi or Nit or Nok or whoever kept sobbing and Martin was singing along tunelessly to a Celtic jig by The Pogues after I'd told the prick not to put any more music on, when the room started spinning like helicopter blades and I barely made it to the toilet before my stomach turned into a live volcano, spewing up all the toxic excesses from a few misspent years on Khaosan Road: of bad drugs and sour beers and sordid sex and ugly camaraderie with these ignorant hooligans.

And when I'd finally cleaned myself up a bit and brushed my teeth five times to get that acrid taste of puke out of the back of my throat, I found that the orgy was already over, even though it was not yet 10 p.m., and almost everyone had passed out, save for one of the young women, dressed now in just her red bra and panties, who gave me some sleeping pills and invited me to lay down beside her, but Mick was on the bed too, almost invisible in the darkness and he put his hand on my shoulder in a brotherly way and said in a near whisper, "You're not nothing and no one. You're a diamond geezer, a top bloke, one of the best blokes I ever met." Unbelievably, he'd actually listened to my confessions, as I'd listened to his, during that week we spent doing smack in his room.

And all I could do was mumble, "Sure, Mick, whatever, man. Look, I'm trying to snuggle up to this girl here, so you can sleep on the floor."

But that gorgeous, honey-skinned phantom, who probably couldn't remember my name either, had her back to me and I couldn't roll her over because she was already asleep, or faking it, and the last I thing remember is that she had her fist clenched around something and when I finally opened it up I saw that the greedy gold-digger was clutching a one-dollar coin from Canada.

The three of us fools woke about thirty hours later to find that the women were gone and so was most of my stuff: the TV, video player, stereo, microwave, my clothes, shoes, jewelry and other appliances. Some criminals we'd turned out to be: drugged, mugged and totally outfoxed by these rice farmers' daughters who had about six years of schooling each.

Nearly everything I'd acquired from three years of "import export" was gone now, except for my passport and bankbook still safely stashed in the pages of *The Tibetan Book of the Dead* (the 1924 edition with an introduction by Carl Jung), and all of my books. That was where the real riches lay anyway.

As a Christian might reach for a Bible in a crisis situation, I reached for a copy of Henry Miller's *Tropic of Cancer*. The book is less a novel than a how-to guide about surviving the depths of degradation and poverty that one man can sink to without losing his mind or his sense of humor. *Tropic of Cancer* is to the staid and overly mannered literature of the 1940s what the Sex Pistols were to the bombastic art rock music of the mid-70s: raw, aggressive and brutally honest.

When Miller moved from New York to Paris with only a one-way ticket on a ship and twelve dollars to his name, he was well into his thirties and trying to start a career for himself as an author after many years of failure and rejection. I could relate to that. It looked like a game plan worth emulating and a welcome respite from the academic school of writing and researching in libraries, of dissertations and giving lectures, of applying for arts' grants, of supporting one's literary endeavors by working as a journalist slavishly conforming to "style guides" so they end up with no styles or voices of their own, whereas Miller did his undercover "research" in the streets, whorehouses and Bohemian bars of Paris, his "style" a series of what read like ranting and rambling diary entries about spitting in the face of art, man and God, about fucking women so they stayed fucked, and about the stupid code of macho honor that permits no backing down, whether from screwing a prostitute when Miller and his friend are too tired to perform or from attempting to cool the simmering hostilities that sparked World War I.

Long before Jack Kerouac and the other Beats hit the road in search of kicks and books, Miller led the way in showing that as a writer you had to hunt down your characters, subject matter, and experiences, because *Tropic of Cancer* is also a kind of literary travelogue. As Miller observed, "The destination of journey is not only a place but a new point of view."

At different points in my life I reread different parts of the book that spoke to my present circumstances. In Bangkok, I had no interest in rereading any of the sex scenes that caused the book to be banned in his homeland of the United States until the 1960s. (We had been living out those scenes—and worse—on an almost nightly basis anyway.) The part I needed to find was where he lost everything in Paris and wound up a homeless bum. Instead of bitching, as many would do, Miller wrote, "I have no money, no resources, no hope. I am the happiest man alive."

It's a great two-liner, but it's not intended to be glib, because he went on to explain that all he'd really lost were his illusions. He himself was still intact.

The more I thought about it the more accurate it seemed. I hadn't really lost anything except for my illusions either: the illusion that Mick was some kind of modern-day Jesse James and Charles Dickens character (he was a middle-class kid who thought he was special and deserved better, same as me); the illusion that there was any rebellion or romance in being a criminal (crime is just another job with more irregular hours and not nearly enough danger pay); the illusion that Bangkok is the sex capital of the world (it's the bedroom farce capital, in my books); the illusion of "heroin chic" (a man passed out with his face in a melted ice cream cone is not a fashion statement); and, the biggest illusion of them all, just because you changed your country, your job, your name and nationality many times over it didn't mean you'd become a different person. The old you is still waiting in the wings, thinking old thoughts, dreaming old dreams, and ready to reprise roles you thought you'd long outgrown and cast off.

Behind me, the two of them were plotting a revenge scenario. Mick said, "I'll knock those slags for six."

Martin said, "Now both me fists will smell like dead women."

Unable to express themselves with anything but violence, taunts and sex, what else could they do?

So they went out looking for revenge while I went back to rereading *Tropic of Cancer*.

That was the last time I saw either of them.

I WAS NOT all that surprised to hear of Mick's death in the months that followed the economic earthquake of 1997, which spread from its epicenter in Bangkok to send shockwaves all over Asia. His passing never made the local or English press in Thailand, but the word on Khaosan Road was that he had either committed suicide or been murdered. Both possibilities were plausible. In the latter case, Mick had made enemies all over Bangkok. He'd been in dozens of fights in the Thermae and the bars of Khaosan Road. And he had constantly violated every single criminal code of honor by discussing everyone else's shady businesses.

That was one theory: an old enemy had returned for fresh payback.

Another theory was that, since the economic crash the crime world around Khaosan had turned info a free-for-all of gangs informing on their rivals and making power grabs, so Mick had been killed after trying to muscle in on someone else's turf, or tried to form his own human trafficking gang.

Those who suspected that he took his own life retold the rumor that Mick's "suicide note" supposedly consisted of him spray-painting "FUCK THE WORLD THIS IS HELL" across the wall of his one-room apartment in big black letters. That sounded like his signature style of hateful hopelessness.

Mohammad also agreed with the suicide theory. "He is having anger management issues for years. Mick was very unhappy with his life and lack of success."

I had to give some credence to his opinion, because the strangest thing about our Bangladeshi boss was that his entire story checked out. Many of the customers we imported from places like Afghanistan and exported to Japan would tell me later when I ran into them, after thanking me over and over again for helping them and their families out, said, Yes, he did have ten sisters, yes, he was the only son and a former headmaster at an exclusive boys' school, and yes, his first name really was Mohammad.

Via email we kept in contact for years after I left Thailand and he relocated to Malaysia, where he eventually had four children with a Malay-Muslim woman. Depending on your prejudices, he was either a pathological criminal or an astute businessman eager to comply with and cash in on market forces. After the economic crash of '97 he changed his whole operation. "My customers are now political prisoners from repressive regimes," he wrote in one email. "Therefore, I am sending them to Canada and other merciful nations where they apply for political asylum and refugee status."

Neither of us could do much mourning for our deceased partner in crime. Mohammad said, in his textbook-perfect English that always came off sounding a little robotic and insincere, "Mick was teaching me many things about football and cricket, for example, the expression 'sticky wicket.' It was not an idiom I had any familiarity with before encountering this sporting chap."

I said, "Mick rolled the most beautifully cylindrical spliffs I've ever smoked. One time, on the rooftop of the guesthouse, I saw him roll this five-paper joint—yes, five papers—that he called a 'Bob Marley stealth bomber.' It took us about a week to smoke that missile."

No, we couldn't mourn the person he was, that miserable, racist, homophobic bastard, that violent thug giving out "Glasgow kisses" and turning men who reminded him of his older, much more successful brother into gargoyles spewing blood instead of rainwater, that nearly illiterate hard man with all his pipedreams, posters of cowboy outlaws and ridiculous conspiracy theories.

But it was easier to mourn the person he could have become, had he not been dyslexic and so uncourageous in the face of failure: the man who coined those tell-all expressions like "phantom fucks," who possessed such deadpan panache, "Court appearance today, Yves?" and lampooned the hypocrisy of those who love reading about criminal activities but are too afraid to commit any themselves, "Virtue is for folks who don't have the balls to do crimes." I liked that Mick a lot. That guy even went out of his way to comfort me on that Christmas Eve when the orgy went awry.

In the days leading up to and after the crash of '97, I know that there were much bigger thugs operating than him, and many worse real estate developers selling properties back and forth between themselves to inflate their prices, thereby creating a bubble economy whose balloon was pricked by greedy currency speculators. There were many more corrupt cops, military generals, thieving politicians and directors of financial institutions who absconded with billions of baht. I know that, you see, but I didn't know any of them personally like I knew him.

And I also know that nobody else thinks of him this way, but in his greed, stupidity, violence, amorality and obsession with being on the winning team, he was the figurehead of that era for me: a larger-than-death figure deserving of his own lengthy obituary.

That is what I do now. After returning to the West I pursued the genre of writing that I have always found the most engaging and meaningful: obituary columns.

As an editor for a large tabloid, I was given *cart blanche* to overhaul and sensationalize the obituary section. No question Henry Miller would have approved of the shock tactics. By way of an example let me share one with you. After an alcoholic garbage man who had served three different prison sentences for assaulting and battering at least eight different women passed out beside his garage in subzero weather and froze to death, I decided, after meeting with the paper's lawyer, to publish a letter (read: lengthy tirade) written by one of the ex-wives he had beaten and never paid alimony to, along with a host of other legal documents and photographs of him posing with a shotgun and a severed elk's head on the hood of his pickup truck. My headline read, "Good Riddance to Bad Garbage Man."

You would not believe the thousands of hate emails generated by that column. To be fair, there were just as many positive responses, mostly from women who had also been victims of domestic violence. Rightly or wrongly, these scandals sell papers and bring tens of thousands of "unique visitors" to our website every day. That's why they pay me the big money and how I can afford to drive an Italian sports car.

Perhaps it was all those years of consorting with criminals in Bangkok, but I have to acknowledge that even the most seemingly despicable of characters, like this wife-beater, had a better side too. His only son phoned me and broke down in tears when recalling how his father had taken him along on all his hunting, canoeing, snowmobiling and cross-country skiing trips as a boy. So the son had become a forest ranger, headed a wildlife conservation group and, after watching his old man drink himself into a floating grave, was a life-long teetotaller. In the interests of fairness, the interview with him ran in a follow up column headlined: "One Woman's Trash, Another Son's Treasure."

Honestly, I think this new series of obituary columns on the fifteenth anniversary of Mick's death, which ties in with the anniversary of that economic debacle, will eclipse the garbage man scandal and create many more crossbones of contention to stick in the throats of our readership. I am already anticipating the hate emails. "How dare you pay homage to this criminal and drug fiend. He was a scumbag." To which I will have to reply, "It takes more than one scumbag to start an economic crisis. In any such era, the scumbags become the defining characters, whereas the men and women of virtue and cowardice settle for writing whiny letters to the editor or waving placards around."

As a tabloid hack, not a man of letters or intellectual, I hope that I'm not overstepping the boundary lines of my profession when I say that this series of obituary columns that you have just read excerpts from are more than just a remembrance of one man's past. They are also obituaries for an era when scores of elite scammers and swindlers propelled an entire nation to record-setting, double-digit economic growth; for a Bangkok boomtown gone nearly bankrupt; for a time in our lives when the most shallow subjects of hedonism and serial sex with as many possible partners became profound obsessions; for a road that was the main drag of trailblazing travellers and Southeast Asia's biggest "safe house" for criminals, before it became sanitized and turned into a glitzy strip for a new breed of young package tourists; and finally, an obituary for the dreams of millions of petty criminals like Mick gunning for the one big score that will turn their lives from little tragedies into Cinderella stories. In the end, they all have about as much of a shot at the big time of the crime world as the secretary buying lottery tickets every week has of becoming a millionaire. Is anything sadder and more commonplace than the striking-it-rich dreams of small-time crooks and office workers who believe that wealth is the cure for all their woes? Entire lives are wasted in such fruitless pursuits—deaths also deserving of obituary columns.

Mick always wanted to do something exceptional. That was another thing we had in common. Given his mediocrity as a student, a son, a footballer, a criminal and a husband, that was not possible. But now he's going to star in the longest-running, serialized obituary column in newspaper history.

By cobbling together different rumors and eyewitness reports, I have finally been able to recreate Mick's last moments, when two of the Brazilians from a rival human trafficking gang came bursting through the door of his apartment with Martin the traitor timidly bringing up the rear.

The Brazilians waved a gun in Mick's face. They demanded that he write out a suicide note. With his severe dyslexia how could he do that? That task fell to Martin. He spray-painted the suicide note like a graffiti tag across the wall, "FUCK THE WORLD THIS IS HELL," and signed Mick's name to it.

Imagine Mick's shame over not being able to write his own

suicide note. On the long list of failures that defined his life, this would be the last word.

But I can't let him die like that. Not under those shameful circumstances. Not in a one-room apartment with a metal sink on the balcony under a laundry line and a rattling air-conditioner, in a building by the river surrounded by all these half-finished condos that still stand as tombstones for an era when the line between businesspeople and criminals has never been thinner, and even the small fry like him thought they'd grow to the size of sharks.

In my books, Mick made his last stand. He went for the gun, the gun went off, he took a gut shot and slid down the wall, staring up at the portraits of Billy the Kid and Jesse James.

It was the outlaw's death he had always craved, and for once that smile of his was not sideswiped by a sneer, and for once that miserable, malicious prick was perfectly happy.

I wonder what Mick would have had to say about all this?

"Fucking hell. Don't trust that Nancy boy with the steam off your piss."

(In Memory of Michael Winston Jenner, 1964-1998)

THE PHANTOM LOVER

For Joellen Housego

How did Ying wind up in an abortion clinic holding the hand of a woman she didn't even like? A woman whose legs were splayed open while a doctor in a surgeon's mask pushed the nozzle of a hose between them.

Benz's nails dug into the palm of her hand as the vacuum began whirring. The vibrations ran up her fingers and into Ying's arms, sending her gaze flying around the room like a trapped and frightened bird, glancing off the acoustic tiles on the ceiling, the air-conditioner, the pallid walls, and the baldhead of the doctor, until her eyes alighted on the colored illustration of a female body. The body had no skin. Her eyes darted past the heart and lungs to the intestines and, for a blurry flash, the enlarged illustration of the Female Urogenital System.

Ying blinked and blew back her long, ketchup-colored bangs. She looked at Benz. The model's face was crumpling like a Styrofoam cup squeezed by an invisible fist. Sucking in a breath through clenched teeth, Ying looked down at the hose sticking out from the sheet covering Benz's torso and thighs. She knew it was rude, knew it was sick, but her eyes were riveted to that rubber hose. It was like watching a rape and a murder all at once.

Slitting her eyes, she forced herself to look at the blank wall. Gooseflesh pebbled the backs of her upper arms. Oblivious to the nails digging into her hand and the sobs beneath the hum, Ying closed her eyes and clenched her thighs together. The whirring of the machine was drilling into her skull and mining it with migraines.

Ying should not be here. She and Benz barely knew each other. At their university Benz was the leader of the glamorous set of actresses, models and would-be beauty queens, but Ying was part of the indie rock scene. All her friends made scathing jokes about Benz every time she passed by in the hallway with her retinue of male admirers and female flatterers in tow. "She isn't even a real beauty queen. What did she ever win? Miss Guava?" "No, Miss Durian." "You know what I heard? Some guy told me she had a boob job and now she's got hair all over her nipples." "That's disgusting." Ying did not join in. She was not a group or classroom speaker and, to her ears, the insults sounded too much like expressions of envy.

Because of a family connection, the two of them had to greet each other at the annual Chinese New Year banquet and at weddings and other big social events, when they forced airhostess smiles and repeated the polite putdowns—"Cool shoes. They look really good on you."—that young Thai women from different social cliques use when they mean to say exactly the opposite.

Yet, there was no intonation of playful ridicule in Benz's voice when she'd called Ying to say, "I need you to come with me, because I know you don't gossip like the other girls do and that you'll keep this a secret. If the tabloids find out, they'll murder me and my acting career will be finished."

She was going to get an abortion and all she could think about was her career? That was the real reason Ying disliked her; Benz was too selfish. She always wore her skirts a little shorter and her heels a little higher than the other girls, she told the loudest and dirtiest jokes, "You know me. I can't keep my mouth shut except if my boyfriend wants a blow job," and she took up more space on the dance floor than anyone else, because she always had to be the star of every social occasion.

Blaming it all on Benz was too convenient. Ying could have said no, but she was always so eager to appease. So she kept complaining to her boyfriend that all her friends at school took advantage of her, getting her to help them with their papers, sing at their parties, and console them late at night after they'd had arguments with their boyfriends, which gave Ying the selfish privilege of thinking she was more thoughtful and generous than any of her friends.

A nurse came into the room. "Doctor...doctor!" He turned his head. "The police are here to raid the clinic."

What? The police? If her parents found out she'd been caught by the police in an abortion clinic, she'd have to stay home every weekend for the rest of her undergraduate degree.

The doctor turned off the machine. "Miss, we're done. Please use the back door and I'll go and distract the police." He looked at Ying. "Lock the door behind me and please be quick dressing and getting out of here. I don't want any of us to go to jail for this."

Jail? Ying knew abortion was illegal in Thailand, but would they really have to go to court and then get jail terms? As Benz got dressed, Ying riffled through the bills in her wallet. Not enough for a bribe, but she could use her ATM card, except if the police and the hardline Buddhists wanted to make examples of them. Nailing a couple of young, high-society women—especially when one of them was a rising star in the movie and TV worlds, and the other was the lead singer of the hottest new indie rock band—would be a publicity coup for the anti-abortion lobby.

Benz opened the back door of the clinic and peeped around the corner. "Okay, let's go."

Ying put on her sunglasses and walked a few steps behind her, so if the police stopped them she could say they weren't together. Hyperventilating, Ying stared at the varicose veins in the cracked street. With each step she was becoming smaller and more hunchbacked, but Benz had not lost any of her catwalk poise. Ying kept waiting for her to stumble, to panic, to catch her high heel in a crack, but her strut and self-confidence did not falter.

In Benz's luxury sedan, painted in the same gleaming white as her skin, they drove down the lane and turned onto a main street. Ying kept glancing in the side-door mirror to see if the police were following them. In anticipation of a siren, her shoulders hunched and her ears pricked up.

Finally exhausted by the dread and stress, Ying sat back in the passenger's seat, letting the air-conditioning freeze-dry the sweat on her face. Neither of them spoke. Neither of them looked at each other.

At the first red light, Benz opened her window to buy a garland of jasmine from an old woman in a baseball cap walking between the cars, carrying a wooden pole draped with them. Benz hung the garland from the rearview mirror. She bowed her head, closed her eyes, and raised her hands in prayer.

While Benz prayed, Ying looked at her. The poise and self-confidence she'd seen in her strut was misleading. Her mascara had run down her face, so her cheeks were dotted with black teardrops. Benz was in such a state of dismay that she hadn't even checked her face in any of the mirrors.

Or maybe, Ying thought, she feels so ashamed and guilty that she can't bear to look at herself.

For the first time in years Ying wanted to pray, too, but that would only make her an accomplice in an incident that had nothing to do with her. While Benz was not looking, Ying popped another antidepressant. The psychiatrist said she was only supposed to take one a day, but this was her third and it was still the early afternoon.

Beside Benz's window was a motorcycle carrying an entire family of four. Sitting at the front, between his father's legs, was a tiny boy. Benz gazed at him through the tinted window. The boy stared back at her.

Turning to face her, Benz said, "Look at the way he's staring at me, like he knows something. I wonder if somebody… passes away, whether or not they can be reincarnated so quickly?"

This was weird. Benz talked about her career and shopping, she gossiped about whom her friends were sleeping with, she gushed about the latest party or DJ set, but she didn't talk about spiritual matters.

Ying could not even think of a response, never mind say anything.

Over Benz's shoulder, the child was staring at her now. Gears gnashing, the public bus in front of them accelerated, spewing exhaust over the motorcycle, so the little boy disappeared as if he'd been vaporized, his spirit rising into the sky, leaving nothing behind but a smudge on her windshield.

Ying spent the rest of the afternoon and early evening cleaning the mirrors in her bedroom and the en-suite bathroom, wiping fingerprints off the windows, polishing the screens of her computer and TV again and again, before writing out detailed instructions for the maid to clean, sweep and dust her entire bedroom without using the vacuum cleaner. Between cleaning sessions, Ying watched the TV news and searched the websites of local dailies to see if there were any breaking stories about the raid on the abortion clinic. She didn't see any, but it was too soon to tell. If the police had arrested the doctor, they might be checking his records now. Then they would arrest Benz or demand a massive bribe. She didn't know her well enough to say whether or not she would implicate Ying in the scandal.

She had not realized that abortion was such a serious crime in Thailand. If they enforced the letter of the law, Benz could be imprisoned for up to three years and the doctor for up to five. For a young celebrity like her, from a well-to-do family a jail term was unlikely, but if the tabloid bloodhounds got their teeth into this story, her career would be ravaged.

The Burmese maid did a good job of cleaning, but the room still felt dirty and dusty. Ying didn't want to be enclosed in a bedroom the size of the backroom in the clinic, but she had to get back to work on a history paper she was writing.

The professor, a young Oxford graduate who kept advising his students to "take more chances and to see the past in the present tense," had lauded her idea to write an essay about the tradition in ancient Siam of branding adulteresses with golden lotuses. In the town square, the male officials used the same branding irons that farmers marked their cattle with to emblazon the women's shoulders with flowers visible above their sarongs, so they would be subject to scrutiny and public disgrace for the rest of their lives.

But it was difficult to find any information about this brutal tradition. The history of Siam and Thailand mostly consisted of royal chronicles about the good deeds of male monarchs. Most of those records had gone up in smoke when the Burmese sacked and razed Ayuthaya in 1763. To get access to the few palm-leaf manuscripts remaining at the National Library would take months and months, the librarian told her, but she only had another three weeks to finish the paper.

So far, in her first year and a half of university, Ying had already changed majors three times, from Sociology to Computer Science and now Thai History. If she couldn't even finish her first semester in history she'd be in for another scornful lecture from her mother. "I don't know what it is with you. You keep changing your major every semester. You rearrange the furniture in your room every two weeks. You change your hairstyle or dye your hair every month. Then you have a new boyfriend every couple of months. *What* is wrong with you?"

With only a few sentences, her mother, adopting stiff, manly postures and deepening her voice, as she did when addressing company boardrooms and giving lectures at international business conferences, could reduce Ying to a child again. Even Ying's voice sounded small and infantile. "I don't know... I guess I'm confused."

"There's nothing to be confused about. Pick a subject you really want to study that will lead to a good career. Then you establish yourself in that career before you get married and start a family of your own. What's so difficult about that? Music is a wonderful hobby and I love hearing you sing at our family karaoke nights at home every Sunday, but it's not a career and that noise you make with your latest boyfriend doesn't sound like music at all."

Ever since her last year of high school, it was the same lecture over and over again. In the same way her mother's features had hardened from all the cosmetic surgery, her attitude had gotten more rigid too. Decades of competing in the man's world of high finance, where weakness and indecision were not permissible, had turned her into a CEO on the home front. Ying didn't bother trying to explain anymore that the life her mother wanted for her was not the life she wanted—except she didn't know what sort of life she did want.

Ying pulled out the list of things she wanted to change about herself. Right after, "Legs too stumpy, need to diet more," and, "Must grow hair longer and use makeup to highlight cheekbones, because face too round," she underlined, "Too uncertain and confused all the time. Must be more self-confident and outgoing."

In the margin, her current boyfriend had scrawled, "Must have sex with Dee Dee at least two times per day and more often on weekends and Buddhist holidays." Reading that usually made her laugh and want to call him. Not now. The word "sex" echoed the sucking noise of the hose between Benz's thighs.

Ying crossed her legs and picked up some of the papers scattered across the bed, next to books on dieting and biographies of dead musicians like Kurt Cobain. On another piece of paper she'd written a few lines, while bored in class, for a new song or poem called "Lonelier Than All the Graves in China," but she'd better not mention that to Dee Dee or he'd complain again: "You write the saddest and most depressing lyrics I've ever heard. At this rate, we're going to have to call our first album, *Songs To Slash Your Wrists To*." Dee Dee thought that was funny. She didn't. Since she could not explain to him how depressed she usually felt, she had to write lyrics and poems about it.

Ying listened to a few songs on her MP3 player, she wiped a few fingerprints off the screen, she picked out one of her uniforms and some fresh underwear for school tomorrow—she did everything but get back to work on the paper. Getting started was always the hardest part.

Finally, she opened the file with all her notes on the computer. Most of the research she'd done was on Thailand's most popular folk epic, *Khun Chang Khun Paen*, about two men who loved the same woman. In high school and at college, whenever they studied excerpts from the epic poem, the teachers always said it was a cautionary tale about a woman who did not conform to society's norms and met a tragic end. Wanthong refused to choose between the kinder and more sensible Khun Chang, and the dashing woman-izer Khun Paen, an adept at the black arts who commanded a magical horse and a baby ghost known as a "golden child."

Ying frowned. She'd forgotten about the child. Wiping the computer screen again, she shook her head to dislodge the sliver of a memory that was actually a hallucination from the abortion clinic: a frightened swallow crashing into the window over and over again until its beak punctured its brain and it fell to the floor in a spray of feathers.

She looked back at the scene she'd transcribed, when the king told his courtiers: "Go and execute Wanthong immediately! Cleave open her chest with an axe and don't show her any mercy. Do not let her blood touch my land. Collect it on banana leaves and feed it to the dogs. If it touches the ground, the evil will linger. Execute her for all men and women to see."

In a current paper she'd found by the eminent historian Chris Baker, he argued that executions were not the typical sentences doled out to those convicted of adultery and bigamy, which usually included caning, fines, and the public mortification of branding the women with golden lotuses. So Wanthong was executed on the same grounds as those guilty of treason. She was a kind of revolutionary, Ying thought, and as Baker had written "a sacrificial lamb."

Beyond that, Ying only had a few more notes on how the term *khun paen* was still widely used to describe a Casanova kind of womanizer, which most Thai men took as a compliment, while "golden lotus" (*dok bua thong*) had been shortened to *e dok* (flower) as slang for a "bitch" or "slut."

Ying's cell phone played a jingle-jangle version of "Smells Like Teen Spirit." Benz. What did she want? It didn't take long to find out. "I really need to see you tonight. Some very strange things have been happening."

"Like what?"

"Remember the little boy on the motorcycle? He's been

following me. I've seen him at least four or five times. I don't think he's a boy at all. I think he's a "golden child," a baby ghost."

A shiver made Ying's shoulders spasm. "That's a strange coincidence. I was just reading about them for this history paper I'm writing about Wanthong."

"Really? She's my favorite character from Thai literature and I'd love to play her. So it's not a coincidence then. Everything happens for a reason or because of karma. This might be a case of 'rocket karma.' Whatever we did wrong is not coming back in the next life, it's coming back now."

"Why are you saying *we*? It doesn't have anything to do with me."

"Because you were there with me and now the golden child is creeping into your life, too."

"Maybe you've acted in too many TV dramas about ghosts." Ying looked down at the scabbed-over wounds on her wrist left by Benz's nails. "Have you heard anything about the police raid on the abortion clinic?"

"No, it's all gone suspiciously quiet. The doctor's phone is turned off and the clinic is closed too. I just hope that he didn't write down my real name in his records. But let's talk about it when you come over."

Holding the phone against her ear with her shoulder, Ying picked at the scabs. "It's almost eleven. I have a history paper I'm working on and tomorrow I have a long day of classes then a rehearsal with my band."

"I've got a friend who writes a lot of my papers. I'll pay him to write yours."

"That's cheating. I couldn't do that." Under her thumbnail, the scabs peeled off. Droplets of blood welled up in the fingernail-sized trenches.

"That's not cheating. In business and politics it's called 'delegating.'" Nobody laughed louder at her own jokes than Benz did. She was her own biggest fan and best cheerleader. But her laughter was shot through with static by a bad network connection. Or was it something else? For an instant, Ying had heard a baby crying. "I'm joking. I know you wouldn't do anything like that. Listen, I'll send my driver to pick you up in thirty minutes, okay?"

Surrounded by servants from a young age, Benz did not make requests; she spoke in commands and rhetorical questions. "I really need to see you tonight. You're the only one who knows about this and I need your advice. You were so sweet for coming with me that I had to make you something special that I know you'll really like."

How could she say no to that?

Ying looked at the list of things she wanted to change about herself, while the wounds on her wrist complained about being exposed to the chill of the air-conditioner. "Too eager to please others. Must learn to be more independent." She had highlighted and underlined that reminder so many times it was almost illegible.

Ying picked up her MP3 player and climbed into the massive wardrobe, which she had soundproofed with cushions and empty egg cartons, so she could practice singing on her own or sing along to the demos they had just recorded for their group, The 11th Hour. She referred to the walk-in closet as "my padded cell in the lunatic asylum of high society." It reeked of the joints her and Dee Dee smoked in there, along with the incense and air freshener they used as smokescreens. Beneath that was the pungent aroma of their sexual sweat which now reminded her of being trapped in a birth canal.

Ying slid the door open, suddenly hating Benz with a fury that could only be released in a song. That self-obsessed woman and her...*decision*...was polluting Ying's music, her thoughts, her relationship, her studies—everything! Tonight she'd have to give her a good telling off and make it clear that they should have nothing more to do with each other.

Already cooling off, Ying's anger ran out of steam when she saw Benz's swollen, bloodshot eyes and blotchy skin. She looked like she hadn't slept in days which, as it turned out, was true. Dressed in a long nightgown with a fluffy pair of slippers shaped like bunnies, Benz had been stripped of her glamorous image. Forever comparing herself to her female peers and often finding herself lacking, Ying felt better now—and guilty because of it—that Benz looked so bad.

Ying had imagined that the actress's bedroom in her parents' mansion would be a shrine to her vanity, wallpapered with photos of herself and posters for her films, TV shows and ads. On the contrary, it looked like a botanical garden overgrown with ferns, vines and spider lilies. Terrariums ran down each wall. Benz's pets were a Malayan pit viper, an iguana, a water dragon, and a bird-eating tarantula. Until now, Ying had thought that one of Benz's nicknames, "The Horror Queen of Thai TV," was a marketing gimmick based only on the parts she played.

It was another surprise to learn that Benz's major was botany; she took care of all the flowers and creatures herself, and she'd painted all the watercolors of nature scenes on the walls.

Sitting on top of the terrarium housing the tarantula was an earthenware pot containing a plant with black flowers that Ying had never seen or heard of before. The plant was hemmed in by the red, jagged-edged flowers Thais call "cobra fangs." This was the present Benz had made for her.

Holding up the flowerpot, she said, "Look at this beauty. The bat lily is one of the world's only flowering plant species that has black flowers. They're really rare. I had to trek about twenty kilometers into a rainforest in southern Thailand to find this one. When I was thinking about what your flower would be, and every woman reminds me of one species or another, I thought the bat lily would be perfect for you. It's rare and dark, beautiful and very remote."

Smiling defensively, Ying said, "Thanks... better to be a bat lily than stinkweed I guess." She laughed nervously. "Actually, my plant is marijuana."

Benz turned to face her and frowned. "I don't find self-deprecating jokes very funny and I don't see why you're so down on yourself and moping around the hallways at school all the time. You have more singing and performing talent than anyone at our university, and I've never seen any woman who moves around on-stage like you do."

Compliments made Ying shy and skeptical; her self-pitying streak, which was a side effect of her chronic case of depression, automatically downgraded them to the level of empty flattery designed to extort future favors from her. Benz appeared to be sincere. But who could trust an actress?

Ying sat down on the edge of the bed, close to the door, so she could keep her eyes on the terrarium and make a quick escape if one of the creatures got loose. Resting her back against the headboard, Benz sat cross-legged, surrounded by a dozen teddy bears and other stuffed animals laid out on a florid pink bedspread. Benz typed away on a laptop, refusing to look at her. Ying couldn't believe that she was this offended by an off-hand remark. Whatever talent she possessed as an actress—and many people thought she had enormous potential—could be rooted in her easily wounded sensitivity.

"Thanks for the flowers," Ying said. "The bat lily is really beautiful."

Benz did not look up from the laptop. "I have to finish typing up my schedule for tomorrow. I'll be with you in a minute," she said, as if Ying was her personal secretary. Here was a woman who held grudges and avenged the slenderest of slights.

After leaving Ying to stew in her guilt for a few minutes, Benz showed her the spread sheets on the computer, where she accounted for every single minute of her day, even taking lessons in Cantonese from a private tutor in the back of her chauffeur's car on her way to and from university. Ying knew that her father was an economist and former Minister of Finance, but she hadn't suspected that Benz had used the template for one of her father's five-year economic plans and applied it to her modeling and acting career. By comparison, Ying's list of things she wanted to change about herself looked like the neurotic outpourings of a spoiled teenager.

Reclining on the headboard again, and pushing her long auburn hair back behind her ears, Benz said, "Everything was going according to the plan, except I didn't mean to get involved with this film director from Hong Kong. You know what he made me do to audition for the role of a prostitute who gets killed by See Ouey in this new serial cannibal movie? He took me to Chinatown where the cheapest and nastiest hookers prowl the streets and had me walk around in this sleazy little outfit while he watched from the van."

Benz leapt to her feet, acting out the whole scene and playing all of the different characters. Watching her was like having a front-row seat at a play. "It was the most embarrassing thing *ever*. Guys were yelling come-ons at me, 'Hey, baby,' some of the other street-walkers were telling me to get off their turf, 'This is my street cor-ner, *bitch*,' an old drunk came up and grabbed my ass.

"And then, as if things weren't awful enough already, Jack Wu took me into this short-time hotel, paid for a room for an hour and when we got inside he offered me three hundred baht for sex. Can you believe it? I freaked, started yelling at him, tried to slap his face, threw an ashtray at the wall. And you know what he did? Burst out laughing and said, 'Okay, you've got the part. You finally understand the character. She's angry, she's disgraced, she's violent.'"

"Sorry for laughing but, you mean, on your first date he took you to Chinatown and made you act like a hooker?"

Benz laughed. "Well, sort of, but no, our first real date came later in Hong Kong when he invited me to watch him editing the See Ouey movie and we hung out night after night in the editing suite and went out for dinner and drinks afterwards, but he didn't make any moves, never even made any hints. So after this went on for a few weeks I invited him back to my hotel for a nightcap one evening and you know what he said?" She crossed her legs, folded her arms across her chest in a manner that was both arrogant and defensive, lowered her voice and spoke with the director's sense of conceited amusement. "You're not a woman yet, you're still a girl. You've never really been in love with anyone except yourself and you've never even had proper sex before. You can always tell when a girl makes that step into womanhood because she loses a lot of the giggly man-nerisms and the pouting little girl faces, and starts to exude a lot more self-confidence. Her walk changes too. It's a subtle change, but she becomes more natural, more comfortable in her own skin and you can see all that in her walk. But the way that you strut around still looks like you're a model showing off clothes on a catwalk."

Benz, who had been staring off into the corner of the room, now looked back at Ying. Her deep brown eyes had the glazed look of the stoned or the lovesick. "Can you imagine any of the guys at our university saying anything like that? With these guys, 'Hey, you're really cute, do you want to come over and have a private party at my place,' passes for a witty chat up line. I guess that was the attraction. Jack is almost forty and he kind of became my mentor in movies and sex and relationships."

"So what happened to him?"

"He wanted us to get married and have the baby. I told him that I'm only twenty-two and I can barely take care of myself. I couldn't take care of a baby and a husband."

"How did he take the news?"

"Oh, he'd already told me that if I had the…you know…he wouldn't ever talk to me again. I've tried to call him about a hundred fifty times in the last two days, sent him many text messages and emails, but he won't respond. He's one of those tyrants who's used to always getting his way and calling the shots. When I tried to tell him that having a baby and getting married was going to mean curtains for my career, he said he'd support me and that I didn't have to work. But I'm too independent and ambitious to settle for becoming a housewife at this point in my life."

"I always found it strange that if life is supposed to be sacred, then why are women who are menstruating not supposed to go to temples or churches because they're seen as impure? Did you see that protest on local TV last week? They had all the female protestors rub photographs of the prime minister between their legs to put some kind of curse on him and oust him from power." Ying was no longer talking to Benz. She was far too self-absorbed to hold a conversation with anyone except her inner selves for more than a few minutes at a time. Now she was advising her academic self who was writing an essay about golden lotuses.

Benz put her hand on Ying's. Her eyes were asking a question or making a plea that Ying could not quite decipher. Perhaps it was, can I trust you? "I have something else to tell you and this is not very pleasant at all. So if you don't want to hear it I think you should go home right now and never talk to me again."

Ying's fingers stiffened. Her spine straightened. "What happened? Was it that bad?"

"Okay. Don't say I didn't warn you." Benz intertwined her fingers with Ying's. She was staring at the bat lily crowning the terrarium with the bird-eating tarantula inside it. "When I was going to the bathroom last night, I had all these stomach pains and…well, there's no easy way to say this, but I, but I passed part of the…umm…fetus."

"What?" In sympathy, Ying squeezed Benz's hand.

Benz nodded slowly. She continued to stare at the bat lily, surrounded by cobra-fang flowers veined with red. "I guess the doctor didn't have enough time to remove the whole thing."

"That's really…I mean…I don't know. That's awful. I'm so sorry." All of sudden the air-conditioning felt too chilly.

Benz patted her hand. She smiled sarcastically. "Oh, don't worry. It gets worse. I mean, what could I do with the…stuff…floating in the toilet? It almost looked like a little rubber doll. Oh, all the blood and cramping, too. I was in such pain that I was crawling on the floor of the bathroom, trying to staunch the flow of blood with a roll of toilet paper. Before I cleaned it all up, the bathroom looked like a murder scene."

From this close, Benz's bloodshot eyes and peeling skin made it look like the model had aged a couple of years in the last few days. "You know that feeling you have when you've been with someone for a while and it's quite serious, but you dump him or he dumps you, and afterwards you know something has died, but there isn't any evidence of it outside your own mind or heart? Looking into the toilet last night was the first time I've felt, well, here's the proof. Talk about love and death."

The woman who everyone had stereotyped as yet another vacuous beauty possessed a level of eloquence Ying had not thought her capable of. Though everyone was so obsessed with her looks and catwalk legs that they barely listened to anything she said.

Ying massaged Benz's shoulder. By degrees, she felt the heat of Benz's bare thigh flowing into her own leg through the jeans she was wearing. By sitting there like this, holding hands, thigh against thigh, shoulder to shoulder, they were propping each other up. If one of them moved or stood up, Ying thought, they would both collapse. It was too much misery for one person to stand alone.

"So what happened after that?" Ying asked.

Benz searched her eyes again, as if looking to confirm or deny her guilt. "What could I do? I couldn't flush my own…you know… down the toilet, could I? I can't take it to a temple to have it cremated because the monks would never allow that. So…" Benz gestured with her head towards a small fridge near the wardrobe. "I wrapped it up and put it inside an old purse of mine and left it there."

"It's in the fridge?"

Slowly and solemnly Benz nodded.

The conversation ended on that mournful note which resonated like a funeral bell inside Ying as she settled down to sleep in Benz's bed, wearing one of her nightgowns. She kept thinking about that little boy on the back of the motorcycle, suddenly vaporized in a cloud of smoke, his flesh and spirit rising into a storm cloud that began raining down thousands of tiny fingers. The fingers crawled across the carpet and over the covers of Benz's bed like slugs, inching their way up Ying's legs and over her knees.

She awoke with a series of spasms that jerked her upright to see that the light was on, Benz was not in bed, and the lid on the largest terrarium was dislodged. At the end of the bed were smears of blood. Skeletal legs scurried over them as the bird-eating tarantula ran across the light fixture on the ceiling.

Ying let out a squeal and bolted for the door. In the hallway all was dark and quiet. Slowly her eyes adjusted to the darkness. Shadows gathered substance and silhouettes appeared: a grandfather clock, a Chinese vase, a rubber plant.

Her mind tried to comfort her by offering the most humdrum explanations for Benz's absence. She was hungry. She'd gotten up to get something to eat. Now she was in the kitchen, but she'd come back to bed soon. Everything was fine. There was no need to worry.

But the longer she stayed there with her back pressed against the wall, trying to merge with the silhouettes and shadows, the stranger the thoughts arising in her mind. The smears of blood at the end of the bed looked like the Thai letters for "mother." The remains of that fetus had turned into a "golden child" and were trying to get back inside their mother. That was why Benz had leapt out of bed and ran off to hide somewhere. Now the remains that looked like a little rubber doll were crawling across the floor, Ying imagined, leaving a trail of blood and bile, to seek out another womb.

Ying looked down at the bar of light at the bottom of Benz's bedroom door. She could go back in there, but the terrarium was open and that spider, the size of a giant's splayed fingers, was scurrying around searching for prey.

Keeping her back to the wall, Ying tiptoed towards the living room, where the windows permitted the night to enter in all its sable mystery. On the walls, the shadows of branches waved at the black-and-white, Chinese-style portraits of dead ancestors, making their eyes blink and their lips move.

The front door was wide open. Out in the front yard, standing in the middle of a circle of silvery light, as if caught in a spotlight on center stage, stood Benz with her head tipped back, transfixed by the full moon. No longer the woman that all the other college girls wanted to look like and all the boys wanted to sleep with, she resembled a sleepwalker in a grandmotherly nightgown, clutching a designer handbag that contained the remains of her aborted child and the only proof of a dead love.

Ying sat down cross-legged on the grass behind Benz, afraid to startle her by saying anything because of an old Thai belief that a person's soul leaves their body when sleeping and if they're woken suddenly the soul will never come back.

From where she sat, it looked like Benz's arm shot up through hundreds of thousands of kilometers of black space to touch the moon. But the figure inside the moon did not look like a goddess or a rabbit as Ying's grandmother had told her. No, it looked more like a fetus curled up in a womb: a silver child with craters for eyes and teeth like a saw.

It was the ugliest and cruelest-looking baby Ying had ever seen. But just as every mother loves her offspring, no matter how sick or deformed, Benz was stroking the infant's cheek and smiling at him.

Out of nowhere, a creature galloped across the front yard on all fours, snatched the purse in its mouth, snorted and loped off into the shadows, as Benz stood there still as a statue. Though she only saw it in silhouette for a few seconds, and by the time Ying could process it the creature was long gone, but it reminded her of that magical horse, with the legs and genitals of a man, in the epic tale *Khun Chang Khun Paen*.

❧ ☙

YING HAD BEGUN incorporating all sorts of anecdotes about abortion into a section of her history paper, and statistics from Thailand, where an average of one hundred women die of complications every year, and another aside about how the lack of sex education classes had spawned the highest rate of teenage pregnancies in Asia today.

But how was all this supposed to tie in with golden lotuses and Siamese adulteresses? As far as she could see they were two separate papers. But she hadn't mentioned that to her history professor in their email correspondence about the paper.

She knew that no male teacher, unless he was too old and impotent, was ever going to turn down topics as provocative as these. If anything, the subject matter and her unconventional approach to it flattered his impressions of himself as an iconoclast in his field and followed his advice to his students about "finding the past in the present and bringing history back to life."

On several occasions, Dee Dee had told her, "You're the most conniving female I've ever met—even worse than my mom used to be."

Ying's never-differing response revealed her stubborn and tenacious streak. "Men always say that about women who are smarter than they are." To spare his feelings and make fun of her pomposity, she'd poke him in the stomach and lick his cheek like a cow before dissolving into falsetto giggles.

Her emails about the paper had generated almost immediate responses and more questions from the professor. "Was Wanthong a victim of a patriarchal society or a victim of her own desire to court the black magician? In my opinion, Khun Paen was the bad boy rock star of his day. As a musician yourself with a musician boyfriend you may want to delve into this a little more deeply."

The professor had been doing his homework on her and that was worrying. Over the course of six or seven email exchanges, the tone of their correspondence had changed from teacher and student to friends and kindred spirits; his interest in her no longer seemed entirely professorial.

On the afternoon of Ying's big meeting with the professor, when she was preparing her notes and rehearsing lines in her head, Benz began sending her a series of text messages, emails and photos from Wat Laksi, the most famous Thai temple for getting exorcisms and dealing with paranormal phenomena. Since Benz wanted to rid herself of misfortune and ward off darker forces, the monk had made her a "golden child" by putting a small icon of what looked like a Siamese toddler, whose head was half-shaven and sported a centuries-old topknot, into a jar filled with holy water. From the photo Ying recognized the child. She had seen similar icons on many Buddhist shrines, often with a red soft drink and candies laid out for offerings. Benz texted: "The abbot is giving me directions on how to feed the baby ghost and what sort of toys I should put out for him. If I don't take good care of him he might run amok and cause a lot of trouble."

Ying wanted to write, "That's ridiculous." She thought about telling her, "Don't be silly." She wanted to share her doubts and be the voice of rationalism, but she knew how distraught the actress was—and who could blame her? She was not in her right mind anymore and the baby ghost had become her surrogate child.

Ying's skepticism about the temple and the abbot's abilities as an exorcist were challenged by the video Benz made, which showed the old abbot, whose arms were covered in sacred tattoos, interviewing a thirty-year-old woman who claimed to be possessed by the spirit of her dead mother. The abbot sat on a dais surrounded by Buddha images and Hindu icons. The woman knelt at his feet, hands raised and palms conjoined in a respectful *wai*, addressing the holy man as "royal father." The woman told him, "She won't leave me alone. She keeps trying to tell me what to do and if I dare to disobey her, then she starts choking me, just like she did when I was a little girl and a teenager or—" The woman began choking. She wrapped her hands around her throat. She rolled across the floor, jerking and twisting and frothing at the mouth as if in the middle of an epileptic seizure. Finally, it took the abbot and three monks to restrain her.

The scenario did not look staged and the jerky video had not been edited. For Ying the video had an extra layer of plausibility, quite beyond the tiny woman fighting off four much bigger males. Because of her own mother's dominion over her life, she could easily imagine her, even from beyond the grave, wanting to give Ying lectures, always finding fault with her daughter's inability to live up to her own impeccably conservative standards of deportment and success in the business world.

She had to pull herself together for this meeting with professor. What did he want anyway? All she could think was that he wanted to have an uninterrupted half hour with this shy and famous-around-campus singer, who never spoke in class and hid behind a fringe of dyed-violet bangs and the most old-fashioned skirts that came down to the middle of her calves.

By contrast, the Oxford-educated historian, with his drainpipe jeans and gelled hair, looked more like a pop star than a university professor. In class, he was always dropping the names of alternative bands and art-house directors and new-wave fashion designers. His office, with all the blurry, abstract photos and geometric prints, looked more New York loft than Bangkok collegiate style.

In his presence she automatically slipped into a superficially more subservient manner by bowing her head and raising her hands together up to her nose for a greeting, by pitching her voice a little higher, by smiling more often; all these mannerisms, performed by rote and reflex, were designed to make herself appear less threatening while showing proper deference to a man of superior social standing.

The professor sat behind a steel desk uncluttered except for an open laptop and a few framed photos. "This is a very ambitious paper, but it sounds as if you've got enough material to write a master's thesis."

Ying stared at her hands. In the frigid air-conditioning, she was alternating sweats with chills, and her mouth was as dry as a textbook. "Maybe. I don't know. Depends on the editing I guess."

"But is the structure really going to be this disjointed? I can't see how all these pieces are going to fit together."

Ying kept looking at her hands, clasping and unclasping them. "The structure is more like a literary novel. I was thinking about *The White Hotel* by D.M. Thomas and how it mixes together an epic poem, a Freudian case study, letters, postcards and this story about a neurotic opera singer whose phantom pains foretell the Holocaust. At the end all the characters are reunited in some kind of heaven or afterlife. Much of it seems disconnected but the connecting thread in that book is psychological and my paper is the same."

Ying stopped talking to her professor and began speaking to her conscience which felt guilty about betraying the confidences of an almost friend. "Because abortion is such a taboo topic, and there's so little sex education or counseling here and no Freudian tradition, the woman in question can't find a way to process her grief except through these old archetypes and folkloric figures like the 'golden child' which appears in that epic poem with Wanthong."

"That sounds reasonable, but speaking of taboos, how explicit is this paper going to be?" There was a leer in his voice that she did not want to look up and see on his face. "As a singer in an alternative rock band I guess you've done a lot of first-hand research on the subject." He chuckled and there was a leer in that too.

Had he really just said something as rude and tasteless as that? Ying could not quite believe her own ears. Was he coming on to her or just expecting a titillating conversation to fill in some boring office hours? In either case, she had to be careful. Only two months ago one of the older professors at the school had been suspended for trying to extort sexual favors from five different female students in return for good grades.

She glanced at the framed photo of the woman on his desk. "Oh, is that your wife?"

Reluctantly, he said, "Yes."

"She's very pretty."

Another pause. "Thank you."

"Well, I guess I'd better head off to my next class now. Thanks for your time and advice."

Since she had artfully dodged his most provocative question, he could not keep a burr of bitterness out of his voice. "Just be careful that the essay doesn't turn into a feminist polemic from a Women's Studies' class."

"Sure, except that in this country, and many other parts of Asia, most people think that Women's Studies means hairdressing and flower arranging." Still at that age when she was doubtful, and a little ashamed of her own intelligence, Ying smiled shyly while finger-braiding a lock of hair on the back of her head.

The professor's amusement and nods of agreement surprised her. "That's very well said. I won't disagree with you on that point, and I do appreciate a historian with a sense of humor and satire. If you ask me, the field has been colonized by far too many dullards who rummage around in the past like antique hunters in a flea market."

Ying thought it was wise to let him have the last word and regain a little "face." Before leaving the office, she made the appropriate gestures of deference to restore his superior social standing and uphold the conventions of Thai society, which she was trying to question and subvert in her paper.

Ying tried to walk off her anger but it kept outpacing her. She was too preoccupied with all the comebacks and barbed quips she could have thrown at him to even notice the running track and the Himalayan cherry trees shedding white blossoms during the warm up for the hot-season meltdown. That reminded her of another line in her list of things she wanted to change about herself. "Must be more outspoken and up front about my feelings."

He wasn't interested in her essay—only the titillation factor. It was hard to put her finger on it exactly, but most of her interactions with her male professors had been colored by their condescension. Dee Dee said, "That's only because you're too uptight and sensitive. So you think they're being condescending when they're not."

She looked over at the entranceway to the Faculty of Science, the oldest faculty on the campus, remembering how, as a freshman, she was told not to walk up the front stairway because they used to store cadavers for the medical students to dissect there, and the students still told tales of decapitated, one-legged ghouls crawling upstairs in the dark of night to find their other body parts. Past that building stood the Faculty of Architecture where a statue of the Serpent King was supposed to be the luckiest place for students to have their graduation photos taken. Outside another faculty stood the shrine to the Black Tiger God. That was one of the most popular places for students praying for good grades.

There she was in the country's oldest and largest university, with all the high-tech laboratories, faculties of engineering and architecture, medicine and agriculture, but around every corner was another strange story, another spirit to be worshipped, or curse to be avoided.

Over Benz's shoulder, the child was staring at her now. Gears gnashing, the red and cream public bus in front of them accelerated, spewing exhaust over the motorcycle, so the little boy disappeared as if he'd been vaporized, his spirit rising into the sky, leaving nothing behind but a smudge on her windshield.

Flying around the room, a swallow, which could see the sky and the trees so near, smashed into the window of the abortion clinic again and again until its beak punctured its brain and it fell to the floor in a spray of feathers.

Ying blinked and shook her head to dispel those memories. Would she ever stop thinking about that day? No, probably not.

If Ying was still traumatized think what Benz was going through? Imagine looking into a toilet and seeing…

Ying pulled out her phone, wiped the screen smudged with her fingerprints and looked at a photo Benz had sent of her new baby ghost. Another text message: "I explained to the abbot about that little boy on the motorcycle who keeps following me. He said it's probably not a 'golden child.' It could be much worse, like one of the 'smoke children' from the Khmer occult. They go all the way back to Angkor Wat and are made in much the same way as the Thai baby ghosts, the fetus is grilled and black magicians utter incantations to bring it to life."

With her it was one text message and one plea for attention after another. Before the… incident … had she always been this needy and demanding? If so, she must have driven many friends and lovers away.

One thing about her had not changed recently; she still spoke in rhetorical questions and commands. Which meant Ying was supposed to go and meet her at the most popular after-dark shrine in Bangkok for women—and a smattering of men—in search of lost loves or a new partner.

The film director in Hong Kong had not answered any of Benz's emails or text messages or phone calls, so she was resorting to one last desperate gambit: offering nine hundred and ninety-nine roses to Brahma, the Hindu god of creation, for whatever he could do to reanimate this lifeless love.

The shrine stood at one corner of the CentralWorld Plaza, a mall stocked with all the Western designer brands and fast-food franchises, home décor shops from Europe, and a Cineplex showing all the latest Hollywood films. Puncturing the skyline around it were the illuminated, syringe-shaped towers of office blocks and some of the city's priciest hotels.

On the benches near the street, where a night bazaar had colonized most of the sidewalks, sat Ying, watching Benz lighting a candle and incense so she could kneel beside her high heels, among the other lonely hearts, to ask the four-faced effigy of brass for a favor she would promise to return with more elaborate offerings. The god was known to favor wooden elephants and live performances of Thai classical dance.

Ying was not sure whether any of those praying were communicating with the divine or just talking to themselves: a sort of spiritual schizophrenia. But if it helped them to concentrate on their desires amid the hum of traffic and the hubbub of the crowds she supposed it was a good thing.

The oppressively warm night and the clouds of sandalwood incense threw a tarp of gloom over the shrine and all the supplicants, many of them university students still wearing their uniforms of black skirts and white blouses.

Only around shrines and temples is there none of that typical Thai mirth capped with toothsome smiles. Making pleas to the Great Beyond is nothing to be scoffed at or joked about, for that could bring about a reversal of fortunes.

The gloomy setting, where conspicuous capitalism had relegated religion to a small outpost beside a septic canal, had already inspired Ying to gobble her fourth antidepressant of the day. Now Dee Dee was pissing her off with all these snide text messages asking why she'd become a nun lately?

Since the afternoon at the clinic two weeks ago, they had not had sex. At first, he'd been okay about it. Some of his text messages were funny enough. "I'm getting so horny that if I have to masturbate people in Bangkok will think there's a meteor shower raining down on the city." But each message was less sympathetic than the last and now he was openly taunting her. "I'm having a drink with Annie A-Bomb tonight."

Ying's anger made her dyslexic. She kept making mistake after misspelling after mistake. Going backwards and forwards deleting and retyping characters only made her madder. "Even her stage name is stupid. She can't sing and she'd fuck a streetlamp if she thought it would get her some gigs and publicity. Annie is such an *e dok*…" Ying stopped. Now even she was using the shortened form of "golden lotus,"

In the middle of that argument, the band's producer sent her a message about rerecording some of her lead vocal tracks on the demo tape. Not again! She'd already spent five weekends in a row recording and rerecording all her parts to appease that perfection-ist, so she'd begun to hate and doubt all of their songs.

Then she received an email from the perverted professor. "I en-joyed our chat today. Please stop by my office whenever you want." Ying stifled the urge to send him a sarcastic reply.

Why did all her troubles always come in clusters? Next her mother was on the phone and when Ying refused to pick up, there was a long text message. "Are you out again? I thought you had an essay to write. I hope you're not thinking about changing your major again already."

And what if she got an F on her paper? What if she had to drop out of history and disappointed her mother and herself again?

Ying's grandmother kept telling her, "Your college days are going to be the happiest and most carefree years of your life." What was she talking about? Ying had never felt so stressed out and inadequate in her whole life.

When Benz came to sit beside her, she took one look at her face and said, "What's wrong?" Ying started to say something, but all of a sudden everything she was thinking and feeling and worrying about broke like a wave over her head so she was drowning and gasping for breath. Then she started crying and put her arms around Benz's neck and cried the tears of a little girl overwhelmed by how tiny and help-less she felt. Surrounded by all these office buildings, malls, shrines, and ivory towers, Ying did not feel so big herself right now, and she appreciated that Benz didn't ask her for any explanations or offer any sound bytes of condescending advice. All she did was sit there hug-ging her like a mother, but when Benz felt that maternal flush she started crying too because Jack Wu was never coming back to her even if she gave a million roses to all the gods in the world's pantheon, and every time she saw a little boy she wondered what their baby would look like, and she should never have hired that black magician to pick up the fetus and concoct a love potion that would make Jack forget the abortion, and she apologized for not telling Ying that she'd been conducting a black magic ritual with the spider and the blood offering on the night of a full moon, and only now she realized how useless it all was, but that's how desperate and heartbroken she'd been, and Ying said with a catch in her throat that it was okay because when she found out that her ex was screwing around on her with three other girls at their university she threatened to have a curse put on him that would make his dick shrivel up and fall off, which made Benz laugh so that tears shimmered on her eyelids.

By the time they were cried out and done hugging they were not sure whose tears belonged to whom and who was wearing whose perfume.

At first, it was supposed to be just a few glasses of wine at Benz's place, but they both needed to relax, so they kept pouring out more wine, dancing to their favorite songs, taking turns playing the stylist and giving each other different hairstyles and makeup that became more and more outlandish the drunker they got. It was like a two-girl teenage slumber party. Since they didn't want to sleep alone and Ying was too drunk to go home, they got into bed together and it started off innocently enough, just a few cuddles for comfort like beside the shrine, but the wine was a love potion too and neither of them could stomach the idea of sleeping with a man right now and risk getting pregnant, and who would not be flattered that the sexiest girl in the university was coming on to them? More than that, she was shoving her tongue down Ying's throat as if she wanted to lick her heart while seesawing her hipbone against Ying's clit (clearly this was far from the first time that Benz had seduced another woman). As aggressive and masculine as she was in bed, Benz was still the sort of generous lover who took her greatest pleasure from pleasuring her partner.

For all the eroticism of their exchanges, it seemed to Ying like an extension of the other night, when they sat shoulder to shoulder on the bed, propping each other up because it was too much misery for one person to stand alone. Since then their wounds had deepened. Only bites, nips and fingernail scratches could cauterize those wounds or at least redirect the pain to other places where it was more bearable.

Did it sound ridiculous, did it sound like sober denial excusing the drunken debauch, Ying asked herself later, to say that she was more aroused artistically than sexually? Aroused by the sleek planes of Benz's face and the pale marble of her flesh, the breasts and abdomen that shifted like Saharan sand dunes at her touch, the Roman column of her neck, the tiny ridges in her lips, and the Cabernet Sauvigon kisses that stained their mouths and throats with red wine as if they were two vampires feasting on each other's lifeblood. Ying was no longer sleeping with Benz. Now she was sleeping with an idealized reflection of her fascination with poetry, history, mythology, and geography.

As it turned out, she would never understand Benz's interest in her, and it would continue to bother her for years. Mostly she would be tempted to see herself, and that night, as one of those typical distractions and sexual experiments of the college years; she was good enough for a quick fuck, but not nearly cool or sexy enough to lavish more time on.

When Ying fell asleep her soul left her body and ventured into a morgue where a man with magical tattoos and spells written in ancient Khmer script covering his arms and neck and even the sides of his face—could this be the black magician Benz had hired?—who was cutting open the stomach of a dead woman, pregnant with child, to use the fetus to create a "golden child" and baby ghost like Khun Paen had once done in that old folktale of epic proportions. He then placed the fetus, wet and pink with blood, on a barbecue grill and lit the charcoal...

Twitching and blinking, Ying woke up in the birdsong dawn with those sudden spasms of disorientation that always shook her after waking up in someone else's bed for the first time in a tangle of limbs, sheets, socks and underwear, their arms and hair still intertwined, not knowing where she ended and her lover began.

Through the gauze of a hangover only beginning to pulse, she saw that, sitting on top of the terrarium housing the bird-eating tarantula, was Benz's designer handbag, which doubled as the coffin for her half-aborted fetus, snatched the other night and now returned. Beside it was a shrine for the baby ghost that the abbot-cum-exorcist had given Benz. But the glass looked like it contained blood instead of a red soft drink.

⚜ ⚜

BENZ TOLD HER that she'd talked to the doctor from the clinic and he'd recommended a temple where they could have the fetus cremated. All she had to do was make a decent donation to the abbot of the temple for "renovations" and he would arrange for the cremation after it was dark and the temple was quiet.

By the time Ying arrived, after having more arguments with her mother and her boyfriend, she felt more liquid than flesh and bone: a witch's cauldron of antidepressants, tranquilizers and diet pills laced with amphetamines. She would try to say something but Benz would snap, "What's that supposed to be? Sanskrit? Could you please get it together? You always fall apart in crisis situations and I need you to be strong right now." The snotty aristocrat was talking to her like a servant again. Had Benz already forgotten the other night and what they'd done together? Did it not mean anything to her?

Ying sulked and pouted. She would have to revise her opinion of Benz again; she was a bitch and a narcissist who used people as secondary characters and foils in her little dramas. When they no longer amused her, she banished them to the sidelines.

Even though Ying was wearing her contacts, the temple, with its colored glass mosaic of the Hindu god Indra riding a three-headed elephant, the golden statues of the bird-woman Kinnaree, the main altar with its jumble of Buddha images (dark now except for the candles), and the whitewashed crematorium with its single smokestack, were as blurry and soft around the edges as if she was not wearing her contacts at all.

Benz was too distracted to notice Ying's state of distress. She kept going off on angry tirades, "I made the right decision, but if I'd gotten better medical care, if the doctor hadn't been distracted by the police, then this never would have happened." But then she'd look at the tiny white coffin and turn her head away to dab at her eyes with a tissue. The coffin was gilded with decorative swirls and crowned angels in flight as if ready to spirit the dead person's soul away to its next reincarnation.

The abbot sat on a dais beside the coffin. As the two women knelt before him with their heads bowed, hands raised and palms pressed together, he intoned baritone blessings in Pali, wishing the infant a safe journey to heaven and a good rebirth as a human being.

As far as Ying could remember, this was almost exactly like going to a real funeral—except the undertakers did not open the lid so the relatives could crack a coconut and pour the water on the face of the deceased as a purification ritual. Instead they slid the coffin into the oven and invited the two women to drop tiny flowers made of sandalwood on top of it. Benz shook her head and dabbed at her eyes again.

Ying could not work out why there was another big white coffin inside the oven and two smaller ones as well. It didn't matter. The flames were mesmerizing. They were like ballerinas leaping and pirouetting, like red snakes wriggling out of the crematorium's concrete floor. The snakes bared their fangs. They gnawed on the coffins, so the wood blackened, the angels melted and the serpents mated.

Something was wrong. The smoke was billowing out because the undertakers could not get the metal door of the crematorium to close. Then the wooden coffins began cracking and splintering.

As fog enveloped them, the "smoke children" swarmed all over Ying like mosquitoes at nightfall in a malarial jungle. Tiny hands pulled her hair, curled around her throat and pushed against her windpipe as toothless mouths brushed against her blouse and sought out her nipples.

As the smoke thickened, the smell of burning flesh pierced her nose, a smell so strong and putrid that it lodged in her throat like a bone. Ying coughed up phlegm and hacked with such force that it felt like there was spittle coming out of her eyes too.

She had to get out of there before she suffocated to death, but she didn't know which way to turn. In a matter of minutes, she had been exiled to the cloudy surface of Jupiter, that gaseous giant, which was hostile to all life forms.

A baby cried, "Mother," then another echoed that cry. Still others joined in until there was a chorus of howling children. These were not the cries of hunger and thirst she had heard from her niece and nephew as infants. Not the bawling of a baby with wet diapers or teething pains. These were the shrill cries of abandonment reserved for those middle-of-the-night terrors when waking in the crib to find all was dark and baby was all alone.

It was the most heartrending ballad Ying had ever heard.

To comfort them, she began humming. The babies kept crying. She hummed a little louder. The smoke children would not stop wailing. "Be quiet, okay? Please be quiet. You're driving me crazy." Ying put her hands over her ears. It didn't help much. The smoke was so thick she could not make out any outlines or shapes and, in the absence of sight, of anything to take her mind off her ears, their bawling was as relentless as a dentist's drill.

Ying's wordless humming turned into the chorus of that song she was working on, "Lonelier Than All the Graves in China," but it sounded empty without Dee Dee's guitar. Where was he? Out with Annie A-Bomb again?

The crying stopped.

Then they appeared.

One by one they swirled through the mist, these infantile phantoms, drifting just out of reach, some missing a nose and a leg, others with no arms, some no more than blobs of flesh while a few had eyes that dominated their entire faces. Now that she saw them up close—saw them for the lost and helpless souls that they were—Ying was not frightened, because they were not menacing.

The most beautiful thing about babies, she felt, was how unlined and uncomplicated their faces were. She had only seen the smoke children for ten seconds and already she knew exactly how they felt and what they wanted:

> They wanted their parents.
> They wanted to be loved.

They wanted something to eat and drink.

They wanted to be cuddled, to not be alone.

More than anything, they wanted to live. Failing that, they wished to die with a measure of dignity so they could be reborn again in a different womb in a better place and another time.

Her mind tried to comfort her. The smoke children had been given a proper Buddhist funeral. They were at peace now. They would not cause any more problems. They had only come to say goodbye.

The smoke cleared for just long enough so she could see that the ugly man with all the magic tattoos and Khmer spells etched on his arms and face was standing close enough to her that she could see the tobacco stains on his teeth. This had to be the black magician Benz had hired. Apart from the tattoos and all the amulets of tiger's teeth around his neck, with his brown skin and flat nose he looked more like a taxi driver from the northeast. That impression was compounded by the look he gave her, envy giving way to resentment before shame won out in the end and he looked away. If he had any real magical powers he would not have backed down so easily, she thought, experiencing one of those rare moments of lucidity that came now and again on every pharmaceutical binge.

The smoke closed like a curtain between them and Ying backed up in the opposite direction. For defense, she held out her hands, the palms facing up, unconsciously miming the standing sculptures of the Buddha in the so-called "position of subduing the demon Mara."

To her right, a tear opened in the sheet of smoke. Benz appeared. Why was she wearing that pagoda-like crown on her head and the old-fashioned sarong and sash glimmering with golden threads? Slowly and sadly she nodded her head, as if weighing the gravity of what she had to say. "I knew my karma was going to be bad, but this is unbelievable. I am the reincarnation of Wanthong."

After weeks of madcap behavior—buying love potions, staging black magic rituals and attempting to bribe the gods of love with nine hundred and ninety-nine roses—had she finally lost her mind altogether?

Even by her drama-queen standards this was over the top, but she had told Ying that Wanthong was her favorite character in Thai literature, and Benz was most herself when playing other people. That's when her real passions came to life. Only by playing the most tragic of Siamese heroines could she find a role big enough to accommodate the tragedy of losing her child and boyfriend.

The fog drifted in again, sealing them off from each other.

The king told his courtiers, "Go and execute her immediately! Cleave open her chest with an axe and don't show her any mercy. Do not let her blood touch my land. Collect it on banana leaves and feed it to the dogs. If it touches the ground, the evil will linger. Execute her for all men and women to see."

Ying tried to call out, to warn her, but she could not. The acrid and hallucinogenic smoke that was smelted of flesh burning, bones melting, and blood boiling had clouded over her mind.

Panting for breath and swooning, Ying stumbled into a room that was freezing cold and lit by fluorescent tubes of light on the ceiling. For warmth she wrapped her arms around herself. As she looked around at all the freezers, the reality sank in by degrees. This was no ordinary room—it was the temple's morgue and all the freezers were filled with cadavers.

At the farthest end of the room, standing with his back to her, she saw the black magician pulling out plastic bags from a long freezer. Each bag was filled with what looked like a little rubber doll or a sexless, shapeless blob.

Another flash of lucidity; he was stealing the corpses of aborted fetuses in order to make the smoke children and golden kids. He looked at her. Then he grinned and whinnied like a horse. So this was also the charlatan who had worn some sort of costume the other night to impersonate that magical horse from *Khun Chang Khun Paen.*

The sound of her own fury, restrained by years of passivity and honed to an amplified shriek on-stage, frightened her; it was the sound of a boat ripping free of its moorings in a monsoon season storm, a guard dog growling, a child waking up alone in the night, a woman warding off a rapist; it was all these sounds she'd heard and stored up and now channeled into one soprano shriek that stabbed his inner ear like an ice pick.

He cringed and looked around. Each time he took a step towards her Ying shrieked again. He stopped and covered his ears. Soon enough, two monks in saffron robes came running in to see what all the commotion was about. While they confronted the black magician, she slipped out the door, to the left of the crematorium.

At this point the smoke was starting to subside a little. Here and there rents and tears in the smokescreen revealed that Benz costumed as Wanthong was kneeling and praying to an image of the temple's founding abbot, when the silver flash of a camera lit up her face and crown.

Who was that?

Benz did not even flinch. She remained on her knees, genuflecting at the base of the abbot's image, as the photographer took photo after photo. Everything about her posture suggested that she was repentant and resigned to her repentance.

Now another photographer approached. These guys had to be paparazzi. Someone had tipped them off.

Ying should do something. She should warn her and shoo the photographers away. But she was too scared. It was too risky. Then her photos would end up in the paper and her family would never live down the disgrace.

Either it was brave or cowardly, independent or traitorous—her memory would rerun these scenes over and over again—but Ying snuck out the back of the temple, where it squatted next to a small forest, one of the many parts of Bangkok where the jungle and the city mate, where creepers climb telephone poles and pythons feed on stray cats.

This was the only way out. At the front of the temple were three police pick-up trucks. Cops milled around them. Their voices and the static on their walkie-talkies blurred into a babble that was unintelligible except for a single note of urgency. This was no routine bust. This was something special.

Looking out from behind the trunk of a banana tree, Ying saw a dozen policemen fanning out to infiltrate different parts of the temple. Much as she hoped otherwise, she did not think Benz had gathered enough strength to escape. It was not the police who would arrest her; her grief and guilt had already done that.

To make her escape, Ying had to navigate an obstacle course of branches that groped her, mud that sucked at her ankles, leeches that clung to her arms, neck, and chest.

As police flashlights swept the outer limits of the temple, Ying crouched down to creep deeper and deeper into the woods. She had to tread lightly. Almost every footstep crunched a twig or dried out leaf.

In her mind she was moving farther and farther away from everyone she had ever known. Her mother, her band-mates and her boyfriend could not follow her. This was a path she would have to find and make by herself.

Already Ying knew she would not be able to see Benz ever again; the actress would have to face the scandal without her. Ying could not help her anymore. It had not been her decision to go to the clinic, it was not her fault that the abortion—*there*, she'd said it at last—had turned out so badly, and she had not arranged the cremation tonight or tipped off the paparazzi either.

None of this had anything to do with her.

Over the next few weeks, as the scandal broke, and Benz was stripped of all her movie, TV and modeling contracts, Ying maintained her silence. This was the modern-day equivalent of Siamese adulteresses being branded with golden lotuses.

For a final display of penance Benz shaved her head and became a nun for nine days in a temple just outside Bangkok. To wash away some of her bad karma, she cleaned the bathrooms of ninety-nine different temples.

The two women only saw each other one more time, and that encounter was very brief. Benz was walking down the university hallway with her retinue of high-society friends, who now looked more like bodyguards than admirers, and she glanced at Ying who looked away first. Benz was not even out of sight before Ying's friends, the other indie rockers, began backbiting her. "You know what I heard? That was actually her third or fourth abortion."

Completely out of character, Ying snapped, "Why don't you shut your fucking mouth for once? You don't even know her." She slammed her locker shut and stormed off to class.

Trailing well behind her, Ying sniffed a micron of her perfume which sparked a memory of a French kiss that tasted like red wine.

The scandal could have been worse, but it was eclipsed by the finding of more than two thousand fetuses at the temple. For years, abortion clinics from all over Bangkok had been using the temple as a morgue and crematorium.

Ying never finished the history paper on golden lotuses. It was too dangerous, too controversial. Her mother would read it. The professor or another faculty member might realize it was partly about Benz. Besides, Ying was bored of history already and wanted to change majors again.

Her silence over the abortion and her friendship with Benz was not broken for another six years, until after she'd graduated with a degree in Library Science and taken a job as a librarian. In between shifts at the library, she worked on a novel called *Golden Lotuses and Bat Lilies* about a 21st century actress who is a reincarnation of a 15th century adulteress and former concubine in the royal court.

Towards the end of the book, she wrote: "Trudging through the dark forest, her clothes sodden and heavy with swamp water, her shoes squelching, a cop's voice garbled and distorted by a megaphone somewhere behind her, Anne could finally identify with Wanthong. In the end, Wanthong was not even allowed the relief of death. She was reborn as an "unhappy spirit" who haunted rainforests and foraged for scraps around town limits. The two of them were sisters now, sisters from centuries apart condemned to a similarly lonely fate: the detested traitor who had not conformed to society's norms by choosing a proper husband, and the spoiled singer who had been forced to take a vow of silence, to never repeat what had happened over the last few weeks, except under the guise of a supposedly fictitious story. Such was the repressiveness of patriarchal power in her country that women could only turn to prose, poetry, plays and songs to relate their taboo woes.

"Still sick, still high from the acrid smoke, Anne felt twinges inside her guts. She stopped and put her hands on her stomach. Was it gas or a stomachache? It almost felt like a baby kicking inside her. Now it felt like the baby was scampering up her chest, squeezing her lungs and, hand over tiny hand, crawling up her throat, until it grabbed the corners of her mouth and pulled them apart like curtains, to emerge in a puff of smoke: a toy-sized version of the little boy on the back of that motorcycle, except now he was riding a swallow with a broken beak. Anne began coughing and coughing. She coughed up a notebook of song lyrics, wadded paper balls of her unfinished essay on golden lotuses, an empty wine bottle she had shared with Bee, two roaches of marijuana, a pair of earrings from a backstabbing, ex-friend she would never talk to again, the black petals of a bat lily, a photo of her and another ex smiling on some sunlit beach, a memory stick full of songs which had never been released, and a love letter to Bee she had never dared to send.

"As they came out of her mouth, each of the abortions dissolved into smoke, like all her big plans, and groups, and love affairs, that came to nothing in the end. On the breeze, her stillborn brainchildren floated away the same as the smoke billowing from the crematorium's white tower. The smoke came from thousands of fetuses reduced to ashes that dusted leaves and smudged windshields, darkened the eyes of the fetus sleeping inside the moon, and left empty graves no larger than a sigh in their parents' hearts."

LIFE AND DEATH SENTENCES

*In memory of Chaovaret Jaruboon, 1950-2012,
a gentleman, a rock 'n' roller, a drinking buddy,
and Thailand's last executioner*

The executioner leaned over the barrel of the sub-machine-gun mounted on a wooden tripod bolted to the floor. He closed his left eye to focus on the target with his right. Then he adjusted the barrel so the target was a perfect bull's eye in the gun sight. From this close he could not possibly miss.

He wrapped his index and middle fingers around the trigger. In those two digits he held all the power that anyone can hold in this world; of life and death, of the government, police and courts, and the power to take revenge for murder victims and their relatives; always believing that he was saving many more lives by taking these ones, because he was a good Samaritan, not a legal assassin, or the guilt would have driven him insane long ago.

Each time he leaned over the gun and wrapped his fingers around the trigger, that surge of power and responsibility made his shoulders hunch and the follicles on his scalp tingle.

He squeezed the trigger nine times. That was the number of shots it took to kill most inmates. The bullets tore through the target painted on a white curtain and sank into the sandbags lined up against the wall.

Excellent. The gun had not jammed or misfired. Everything was in working order.

He stood up. He got a fresh magazine of fifteen bullets from the locked filing cabinet in the corner of the execution chamber. Each of the bullets he inspected by hand and with the trained eyes which had sent seventy-nine men and two women to their rebirths from this small chamber on the grounds of Bang Kwang Central Prison.

Boonchu could not afford to make any mistakes today. Today was special. Today, he'd told his wife, was going to be an "elephant fair": a very big day. The prime minister had ordered the first executions to be carried out in the government's "War on Drugs" of 2003. Among the prison's populace of seven thousand inmates a rumor had spread like HIV, making its way to his office in an hour, that this was going to be the biggest bloodbath in the jail's history.

AFTER CHECKING THE gun, he returned to his office, feeling a few centimeters taller and a dozen years younger. The in-tray on his desk was already full. One envelope was stuffed with bills, a kickback from a mobster who ran one of the illegal sweatshops in the prison. Beneath his desk, Boonchu pocketed the bills, wondering what all these rich kids would think if they knew their brand-name trainers had been produced by Asian inmates, working seven days a week, for the equivalent of ten dollars a month. Would they find that as amusing as he did? Probably not. Outside these prison walls, topped with brambles of barbed wire and manned by guards with hunting telescopes on their rifles, gallows humor inspired a lot more grimaces than guffaws.

Also on his desk was a death certificate for an African drug trafficker who had died the night before. As a former guard, removing corpses from the cells had once been his job. Since the bodies could not be moved at night, they had to wait until morning. By then rigor mortis had set in.

He read over the death certificate, remembering all the times he'd had to use a hammer to break the frozen-stiff fingers of an inmate before they could be fingerprinted. Each hammer blow, he imagined, had toughened him up so he felt like he was encased in concrete, not flesh, his bones reinforced with metal bars. For the past three decades, he had looked out at the world through this invisible cage no one else could see.

That was nothing special in the penitentiary. All the guards and prison officials had built up their own fortifications to put a wall between their personal lives and the squalor of what was the size of a town built on violence, vice and pestilence. Some used alcohol as a moat, others gave themselves to adultery and gambling, Boonchu turned to his family and took up cooking.

The official cause of death was a drug overdose, but the prisoner could have been killed by another inmate or a guard. In his early years as a guard Boonchu had tried launching a few investigations into human rights abuses, but they never went anywhere and neither did his career. Once he'd learned how to keep his mouth shut and become a yes man he had risen through the ranks, until he was now the prison's Chief of Foreign Affairs in charge of overseeing the eight hundred and twenty foreign prisoners.

Since the Africans had dark skin like him and were doled out the worst treatment by the guards and the other inmates, he arranged "contact visits" with their wives and other discreet favors. Using the kickbacks from mobsters, he made anonymous donations to an NGO that purchased medical supplies for them. What good had it done? The idiots kept winding up in prison and dying of drug overdoses, or killing each other, didn't they? It was useless. Fuck it and fuck them. From now on he'd keep the money for his daughters' educations. That was for the greater good. All he'd been doing was bribing his conscience, like the gangsters bribed him.

From 10 a.m. until noon, the warden had organized a series of interviews for him with journalists, mostly from the local press. As usual, the warden had written out a series of instructions to follow: "Toe the party line. Repeat what the prime minister said, 'Drug dealers have been cruel to our children so we must be cruel to them.' Praise the director of the Corrections Department and myself for all the improvements in the jail, such as correspondence courses. Do not cast any doubts on the death penalty."

Every time he had to do any press he was gagged by similar orders. Once, just once, he wanted to speak out, to say how he really felt. Behind those concrete expressions he wore and inside that cage of bones dented by a thousand hammer blows, was incarcerated a boy, a prisoner, a different self, who wanted to be heard, too; but he was always overruled by the authorities who made him repeat the same anecdotes to the same reporters that he'd been repeating for years now. Sometimes he wondered if he even believed himself anymore. How many times could he repeat the same statements before they became lies?

His imposing size and the way he swaggered into the office used for interviews made it a little too tempting for most of the journalists to see him as anything but a grownup version of a schoolyard bully. That tension in the shoulders and jaw made it look like he was always about to fly off the handle—tension that worked its way out in different quirks and gestures: cracking his knuckles, grinding his molars, drumming his hands on the table to a rock song on the radio in the next office. None of the journalists could say with any certainty whether it was anger or anxiety that bubbled up to the surface of his skin and simmered there so his dark skin gleamed like polished mahogany. To confuse them even more, he alternated between mumbling while staring off into a corner of the room and speaking in such a formal tone that he sounded like a student reciting passages he'd memorized by rote to a teacher.

In the background, an old cassette of his played rock standards by Elvis, Gene Vincent, Eddie Cochrane and Chuck Berry; these were the tunes he'd grown up with and used to learn English. At times, a favorite melody would make him smile and he'd drum his fingers on the desk, enjoying the music more than the interviews.

He pulled himself away from "Summertime Blues" and turned to the journalist. "Let me give you an example of why the death sentence is necessary. I've only had to execute two women…" He looked off into the corner of the room. "Yes, two. It's not easy, no, it's not really easy to discuss." Apologetically, he mumbled, "They had families and loved ones too." He looked away again and his voice turned robotic. "But we have to face the unpleasant facts. Both of them deserved to die. One of them killed an infant, gutted the poor child like a fish, then packed her full of heroin and tried to carry her across the border into Malaysia. The other woman kidnapped a child. Her and her accomplice buried that boy alive and he choked to death on dirt. What can we do with people like this?"

The reporter looked up from his notepad and across the long wooden desk where Boonchu, dressed in his beige uniform with black epaulettes and golden buttons, sat framed by a Thai flag, portraits of Their Majesties the King and Queen, and a wall-mounted shrine with a Buddha image. "So you think these two women deserved to die?"

He stared off into the corner again. Was there a lack of feeling in his voice or was that just resignation and boredom talking? "It's not important what I think. It's only important what the police and the courts and the judges say. In the end, they are the ones who decide. I have nothing to do with that process."

"So you don't have any personal opinions on the subject of capital punishment?"

He cracked his knuckles again. He twisted his lips from side to side. "I have no personal opinions, no, only what I just said that in certain cases capital punishment is necessary. If anything, I believe that we have saved many more lives by taking these ones, because…" He looked off into the corner of the room again. "Because I'm a good Samaritan doing a difficult job that many people resent. Other than that I let the legal experts decide. We must trust their superior judgment."

This was as much as his conscience would ever permit him to admit. To confess to any personal culpability, to even suggest that there was an element of choice at work, would be the first step in dismantling the life he had built, which was a different kind of prison: the job, the marriage, the thirty-year mortgage, the three daughters, and the past he never spoke of to anyone, not even his wife of thirty-five years.

Throughout the interviews that day, he kept his hands folded over his enormous stomach. The press corps assumed he was ashamed of his beer belly.

That was not it. Through an act of concentration and willpower he had learned from an abbot and meditation master at the temple where he ordained as a monk for nine days before his wedding, Boon-chu directed all those arrows of stress and sorrow away from his head and heart to a place in his stomach where he did not have to think about them. There they remained, eating through his stomach lining. At first it was only upset stomachs and outbursts of gas. Later it was ulcers. Finally cancer.

Not long before his death, just two years into his retirement, Boonchu's stomach had swollen up to the size of a pregnant woman about to give birth to a ten-kilo tumor. The nurses thought he was hallucinating on painkillers when he kept crying out, "That Siamese fighting fish I swallowed has given birth to a hundred other fish that are tearing out my stomach. Please stop them," but he was just remembering his childhood.

AT AN AGE when the worst thing that could happen to most boys was falling off their bicycles, or falling out of a tree and breaking an arm, Boonchu was already running errands for the gangsters, drunkards and hitmen who converged at his father's gambling den for Siamese fighting fish, which also doubled as the family home, where his father bred and trained the combatants himself. Behind their old wooden house, the backyard was filled with dozens of large earthenware urns containing the fry of the fighting fish. All over the house—even on the toilet tank—stood glass bottles, each containing a single fish. Pieces of cardboard separated the glass cells. This prevented them from going into a fighting frenzy when they spotted a rival, but could not stop the fish from trying to attack their own reflections in the glass.

The creatures with the longer fins, named after a Chinese emperor's robes, and the ones with the shorter fins who were trained to fight, came in the same iridescent shades of green and red, blue and purple as the soap bubbles he chased and popped in the backyard. The boy spent long hours watching his own reflection in the glass as the fish glided through his eyes and across his forehead, their fins unfurling like sails. He pushed his nose against the cold glass and puckered his lips to imitate them blowing bubbles. He gave them the sort of names that boys give to their cats and dogs and talked to them in a language he invented. But the *pla gat* ("biting fish") remained as remote as a dream, floating in their private prisons. They only acknowledged him at feeding time when he fed them dried worms or living brine shrimp, and when he pressed a finger against the glass they would try to bite it.

Even before he could read and write his father had taught him how to develop the fighters' stamina by putting a male in with a female for every fifteen minutes every morning and evening so he could chase her around. To toughen their scales, he showed his son how to put Indian almond leaves in the water.

In the backyard, under the shade of a jackfruit tree pregnant with fruit the size of cannonballs, the gamblers placed bets on dozens of fights going on simultaneously, the male combatants nipping at each other's fins and scales for hours on end while the men sat around drinking, smoking and talking about things he barely understood. "If you put a gun in a woman's cunt and pull the trigger, would the bullet exit through her tits, her mouth, or the top of her head?" "Depends really. You mean she's laying on her back?" "Say I just fucked her and she's not leaving fast enough." Boonchu piped up with an expression he'd heard in the gambling den, "*Mia dai mai seea hai tao lao hok* (If my wife died it would be less of a shame than if I spilled my liquor)," and all the men cracked up.

When not playing the joker, he served as the gopher, fetching beers and cigarettes for the gamblers. It was his job to release the losing fish into the canal behind the house and remove the dead ones from the jar whenever there was a kill, mostly in the first few minutes of the fight when the fish tried to tear each other's gills off.

The viciousness of these creatures went against everything their teacher was telling them about Buddhism at school. After the students stood at attention around the flagpole for the Thai national anthem and royal anthem, they had the morning prayer session, repeating the Buddhist sutra about how every creature is born, gets old, suffers and dies. Afterwards, they had to close their eyes, stand at attention and practice sending out *pa medha*, "loving kindness," to all sentient beings.

The boy sent out *pa medha* to the fish so they would stop fighting, to the gamblers so they would stop gambling, and to his father, so he would stop drinking and cursing all the time. Most of all he sent out "loving kindness" to the mother who had abandoned them—taking his baby sisters with her—in the hope they would return.

Nothing changed.

In the temple, kneeling before the main Buddha image, candle wax running down his fingers, he made extravagant promises to the Buddha that if his family was reunited he would set all the fish free by pouring them into the canal that ran behind their house.

That had no effect either. The gamblers kept gambling. The fish kept fighting. His mother and sisters did not return, and his father kept drinking and insulting him. "Your slut cunt whore of a mother must have fucked somebody else because no kid as stupid and slow and fat as you could possibly be mine."

By the age of ten Boonchu had given up on Buddhism and finally become popular with the bad boys at school by teaching them a trick one of the cock-fighters in the gambling den had shown him: how to jam a lit firecracker in a frog's mouth so when it exploded its head erupted in a geyser of blood and brain tissue.

The boys thought this was the coolest thing ever. They were his first circle of friends, the boys who were either too cool or too stupid to study, who could not, or could not be bothered, competing on the sports field.

To keep them as friends he had to keep upping the ante. So he stole from shops, pulled dangerous stunts on his first motorcycle, swallowed live fish, got in fights, stole liquor from his father to give them, and showed off his collection of Siamese fighting fish. "When they try to tear each other's lips off like this it's called a 'spiral kiss.' So you faggots better be careful with your boyfriends."

Years later, when the warden asked a roomful of guards if there were any volunteers to take over the position as executioner, only one man stepped forward.

What he could not bring himself to admit to the journalists, because he could scarcely acknowledge it himself—it sounded too weak, childish, pathetic, not at all like the tough personae he'd cultivated—but the real reason he'd become the executioner was to be the best at something, no matter how sinister, to gain the admiration of his peers, and to show the world that he was not the gutless, incompetent idiot that his father said he was.

THE REST OF the interviews were boring. All the reporters wanted were the usual blood and carnage stories. So he repeated them by rote. The fire in the jail that claimed several hundred lives (most burned alive in their cells). The inmates who commandeered a laundry truck and tried to drive it through the front gates (all five shot dead by the guards). The legendary serial cannibal who spat on the robes of the monk giving him a final blessing.

He took the warden's advice and repeated the prime minister's remark about the reasoning behind the "War Against Drugs" which had now claimed the lives of some two thousand five hundred alleged drug dealers, who had been shot dead by police and other drug dealers over the last three months. But he said it with such little conviction that anyone could have heard a few undertones of opposition in his voice. "Drug dealers have been cruel to our children, so we must be cruel to them."

He added: "I think we need to look on the positive side too. Thanks to the warden and the director of the Corrections Department there have been many improvements in the jail, like corre-spondence courses in seven different subjects."

The only journalist who proved to be at all different or interest-ing was a lanky Australian guy with a soldier's haircut who was dressed in army clothes. The earrings he wore looked as gay as the jail's ladyboy hookers, and he wasn't the sort of man Boonchu could ever be seen with in public, but at least he spoke some Thai and wanted to know the man behind the sub-machine gun. Unlike all the other reporters, he actually took notes when Boonchu told him that his favorite pastime was cooking, and every morning he woke up at five to go to the fresh market to buy meat and produce so he could have breakfast on the table for his wife and daughters by seven.

One of the strangest things about being the executioner was that most of the men he met, when they found out what his job was, wanted to outgun him with their own tales of violence and bravery under fire. This guy was no exception. He told Boonchu a long story about how he'd been shot on the streets of Bangkok during the "Black May" political crisis of 1992.

Smiling, Boonchu taunted him in a good-natured way, as he did with all the macho men who wanted to win his respect but only received his mockery. "Yes, you make protest while I sleep. Can you believe I never vote in election, never believe in politics? Maybe you are more strong than me. You want my job?" Boonchu tipped his head back and laughed, so he could see all the dead flies lying at the bottom of the light fixture.

"No, thanks. I don't have those kind of killer instincts."

"Yes, you do. Everybody can know sometimes. Maybe your fam-ily is threatened, somebody kidnap your wife, kill your baby, then you find out. Sure."

Boonchu leaned forward. He lowered his voice. He would not dare to steal the spotlight and show up any of his seniors and supe-riors on such an important day, but he could at least hint at his surprise. This guy could get the word out to the international press and the scientific community. If the experiment worked, it would make the "War Against Drugs" look trivial. "You want to know something secret? Off the record, I am a scientist, ichthyologist."

The Aussie lowered his voice to a whisper too. "An ichthyologist? What's that?"

"Expert on fish. I make big experiment for many years. Maybe I can tell soon and give you exclusive story, if you want."

"Absolutely. I'd be well up for that. You know, I have to say, for a professional killer you seem like a very nice guy."

"Yes, I must say, for a journalist you are a nice man too." The belly laugh made his hands tremble.

The phone on the desk rang. It was the warden. He said, "Lockdown at 3 p.m." That was the code they used; whenever executions took place the prison was locked down an hour earlier than usual. "Today, we need your team to pick up six men."

"Six? We've never had that many in a single day before."

"I told you. The prime minister wants us to set some stern precedents in the War Against Drugs. Let's make sure our department is not the weak link in the chain of command or our careers may get the death sentence too."

The warden read out the names and numbers of the inmates so Boonchu could write them down. Even after all these years, the way that the warden could recite the roll call of the condemned, like he was ordering a meal in a restaurant, chilled the sweat on the executioner's forehead.

ALL OF BOONCHU'S sex education classes came from watching the fish mate. During the breeding season, when a male and female were put together, the male would build a bubble nest in one corner of the tall square glass. Then he'd wrap his fins around the female to fertilize the eggs while they swam back and forth in a languorous mating dance that could last for half an hour or more. One by one the male would then extract the eggs and swim up to place them on the bubble nest.

The boy said, "Look, dad. Who'd ever think that creatures so mean could be so gentle?"

"Just you wait, kid. The sweetness never lasts for long in any love affair. It gets ugly again really quick." His father took slugs from a bottle of rice liquor in between puffs on a cigarette made from tobacco rolled up in a dried banana leaf. "Look at that! Exactly like I told you. The female is trying to eat her own eggs. That's all you need to know about women. They're as nasty as a kick in the balls. You know something, I think your own mother wanted to have you aborted. If it weren't for me you wouldn't even be here. So show some gratitude and get me another bottle."

The boy fetched the bottle from the fridge. His father was right. He was dumb, he was ugly, he was fat. He didn't deserve anything better. If it were not for his father he would never have been born. It was lucky for him that the old man tolerated him at all.

And he could be generous too. To celebrate Boonchu's fifteenth birthday, when he reached the legal age of consent, his father took him aboard one of the floating brothels that cruised the canals of Bangkok until the mid-seventies, so he could lose his virginity.

Much to the bafflement of his father and the two gangsters they were with, he chose the oldest prostitute—almost twice his age—on the boat.

Each of the cubicles, partitioned off with plywood, had a mattress on the floor and a sink for washing. The sound of thighs slapping against each other merged with the waves lapping against the hull. In those airless cubicles, cooled by ceiling fans, the sweat took on an even sharper and fishier smell. Combined with the rocking of the boat, he felt drunk and queasy, not aroused at all.

It was embarrassing. He did not know what to do with this woman. He'd never hugged or kissed anyone before, never seen any pornography except a few old magazines. All he knew how to do was wrap his arms around her like the male fighting fish wrapped his fins around the female, to nip at her neck and shoulders. Before she could even get his pants down he'd passed out. When one of the gangsters came to check up on him, the light from the hallway fell on Boonchu sleeping with his face buried in her bosom, his arms around her waist, like a little boy who'd awakened from a nightmare to take refuge in his mother's embrace.

Three months later they were married. On his seventeenth birthday his first daughter was born. The year after that he began working as a prison guard because he needed a regular job with a decent salary and benefits, like health care and a pension, to take care of his family.

Beaten down by his father from a young age, and performing tricks on command for the other kids like a bear in a circus, this mama's boy made the perfect civil servant: obedient to his seniors and superiors (all of the older men became surrogate father figures to him), unquestioningly loyal and willing to do anything to appease them, even the job that nobody else wanted.

He wasn't really the executioner. Those death sentences were decided by the cops, the lawyers and judges. He was only the authorities' triggerman; he was their scapegoat, their dupe.

But the journalists and crime reporters who trooped through the meeting room that morning, true to their shallow and moralistic profession that frames complex issues like capital punishment in the black and white newsprint of five hundred-word op/ed pieces, persisted in seeing something macho, something dangerous in this man and his profession.

As Kendall was leaving, he said, "I couldn't do what you do, mate. You've got the toughest job in the world."

Boonchu smiled sadly and folded his hands over his enormous stomach. "No, it's the easiest job in the world." He held up the index and middle fingers of his right hand. "All you have to do is point the gun and go click, click, click, click. The hard part is what comes after."

ALL THE GUARDS and prison officials referred to the death chamber in quasi-Buddhist terms as the "room to end all suffering." It was surrounded by trees, freshly cut grass and flowerbeds brightened with red and yellow dahlias. These were some of the last sights the condemned men and women would ever see, after they received a blessing from a monk and the offer of a final meal, before they were led into the rectangular chamber that was the size of a windowless, one-bedroom apartment.

The building's Thai name and its garden had drawn the flak of Western journalists who saw them as the whitewashes of a barbaric injustice system. Seen from a local perspective, however, was there not a Buddhist sense of compassion operating here? That the condemned man or woman's last moments could be made a little more pleasant in the presence of all this foliage and the butterflies which flew up and over the brambles of barbed wire; even an inkling of the Buddhist belief that human nature is subject to the same law of impermanence that governs the natural world.

Off to one side of the chamber stood the "spirit house": a miniature Buddhist temple on a pedestal that served as a shrine and a home for the prison's guardian spirit. Before each execution took place, Boonchu and the rest of his team, holding candles, incense and lotus blossoms, asked the deity for forgiveness while praying that the ghost of the deceased would not come back to haunt them, because they were not killing him out of malice, they were only doing their duty.

The two guards who led the prisoner inside the death chamber then blindfolded him and tied him to a wooden cross. The guards put offerings of incense, a candle and a lotus blossom in his hands and tied them together with the sacred white thread that Thai monks use to bless people or ward off evil. Behind the cross was a ceiling-high bank of sandbags darkened with bloodstains. The sub-machine gun, mounted on a wooden tripod bolted to the floor, was the long arm of Thai law pointing an accusing finger at the condemned person's back.

The first five executions that afternoon went off like clockwork. After almost twenty years on the firing line, Boonchu was stunned that he could walk into the death chamber and no longer be terrorized by all the memories and ghosts which had once lingered there to ambush him: prisoners screaming abuse or pleading for their lives, leg irons rattling, screams and gunshots, that horrible woman who gutted the baby and packed her full of heroin shouting, "I'll kill you in my next life, you fat, ugly buffalo!"

All was silent now. Either his conscience had made peace with the job or he and his team had become calloused old hands going through the motions on an assembly line of death.

The trouble started when the guards led the last dead man walking into the chamber. He twisted out of their grip and fell to his knees in front of Boonchu. He began stammering in mangled Thai, broken English and some hill-tribe language, "Please, sir, I'm innocent. I didn't know what was in the truck. I really didn't know. They just paid me ten thousand baht to drive it."

When Boonchu had read through his file earlier today this was the case that had bothered him the most. The inmate was only twenty-five. He had four years of education and came from a hill-tribe in Burma that Boonchu had never heard of. He'd been arrested driving a truck with fifty thousand methamphetamine tablets hidden in the back at a border crossing between the two countries. The kid claimed he didn't know what the secret cargo was, an alibi reiterated by most drug dealers, but in his case it would not have been difficult to dupe someone with such little education.

When the kid started weeping and wailing for his mother and sisters Boonchu walked out of the execution chamber. The warden was right behind him.

The executioner stood in a trench of shade cast by the building's eaves, smoking a cigarette and staring at the blindingly bright flowerbeds.

The warden said, "*What* is going on?" He looked at his watch. "We're now almost four minutes behind schedule."

Boonchu did not look at him. He kept staring at the red and yellow dahlias. "I don't feel good about this one. The kid is only twenty-five. I've never had to execute somebody that young. Think about it. Think of all the mistakes we made at that age and nobody ever killed us for them."

"I agree with you. It is a tragedy that someone so young should turn to trafficking in narcotics. Personally, I blame it on greed and laziness. Young people today just don't have the kind of work ethic we had. They expect all the riches in the world without having to work for them. But if we can make an example of this one that should stop hundreds more young people from entering the drug trade. Think of the long-term benefits."

The warden and the executioner were a study in anatomic contrasts, the former as pale, slender and balding as the latter was dark, stocky and hirsute.

The warden had the tunnel vision of the lifelong bureaucrat, focused like a magnifying glass on the most microscopic of tasks that fell under his jurisdiction, but blind to any of the bigger issues outside of his department. He could not even see any of the foliage that Boonchu was staring at. Right now he could not see anything except the hands of his watch, because their schedule had been delayed and he would have to answer for it.

Boonchu said, "I used to believe it when we told the journalists that capital punishment was a deterrent, like that old proverb about 'killing the chicken to scare the monkeys,' but the prison population… I don't know… it's bigger, much bigger, maybe even double or triple since we started here." Why could he never remember these statistics and facts when he needed them? "And the men on death row, there's more of that, I mean them, too. It's bad, it's worse than ever."

"It's not our fault that society keeps getting more violent and people are becoming more and more materialistic all the time. Then they turn to crime to satisfy those base instincts and cravings."

A former lawyer, the warden began building up his case, like he was in front of a judge. "At least we're better than the barbaric Chinese is all I can say. Last year, they executed close to thirteen thousand people, and those are only the semi-official figures. Many of those executed have their organs harvested to sell on the black market. Up until a year or two ago, the Chinese had mass executions in sports stadiums. Soldiers walked along lines of men and pumped a single bullet in the back of their heads while they knelt on the ground. Then the government sent the family of the deceased a bill for the bullet. Nice touch, huh? Now they have these vans, these execution chambers on wheels, so as soon as person is sentenced to death they march them out of courthouse and into the van, inject them with lethal chemicals and they're dead in ten minutes."

The warden put his arms behind his back and walked to and fro.

"Singapore now has the highest per capita rate of executions and in the state of Texas alone there are more men on death row than in our entire country. So let's put everything in perspective and be thankful that we've still got more of a Buddhist sense of mercy and decorum here in the kingdom of Thailand."

"One way or another, the condemned all end up dead. So what's the difference?"

This time Boonchu would not be cowed by the warden's intellect and eloquence. He would not grovel when the warden said that the prime minister was waiting for the word on the last execution of the day so he could hold a press conference to say what a success the "War Against Drugs" had been thus far. "Fine," Boonchu said. "Tell him to come down and shoot the last man."

"*What* is eating at you now?"

Boonchu refused to look at him. He kept his eyes on the gilded spirit house. A pair of pigeons were eating the offerings of food that he and his team had left for the guardian spirit. It was funny, sadly funny, how religion and prayer were just as useless now as they'd been when he was a boy.

"What's eating me? Oh, thirty-five years in jail and more than eighty executions. I feel like a prisoner too, a prisoner doing a life sentence with no chance of parole."

"I don't think you'll have to worry about that for much longer. After today we're both going to be out of work. Here we are five or six years away from collecting our pensions, and you have to throw it all away for some ignorant hill-tribe kid and your latent guilt complex."

He turned to face the warden. Women thought Boonchu's most attractive feature was his large, deep brown eyes. His body and face had aged, but those deer-like eyes had retained a glimmer of boyish innocence. "Can I ask you something? What did you want to be when you were a boy?"

The warden looked at his watch again. He sighed. "Oh, I don't know. I was quite keen on Formula 1 and used to fantasize about winning the Grand Prix at Le Mans, taking the checkered flag, opening a bottle of champagne and spraying it all over those sexy models, not the most subtle kind of Freudian symbolism. And you? What did you want to be?"

At long last, the prisoner within, the boy, the shadow self, spoke up, "I wanted my father to love and respect me, and I wanted my mother and sisters to come back. Those were my only ambitions then and I didn't accomplish either of them."

Over a three-decade career as a lawyer, judge, prison authority and advisor to the Ministry of Justice, the warden had honed his greatest and most dubious talent: how to exploit people at their most vulnerable while making it look like he had their best interests at heart. After all, a person facing a death sentence is not going to argue when his lawyer demands another large sum of money. "And look what happened! From that misery you created your own happy family. You've got three beautiful daughters, you're still married after all this time, and everyone knows you don't cheat on your wife, which is more than you can say for most of us. You, my son, are a paragon of one man's triumph over adversity, and you will not let your family down now. You will not turn your back on them and forsake your career. You will not let me down either, or the director of the Corrections Department, or the prime minister. When it comes right down to it, you are the bravest man in this prison system, the man who's lasted the longest in this job. When we finally switch over to lethal injection next year, you will go down in Thai history as not only the last executioner but the greatest and most heroic of them all!"

The warden had fenced him in. Boonchu looked at the guard tower. He looked at the tangles of razor wire crowning the wall. He looked up at the blue sky and over at the gilded spirit house where the birds feasted and chattered. He looked at the cellblocks and finally, reluctantly, at the "room to end all suffering." Who was he fooling? There was nowhere he could go. This was it. This was his life and his career.

He felt like a Siamese fighting fish trapped in a glass cell. It only looked like he was free, but everywhere he turned he kept running into barriers.

Most of all he could not escape the truth. The warden was right. It was exactly as he said. Boonchu was not that fat, ugly, slow-witted kid from a broken home. He was the record holder, the greatest and most heroic executioner of them all, a loyal husband and father, a man who had triumphed over adversity.

Now he must do his duty and not let his family, country and superiors down. They were all counting on him.

Boonchu dropped his cigarette and ground it out under his army boot. "Okay, but this is the last one. Let's get it over with. Let's rock 'n' roll. Then I'm done with this job forever."

When he walked back into the room, two of the guards pulled a white screen between the gun and the man tied to a wooden cross. Then the doctor drew a target on the screen where the prisoner's heart was.

Boonchu leaned over the Heckler and Koch nine-millimeter sub-machine gun made in Nazi Germany during World War II. Looking into that gun sight was the only thing he had ever enjoyed about this job. For it was then that all of his conflicting feelings about his life and work converged: the guilt he felt about taking all these lives and the knowledge that so many of these people were pathological criminals and killers who could never be reformed; the pride he took in setting the record as the longest-serving executioner and the shame that his career as a prison reformer had been a failure; his confusion about living in a country where all the school kids practiced basic Buddhism every morning and yet capital punishment was still on the books; the hatred he felt for his father, whom he had shot a dozen times already in the form of other men, and the hope, however futile, that they could reconcile in a future life.

To his right, a guard held up a red flag, like a signalman on a railway platform. (The journalists, barred from this chamber, would have been surprised by how bureaucratic and banal the executions were.) When he dropped the flag, Boonchu moved the toggle switch from single shot to rapid-fire. .

That sudden surge of power and responsibility made his shoulders hunch and the follicles on his scalp tingle. He could not take any chances. He had to empty the entire magazine.

The bullets tore holes in the screen, as the echoes of the gunshots ricocheted off the walls, destroying his moment of perfect peace.

All the rest happened by the book. The doctor pronounced the inmate dead and the officials lined up to sign the form. By law they needed at least eight witnesses. According to his rank and seniority, Boonchu lined up behind the director of the Corrections Department and the warden.

After an execution, he and his team usually went out drinking together, because nobody wanted to be alone with their guilt and ghosts after that, and none of their families could understand what they had been through. But today he had something more important to do.

He walked out of the death chamber alone, mumbling to himself, "You poor kid. You poor, stupid kid," but he did not know whether he was talking about the young man he'd just executed by pumping fifteen bullets into his back from only a few meters away, or the prisoner trapped inside himself.

IN HIS OFFICE in a backroom of the family home, where his wife and daughters were not permitted to enter, Boonchu had been carrying out an experiment in ichthyology for almost the entire two decades he had been the executioner.

At first, it was only a bet with his wife that he could breed a new strain of fish that would no longer fight. As the experiment continued, he thought it might have wider applications. One day, scientists might be able to apply it to larger animals, even humans.

The thirty-five, short-finned, Siamese fighting fish swimming back and forth in the glass bottles were the offspring of nine or ten generations of fish which had never fought, never been exposed to other fish except for mating, and never seen any violence whatsoever. By now these males must be docile. Even when he put them together they should not fight. They would be able to co-exist without resorting to any aggressive behavior at all.

Wouldn't that make for a beautiful world? No wars, brawls, muggings, homicides. No wife battering or cases of road rage either.

He scooped up a red and blue fish and put it in with another male. As soon as they spotted each other their gill covers flared and they began circling and nipping at each other.

He put two other fish together and they had the same hostile reaction to each other.

Shaking his head and sighing, he kept pairing the males off in their glass cells. He couldn't believe it but every last one was still a fighter.

Boonchu rubbed his temples. What had gone wrong? The beer tasted bitter now. His experiment was a disaster. He would not have any exclusive stories for that Australian journalist. His new breed of fish were still vicious, territorial bastards. Nobody could breed that out of them.

Out of habit, he stood up when the national anthem came on the radio at 6 p.m. He mouthed all the words but did not sing them aloud.

The news started as he poured himself another beer.

Boonchu was not sure if it was a fair experiment, though. In the rivers and rice paddies, the fish could not kill all of their rivals or they would have become extinct by now. It was only when they encroached on each other's territory that they attacked each other, or when they were put into a glass jar together, like prisoners in cramped cells, that they fought to the death. Who could say what they were really like out in the wild? Aggressive, sure, they had to be to survive, but not all the time.

He did not know who was to blame. The fish or the gamblers? The prison or the prisoners?

Not even an amateur ichthyologist like him, who had spent so much of his life around these creatures, knew why they fought. Was it out of self-defense or hostility, a territorial instinct or sheer boredom? He could not say for sure.

His experiment didn't prove much except that he was still as stupid as he'd been as a boy. It was good that he'd started working in the jail. Otherwise, he never would have made it as a scientist or ichthyologist.

On the news, the announcer read out the usual list of atrocities: another suicide bomber in the Middle East, more American and Taliban casualties in Afghanistan, a gangland slaying in Hong Kong.

Over the course of his life, the news had stayed much the same and very little had improved. Not himself. Not the world. Nothing. So why bother retiring from the firing line? The average suicide bomber took out more people in two minutes than he'd taken out in twenty years. The average army general had much more blood on his hands than he did. Compared to these men he was an amateur.

With his index finger, the executioner mowed down the fish, which were still attacking each other, and mimed shooting the radio too. "Go ahead and kill each other," he muttered. "That's all you're good for anyway, and I guess it's all I'm good for too."

Boonchu thought about emptying all of the fish into a bucket and throwing the radio in to electrocute them. Hey, I should tell the warden about this mass execution technique, he thought, it sure would save the government a lot of money. The cruel kid he'd once been, and still was sometimes, sniggered.

Some other day he might electrocute the Siamese fighting fish.

At the moment, he had to get another beer and make supper for his wife and daughters. By now the chicken would have defrosted, the three girls would be home from university, and he should start getting the ingredients together to make his famous "sweet green curry" with morning glory fried in garlic and chili on the side.

The executioner switched off the light, leaving those beautiful fish with their iridescent scales to nip and tear at each other in the dark, like all the conflicting impulses doing battle, forever at odds inside his swollen gut.

THE VICIOUS
LITTLE MONK

For Ginger, Fang and Ruth Abramson

For decades I disliked cats. They were not loyal or affectionate. They were too vain. They treated their owners like meal tickets. Other than rodent control and possessing a certain feline grace, they served no purpose that I could ever see. At least they sensed my indifference and avoided me.

But my wife loved them. She could never pass the most flea-bitten feline without saying, "Hello, kitty," and kneeling down to stroke it.

She also insisted on feeding the strays that lived in the fluorescent-lit parking lot in front of our apartment. Among the litter was a chubby black guy with green eyes who would only come as far as the front door where she would leave his plate of food. Blackie came, he ate, he high-tailed it.

Another furry freeloader that was the local gangster of the feline posse always showed up with patches of missing fur and fresh wounds. He loved to jump on the kitchen table, searching for scraps. No matter how many times she put him down and said, "No, Mucker," he would leap onto the table again almost immediately.

One night, when we came back from a dinner party, there was a new cat waiting with the other two. He was not as afraid or aloof as Blackie, but he wasn't as psychotic as Mucker either. More curious than cocky, the new cat sauntered into the apartment. My wife left some sardines for him on a separate plate.

At first, I didn't think much of him. He had dirty white fur with a few islets of ginger on his back and head. In place of a tail he had a ginger pompom.

After finishing his food, the new guy lay down on the mat of rice straw stitched with the outlines of wild Asian cattle on a red and gold background. Just what we needed: another feline layabout to spread fleas and discontent.

I picked up the broom to sweep him out the door when I noticed that he had a snaggletooth. Not only that, two of his other fangs stuck out at strange angles. A cat with buck teeth? I had never seen an animal with this abnormality before. So I knelt down to take a closer look.

As a child I had terrible teeth, too, no nicer than his.

As a compulsive fantasist, I spun off a brief history of the cat's life in less than a minute. He was the runt of the litter, the odd feline out. Through no fault of his own, except that he looked different, the other cats shunned him. Even his own parents and siblings had abandoned him. So he became a loner, masking his feelings of shame and hurt with violent outbursts. Looking for companionship, not free handouts, he turned up on our doorstep.

My wife claimed that cats are highly intuitive creatures. Now that I was looking at him with compassion rather than hostility, now that he "sensed" he had nothing to fear from a fellow outcast, the cat rolled over on his back, offering his stomach for me to pet.

From experience, I knew that these are cruel, devious creatures who love lulling people into a false sense of security only to bite and scratch them. Around felines, caution has to be the watchword. Tentatively, ready to pull my hand away at any second, I stroked his stomach. He seemed to enjoy that, made no attempt to scratch or bite me, and even licked my hand a few times.

It was more affection than I'd gotten out of my wife in months and months.

Night after night, the white and ginger cat returned, staying for hours at a time. When I was working on the computer, he would jump on my lap, curl up in a ball and catnap.

Even when his mouth was closed he had an overbite of two fangs. So I named him after one of my first favorite books: a wilderness adventure by Jack London about a wolf called *White Fang*.

Fang did not care for my wife. He never went near her. His feline intuition must have told him that she was mean, selfish, vain and not to be trusted.

This was the first cat who had ever preferred me to her. At least it gave us something to talk about. For months, maybe years, there hadn't been much to discuss. Occasionally she'd make the effort, but any time a woman says to a man, "We have to talk about our relationship," I find it's best to avoid such potentially painful subjects by smiling and replying, "It's fine. There's nothing to discuss. Why don't we go out for a drink and invite some friends?" As a diversionary tactic it's not bad. It's just that after you use it ten or fifteen times over the course of a few years it begins to sound like you're putting off the inevitable and prefer the company of other people.

AFTER SHE WENT back to her homeland to spend Christmas with her family, White Fang moved right in. Every afternoon when I awoke and came downstairs to turn on the ceiling fan, that was his cue to begin mewling outside the front door. Upon entering the living room, he would walk straight over to the red and gold mat and scratch it with his claws for thirty seconds or so, marking his territory I suppose.

He ate from the plastic plate, but he would never lap water from the other dish. Instead, he'd go into the bathroom to lick the drippings from the showerhead or the leaky pipe off the floor. Or he'd leap on the counter to lick water out of the dirty cups in the kitchen sink.

His agility astonished me. From a near-vertical angle, the cat leapt a distance at least four times greater than his own height—a feat no Olympic champion could ever equal—and he never missed that jump. Not once did he miss.

I couldn't break his habit of getting water from the bathroom or sink. In fact, I couldn't even get him to respond to his name. No matter how many times I repeated it, either loudly, softly, or somewhere in between, he refused to acknowledge it. Translating his name into Thai didn't work either. I fared no better in teaching him any verbal commands or tricks.

Apart from the female homo sapien, this was the most stubborn and capricious creature I had ever encountered.

Of course, I didn't have enough experience around them to realize that you don't train cats: they train you. When Fang lay down near my feet that meant he wanted his belly stroked. If he bit me on the ankle that meant I should pay more attention to him. When he rubbed against my leg as I opened the fridge (a typical feline in this respect) that meant he was hungry. If he wanted to come upstairs he would sit at the bottom of the stairs and begin mewling. Only after I knelt down at the top of stairs, cajoled him for a while, "Come here, Fang. That's a good boy," rapped on the stairs with my knuckles, clicked my tongue against the ceiling of my mouth and cursed him a few times, "C'mon fur face, get the hell up here," would he consider sauntering up the stairs in his own sweet time, immediately laying down on his back for another belly rub.

After only about two months, White Fang had turned me into an obedient pet.

Watching the cat strut around the apartment, I got the feeling that in his estimation he had granted me the privilege of living with him, not the other way around. I came to admire his arrogance and independent streak. For hours on end, he would disappear in the apartment. Sometimes I'd find him sleeping under the bed with all of his legs akimbo. At other times he was more elusive, searching out the darkest corners of the wardrobe to use as a den.

Fang was a moody, solitary, mostly nocturnal creature just like me. I ignored him. He ignored me. We had an understanding.

The term "lone wolf" is an oxymoron, because wolves are pack animals. Cats are the real loners of the wild realm. Better to call Fang and me "lone tigers."

On a primitive, non-verbal and non-intellectual level—there are far deeper oceans of thought and feeling than can ever be plumbed by the most profound language and advanced technology—the cat "sensed" I was in bad shape, because he would not let me out of his sight. When I went to the bathroom he would come and lay beside my feet. When I went to the computer to exchange a few more acrimonious asides with this callous, ungrateful, traitorous, out-and-out bitch whom I no longer recognized as my wife, nor even as a human being, Fang would jump up on my lap for a catnap. When I slunk back into the bedroom to crash out in another coma of despair he would leap on the bed and lay down beside me. Sometimes he'd get bored and wander off, but ten or twenty minutes later he'd be back, jumping on the bed and mewling. I had never heard him make these noises before. White Fang was trying to communicate with me. I have no idea what he was trying to say, but it was a wakeup call, it was a welcome distraction from all the rest of the distress.

At times, I could have sworn that the cat had put me on some sort of "suicide watch."

One afternoon, I woke up to find him sleeping on his stomach with his face snuggled in my armpit. It was like a sight gag from a slapstick comedy. I smiled and stroked the long ridge of his spine. Fang woke up and began licking my armpit. "Look at you, a cat with an armpit fetish. You are a little freak, aren't you?" Fang continued licking my armpit. His sandpapery tongue tickled a chuckle out of me.

It was the first laugh I'd had in eons.

So much for my prejudice that cats are not loyal. This guy was as loyal as any dog I ever had, a superior hunter, and a dozen times smarter.

As a reward, I stroked the furry bridge of his nose with my index finger. That was his most sensitive spot. Fang especially liked it when I rubbed the tip of my nose against the bridge of his. He'd close his eyes, purr like a little outboard motor, try to rub his wet little pink nose against mine and exchange "Eskimo kisses."

I guess the cat was lonely or something.

Since men don't talk much about their divorces, I don't know whether this was unusual or not, but in place of the melodramatics in mainstream movies, TV shows, pap songs and generic fiction, the arguments and hysterics, the romantic flashbacks and attempted reconciliations, there was just a guy who'd become so emotionally shut down, and reduced to such a barely functioning beast, that he could only relate to a cat.

HAVING NO ONE I wanted to talk to, and nothing I felt like writing, I spent my afternoons and evenings lying on the mat near Fang, taking a series of disjointed notes entitled "Apartment Study on the Domesticated Feline in Semi-Captivity." Except the title quickly proved to be problematic.

The first time the cat attacked me I was startled. One minute he was dozing in my lap, the next he'd flipped over on his back and was tearing at my hand with his crooked fangs and the fully extended claws on his back legs.

I challenged him to a duel with my eyes. He didn't look away, he didn't back down, he kept right on scratching and clawing me. There was no reasoning with, and no talking to, this little savage, who had still never acknowledged his name.

This was not a domesticated feline. This was a half-feral animal which had never really been tamed.

Not two minutes after the attack, adroitly balancing on his bottom and one forepaw, Fang sat there licking his other leg clean.

For long periods of time he would lay on the ground with his head on his paws, neither fully awake nor asleep. As a noodle vendor pushed his cart down the lane, tapping a wooden block to announce his presence, one of Fang's ears would swivel in that direction. When a motorcycle hurtled past, rattling the windowpane, he would twitch.

The cat lived in the present. He had no past. He never worried about the future.

In ancient Siam, these creatures were held sacred. To kill a feline was deemed as heinous as killing a novice monk. That's why they are still referred to by the nickname of *phra noi* or "little monk."

Those wise men and women of ancient Siam had described that side of him perfectly. Laying there in quiet concentration he was like a monk practicing meditation.

The cat couldn't care less about any of the things that I was worrying about: love and work, success and money. As my old mate Mick would have said, were he still alive, "He don't give a rat's arse about all that bollocks."

Fang watched the female strays walk through the parking lot, but he didn't chase after them. No amount of coaxing from me, "Put out the love vibe, man. At least one of us should go out and get some pussy," or insults, "You are the most useless and slothful creature on the planet," or self-pity, "You and me are about as appealing to females as yeast infections," made the least bit of difference to him.

His existence was one of monastic simplicity. How little it takes to sustain life: food, water, shelter, a little companionship. Everything else is superfluous. Everything else, if worse comes to worse, can be eliminated.

In a divorce, it's best to purge as much as possible, for even the most basic utensils—the pestle once pressed into service as a makeshift sex toy and the cutlery that was a wedding present from a now deceased relative—have been imprinted with all sorts of personal, and now painful, associations.

So I threw out boxes and boxes of junk. I had to get back to the animal necessities of life and sharpen my survival instincts like he sharpened his claws every hour or two.

When a new job came up in Hong Kong, I decided that the cat had to stay. He was another totem of remembrances I longed to forget.

On the day of my departure, I explained the situation to White Fang in the parking lot. "You're not really an apartment cat or a domesticated feline. You need your own territory and plenty of room to go roaming at night. So it's best for you to stay here," I said in that matter-of-fact tone people always use when they want to break someone else's heart and let themselves off the hook of guilt. *It's all for your own good. I only want you to be happy.* Which is the worst sort of self-serving fraud—tantamount to a denial of any personal liability.

The cat must have understood all this about as well as I understood any of my wife's reasons for leaving me, meaning not at all.

At the front gate, I turned around and called, "Fang."

Wouldn't you know it, but after nine months and a thousand repetitions, the cat finally acknowledged his name.

IN THE GENTRIFIED fishing village of Sai Kung where I took up residence, I usually saw a few stray cats when I was coming home from work at night. Most of them ran away when I approached. Some of the more feral ones tried to scratch me if I got too close. Only a few stuck around for a couple of pats before they wandered off too.

Even if I lived with one of the friendlier cats for a year, I couldn't imagine any of them wanting to sleep with their faces snuggled in my armpit.

All of them were felines. None of them was White Fang.

He was as irreplaceable as any friend or spouse.

When I started missing the cat it was often in concert with The Only Ones' ballad "Out There in the Night." For the longest time, I'd thought it was a lament for a lost lover, but when I did an interview with the singer, Peter Perret, he said he'd actually written the song about his cat, who disappeared one night and never came back.

To improvise a little on the chorus, "Sometimes I think of White Fang out there in the night," and I worried that he was back in the fluorescent-lit parking lot, lying beside the wheel of a car, the dirt and oil graying his white fur as he waited for a partner who would never return, with no one to give him any more "Eskimo kisses" or show him any affection at all.

Or has the bitch—sorry, I meant the "little prick"—forgotten all about me and everything I ever did for them?

That wasn't fair. I guess it's possible that the "little monk" with crooked fangs felt more like, and Buddhism insists that all living creatures have feelings: *Why was the two-legged animal so kind to me only to abandon me in the end?*

He'll never know and, all alibis aside, neither will I.

TSUNAMI

For Julia Lazarus, we'll always have Cadaques, and Ed Bovard,
thanks for the homecoming way down south

Yves looked up from his paperback to see that the tide had gone out by at least fifty meters. That was strange. The last time he'd checked the bay was filled with swimmers scissoring through a sea the color of melted-down sapphires and waders kneeing through foamy waves that fizzed along the sand to scuttle hermit crabs and leave shells in their wake.

Now tourists were walking around on the seabed and locals, protected from the sun by trousers and long-sleeved shirts, were picking up fish flopping around in the muck and stuffing them into bags and pockets.

The silence was also odd. A short while ago the air had sparkled with birdsong. Along the shoreline he'd seen herons and kingfishers using their beaks as spears and spades. Now it was quiet and the birds had flown.

Where were his wife and Stephan? He scanned the seabed and ocean. He looked over each shoulder at the hundreds of sunbathers laying on towels or deck chairs. Many of them had also noticed the sea receding and heard the silence that was like a held breath.

Yves got to his feet and put on his money belt. Somebody shouted. He looked towards the shore. All the people in the bay were running towards him. Squinting into the sunlight, far out to sea he saw a gigantic wave approaching.

Yves ran towards the shore to find his wife and oldest friend as tourists clambered out of the muddy bay and ran past him, shouting warnings in a dozen different languages.

The bay was almost empty now and he couldn't see Zara or Stephan anywhere. They must be in one of the beachfront restaurants having a coffee or fruit shake.

He put his hand over his eyes to cut the glare. This was no ordinary wave. It was the size of a waterfall, white as lightning and loud as spring thunder.

Yves ran towards the line of resorts and restaurants, his sandals slapping against his heels.

He would be condemned to remember this moment for the rest of his life and feel the guilt nibble at his conscience; the moment he abandoned his wife, and Stephan, and his reason, in favor of a blind terror and survival instinct that overrode everything else.

WATERMELON KNEW it was a mistake to go out on the jet-ski without paying proper respect to the Water Goddess first, but ever since she'd gotten engaged to Wade she had stopped performing many of the old rituals like that, because he would make fun of her, "What in the heck are you doing now, sweetie?" with that mocking tone in his voice.

He didn't understand anything about Mother Nature. It was important to show her respect and treat her with caution. Her moods were unpredictable.

The Water Goddess was a changeling. She could inhabit millions of different forms: an octopus or a manta ray, a coral reef or a purple sea anemone. All of them were alive and all of them were part of a bigger entity known as the ocean. Calling her a goddess was short hand.

But Wade had spent too much time in cities to understand any of this. He could not smell the rain minutes before the clouds ruptured. He didn't know how to see the forecast for an entire rice harvest in a single stalk of rice. He was unable to hear the warning sounds in the number of times a gecko burped or see future prophecies in his dreams.

Three nights before the tsunami hit she had told him that they should leave the resort, that something bad was going to happen, because in her dream the ocean had spewed up everything it had swallowed: fishing trawlers and sailors' skeletons, mountains of garbage and plastic, coconuts and battleships, in one great "Churning of the Ocean," like had once happened in that Buddhist story about the search for the ambrosia of immortality.

Wade laughed. "What? Like that sculpture in the Bangkok airport showing how the world was created by all those gods and turtles and serpent kings crawling out of the waves?"

Watermelon said, "We cannot know for sure. Everything is always changing in Buddhism."

Yves, who said he was her older brother and defender, came to her rescue as always, which was both kind and condescending of him. He was always talking about ideas and metaphors that were supposed to be one thing but somehow applied to something else, or substituted one theory for another. "Sounds to me like that Hindu creation myth was a few thousand years ahead of Darwin's theory of evolution and how life first arose in the sea and only evolved on land later."

Yves and Wade would conduct their boring debates for hours. It was like watching a ping pong game except the points were harder to tally. Their arguments went around in circles and never came to any conclusions. That was Buddhism, too, all these wheels within wheels spinning around forever and ending up nowhere.

The Western men she had met in the different go-go bars where she had once worked all loved to talk about progress. That was their favorite subject: new computers that were faster, new phones that were smarter, new cars that were more energy efficient and new planes that could carry more passengers. She would not be rude and tell them they were mistaken; none of these inventions changed the cycle of life even one little bit. No one could escape from the Buddhist Wheel of the Law and the endless cycle of birth, aging, suffering, death, and rebirth.

They were so busy analyzing life that they couldn't enjoy any of it. While they prattled on about politics and buying real esate, she was savoring the delicate combination of flavors in a sour tamarind soup with shrimp. The cook had used flowers from the hummingbird tree, or scarlet wisteria, in his recipe. She and the waitress, who was also a northern girl, and had the soft voice and gentle demeanor that are their genetic birthrights, talked about how the flowers made the flavor linger on the tongue for longer and gave the soup a richer smell.

As a girl, she had learned the art and the necessity of making herself almost invisible in the company of men. The Western women she talked to, or who used to try and pick her up in the bar, didn't understand that this invisibility was not negative. It allowed the women to strengthen their ties, because they controlled the family and finances anyway, and it allowed her the time to cultivate her inner life. Like a plant drinking in sunshine, she absorbed all the most pleasant aspects of what was happening around her: the ocean sighing and tossing in its sleep, the breeze fluttering past that caressed the hairs on her forearms, the candlelight burnishing the wooden table, and all the smiling people on holiday dressed in bright colors.

Yves, who was always asking her all sorts of penetrating questions and borrowing her responses to put in his stories, had once asked her, "Why don't you get bitter and turn to drugs and drink and despair like so many of the other bargirls do?"

"Because my inside life is very strong and I must be strong for my daughter. I take care my inside life and plant new seeds like a garden, only beautiful seeds, nothing ugly, nothing violence, only soft lights, nice food and gentle music. A flower looks soft, but it's very hard. The monsoon rains come and beat the flowers down, but they bend and not break. Maybe it not make sense for *farang* people, who always get so loud and angry and aggressive, but Thai people understand that you must be very soft to become very strong."

In between topping up their drinks, as quietly and unobtrusively as possible, she marveled at the sky. With each passing moment it darkened a little more. In the mountains where she grew up the dusk was never this blue. The only shade she'd ever seen like it was the dye from the indigo plant her mother used to make woven cotton shirts for the men who toiled in the fields.

Now and then, as a matter of politeness, Yves or Wade would ask for her opinion on some boring political subject, but she'd only repeat that old Thai expression, "Politics is an illusion, but rice and fish are real." They did not have to know that it was one of her late husband's favorite expressions. Repeating it aloud was a homing signal for his spirit, so they could find each other again and be reunited in a future life.

At least he wasn't as dull as Wade, whose main hobby was traveling around in circles via car, motorcycle, all-terrain vehicle, go-kart or jet-ski. To keep him happy, there she was, fully dressed and wearing a balaclava to protect her skin, circling the bay at Khao Lak on a whiny jet-ski that skimmed the waves like a dragonfly. A mist of sea spray dusted her lips with salt.

Arcing into another turn, sunlight sparkling off the foam-flecked waves, she saw the wall of water approaching, only a few hundred meters away. Watermelon banked the jet-ski towards the shore but another wave sideswiped her, pitching her headfirst into the water. Furiously dogpaddling, she propelled herself towards the jet-ski with saltwater stinging her eyes. Finally she climbed back on the jet-ski, gunned the throttle and pointed it towards the beach.

Looking over her shoulder, she saw the wave bearing down on her. She took off her Buddhist amulet and held it up in the direction of the water, screaming the same mantra over and over again. But even the Buddha and the Water Goddess must have been deafened by this dragon-loud roar.

ON HIS DAY off from bartending at a five-star resort, Yai would sit on the beach watching all the white women sunbathing and walking around in their bikinis. In his eyes, their semi-nudity was both heroic and blasphemous, as they openly flouted all the rules and taboos of Thai society. Even watching them lying on their beach towels, nipples upturned to the sun, or staring at their hips in the tiniest of thongs bisecting their buttocks as they sashayed across the sand, suggested a degree of freedom that was intoxicating to behold. If one only had the courage to be that brave and open to the elements and all that life offered, what would not be possible?

He had often heard tourists, especially the American Marines on Cobra Gold, talk about freedom, but this was the only proof he'd ever seen that there was such a thing.

The statuesque blondes from Scandinavia, California and Australia's Gold Coast were his favorites. They had the sea in their eyes, the waves in their hips, and their hair looked like it had been woven from sunbeams. On the beach, they looked so natural and at home that they had probably been leopard sharks and manta rays in a previous life.

At the bar, during his nightly shift, his old friend Yves pestered him. "Stop obsessing over these blondes and go and talk to one."

"They not interesting in me. They want only rich, good-looking guys."

"Well, they certainly don't want men with no self-confidence or pride. So I guess you'll just have settle for porn movies about Swedish air hostesses."

"Why I want look some guy with cock same same baseball bat fucking some girl like he's doing pushups in the gym? Nothing sexy in porno movie. I'm not sure if they want to make love or lose calories. Not my style."

"Yes, some men go to an art gallery or a church in search of beauty and transcendence, or they look to politics and human rights for freedom and higher ideals, but Yai goes to the beach and leers at blondes in bikinis." Yves made fun of him in such a playfully Thai way, constantly grinning in between clauses, that he could not take offense.

But the former snake-handler's days off on the beach were also a torment, for he could no longer walk around in nothing but beach shorts and a saucy grin like these lucky white guys did. His arms, chest and legs had been scarred by so many snakebites that he had to cover up as much as possible. And he had to wear a baseball cap too, because his skin was already beer-bottle brown. The sunglasses allowed him to peek in privacy.

After an hour or two it was like window shopping in a mall where he could not afford to buy anything—more torture than pleasure.

As Yai came out of the bathroom in the resort, parting a curtain of seashells hanging in strings for a doorway, he heard screams coming from the beach. Out on the sand it was pandemonium. Some tourists ran towards the main road, while others stood there pointing out to sea at this massive wave coming in. An old Muslim vendor carrying shoulder poles strung with inflatable cartoon animals scurried past, yelling something in the southern Thai dialect that Yai could only halfway make out: "Run for your lives! It's the end of the world. Allah is punishing all the sinners in this beach resort."

Most of the Thai staff from the resort were right behind him, fearing a natural disaster that forecast a supernatural apocalypse. Yai was not so easily cowed. He jogged towards the shoreline, flip-flops sinking into the sand with each step, keeping an eye out for Yves and some of the other hotel guests who were his regulars at the Sea Breeze Cocktail Lounge. Except for some parents frantic with fright as they searched for their children, and friends beach-combing for friends, nobody was walking *towards* the water.

From his vantage point, the wave looked to be about a kilometer long and ten to fifteen meters high. The last stragglers, locals carrying buckets of fish and a dozen or so foreign adventurers, were now scrambling through the mucky seabed towards the beach.

Yai was turning around when he heard a kid cry out for help. Near the shore, dressed in a turquoise bathing suit, a little girl was waving at him. Yai ran over to her. She was limping around on one foot. It looked like she'd twisted an ankle. With her platinum hair and blue eyes, she could have been the daughter of one of those

Viking goddesses, and she had the standoffish disposition to match. "My mom told me not to talk to strange men."

"I'm not a strange man. I am a superhero, same as Spider-man." Yai laughed and smiled at her, but this petulant little princess stood there looking at him like he was a waiter or a bellboy.

"Spider-man isn't Asian. He's white." Even the little Western girls treated him as an inferior.

"Listen," he said, an edge of anxiety slicing through the words, "do you see that wave coming? Do you see how close it is?"

"Is that the waterslide?"

Yai knelt down with his knees on the sand so his eyes were on the same level as hers and shook his head. "We have to run away now. Your parents are waiting for you. Can you walk?"

She put her weight on her right foot and cringed.

"Okay, climb on my back."

With her arms around his neck, Yai ran across the beach towards the line of resorts and the road that lay beyond them. Every few seconds he looked over his shoulder. In the distance, when he first saw it, the wave had appeared to be almost frozen or moving at a very slow speed. As it came closer he realized that it was moving as quickly as a herd of stampeding horses, hooves thundering.

Yai could not outrun it. The only thing he could do was shinny up a palm tree, the girl's hysterical cries drowned out by the water washing over them.

YVES WAS TRYING to rescue his laptop when the wave punched through the window of his bungalow and slammed him against the wall. Within a few seconds the water was up to his throat, then it was over his head and he was spinning around in a whirlpool.

He swam to the surface, gasping for breath and grabbed on to a foam pillow. The water was rising so quickly he did not know what to do. If it kept coming up at this speed he would drown. If he tried to swim out through the window he might get caught in the debris and drown.

Yves dipped his head beneath the surface to check the visibility but the water was too turbid to make out anything except a grey swirl of particles.

For now the only saving grace was that the bungalow had a high, triangulated, Thai-style roof.

Couldn't he think of any famous last words? A verse from Poe or Blake on mortality? Even a single line from Sylvia Plath? No, the only words on his lips were *holy shit* as he plucked one of his wife's hairclips from the water. A strand of her red hair was caught inside it. This was his only talisman now. He held it to his lips and murmured her name, like a deathbed prayer to a higher power.

NOTHING HAD prepared Watermelon for this level of savagery, delivered with such inhuman indifference; not the sodomy with the golf clubs and the punch that broke her nose, not the boxer who had fist-fucked her, or the Japanese sadist who'd bound, muzzled and beaten her with a length of garden hose, nor even the half dozen Arabs who had taken turns with her ("Twelve fucks for the price of one," the ringleader said). None of those ordeals came close to this, even if the sense of helplessness, of crying and pleading for mercy that never came, was exactly the same.

This was like a dozen, like fifty, like a hundred rapists all having their way with her at once. They were opening new orifices all over her thighs and across her chest then filling them with spears and torches. They were shoving their fists down her throat and ejaculating blood all over her face. They were drowning her in the salt-water of a billion tears, pulling her hair back so she could grab a wheezing breath and then plunging it back under the surface.

She screamed into the teeth and the rabid mouth of the tsunami, but she could not hear herself above the water. She pleaded with the Water Goddess to either save or take her life, just like a hundred thousand other people were praying right now: to Shiva and Allah, to Jesus and the Buddha, to famous monks and elemental spirits. For there are no atheists in the midst of a natural disaster; everybody prays to someone.

Whether by luck, chance or divine intervention, an inflatable doll of Winnie the Pooh floated past her. She grabbed on to the grinning bear and clung to it like a life preserver.

When the great mass of roiling brown water finally retreated, it tried to pull everything back into the sea with i—cars and bodies, furniture and drowned livestock. With her broken, splayed fingers (the shock and adrenaline had numbed the pain for now), she paddled her way into the tangled roots of a mangrove tree, where she took shelter in a memory of her mother rocking her back and forth in a bamboo cradle tied to the stilts propping up the family home.

For a long time afterwards it would seem like the tsunami had dragged the best parts of her back into the sea with it, leaving behind a broken doll washed up on the beach after a summer vacation and left to rot beside chunks of sun-bleached driftwood and plastic water bottles half buried in the sand.

THE WATER HAD come up to Yai's waist and he was starting to slide down the knobby coconut palm. To make his balancing act even more precarious, the girl had wrapped her thighs around his throat and had his hair gripped in both of her hands.

Yai had heard that people in life-threatening situations see their entire lives flash before their eyes, like a film strip of images and memories whizzing past. But the only thought running through his mind was an old fantasy that he'd first imagined back at the Snake Farm on Phuket: his triumphant homecoming, when he rode that Harley Davidson into his village with his pretty blonde wife on the back. All his family, friends and neighbors emerged from the shade beneath their houses to admire him, all thinking the same thing, "Yai has finally made something of himself. He's got money, a good job, and a beautiful wife."

But that would never happen. He'd never be anything more than what he was now: a bartender, a drug dealer, and a servant of rich tourists who mostly treated him like a second-class citizen from a

Third World country.

Long before the wave came he was already broken, already finished.

But the girl was still young. She still had a chance.

With his last reserves of strength and self-loathing he pushed her towards the cluster of coconuts at the top of the tree.

LESS THAN HALF a meter from the ceiling of Yves's bungalow, the water stopped rising. Within a few minutes, it began draining.

The joy of still being alive, of setting foot on land again and taking in deep breaths of air, of seeing a sun of white gold and a blue sky, overwhelmed him for a few minutes and provided a buffer zone against the devastation.

All the resorts and bars and restaurants on the beach looked they'd been flattened by a blitzkrieg. Only the foundations were still visible. Everything else had been reduced to rubble. Yves's bungalow was the only one in sight that was still standing.

Not a single person, animal, bird—or even an insect—was in eyeshot. It was like Armageddon had come and gone and he was the last man standing.

Picking his way through the rubble of collapsed walls, legless deck chairs, overturned umbrellas and refrigerators bleeding soft drinks, Yves thought, "This is a great story. Maybe the best I've ever stumbled across." How quickly his gratitude for being spared had sunk and the old egotism risen to the surface. Immediately he rebuked himself. "Don't be a selfish prick. Look around for survivors and find Zara and Stephan."

Walking anywhere meant navigating an obstacle course. Nails stuck out of planks. Chunks of glass sharp as shark teeth glinted in the sunlight. Pools of water and sand sucked at his bare feet.

From somewhere he could not see, he heard a child calling out. He looked around at the piles of rubble. He didn't see anyone. Was she buried alive in the debris?

"Up here."

He looked up at the coconut palm with the crooked trunk. Sitting on the cluster of green coconuts, like an angel atop a Christmas tree, was a little blond girl. She waved at him. How did she get up there?

Beneath the tree, partially hidden from Yves's view by a sign that read "Dance the Night Away at New Year's Eve Party," knelt one of the waiters from the Seabreeze Cocktail Lounge beside a man stretched out on the wet sand. Few things disturbed Yves like seeing another man crying. Under normal circumstances, he would have pretended not to see him and walked in the opposite direction, but the two of them and the little girl on top of the tree were the only people on the beach.

The waiter was still in his uniform of brown slacks and a beige shirt. His name tag said Winai. He was probably in his early twenties but the tsunami had turned him into a toddler throwing a temper tantrum. In between spasms of tears and digging up handfuls of wet sand that he flung at the sea, he kept babbling in three or four different languages. Yves could only pick out a few words, "My friend Yai he good man. He take care bar very good. Before he working Phuket long time."

But the man sprawled on the sand beside him could not be Yai. He didn't look anything like him, the most obvious difference being that this man did not have a face. Instead he was wearing some kind of demoniac mask from a supernatural festival. Daubed with crimson paint, the mask was punctured with holes where the eyes and nose should be.

Yves rubbed some greasy sweat from his forehead and puzzled over the mask. Today was Boxing Day. There weren't any festivals on. There wasn't, as far as he could remember, supposed to be a costume party at the resort.

So why was he wearing a Halloween mask?

Where had the wave come from?

What happened to Zara and Stephan?

Who was the little girl in the tree?

Yves bolted for the main road. He ran past artificial Christmas trees dripping with seaweed, leapt over a fallen motorcycle which had been torn in half, dodged around a pair of legs sticking out of a collapsed doorway and goggled at the sight of a Royal Thai Navy gunboat washed up at the base of a limestone cliff a kilometer from shore.

Even running as fast as he could, his sandals spitting out sand, he still couldn't leave behind all the scenes of carnage and all the question marks lodged in his brain like thorns, because there was no longer a road winding through the town, there was no longer a beach community here at all.

Everything had been scattered helter-skelter like pieces of a jigsaw puzzle thrown to the wind by a race of giants.

And in the days, months, years to come, as the survivors tried to put their lives back together and struggled to make sense of this senseless catastrophe, they would all be struck at different times by the terrible knowledge that the pieces they were looking for, like all the bodies washed out to sea or pulped by the pestles of trees and concrete pillars in the mortar of the earth, would never be found.

❦ ❧

THE BIGGEST GOVERNMENT hospital was some fifty kilometers away in the provincial capital of Takuapa. By noon every bed was taken, and the waiting room and corridors were full of the injured on stretchers, in wheelchairs and sitting on plastic chairs in a lobotomized daze.

Yves sat in a corner of the waiting room, switching between the foreign news channels. Every hour the body count rose. At first it was only a few hundred, then a couple of thousand, but as more reports flooded in the death toll climbed steeply. On the BBC, the font read in big letters "ASIAN QUAKE." Underneath that, in smaller letters, it said, "Area from Indonesia to Africa affected."

An anchorwoman with a Christmas tree behind her looked grim. "Good evening. More than 11,000 people are thought to have been killed in southern Asia after an undersea earthquake off the coast of Sumatra triggered enormous waves across the Indian Ocean. The quake measured 8.9 on the Richter scale, the biggest in the world for forty years."

Maps with arrows showed the number of fatalities around Sumatra (3,000), the Maldives (20), Sri Lanka (500) and Thailand (300), in between jerky, amateur video clips replaying the same scenes of waves washing over beach resorts and sweeping people and cars away.

"Let's get the latest from southern India. The BBC's Mathrew Grant joins us on the line from Madras. Mathew, what is the latest you have on the casualty figures there?"

"The latest figures from Tamil Nadu are 1,700 people have been killed," said a voice over top of another amateur video clip of an old man in bathing trunks being carried away two young men, and a white woman in a bikini being lifted onto a helicopter."

"We've had reports about the number of bodies being washed up on the shore. How are they coping with this?"

"I was down on the beach here, and it was a chaotic and tense atmosphere. People are struggling to understand what's happened. It's just an incredible shock."

It sounded to Yves like the situation in India and Sri Lanka and Indonesia was much the same as in Thailand: *bedlam as unusual.* He wrote the phrase down in his notebook, but he could not concentrate on writing anything more. He was too nervous, the hospital far too noisy.

The news reports disturbed him, but not on an emotional level where he wanted to be disturbed. They disturbed him because of the reliance on body counts, statistics, and scientific data. In straining for objectivity—and this would happen over and over again in most of the news coverage—they had lost sight of their humanity.

He kept waiting for his wife to hobble into the waiting room with an injured leg—and there he'd be, ready for a tearful reunion and a healing hug. He kept waiting for Stephan to stroll in, remarkably unscathed as always, a man who had been immune to boyhood injuries on the hockey rink, who walked away from spectacular wipeouts on the ski hill and never so much as sprained an ankle. For once, Stephan, a pathological exaggerator, would not have to invent any more tall tales, like the one about the female cop, who was trying to arrest him for drunk driving, but who supposedly let him off and then slept with him the very next night. "She told me she has never experienced four climaxes, what the French call 'little deaths,' in one night. By the last time she was screaming louder than a police siren and I was whispering a stanza by Baudelaire in her ear. Is there a finer erotic poem than 'Head of Hair'?

"Languorous Asia, scorching Africa/A whole world, distant, naked, nearly dead/Lives in your depths O forest of perfume/While other spirits sail on symphonies/Mine, my beloved, swims along your scent.'"

Yves had always been stunned by his ability to commit entire poems to memory and then recite them with the passion and conviction of a preacher doing a Sunday sermon.

Behind his back, their mutual friends, brother writers and fellow professors, would mock him. "He is the bard of bullshit," was a typical slur. Yves would always come to his defense. "No, he's got an incredible imagination, and he makes no distinction between his poetry and his personal life. He wants them both to be just as dramatic. What's the difference? The fantasy is every bit as revealing of his character as the reality."

He could relate to Stephan's desire to be a man of action, not a bookworm and introspective slug. By drinking, womanizing and playing thrill sports, Stephan could still be a man's man and a poet too, following in a long line of literary degenerates and Hemmingway surrogates.

After surviving and inventing so many different scrapes with mortality, like falling through the ice of a lake while out cross-country skiing and almost drowning, or getting into a knife fight with a man whose wife he was having an affair with, Stephan would always say, "I cannot be killed by conventional weapons."

The tsunami would certainly qualify as an unconventional way to die. Until a few hours ago, most of the world had never even heard this Japanese word before. Only now, after geologists and bureaucrats were giving interviews on TV, lending scientific heft and credence to a story that was flimsy with any hard evidence or facts, did the world learn about the underwater earthquake. On the BBC, Dr

Roger Clarkson of the British Geological Survey said, over top of animated waves rolling across the screen, "You can't tell when an earthquake like this will strike. At sea the waves can reach speeds of 400 miles per hour, but they're only a meter high. As they approach the shore they slow down but rise to ten meters or more."

Whenever somebody else limped in to the waiting room or was wheeled in on a gurney or pushed in a wheelchair, Yves steeled himself for the inevitable. Both Zara and Stephan would be bloodied and bandaged, possibly incapacitated by injuries that were life-threatening, maybe dismembered or even dead. Perhaps they were fine, nothing more than a few abrasions and bruises. But the endless see-sawing between hope and fear had created a friction that was chafing his nerves and grinding him down with exhaustion. His eyelids drooped. His vision got blurry. His shoulders sagged. He needed to rest, to find a bed.

After hours of waiting and dozing off, watching the news channels show the same footage of debris circling in whirlpools and widows weeping over dead babies, while the body count grew, Watermelon's fiancé walked in. It didn't matter that they'd only met a couple of times and didn't know each other very well. The normal rules of engagement had been cast aside as the survivors developed the sort of camaraderie reserved for soldiers who'd survived a major battle.

Wade (short, squat and wearing a baseball cap) walked over and gave him a bear hug. "Hey buddy, how ya doin'? Great to see ya in one piece."

"Yeah, you too. Where is Watermelon?"

"I was hopin' you could tell me. How's your old lady?"

"Missing in action."

"And that Quebecois guy who wrapped the sports car around the power pole?"

"Also MIA. You remember Yai, the bartender from the other night? He's missing too. Most of the mobile networks and phone lines are down. I hate to think what's gonna happen if the power goes out and the water supplies dry up."

"Don't worry. The Thais'll take care of it, eh? They're good people. I'm sure our old ladies and buds will turn up sooner or later. We ain't up Shit Creek without a paddle just yet." Wade took off his baseball cap to wipe the sweat from his forehead and bald head. "So let's say a prayer for the missing, stop fuckin' around, and see if we can lend a helping hand around here."

Wade looked around the waiting room, meeting everyone's eye and smiling at them in a reassuring way. He said "hello" in Thai and smiled at all the doctors and nurses passing by, too. "Okay," he said. "Follow me." He walked down the corridor, ducking into all the rooms, exchanging smiles and greetings with any of the patients who were still conscious and any of their friends or relatives standing by their bedsides. It didn't matter to him what their races or ages were. With the old Chinese lady who could not speak English and was playing solitaire on her dinner tray, he taught her a couple of card tricks that made her smile. With the young girl from San Diego whose right leg had been severely gashed and whose parents were still missing, Wade sat down on her bed and looked at the bandaged leg. He said, "Don't worry about that none. You're gonna grow up and still be a beautiful woman one day." She smiled and blushed. "You know what, Rosalyn? I'll bet you like horses, don'cha? Yep, that's what I thought. I love 'em, too. So I got a little present for you right here." Wade took a card out of his wallet with pictures of mountains, horses and ski hills. He handed it to her. "Up in Jasper at the resort where I work we got lotsa different horses for trail riding. Once we find your parents and you get better, then we're all gonna go trail riding together. How does that sound?"

Yves had always been in awe of healers, those doctors and nurses who tend to physical injuries, and those sympathetic souls like Wade who provide emotional healing in times of tragedy.

Within a matter of minutes, the girl had bounced back and was looking at Wade as if he were a long-lost family member. At the door he said, "All righty, Roz. I'm gonna check up on you again in an hour or so, but what I want you to do is keep looking at that card and thinkin' about them horses and ski hills. Chin up, sweetheart.

Soon as we find your parents we'll send 'em over in a jiffy."

Wade continued making his rounds. He got the graying Japanese golf pro, uninjured but almost catatonic with grief he could not describe, on his feet to help him improve his swing using a crutch. With the Yugoslavian grandfather, whose English vocabulary was also minimal, Wade did impersonations of Donald Duck and other Disney characters. For the twin teenaged brothers from Finland whose missionary parents had both been killed, he recited Biblical anecdotes and sayings. "Jesus said that who so shall believe in me shall enter the kingdom of heaven and enjoy everlasting life."

In between these encounters, he kept throwing challenges at Yves. "C'mon. Get in the game, bud. Nobody cares if you got anything clever or witty to say. I certainly don't. They just wanna hear some kind words or dumb jokes and have somebody tell 'em everything is gonna be okay."

Part of Yves's reticence stemmed from the fact that he couldn't bring himself to admit he had been wrong about Wade, and part of that harsh judgment stemmed from his jealousy of Watermelon's new fiancé. Their brotherly/sisterly routine had not fooled his wife or Wade.

His first impressions of Wade had not been favorable. The guy looked like a cartoon of a Canadian redneck on vacation: the loud beach shorts, the Singha Beer singlet, the faded tattoos of hot rods and bare-breasted pinups, and the baseball cap with the Moosehead Beer logo and two yellow antlers sticking out of the crown. He talked louder than anyone else in the bar, and if he liked what someone had said, he'd say, "Now you're talkin'," and hold out his hand to offer them a handshake, "Put 'er here, bud." Then he slapped them on the back, nice and hard, to show his dominance over the pack as an alpha male. Whenever Yai put on a hard rock song he liked, Wade would start head-banging and playing air guitar. "I love AC/DC, eh? Right up there with Led Zep as the best band ever I reckon." He told long rambling stories about getting up at 4 a.m. to clear the latest blizzard with his snowplow, and getting high before hitting the road. "First joint of the day is always the sweetest." He mimed taking a drag. "Then I step on the gas and give 'er." Wade told them, and half the bar who was forced to listen to this loudmouth, how a cougar had chased him when he was mountain-biking in Jasper. "I saw him runnin' alongside the trail. Every year we lose two or three mountain bikers to those cocksuckers. Usually they hide on top of a rock and pounce when you ride past."

Stephan, wearing his sunglasses on his head and a Thai silk scarf around his neck, kept baiting him. "Maybe you can go out and wrestle some water buffalo tonight, uh? Have a Thai rodeo."

"Oh, I get it. Hearty fuckin' har har. The east coast Quebecois liberal who keeps stealin' all our oil and taxing us up the wazoo for it, now wants to put us down for being salt of the earth. Well, you got another think comin', buddy."

"So now you will take me outside for some rough justice and fisticuffs to prove what a macho man you are. I am not scared of you, my friend. In Quebec we have the Hell's Angel's. They are my hash-ish dealers and I learn many fighting moves from them."

Yves told Stephan to shut up in French. Half the other tourists clustered around the bar were staring at them now, while Yai pre-tended to be washing glasses so he could continue sneaking peeks at a couple of Scandinavian women wearing tie-dyed tops and denim shorts.

Yves looked out at the dark sea. He looked over at the glass case behind the bar where all the bottles of spirits were illuminated by soft lights, their contents glowing like magic potions in an alchemist's lab (he gauged his alcohol intake by how fanciful his metaphors became, which meant that by now he was really plastered). He looked around the lounge at all the tourists tanned prawn pink and golden brown happily discussing the highlights of their itineraries.

What he wanted to avoid looking at was the two bickering drunks.

Wade tapped him on the shoulder. "Can you help me out here and call this guy off? I mean, what's this clown yakking about any-way? Last time I had a fight was back in Grade 5 or 6. I'm a pacifist, eh? Even when I'm channel surfing and some violent action movie comes on, I keep flickin' those channels."

In the hospital, Wade continued to surprise him. He possessed a depth of compassion that Yves could not fathom. Like a lot of intellectuals, Yves had a habit of overcomplicating people and over-analyzing situations. Wade was too straight-forward for that kind of character study. He loved being around people. They saw that and responded in kind. It was no more complicated than that.

But Wade would not be a pacifist for much longer. After the tsunami receded, its undercurrents continued to ripple through the survivors, changing them in ways they could never have foreseen. Those changes began to make themselves felt when the two of them volunteered to be part of the cleanup crew at Khao Lak. After asking the famous forensics expert with the porcupine quills of punk hair, Dr Pornthip Rojanasunan, what they could do to help, she suggested that they use Wade's camera to take as many photos as possible of the dead. "In this heat, the bodies will not last long. We need photos of tattoos, earrings, watches, scars—anything that family and friends can identify."

It was only twelve hours after the waves had hit and nobody knew who was supposed to be in charge. Soldiers, cops, civil servants, nurses, field staff from several Christian NGOs, rescue workers from private Thai firms, and dozens of would-be volunteers, both locals and foreigners, were milling around the trashed town and the beach, strewn with debris. Wade managed to rent a dirt bike from the one rental shop which hadn't been inundated. His take-charge attitude impressed Yves, who was still in a state of shellshock, like many of the other survivors wandering around, jittery from too much coffee and dazed by too little sleep.

"Hop on the back. Crisis management is my specialty, eh? At the ski resort, whatever goes wrong, if a blizzard snows in the main road, or a pipe freezes and breaks, or a shitter gets blocked up, if Wade can't fix it, then it ain't broke. That's our motto."

It was a good thing that Wade had been a motocross racer in his teens, because the "road" out of town was an obstacle course of uprooted trees, boulders, long-tail boats broken in two, cars laying on their roofs, and bodies—bodies strewn everywhere like fallen soldiers on a battlefield. Wade stopped the bike. "I'm drivin' and you're shooting. That's the deal, bud."

The fetid smell of damp and rot, as if the sea had puked up its guts, swam on the breeze. Yves dismounted. He looked at the ocean. It was calm now. The sun was sparkling off those sapphire waves. The water was one hundred meters away. This was as close as Yves could get without panicking. Even so, he could not turn his back on the sea, for fear it would pounce like one of those mountain lions Wade talked about.

Cautiously, Yves approached the first body, a young boy in a cartoon T-shirt, lying on his back in a crucifixion pose. The boy looked like he was sleeping not dead. Framing that angelic face streaked with mud, Yves pictured him unwrapping his presents and singing "Jingle Bells" and "Silent Night" on Christmas the other day. He put down the camera. This was going to be harder than he'd thought.

Since he had no experience in this kind of photography, he had to follow the advice of an Australian photographer he sometimes collaborated with. Kendall had told him, "When I was shooting all those corpses in the streets of Bangkok in 1992 I used the camera like a shield. It was a buffer zone between me and the victims. What I do is concentrate on the technical details, the composition, the lighting, etcetera. You can't think to yourself, 'Here's a young Sheila cut down in the prime of life before she even graduated from uni,' or this job will drive ya bonkers, mate."

Kendall was right. He could not allow himself to view these cadavers as people who had, until yesterday, lived, worked, cracked jokes, got married, rode bicycles and made love. So Yves pretended he was a European art photographer taking experimental shots of a tropical beach where nature had mutated into all sorts of strange forms. Those arms and legs scattered across the sand were driftwood, that mane of hair seaweed, the torso a tree trunk, that spray of blood across the deck chair a masterpiece of abstract expressionism, the hook of an anchor sunk into a scalp was based on the Christian symbolism in *Moby Dick*, those blue eyes were marbles, that hand a tree branch, the woman who looked a little like Watermelon, dismembered and sprawled across the roots of a mangrove tree sticking up out of the sand, was part of a fertility shrine to the Water Goddess.

It was an exhausting game, worn down by overkill and the thirty-five Celsius heat, which fell apart whenever they met the other beachcombers, usually looking for their families and friends.

Squatting like a duck in the shade of an orange fishing trawler beached on a sandbar was a Thai-Muslim fisherman who had lost his home and all seventeen of his relatives. All he had left was the shorts, sandals and a chain of amulets he was wearing. A wiry man whose muscles were sailor's knots and whose skin had been charred by the sun, he pointed at the shoreline where nothing remained except a couple of wooden posts sticking out of the sand. Yves had trouble following the rapid-fire southern dialect, and Wade only knew a few words of survival Thai, but the fisherman seemed to be saying that all fifty of the houses along the shore, including the school, where a few dozen students were in class when the tsunami struck, had been washed away. He kept looking back at the sunlit beach, as if expecting the village to materialize again as quickly as it had been rubbed out by that eraser of water, then he'd repeat the same line, "There used to be a village here, a school, my home and family, a pier, all our fishing boats. Where have they gone?"

This would be the undertow of almost all the conversations that Yves and Wade would have with their fellow survivors over the next few months: how tenuous life was, how quickly it could all end, and how anything you could possibly build could be destroyed just as easily. Some fell into a black hole of listless despair for months afterwards, like Watermelon. She didn't want to go out, didn't want to talk to anybody, didn't feel like pursuing any of her old passions for making jewelry and shopping for clothes and antiques—because it was all futile. Why bother? If another disaster didn't destroy all the things she'd accumulated, then an accident like the one that killed her first husband would ruin her love life, and even if those could be averted, old age and death trumped everyone in the end. She was better off staying home to practice meditation and study Buddhism. Only those eternal truths and everyone's karma, their balance sheet of good and bad deeds, could survive. All else was ephemeral and doomed to pass.

In the backwash of the catastrophe, Yves would alternate being overly cautious (not jaywalking and even refusing fish because of a fear he would choke to death on the bones) and returning to smoke, drink and party like there was no tomorrow, because maybe there wouldn't be.

Before showering, he would leave the bathroom door ajar and then place his clothes, wallet and shoes on the toilet seat. In case of an emergency, he was ready to bail out immediately.

And there would be many such emergencies in the weeks to come when the aftershocks jolted the survivors out of their beds at two in the morning and someone screamed "Tsunami!" Bolting down hallways and through parking lots did them no good, because they could not outrace the flashbacks that projected themselves on the pavement, across billboards, up the sides of buildings, and turned the sky into a cinema screen where their memories played like drive-in horror movies and the taste of their own sweat tossed them back in the sea to be drowned and revived, and drowned and water-boarded, over and over again.

WADE KEPT HIMSELF busy making a map for the rescue workers of where the bodies were. He had not yet spoken to anyone about where he'd been on Boxing Day. That morning he had gone on a snorkeling trip via longtail boat, with a young couple from Scotland and a Swedish mother with her three daughters. Wade did not remember anything about them except that one of the three blonde girls had a pink T-shirt that read "I'm Crabby" with an illustration of a crab on it. En route, the diesel engine spewed black fumes, the girls shrieked and giggled, while the adults made the usual traveler talk about where they'd been and what they'd done, what destination was next on the itinerary, and different hotels, bars, restaurants and tours they recommended.

They had not reached the first coral reef when they caught sight of the wave coming towards them. At first the boatman had turned around and tried to outrace it. When the wave began spitting on their necks and bearing down on them like a dam on water-skis, the boatman made a risky move to turn the vessel around and try to ride the wave like a surfer. He got a few meters up the wall of water before gravity took over and the front of the boat reared up and flipped over backwards. The three girls were tossed over Wade's head. Their mother leapt up to catch them but the boatman's propeller sliced down and cut off her right arm just above the elbow. From Wade's perspective, as he dove off the side of the boat, it looked like the sun had spurted a geyser of blood.

Buffeted by waves, Wade tried to bandage her arm with his T-shirt, but she kept begging him in Swedish, English, and the sobs of a mother who has lost her children and her reason to live, "Don't waste time on me. I am dead already. You hear me? I am bleeding to death. Please try to save my daughters."

Wade tried one free dive to search for the boat and the three girls, but the sea was too deep and far too murky. By the time he surfaced the woman was gone and so was everyone else. Either she'd summoned a last gasp of maternal love to search for her daughters or bled to death and sank along with her final wish.

Through a turbulent sea, Wade swam five kilometers to shore with what was later diagnosed as a broken collarbone. Shock had numbed it, so the symptoms, even the pain, hibernated for a few days. But the collarbone never mended properly. For the rest of his life, whenever he got in the shower, or the sea, the liquid caress of water set off depth charges under his skin: tiny explosions of pain, each connected to a memory of that fatal odyssey.

Flares of anger also aggravated it. Nobody had ever pissed him off like the bureaucrats, with their endless requests for more paperwork, who kept turning down his requests for grants. To help the locals keep their heads above water after the disaster had destroyed tourism in the Andaman, and to resuscitate the scuba-diving business, Wade eventually set up a foundation to train locals as dive instructors. He named the foundation after Watermelon, using her real Thai name, Chariya Attapakee.

"Listen to this one, bud, same as all the others." His lips moved when he read the email to Yves. "'We regret to inform you that your proposal does not meet our criteria at the moment.' Now how do you like that? Here I am, an honest businessman trying to help the local economy and give people jobs, but the fat cats won't play ball. All these lazy useless fucks from the big aid organizations do is drive through in their SUVs, roll down the window for a minute, look around and they have the nerve to call that an inspection tour. Then they drive back to Phuket to eat in a five-star restaurant and stay in a luxury hotel. I'm on to these guys, eh? What they do is get what's called 'preferred provider status', which means they only have to kick in twenty percent of all the donations they receive. Imagine the millions and millions of dollars being donated right now and eighty percent is going to feed these fat cats and their bureaucratic machines. For crying out loud, Yves, it's a fuckin' disgrace."

Wade's constant tirades against bureaucrats were difficult enough to endure; watching him assault a Thai police officer had been much worse. That happened on the third day they were out doing experimental art photography on the beach. Yves had taken to giving the photographs names that belied their morbid nature: "The semiotics of the sandman"; "Deconstructionism is not humanism"; "Still life with coconut shells"; "Three limbs in search of a body." The cold nature of highbrow art that bypasses the heart to go straight for the head served as a dyke to keep any of his personal feelings at bay.

But all the feelings that he and the other volunteers dammed up would burst open like blood blisters in the oddest of places at the most unexpected times. Coming back through the airport at Phuket on a late night flight almost three weeks after the waves hit, Yves looked around at all the posters for missing persons—hundreds of them, pasted to pillars and thumbtacked to notice boards. He pulled out his notebook to jot down a few details.

At this point, there was no chance that any of the missing were still alive. The faces that stared at him from color photocopies and black-and-white mug shots were all deceased. So the posters, mentioning their names and nationalities, physical descriptions and where they were last seen, read like obituaries in miniature. As a journalist who had spent years crafting the most sensationalistic obituaries for a large American tabloid, this angle appealed to him.

Through taking notes and photographs, he had worked his way through a cross-section of children and adults of Asian and European ancestry, when he stopped before a poster for a middle-aged Hungarian woman. Her badly photocopied image was washed out, her personal details inked in a shaky hand. By who? Yves wondered. Her child? A husband or sibling? "Piri has a big mole on her neck."

As he had now seen hundreds of times over, after a corpse sat in the water for a week, it was so bloated and misshapen that, on first inspection, it was hard to tell if it was male or female, Asian or Caucasian. What forensic scientists refer to as "skin slippage" makes facial features unrecognizable. Hence, most of the corpses had to be identified through DNA, dental records, or tattoos. A mole on her neck would not be visible three weeks after she'd drowned.

The mounting sense of hopelessness he felt, reading over these pleas for help when it was already too late, reached its pit of despair when he read the words scrawled in capital letters at the bottom of the poster: "I LOVE THIS PERSON. PLEASE HELP!"

Finally, after shooting hundreds of photos and writing thousands of words, here in this almost deserted airport, late at night, surrounded by the paper ghosts of the missing, the dead, and those whose bodies would never be found, Yves had to hang his head and weep for the first time since Boxing Day.

❧ ☙

TO CUT THROUGH the mountains of rubble and find anyone buried alive, the Thai authorities brought in elephants to serve as bulldozers. The grey Goliaths were soon pressed into service as corpse carriers; the rescue workers strapped bodies wrapped in white bandages to their tusks so the beasts could forklift them out of the overgrown jungle.

Those scenes, surreal at first, quickly became commonplace for the volunteers working around Khao Lak, which had become the biggest cemetery in all the tsunami-struck parts of Thailand.

Throughout the end of 2004 and into the early parts of the next year, the weather did not mourn the dead with showers and skies carved from headstone granite. All along the coast of the Andaman Sea, it remained eerily beautiful, the sun beaming, with only a few scraps of cloud that reminded Yves of torn tissues in a widow's hand.

The two of them were rounding a cape on day three of the experimental art photography shoot when Wade spotted a Thai cop in his brown uniform stealing something from a dead woman lying beside a coconut palm. For a guy who was so short and stout, Wade moved with incredible speed, barreling across the sand to tackle the cop as he tried to flee. By the time Yves ran up beside them, panting for breath, Wade was sitting on the cop's back trying to handcuff him with his own cuffs. His face red from rage and the heat, Wade looked at up and said, "Of all the lowdown things I seen in my life, this weasel takes the cake."

Yves panted, "Listen, man, I think you've got this backwards. You can't bust a cop. He's the one who's supposed to be making the arrests."

"You seen this scumbag stealing from the lady same as I did. I mean, come the fuck on, stealing from the dead? I got a good mind to whale on this guy." Wade's collarbone was trying to poke its way out of his skin.

"Do not hit him, whatever you do. The cops will put death warrants on our heads."

"He's squirming a lot but I can't tell what he's sayin'. Can you translate?"

"Umm, I think it's something like, 'Get off my back, you monitor lizard.'"

"Tell him I'm making a citizen's arrest and I'm gonna haul his grave-robbing butt off to jail."

"Wade, listen, there are probably about thirty million Thai people who would applaud you for trying to arrest a corrupt cop, and a few hundred thousand who would want to see you given the highest civilian honor if you could actually put him in jail. But the reality is that this guy will have his cop friends hunt you down and get you deported, or worse, maybe a lot worse, like dead worse. Understand?"

"You betcha, but somebody's gotta stand up to these crooks and call a weasel a fuckin' weasel. What's he saying now?"

"Let's see. 'I will open an umbrella in your mother's ass, you monitor lizard.'"

"Nah, he ain't sayin' that. Come on. Be serious."

It took ten minutes of arguing with Wade, while the cop ate sand, to convince him to take the cuffs off. Even so, Wade demanded restitution. He made the rogue give a respectful Thai *wai* to the corpse and put the wristwatch and bracelet back on her. Then he confiscated all the bullets from his gun.

Many of the volunteers and survivors described the post-wave melee in bipolar terms: the best and the worst of humanity they'd ever seen. The worst stooped to plucking gold fillings from cadavers' mouths with pliers and the best sought to eradicate all barriers of race, religion, class and economics. In the supply lines that formed outside the government offices, hospitals and clinics, high-society Thai women worked elbow to elbow with Burmese maids and Cambodian fishermen, who passed packages of water bottles and instant soup to teenaged backpackers from the West who handed them off to wealthy tourists from Asia and Europe.

Doctors and nurses and medical technicians from all over the world flew in to help out for free. Teams of volunteer divers combed the seabed for corpses, picked up trash and uncovered coral reefs. (The Irish dive-master who headed up that ad hoc crew found all of his framed family photos, which had been washed into the sea when the wave hit his dive shop on Koh Phi Phi.) Thai university students, who spoke English, Chinese, French, Japanese and other languages, helped to translate for new arrivals searching for friends and family members. Donations flooded in from across the globe. Musicians staged benefit concerts. Local and international celebrities arrived to lend their household names to the cause and pose for photos while handing out supplies and visiting the injured in hospitals.

It was one of the most incredible outpourings of compassion and goodwill any of them had ever seen. Wade and Yves heard the same comment, "If we had this level of cooperation every day, most of the world's problems could be solved in a couple of years," and variations on the same question, "Why does it take a tragedy of this magnitude to bring people together for a common good?" again and again.

THE GRISLIEST VOLUNTEER work was carried out at Wat Yanyao in the district capital of Takuapa, where Dr Pornthip and her forensics team were in the midst of identifying several thousand corpses. Besides all the monks, soldiers, cops, translators, journalists, families searching for loved ones and friends looking for friends, milling around, the members of different Disaster Victim Identification Units from a dozen different countries had also set up command centers under awnings beside the century-old temple with its fanciful mosaics of Buddhist iconography and its single-smokestack crematorium.

Wade and Yves were on the crew unloading the cadavers, wrapped in white gauze body bags, from the backs of trucks, to lay them out in the temple grounds so they could be identified by friends and family members. The forensic teams sprayed the bodies with fungicide and put pellets of dry ice on them so they wouldn't decompose too quickly. As the ice melted, an eerie mist drifted over the dead. Worst of all was the stench of rot mingling with seawater, which speared through nose plugs and closed eyelids to lodge itself in the back of the brain, where it lay dormant for years, waiting for a chance encounter with a seafood market or sex on a tropical night to cause flashbacks of rips appearing in that veil of dry ice, showing blackened limbs sticking up at grotesque angles like dead trees in a petrified forest and chickens pecking out the eyes of corpses.

Most of the volunteers wore white rubber outfits, surgeon's masks, rubber gloves and boots. Creeping from corpse to corpse,

Yves knelt down to inspect them. Each had been tagged with a "DVI Body Number" by a Thai soldier. At this point, seven day days after the tsunami, he had to steel himself for the sight of his wife and Stephan. He just hoped that they didn't look too banged up. For a woman of Zara's statuesque beauty, who prided herself so much on her great looks, the final insult would be ending up like these other victims: their genitals swollen like balloons, their faces purpled and blackened, their chests torn open to reveal internal organs and the spaghetti of intestinal tracts.

Was this Stephan? The long blond hair looked familiar, but the face, if you could call it that, consisted of a mouth left agape by a final scream that revealed a picket fence of broken teeth and a flattened nose. Both eyeballs hung from their sockets by threads of flesh.

Yves lowered his face until it was no more than a few centimeters above him. The tongue wriggled and the dead man moaned, "Yves... Yves."

He ran over to where Dr Pornthip was standing. "Hey doctor, doctor. Listen, I know this sounds crazy, but that man over there isn't dead. I swear he's not dead. He just moaned something that sounded like my name."

The wild-haired forensic scientist, dressed all in black as usual, smiled sympathetically. "I know it sounds like that, but it's the gases escaping from the body. Sometimes they move the vocal cords, so the bodies appear to be speaking. It's normal."

Normal or not, Yves was too spooked to go anywhere near those bodies for the time being.

He did not hear anything about Zara and Stephan until a few days later when one of the high-society Thai ladies bringing medical supplies to the temple loaned him her cell phone to call an old friend in Montreal. Outside of his new inner circle, consisting solely of fellow survivors and volunteers, he had spoken to no one except his mom and brother. Even with his family it had been a struggle, for his experiences were so far beyond anything he had ever experienced, or even imagined, he could not begin to describe what he'd been through. The intensity of the waves, the sense of helplessness, of being a baby again but with the brain of an adult, did not make for polite conversation or easy explanations. Putting too much emphasis on the dangerous elements sounded like boasting, when his survival owed more to luck than manly bravado. How to explain the fact that he was in the only bungalow out of forty or fifty in that resort which stood up to the waves and did not collapse? Why did the water stop flooding the bungalow only about ten centimeters before it reached the roof?

He didn't know. He couldn't explain it. Some of the other Thais volunteering at the temple attributed their survival to the power of their amulets. One local businessman said, "This monk on my necklace has very strong magic." But the only "amulet" Yves had possessed was his wife's hairclip, a few of her red tresses caught in its plastic teeth. He kept it in his pocket for a lucky charm, the same as he'd kept a rabbit's foot when he was a boy.

Standing in the shade cast by the temple's ornate eaves, lotus-shaped bells hanging from them and tinkling in the breeze, Yves fingered the hairclip as he tried to speak to an old friend who had suddenly become a distant stranger. The crackling connection only accounted for half the distance between them.

"Thank God you're still alive," said David.

"I don't know what God has to do with it. Can't say I've had any religious experiences down here except for meeting a few saintly volunteers. But the missionaries are pouring in now with bibles and scouring the area for lost souls. Trust them to hit people up when they're at their weakest and looking for answers."

"I meant it as a figure of speech not an ontological statement."

"Sorry. I don't know what to say. All I do know is that I'm very very lucky to still be here. So I feel like I owe it to the deceased and their relatives to stick around and help out. I just wish I knew what happened to Zara and Stephan. I've been searching for them for days now and asking around and nothing. Have you heard anything?"

"Yes, and I'm delighted to be the bearer of good tidings and not Charon ferrying the dead souls to the other side of the river Styx." David paused dramatically, allowing his eloquence and drama school training to impress. "I talked to them on the phone yesterday."

Yves threw his arm in the air and smiled. "Yes! That's great! It's a miracle. It's exactly what I wanted to hear. Where are they?"

"They got airlifted to a hospital in Bangkok. They're banged up a little, but their injuries are not life threatening."

"They're in Bangkok *already*? Why didn't they wait around for me?"

"I would imagine that they didn't know where to find you. From the TV footage I've seen, everything looks like a complete and utter shambles down there. Do you have electricity and running water?"

"Yes, we've always had electricity and running water, but if you watch the news networks showing the same footage over and over again, you'd think all of Southeast Asia is a disaster area."

"Yves, I know this is probably not the best time to discuss such a delicate subject, not that there ever would be a good time…" David laughed nervously.

"What delicate subject?" Yves was listening to the static of his only connection to his homeland with such intensity that he did not see another refrigerated truck full of bodies drive past him. "What's going on, man? What are you talking about?"

"I had been meaning to bring this up earlier and so did a few of our other old comrades in art. But, well, since there is no easy way to say this, I won't throw up any more obfuscations. Zara and Stephan have been having an affair for the past year or so, and they're planning on moving in together soon and making their relationship official."

Yves was too dumbfounded to speak.

"Are you still there? Come in, come in…"

"An affair? Moving in together? What the fuck are you talking about?" When David did not answer, he continued. "This is outrageous. This can't be true. It's impossible. It's not *possible*, do you hear me?"

"Things happen, situations change."

"Things *happen*, situations *change*? We've been together on and off for more than eleven years now. This is not a thing that's *happened* or a situation that's *changed*. This is tantamount to a Judas kiss, the worst possible betrayal imaginable. Do you understand what I'm saying?"

"Sure, but don't shoot the messenger is all I'm saying."

"I'm not going to shoot the messenger. I'm going to shoot both of them. In Bangkok, me and my old friend Mick, do you know how many hit-men we used to know? Do you know how easy it would be to get both of them killed? All it would cost is about a thousand bucks a head. That's it." When David said nothing, he continued, "Thanks for telling me. Take care."

Yves threw Zara's hairclip at the rows of bodies.

He borrowed Wade's motorcycle without asking him and drove down the coast in search of the only person on the planet he wanted to see right now.

The old fisherman who'd lost seventeen relatives was sitting in much the same place as when they'd first encountered him: squatting like a duck in the shadow of a beached fishing trawler. Either he didn't recognize Yves, or recognized him and didn't care, or maybe he'd gone mad already, because he launched into exactly the same spiel that he'd first given them. Maybe he kept repeating it because he couldn't believe it himself, just as Yves could not believe that Stephan and Zara had been having an affair and were now planning on moving in together. Pointing at the beachhead, the fishermen said, "There used to be a village here, a school, my home and family, a pier, our fishing boats. Where have they all gone?"

Yves told him in Thai, "I don't know but I understand how you feel. My old life is gone too… gone with the wave."

Both of them were straining and squinting so hard to see what wasn't there anymore that they failed to notice that the water had also wiped the slate clean. It was a time of endings to be sure, but it was also an era of new beginnings.

SERPENTS SLITHERED ACROSS the moonlit window of his hotel room. This had to be a sign. It had to mean that he was near, that he was listening, maybe even waiting to be reborn again.

"I'm sorry I was so slow getting to you."

Through the screen came a whisper of wind. Or was it a voice? A soft voice calling from the other side of sleep and death.

"I'm sorry but I had to try and find my wife and an old friend first."

What was the voice whispering now? "It's okay. I forgive you." Was that it?

"Thanks for understanding. But there's something I'm curious about. What's it like on the other side?"

The wind died down. The serpents turned into tree branches waving at the window.

"Are you in a better place at least? Is it okay over there? Do you think we can meet again on the other side or in the next life?"

The silence that pressed in on him was vast as the night and as infinite as death.

As the fatality count surpassed the two hundred thousand mark, conversations like this, between the living and the drowned, between relatives and the dearly departed, echoed around the world in a hundred different languages: through cathedrals and mosques, at Hindu shrines and Taoist temples, through Western funeral homes and Chinese cemeteries on hillsides, in dreams of happy reunions in heavenly places and nightmares clouded by the diesel fumes of long-tail boats pulling strings of cadavers behind them, like freshly netted mermaids and shrimp-men.

WHEN KENDALL FIRST BEGAN working as a staff photographer at a daily newspaper in Sydney he got all the most boring assignments: contract signings, Christmas parades, product launches, and ribbon-cutting ceremonies for new shopping malls and office towers.

The senior editors and veteran reporters at the paper snubbed him. Most of them were gruff alcoholics, rough as guts, who went out drinking every night after they'd "put the paper to bed" and nursed their hangovers the next day with endless cups of coffee and cigarettes. In the smoking room, they bantered about the stories they were writing or editing and the latest newsflashes from the wire services while Kendall sat there leafing through that day's paper. By eavesdropping on them and keeping his mouth shut, he tried to learn what he could. From all their bitter asides, "The cops are worse than the fucking criminals these days"; "give me more cunt and less culture in the features section"; "here's the headline of the year we can't run, after that French bloke escaped from custody in New York, Bernie called it 'Frog Legs It'"; "the only difference between op/ed pieces and fairy tales is that some kids still believe in fairy tales"; mostly what he picked up was a strain of cynicism that ran so deep it became the bloodline and the pulse of the news industry to him. He could hear it in the hum of the printing presses, read it between the lines in every story, and feel it rippling through the newsroom in all those craggy, smokers' laughs.

But after a year on the job he could not blame them for it any longer. Working at the paper was depressing. Every day, the front section was filled with one horror story after another: a typhoon in the Philippines that left thousands homeless, a ferry sinking off the coast of Indonesia with hundreds lost at sea, mining disasters in China, a psychopath going ballistic in Tasmania and shooting thirty people, a fortune-teller and serial rapist in Hong Kong targeting schoolgirls, a son killing his father with a shovel in small-town America, Muslim extremists making videos of the men they beheaded: oceans dying, icecaps melting, crops failing, children thin as stick insects starving, another war starting.

Who publishes good news in a daily newspaper? Do-gooders, except when they're celebrities or tycoons, are bad news for advertising revenues and circulation figures.

Day after day, week after week, the same kinds of stories appeared, using the same structures and the same clichés. If you changed the dateline and the byline, swapped a few names and details, the same articles could run over and over again. The endless recycling of clichés and headlines made the bad news seem relentless. There was no respite. It was enough to turn the sunniest optimist into a bleary-eyed cynic and alcoholic.

None of this upset him like the "The Weeping Widows and Starving Orphans Pool." It was a game that the sub-editors on the front desk played. Every time one of the subs got a photo of a widow or orphan on his page, he put five dollars into a beer mug. At the end of the month, the sub with the most photos of those two subjects on his pages won the pot. During the outbreak of the most recent wars in Afghanistan and Iraq, when the widowed wept over corpses and coffins, and orphans ran amok, the pot fattened to more than two thousand dollars.

In the pub one night, he gave the three subs a tongue-lashing. "This pool is a fucking disgrace. It's not on. It's cashing in on other people's misery and making a mockery of the dead and journalism too."

The balding sub, a twenty-year veteran of the paper, who always looked slumped in front of a computer, said, "Who let Peter Pan in here? He's too young to drink."

The only response was a few gruff laughs. Otherwise, nobody even turned their head to look at him. Instead, they continued watching the Aussie rules football match on the wall-mounted TV. Their eyes had the brightly empty glow of a computer screen, dulled by thousands of stories about wars, famines and natural disasters, and millions of megapixels of weeping widows, starving orphans and dead bodies.

Nothing Kendall said about ethics and journalistic integrity elicited any response from them. Now and then, one of them would say, "It's my shout," and order another round, but nobody except the bald guy said anything: "We have to keep shoveling the shit and filling those pages."

"It's not shoveling the shit. It's mining grave dirt."

"Grave dirt is pay dirt in this business. That's the first rule of TV news. If it bleeds it leads."

If it bleeds it leads? Had the news business really been dumbed down to such childish expressions?

Yes it had and, as he soon found out, that was benign compared to the sewer-like depths that some editors would wallow in to get fresh blood and dead meat on their front pages.

His first break on the paper came when he had to replace the crime photographer for an afternoon. The editor assigned the reporter and him to do a "death knock." Kendall didn't know what that was. So the reporter explained it to him as they drove to a satellite city of Sydney on the periphery of the mountains. "It's like this. We're supposed to get the mother or father at the front door. Then we break the news that their son has drowned in a backyard pool. I get fresh quotes. You take a couple of pictures of them breaking down in tears."

"What if they don't want their photos taken?"

"That's another sticky wicket. But here's how I handle death knocks. I go to the pub, have a few pints, go for a feed, call back the editor and tell him the family didn't want to talk. And that's the end of the story, sunshine. Intruding on families grieving is not my cup of arsenic. As a father myself with two young boys, covering stories about children dying gives me the wobblies."

This fella, who had a face full of death knocks and a voice like a gravel pit, did not seem like the type who'd be easily intimidated.

They drove past a beach that was half deserted because of a recent shark attack. Kendall said, "Aw let's give it a go and not pike out. Never done a death knock before and I could use the experience."

"Aren't you the pretentious bugger who gave the old hands a bollocking the other night in the pub?"

"Aw yeah, but as a member of the human race I fully assert my right to be a self-righteous hypocrite when too rotten drunk to know better."

The crime reporter laughed. "Dinkum. Fucking oath, mate."

Outside the front door of the house, Kendall stood a little to the reporter's left. From here, he could take a portrait shot with some suburban trimmings, the vase of plastic flowers and the sign about a guard dog, to set the scene a little.

The young guy who answered the door looked like a bodybuilder. The reporter had only begun to introduce himself, when the man cut him off. "You're the fifth lot of cunts we've had at our front door today. Don't you fucking ghouls have any sense of human decency at all?"

Anger flared up in his cheeks and outlined veins in his forehead. Kendall had to get this shot. He raised the camera to focus it and set the exposure. The man took a step forward and swung a right that smashed the lens. As he was falling backwards, Kendall triggered the shutter. He landed on his tailbone first, then smacked the back of his head on the sidewalk and was knocked out cold for a few minutes. When he came to, the crime reporter said, "Welcome to the news business, sunshine. Glad we didn't pike out, are ya?"

After Kendall developed that roll of film in his dark room, he didn't care that his camera was destroyed, that he had a black eye which would last a week; he didn't even care that the editor knew that the news of the boy drowning was hours old already and had not bothered to warn them. He didn't care, because it was the best picture he'd ever taken. The black and white image, shot through a cracked lens, showed a fist held aloft. Over one of the knuckles peered a single out-of-focus eye. The fist waited menacingly. It would strike again.

During the workshops he would later do, by way of an introduction to his work, he would always start off the slide show with that image. "It was a lucky shot. It was a fluke but I was in the right position. I knew where I had to be to catch the light and frame the subject." To get the students to relax he'd throw in the same joke. "Oh, by the way, that was me getting smacked in the head for being a ghoul and a vulture, which was well deserved. Trust me when I say that photojournalism is another school of hard knocks."

He would move on to other shots he'd taken of angry faces at a political protest in Bangkok, limbless landmine victims in a veteran's hospital in Phnom Penh, a Vietnamese karaoke hostess putting on her make up in a cracked mirror, a tribesman in Sumatra holding up a severed leg he was ready to bite into. "After that first minor epiphany as a rounds man on the crime beat, that became my style, getting in close with a wide angle lens to find my own angle on events, no other camera bodies or lenses, no filters, no tricks in the dark room, no photoshopping afterwards, and no color either. If you're subject matter is strong enough and your compositions solid, you don't need to shoot color. Personally, I find colors too distracting, especially in Asia where they love all these gaudy shades, fluorescent lights and neon signs."

Then he would move on to his first black and white shots of Bangkok: a man with no legs propelling a makeshift bicycle by using his hands on pedals mounted on top of the frame; two dogs stuck together after copulating in a narrow lane filled with laughing schoolchildren in uniforms; a miniature Buddhist shrine on the dashboard of a luxury car; a laundry line in a back lane. "To me, Bangkok is the most photogenic city in the world because of its jarring contrasts. And I need to live in a place where life is all around me, where I can walk down the street and be surrounded by people, animals, little restaurants and noodle stalls on wheels, laundry lines strung on metal fences outside empty lots where locals go to pick wild herbs, a real place where folks live, work and raise families, not in a suburb where I grew up, where you don't even see your neighbors because they live in another fortress with three burglar alarms and two guard dogs."

During question time at every single lecture or workshop, someone would always ask, "Why don't you wear a watch?"

"Nothing sadder than watching the time passing, I reckon. That's part of the reason why I love photography so much, because you can freeze time and preserve those moments forever. Through the camera and film we've been given an almost god-like privilege of rendering folks and scenes immortal. It's a privilege that should not be abused or used frivolously to prop up one's vanity."

During the workshops and slideshows he'd throw in all sorts of personal anecdotes to illustrate his points and add a few lighter tones to the dark portrait that had been painted of him by his many detractors, mostly other photographers jealous of his success. "Unless you have empathy with the people you're photographing, all the techniques and expensive gear won't help you a jot. I became interested in photography after my Gran gave me one of those old Polaroid cameras for a Christmas prezzie one year. I used it as a diary. Anything that was happening around me, all the kangaroos around my uncle's farm, and the one that reared back on its tail to kick me in the chest, I photographed. But I wasn't conscious of how powerful the medium was until my dear old Gran got sick and I was visiting her in the hospital. As a lad I was obsessed with comic books and thought I could develop a superpower too. Mine was this. I wrapped my hand around her skinny old wrist to give her a kind of transfusion of my youth. That way she could get younger and I would age quickly enough to get my driver's license next year. For hours I'd watch the second hand on her watch circle the numbers and listen to the minutes crawl past. The ticking grew louder than her labored breathing, louder than her pulse, even louder than my own heart. It's relentless, the time passing and feeling powerless to stop it. But my superpower didn't work and when I woke up one morning after a long kip, she'd passed away already, they'd taken her to the morgue and the bed was made up. It was like she'd never been there at all." Something caught in his throat. He paused to take a sip of water. "That's when I stopped wearing a watch. I will not live my life marking time like it's an office or factory job. I mark time through these photographs and shoots and whatever relationships develop from them. At the end of the day, we don't have much to remember our loved ones, except our memories and these old Polaroids you can see here of Gran playing poker and drinking beer. Sometimes I'm not sure if I'm memories are constructed from photos or is it the other way around?"

KENDALL WAS ON HIS WAY to teach another workshop in Europe when his connecting flight was delayed in Singapore because of the tsunami. In the airport lounge he overheard a journalist shouting into his phone. "Can you believe this? I'm gonna miss the story of the century so they can send me to cover a coup in Africa? Like I need another African uprising on my CV, right? Time I get back to

Asia in another two weeks or so, the tsunami will be, uhh, pardon the pun, dead in the water." He laughed. "Sorry, haven't slept in fifteen hours now and the nerves are fried rice."

Kendall got his attention. "G'day, haven't I seen you on TV before?"

The pretty boy smiled. Kendall reckoned that he must have been hired for his looks and smooth voice, not his reporting skills or dedication to the news. "Hold on a sec," he said into the phone. He looked like he was getting ready to sign an autograph.

"I'd just like to say fuck you, you egotistical wanker."

"Who the hell are you?"

"The ghost of journalism's conscience and integrity."

Such was the fearsomeness of his presence, and the self-righteous anger in his voice, that few men dared to argue with him. The soldier's haircut, the earrings, the tattoos and military fatigues gave other journalists the impression that they were not dealing with one of their own, but a guerilla and sniper from some militant media watchdog.

Hastily, the foreign correspondent retreated. He kept shooting glances over his shoulder to make sure he wasn't being followed.

Kendall had missed working on the front lines of photojournalism. Following the breaking stories and playing a part in the world's biggest events was a lot more exciting than teaching.

On a whim, he changed his ticket and got rerouted through Phuket. At Patong, where the waves had washed across Beach Road and drowned dozens of guests eating breakfast in basement restaurants, the authorities had already cleared the roads of cars, motorcycles, and buses. But piles of debris still stood like grave mounds, and chunks of the road had been chewed up and spat out. That was not the strange part, though. On a beautiful sunny afternoon like this in the high season Phuket's most popular beach for tourists should be teeming with tourists. But it was more like a ghost town, the streets deserted, shops closed, and the mood subdued.

The only people in abundance were journalists, touts and tuk-tuk drivers (the last two almost interchangeable, which made the former look more dubiously opportunistic by proximity). To get to an internet café he had to walk a gauntlet of drivers, all calling out variations on, "Hey boss."

The first person he recognized there was a stringer for a British daily. Jane had covered the genocide in Rawanda, among many other conflicts, and had the machete scars to prove it. In bars in Phnom Penh, Bangkok and Jakarta, they had compared their battle scars, which used to be the medals of honor and badges of courage among foreign correspondents, before embedded journalists and internet commentators reduced most of them to relics and anachronisms.

Jane wore her usual get up, a fisherman's vest with a dozen bulging pockets in the front. Her ponytail stuck out the back of her New York Yankees baseball cap. "Compadre," she called out as soon as she saw him, "answer me this. Are the papers getting worse or am I just getting older and even more bitter? First story I filed was quite a sensitive, well-balanced piece with some powerful details about a school around Kamala flattened in the middle of a class. But in paragraph fifteen or so, I mentioned that a couple of bars had reopened and there were a few bargirls around. Here's the headline." She put her face up to the computer and squinted at the screen, "'Prostitutes and Jet-skis Return to Patong.' Gimme a break, man."

"Isn't that the paper Orwell used to work for?"

"Yeah, he must be break-dancing in his grave or laughing and saying I told you so. John Pilger, one of your guys, used to string for them too. After Murdoch bought the paper and turned it into a tabloid, Pilger said the front pages went from hard-hitting news to contests like, 'Wingo Bingo, win George Michael's trousers.'"

Kendall wished he could be more like her and learn how to laugh at the crass side of the news business. But he saw nothing amusing in wasting his life on a profession that was more and more tasteless, heartless and irrelevant.

Among journalists Jane was unusual in that she'd actually talk about what stories she was working on, and share her contacts and sources. On this occasion, she even offered to give him a lift over to Khao Lak in the car she'd rented. Jane had hired a Thai fixer they could both use, if he paid for the gas. "It's the usual deal," she said, when starting the car, "you scratch my back and I tickle your balls."

Kendall blushed and looked out the window at a local man cycling past with a live beehive on the back of his bicycle, behind a mini-van with posters of Thai boxers wearing garlands around their necks and a loudspeaker announcing the Muay Thai matches that night.

"Relax, buddy," she said. "Last time I got laid was during the fall of the Berlin Wall to the sound of riotous applause. I swear it was like having cheerleaders at our bonking session. No shit."

To be polite, Kendall laughed along with her. He was glad for the company. Having a trusted mate and colleague around was the only shock absorber when covering a story like this.

Along the coast, on a serpentine road that wound past the Snake Farm, mansions on the "Millionaire's Mile," rocky bays, secluded beaches and rubber tree plantations, the tension grew as they followed the trail of devastation: beach bars gutted and left as concrete skeletons, bungalows with their windows punched out, coconut palms bent at the painful angles of broken limbs.

The two-hour drive gave him enough time to read over all the stories he'd printed out for background details. They stopped once for water and snacks. Kendall walked around the parking lot of the convenience store to see what interview subjects and story angles he could find. Journalism was like detective work for him, hunting down clues, interviewing eyewitnesses. That was the fun part. But he would not play any cloak-and-dagger games with anyone. After some small talk, he introduced himself to the elderly eco-tour operator by saying, "I'm a photojournalist working on some pictures and stories down there. What do you think I should shoot and report?"

"First off, you could get your facts straight. My phone is ringing off the wall from friends and family back in the States who think I'm stranded here and about to die. On Phuket, we've got electricity, food, and running water. Most of the island is dry as a bone. But if you guys keep showing the same footage over and over again, what are people supposed to think? I mean, Christ, how many times did they have to show that footage of the planes hitting the Twin

Towers? We get the point, okay? The public is not retarded. So you can stop treating us like idiots."

Kendall jotted down notes with declining enthusiasm. He would not be able to sell this story. Two angles are almost always out of bounds in journalism: any criticism of the media itself, and any attacks on corporate advertisers. He looked up, "Anything else?"

"We've been through a lot down here, like SARS and the bird flu. Both were non-events, but you guys blew 'em up so big that all the tourists stayed away and I had to lay off half my staff. All I'm asking is don't punish us again. You guys come down here and shit —it's like getting hit by a second tsunami."

Kendall laughed but the other man did not. "Fair comment. I thought we were supposed to be the fourth estate but maybe we're just the second tsunami."

That guy's quip turned out to be the most prophetic quote of his short stay down south. He was not surprised by the devastation that he saw in Khao Lak, because he'd prepared himself for that. But he was surprised by the number of media on hand, and the number of tourists who thought they were now "citizen journalists" because they had a digital camera or a smartphone and a website or blog. Beside every ruined resort, behind every overturned car, next to every rescue team with hunting dogs, was somebody taking photos. He couldn't even frame a shot without another photographer getting in the way.

Down by the beach, at a makeshift pier the authorities had constructed to drop off bodies, the situation was more extreme. At press conferences and rock concerts, outside courthouses and parliament buildings, Kendall had fought his way through rugby matches of journalists bumping elbows and egos, but this was absurd. This was a travesty of media ethics he hadn't seen since that near-death experience catapulted him into the Festival of the Hungry Ghosts with those Eurasian vultures shadowing him everywhere and growing out of that poor Vietnamese woman's feet.

As the fishermen dragged corpses tied together with ropes behind their long-tail boats to the pier, because they considered it bad luck to bring them onboard, and the authorities fished them out of the water to wrap them in white bandages, a scrum of fifty or sixty photographers all jostled each other as they jockeyed for close ups. Fighting to photograph a murderer or rock star was only a reflection of the public's voyeurism, but competing to photograph corpses was, in his eyes and viewfinder, like vultures getting in a flap over dead meat.

When he finally met up with Yves, his old mate and collaborator, at the bar and restaurant down the street from Wat Yanyao in Takuapa, Yves asked him why he wasn't taking any photos. Kendall said, "It's the smell."

"Of all the bodies?"

"No, all the photographers."

Yves laughed. "I can always count on you to have a sardonic take on the bullshit and conmen in this business."

The waitress poured more beer in their glasses and added ice cubes to them from a metal bucket on a stand for beverages at the side of the table.

"I called up a photo editor in Oz and she told me she's already got a thousand free images from citizen journalists she can use. The standards have fallen so low now that it doesn't matter that half of 'em are crap and the other half are the usual clichés about weeping widows and starving orphans. Your feature in *The Australian* was the only original story I've read so far. Fucking ripper yarn, mate. Good on ya. That old parable about the Sheila whose husband died and she comes to see the Buddha about it is something I never heard. Then that search for the person who put the poster up for that missing woman in the Phuket airport really tied it all together."

Kendall had forgotten how uncomfortable Yves looked when anybody asked him about his work or personal life and how he covered it up with a series of mumbled niceties and by ducking for cover under his crow's nest of black hair. "Uhh, cheers, thanks. I appreciate it. Guess it turned out okay in the end."

"What happened in the end? Did they find that woman?"

Whenever Yves got onto one of his two favorite subjects, spirituality or the macabre, Kendall had noticed how he rose out of himself. His spine straightened. His grey eyes were piercing as nails. He kept gesturing with his cigarette for emphasis and running his hands through his hair. And he buried any of his infrequent, personal confessions in the middle of these spiels. "No, Piri is still missing, but the parable is about someone grieving who should not be left on their own, and her brother, this really morose truck driver, is still searching for her. I had this little old Thai lady for a psychiatrist in Bangkok who was treating me for severe depression. I know more about psychiatry than she ever will, but she was very kind and sympathetic, and she told me that parable, which I then repeated to the Hungarian guy and introduced him to some other people looking for their missing relatives. So they all formed an ad-hoc support network. Only the grieving can understand that level of grief and anxiety. That's what the Buddha was talking about. The parable is a very shrewd piece of psychology. That's why he used to insist that Buddhism is more of a science than a religion. But anyway… what's up with you? Are you gonna do any more photos down here."

"I can't be fucked taking any more pictures of the tsunami, and I'll never shoot stock for any online agencies. I have too much pride and I've won too many awards for that. Aw it's like… I don't know where I fit into journalism anymore. It's all about free content now or the coverage is by rote. The fucking press applies the same fucking boilerplates to every fucking disaster."

The waitress refilled their glasses with more beer. Kendall thanked her in Thai and they exchanged smiles. It was good to be back in Thailand again, the friendliest and most hospitable country he had ever visited, with the prettiest girls.

After lighting another cigarette from the cherry of his last one, Yves said, "That was impressive, man, three f-bombs in one sentence. You Aussies still have the market on cursing cornered, I'd have to say. But I know what you mean. All the stories on the news networks and on the wires are predictable. There's the environmental angle on coral bleaching and coastal erosion and mangrove forests serving as a breakwater against the waves. There's the business story on all the resorts destroyed and the number of tourist arrivals plummeting. There's a heartwarming story about the Moken, those sea gypsies, helping to evacuate tourists from another island, and elephants rescuing some other people. But it's hard to do those human interest stories on TV, because it's difficult for most people to act natural on camera. So those episodes come off looking a little flat. Oh, here's tomorrow's news that everyone will be repeating." He pointed at the TV screen, where a press conference was taking place. "Looks like the government is announcing that they're going to build an early warning system which will prevent future disasters."

Kendall thought that Yves had his wits about him. He didn't look any thinner or paler or more or less Goth than ever. On the surface, he didn't seem to have been adversely affected by the disaster, but he said little about what had actually happened to him. Every time Kendall brought it up, apologizing as a disclaimer, "Sorry to mention it again…" he would shrug it off by saying, "It wasn't that bad for me. I got off quite lucky in some ways." He would then lapse into anecdotes about his Khaosan Road days that Kendall hadn't heard him speak about in ten years. "You know who I've been thinking about lately is Mick. You remember him from the Ploy Guesthouse, don't you?"

"You mean the hooligan with all the football tattoos of the Man U Red Devils on his arms? That psychopath who used to head-butt blokes in the Thermae all the time."

"Mick never gave anybody a Glasgow kiss who didn't deserve it. He was a thief of honor."

"One night me and him were on a bender at the bar in the Hello Guesthouse where those two deaf mute tarts used to work, and we got rotten drunk, completely rat-arsed. On the way back to the Ploy, Mick had to take a slash so we wandered down that alley behind Khaosan, and Mick pissed all over this stray dog sleeping in the soi. What sort of bloke urinates on a dog?"

Yves laughed for about thirty seconds, well beyond the point of amusement, and closing in on the fringes of psychosis. "Oh, that was Mick. He wasn't serious. He was just taking the piss, so to speak, or taking a piss." Yves began laughing again.

The photographer knew a few things about post-traumatic stress disorder (PTSD). One of the first signs was evading the event which had caused it by refusing to talk. Another warning sign, the doctor had told him, during the months and months of psychotherapy sessions he'd undergone after getting shot in Bangkok, was spending too much time alone brooding over it.

As another volunteer at the temple, Kendall noticed that Yves was disappearing for days a time. He wouldn't answer the phone in his room. He wouldn't come to the door. His only repeated alibi was, "I'm sick. I've got some kind of stomach flu."

He would not admit to anything else, except once or twice he said, "You know, I have to keep the bathroom door open whenever I take a shower, and I go around constantly making sure all the faucets are turned off, because I have this fear I might drown in my sleep."

As delicately as possible Kendall would say, "You might want to talk to a doctor about that. After I took that bullet I was spun out and had the wobblies for months, even thought my camera was haunted for a while."

"Hey, I appreciate your concern, but I'll be fine in a few weeks."

Kendall did not think it was fair to mention that he had once thought the same thing, too. But he wasn't fine in a few weeks. PTSD does not work that way. In many cases, it has a haunting, almost supernatural quality. Years after his near-death experience, in a flash, triggered by a black and white photo or a headline that mentioned AIDs or cannibalism or political protests, Kendall would be transported back to that darkroom in his dreams where all of his most disturbing images, the ones he'd shot, and the ones he'd only thought about shooting, turned into ghostly negatives to torment him: the AIDS patient, the kangaroo, the Sumatran headhunter, and the teenager who had almost gotten his head bashed in by the butt of a soldier's rifle because of his neglect.

Whatever his other failings, he had made an effort to save the kid. It was more than he had ever achieved as a photographer.

By volunteering at the temple he could create some more good karma, which also allowed his conscience enough wriggle room to take covert shots of the bodies misted over with dry ice, while going back and forth in an argument with himself… *you're a sick fuck, mate, but people need to see the truth.*

These were the first shots he took down south that he had not seen before. But none of them would ever appear in any daily newspapers. Even the tabloids would not go this far, because the true horror of the aftermath was too unpalatable for most readers and advertisers to stomach.

When Yves was doing an interview with him about his book of photos, *Flashpoints in Asia*, Kendall said, "Most of the pictures in this collection were not published in the mainstream media for a very simple reason. The truth hurts. The raw, unPhotoshopped truth about wars, famines, and natural disasters is hideous. It's grotesque. It's hard to face. But I reckon nothing will change for the better until we do face up to it."

Whatever foolish and naïve hopes he had cherished in his youth of photography as an agent of political and social change had perished years ago, when his first and only book thus far shifted around half of a thousand-copy print run.

All those images of weeping widows and starving orphans he refused to take appeared again and again in the press yet nobody gave them much more than a sidelong glance. Then the reader flipped the page, or changed the channel, or scrolled down the webpage, to look at ads for new shoes, new gadgets, and new cars with blandly attractive models standing beside them.

The photos changed nothing, but at least they gave people something to look at between shopping sprees.

Kendall wished he could find the balding sub-editor who once told him, "We have to keep shoveling the shit and filling those pages," not to argue with him again, but to commiserate and shout him a beer.

THE WATER SURGED AROUND and over him, but Yai kept his grip on the knobby trunk of the palm tree. Darts of pain shot up his arms and legs to hit bull's eye after bull's eye in his brain. He lost his grip.

The water was too muddy to see much. He couldn't tell up from down or right from left as he spun around in a whirlpool until his lungs were ready to burst. Then he saw it, a portal like a ship's window. It did not have a handle. The only entrance was a cervix-like tear in the middle. He pulled it apart like a pair of curtains and collapsed on the floor in a puddle.

Once he got his breath back, Yai looked around the room. It resembled a museum. The only difference was that these were exhibits from his own life: the first toothbrush his father had made him from part of a brush and a piece of bamboo, his old school uniforms hanging from a nail in the wall, his first pet, a rabbit named Bugs Bunny, stuffed and mounted in a glass case.

No one was there. The only human presences were in the photographs of family members, schoolmates on his soccer team, and fading color portraits of girlfriends whose out-of-fashion clothes and out-of-date haircuts gave them a sad air of nostalgia and of youthful dreams unfulfilled.

Normally those pictures would have set off all sorts of emotional tripwires and inspired other reminiscences. Not now. In this museum of his life, his feelings were dead too.

Room after room was filled with the junk and the photographic evidence of his life, but there was no life in it. He thought of all the time and money he'd spent (wasted really) accumulating all these possessions that meant so little to him now.

The romances and fights, the friendships and jokes, all the showing off and drinking – what good was any of it now?

He tried to call out but could not make a sound. He took a deep breath, but could not smell anything. He listened but heard nothing.

What sort of karmic punishment was this? Was being bored to death his fate? Had he not been evil enough to warrant the torments of hell nor good enough to merit a holiday in heaven? Would he not be reborn at all?

Anything had to be better than this noiseless, scentless, tasteless, joyless, museum of memories where dust motes were frozen in the air.

Yai walked back to the entrance—he could no longer even take pleasure in the simple joy of movement—and tried to pull those curtains apart. They barely budged. He could only pry them a little ways apart. But if he pushed his head against the crack, like it was the doorway of a womb, and pushed and pushed, compressing himself as serpents do to squeeze into and out of the smallest spaces, then he could slither through it and back into the turbulent water, reborn again.

But he was not reborn into a different body or a different time or even a different place. The room in which he woke up on the floor looked like one of those typical old Sino-Portuguese hotel rooms in southern Thailand, a little down at heel, with clunky rosewood furniture, and a ceiling fan chopping the hot, thick air into cooler and thinner blades that needled his face.

Hanging from the ceiling fan was a suicide, her black tongue hanging down to her chin.

Stacked up on the bed like cordwood was a half dozen other bodies. Each of them, he knew without thinking, was another person who had died in this room.

He had returned from the dead lands with his vision altered. Even the air itself swam with microorganisms flying to and fro. The only experience he could compare this to was looking through a microscope for the first time and seeing all the tiny life forms that existed in a single droplet of water.

The wall burst open in a spray of splinters and wallpaper, as the Serpent King used his crested head like a bulldozer. In a baritone voice that squeezed Yai's intestinal track in a cold fist, he intoned, as if chanting a Buddhist sutra, "You are dead and you must stay with us now. We can't have anyone returning to tell people what the afterlife is really like. Entire religions, philosophies, justice systems, and moral codes would crumble if people knew the truth."

Yai would not go back to that museum of lifeless memories. He ran down the hallway, past a businessman whose briefcase was dripping with blood money, past a cleaning lady whose aborted fetus clung to her neck, and past a boy who had his grandfather's decomposing head growing out of his shoulder, while moths, mites and the skeletons of sparrows filled the air like down from a burst pillow.

Was there anywhere he could run to that was not contaminated by death and decay?

KENDALL DID NOT KNOW what to make of these emails that Yves was sending him. Were they supposed to be extracts from a novel? Were they supposed to be real? Were they yet more proof that he was suffering from a severe strain of PTSD?

The only note accompanying them any of them was, "I'm trying some experiments in 'automatic writing.' It's like going into a trance state. Some people have experienced writing in different languages, becoming possessed by demons or even communicating with the dead."

At the temple, in between shifts, Kendall mentioned these emails to Wade, who said, "Things were gettin' weird even before the waves hit. With Yves and his wife, or ex-wife, those two are quite the fucked up couple, and Watermelon, and their French buddy, something was goin' on there that didn't seem right. The stories Yves has been telling about the waves hitting don't add up either. One minute he's floating around in his bungalow, the next he's on the beach walking around? The water didn't drain that quickly. Frankly, there's so many holes in his story you could open a whorehouse with it. But I'm gonna get to the bottom of it if it's the last thing I do."

"Fair dinkum, but don't fuck with him." Kendall pointed his finger at him like a gun. "He's an old mate of mine and you fuck with him then you fuck with me."

Wade held both of his hands up with the palms facing out. "Hey, chill out, Mr. Hair-Trigger Temper. Nobody's talkin' about fucking with anyone else, least of all me."

"Good-o. Just so you understand a little more what our connection and history is, journalism is a cutthroat profession full of mercenary arseholes. But he's by far the most generous fella I've met in this business. He helps other people get their stories and photos published. He edits people's stories for free, writes hundreds of reviews every year of books, exhibitions, albums, you name it, and if it wasn't for him I wouldn't have gotten a publishing deal. He helped me get more promo for that book than anyone else. So he's a good bloke and you better not do the dirty on him is all I'm saying."

Wade wasn't really sure what to make of this guy. He projected the kind of rage that went both ways. It could be inspiring. It could wake people up when he projected it outwards. But if it backfired, if it got clogged up like a shitter that was out of order, it could do him a lot of harm. Wade figured it was about fifty fifty with this guy.

After they'd known each other for a few days, Wade would rib him, "You missed your calling in life, bud. You shoulda been a preacher or a dictator."

"Dinkum, fucking oath, mate." This appeared to mean that Kendall agreed with him—at least he was smiling—but then he'd turn back to Yves and continue his tirade about politics or weeping widows and starving orphans. He spoke as if he was certain of every syllable, as if he believed in what he said with every atom of his body and every cell in his brain. Wade could see how he'd be a hit on the lecture circuit and at photography workshops, but his conviction and passion had taken an enormous toll on his health. The guy had worn himself down to skin and gristle. He looked like a scarecrow in army fatigues, his face gaunt and haggard.

After they found Yai's body, Wade told him not to tell Yves about it. He was already in a vulnerable position with a fingertip grasp on sanity. One more loss might push him over the ledge.

Because all of Yai's fingers had been torn off and his teeth knocked out, the only identifying marks on his body were the snake bites running up his arms and down his legs.

His cadaver was laid out on a white sheet, alongside dozens more of the dead. Wade bent down to look at the stumps of his fingers. He looked up at Kendall. "Man that guy wanted to live. He was holdin' on to life with everything he had. I'll say that for the guy, he put up one helluva fight. You betcha."

Kendall had been around enough men in war zones and crime

scenes, prisons and riots, to know that Wade was reassuring himself right now. He believed that courage was the most important quality for a man to possess. It gave meaning to life and lent perspective to death. Without courage a man was not a man; he was a coward, a sissy, a failure.

Kendall had also been around enough dead bodies to find no honor in death, no heroism in self-sacrifice. "Whether you die for your country or a woman or in a stupid drunken accident, you still end up dead," he'd once told Yves during an interview. "If I had to choose between a posthumous medal and one more day of surfing and whale watching around Perth, it wouldn't be a choice." He smiled. "Surfing is the only thing that's better than sex, but I'm Australian, so I would say that, wouldn't I?"

Standing by the rows and rows of the dead, laid to rest in white cocoons, all he felt was a perverse gratitude that the cadavers were not his. But in the same way he told religious people he was an agnostic and would not mock their beliefs, he did not dare to contradict Wade. Even atheists have commandments that they live and die by.

Kendall did not raise the subject of Watermelon's disappearance either. It was delicate in several ways. Among the expat men of Thailand the standard question asked of couples, "So where did you two meet?" was off limits, because they'd often met under less than wholesome circumstances.

Kendall had only met her on a couple of occasions when she was the mamasan of that blowjob bar on Patpong 2 called the Star of Love. From what little he could remember of those drinking sessions with Mick and Yves he was impressed by how quick witted she was and her smiling resilience in the face of Mick's constant taunts. "What makes your pussy wet, love?"

"When I take a shower."

She was not even cowed by this other huge hooligan named Martin who demanded a blowjob or he would tear the place apart. She crawled under the bar: a large wooden box with a curtain at the front. Kendall could not see what was going on, but Martin soon shut up. His eyes closed. He rocked back and forth on his stool.

After he had climaxed and staggered out the front door, she crawled out. In her hand she held up half a cantaloupe with a hole in it. "First man who ever pay a thousand baht to fuck a fruit," she announced to riotous laughter from all the bargirls and customers.

A week after Kendall arrived Wade finally brought up the subject of his fiancé's disappearance, when they were sitting on wooden caskets drinking vodka at Col's Coffin Cocktail Lounge. "What I'm thinkin' now is she got airlifted out to another hospital, came down with amnesia and can't remember how to contact me. Well, shit happens, eh?"

In his mind, Kendall ran through a list of possible replies. Best to look on the bright side. Keep the faith, mate. Like they say, hope springs eternal.

Each he discarded. Finally, after not coming up with a single comforting thought he would dare to repeat, so trite and unconvincing did they sound, Kendall looked up from the dregs of his thoughts and drink to see that Wade was gone and twilight had settled over the temple like a blanket of dusk blue tossed over a terminally ill patient.

COLIN CAME RUNNING AND Screaming across the temple grounds. He paused to give the men "high fives" and hug the women. "Pardon me for acting like a Yank and screaming 'woo' but it's a miracle, a bloody miracle. A fishing trawler just rescued an Indonesian teenager in the middle of the ocean. He'd been clinging to an uprooted tree for ten days. Badly sunburned and dehydrated, but he'll live. Isn't that brilliant? Best news I've heard all day."

It *was* brilliant and no one was happier to hear about another miraculous survival story than the forensic teams and Disaster Victim Identification Units surrounded by death.

At the same time, Kendall could not help but notice the way that Wade and the Hungarian truck driver Yves had profiled, who was still searching in vain for his sister, wrestled with the news, their joy quickly rubbed out by envy. They wanted the miracle survivor to be their loved one. It was perfectly understandable, Kendall thought. In their position, he would have felt the same.

As the news broke, many of the volunteers were thinking the same thing but nobody wanted to say it aloud and make it real. Two weeks into the search and salvage mission, this would be one of the last castaways found alive. After this they would only be fishing out bodies.

AT THE TEMPLE, WADE saw all the volunteers lose it in completely different ways. His own breakdown had come quite quickly: attacking the policeman he'd spotted looting the corpse. It was painful to relive, thinking how close he'd come to grabbing the cop's gun and bashing his teeth in with it. But that was his way of dealing with things. He said to Yves, "I have to face things head on. Shit or get off the pot. That's my motto." It was the same as putting his fingers down his throat to puke after getting a little too drunk. Better to purge himself early on before the poisoning became too severe.

He wished some of the other volunteers had gotten the bad blood out of their systems before it turned toxic. Christ, the way some of these men behaved, UN guys, bureaucrats, bigwigs, paper-pushers who'd never seen any real action before, and there they were screwing the asses off two or three bargirls a night over on Phuket, then coming back to work on no sleep, still stinking of booze. It was embarrassing. No respect for their jobs or countries.

After yet another all-nighter, one of the bureaucrats from a big-name aid organization, driving a rented Range Rover on his five-star expense account, reported to work with the coffee machine from his hotel room. He set it up on a wooden coffin. From his duffel bag he pulled out cups, bottles of milk, sachets of sugar, and spoons. The young Englishman with the racing-stripe sideburns then made a sign out of a piece of cardboard. He hung that from a bamboo stake he drove into the ground. The sign read, "Col's Coffin Café: It's Dead Good."

By this point a group of monks just returning from their early morning alms round had gathered around the coffin where the ginger-haired Colin sat making coffee for the other volunteers. Down the first row of corpses a chicken strutted spasmodically. One of the orange-robed monks chased it away. "Anyone fancy a side order of chicken?" asked Colin. Much to the amusement of the monks, he began making chicken noises. Then he winked and grinned at his colleagues. "Feeling a little peckish are we lads?"

Wade, who had just slept in a plastic chair for the past three hours and was still not sure if he was awake or dreaming, cupped his hands around his mouth and called out, "Nah, I'm chicken."

All the foreigners roared.

With mock outrage, Colin said, "I'll have you know, sir, that this is the finest corpse-fed chicken in Southeast Asia. Tsunami Poultry, ask for it by name at posh supermarkets."

One of the tattooed backpackers yelled, "It's CFC, dude, Coffin-Fried Chicken."

These jests were in response to the latest stories making the rounds that the fish served in restaurants in southern Thailand had nibbled on corpses. What had started with one local tabloid had then been picked up and repeated by so many different websites and blogs that the news networks began repeating it verbatim, with no proof whatsoever.

None of the volunteers were making fun of the dead, nor mocking Buddhism. The monks understood that even with their limited English skills. This was the gallows humor of combat-fatigued soldiers and Emergency Room nurses, of cops and coroners working overtime, for whom laughter is the safety valve that releases all the hypertension so they can get back to work.

The jokes got sicker as the volunteers got drunker during the nightly drinking sessions at the curbside restaurants down the road from Yan Yao Temple, where the volunteers and DVI teams sat on plastic stools only a few meters away from the passing trucks carrying rubber tree logs, pineapples, sugarcane, and massive bronze statues of the Buddha.

The volunteers divided themselves up along racial lines. The Thais had their tables; most of the laughter came from their direction. The other Asians, mostly Japanese and Koreans, had theirs; between the older folks there was an uneasy truce among these former enemies. The Brits and the Irish had cornered the two tables closest to the TV for the football matches. Wade and Kendall sat at the table reserved for North Americans as well as a smattering of Aussies and New Zealanders, and Yves moved between all the tables, getting quotes and checking facts.

The nightly "entertainment" consisted of a TV showing local soap operas, game shows, ghost serials, martial arts dramas, and English football with Thai announcers. In this provincial town, where the newsstands at the local bus station, next to a ramshackle wooden market, did not stock any English-language magazines or newspapers, Thai songs dominated all the karaoke machines. The videos accompanying them were like soft-core porn: Thai women in bikinis walking down beaches and wading into the water to splash themselves with it in slow motion.

Every night another fearful rumor spread from table to table. The next aftershock would be bigger than the original earthquake. Outbreaks of cholera, typhoid, and tuberculosis were imminent. It was no use leaving now; all the volunteers had been infected already. Local papers said the forensic unit of the Thai police had accused Dr. Pornthip and her team of mistakenly identifying hundreds of bodies. They wanted to move the identification center from the temple to Phuket, where they would be in charge. Around the tables where the Asians sat, they swapped ghost stories of the drowned returning to haunt the beaches, waterways and the temple's mortuary. They recited these tales with the same mixture of credence and fascinated dread that the Westerners reserved for the rumors of pandemics and aftershocks in the offing.

As if all of that wasn't weird and worrisome enough already, now everyone was too freaked out about the latest stories of corpse-eating fish to order seafood in the restaurant.

"Better stick to the beer diet," said Wade, and Kendall nodded.

After a couple of weeks of rumors, hauntings, aftershocks, coffins used as coffee tables and dead bodies that appeared to be talking, all the black humor had turned very bleak and all the laughter had a desperate edge and lunatic-asylum hysteria to it.

Colin, the ringleader of the British and Irish crew, insisted that he was expanding his business empire with a new venture. "Here it is, lads, the new frontier in post-tsunami businesses, Ned's Bordello for Necrophiliacs. We've got a few thousand tarts over there for those sick fucks."

Above the clatter of utensils on the alfresco wok, insects caroming off the fluorescent lights, and the off-key warble of a Thai songbird venting her spleen and heartbreak through karaoke, Colin's friends were moaning, "Bloody hell, give it a rest, Col."

Yves looked at Wade who had taken off his baseball cap to wipe the sweat from his bald head. He said, "Man, I gotta take a break from this insanity. Listen to Colin. Now he's rehashing some old comedy sketch by Peter Cook and Dudley Moore, aka Derek and Clive, about how dead popes excite them and give them the horn, ie, a boner. I think Col is about two days away from a serious stretch in a loony bin."

"For sure, he's way outta line, but the way I see it, this is a whole new ballgame. Nobody's ever seen anything like it before. So how are they supposed to react? All bets are off and all crazy possibilities are on."

"Nice of you to excuse the loony, but I'm still gonna bail out for a few days. Don't worry. I shall return to my sorry lot in life and do my meager part." He managed a smile. "I won't chicken out on you or Col and the lads." He put some bills on the table.

"You're not gonna go after Zara and Stephan now, are ya? Tell me it's not about all that macho crap and blood vendettas, like life is a blues song and you gotta go kill the guy who stole your gal, eh?"

"Don't speak of the dead. It's blasphemous. To me they both died in the tsunami."

"Okay, however you wanna play it, bud, just as long as there ain't no bloodletting, is fine by this ol' pacifist." Wade looked at the bills, sitting beside a plastic container for a toilet roll and a little tray with condiments like dried chili, fish sauce and sugar. "That's too much. You always pay more than your share. Here…" He gave him back a red, one-hundred baht note with the king's face on it. "So where ya goin'?"

"I'm going back to Bangkok to find my cat."

WADE WATCHED HIM GO and said nothing except, "Take 'er easy. If ya need anything gimme a shout on the cell."

None of his previous experiences, working in nickel mines and on oil rigs, managing a heavy metal band and driving a snowplow, had prepared him for this. He had no advice to offer, no remedies to dispense. This was uncharted territory. The aftershocks from the third largest earthquake ever recorded on a seismograph (9.1 on the Richter scale) had stopped after a few months, but they continued rippling through the survivors, and all those who'd witnessed the deaths and the devastation, for decades to come.

The most disturbing case Wade had come across was Sophia's: kind, hilarious, outgoing and seemingly indestructible Sophia. Yves had pointed her out in the provincial hospital in Takuapa, two weeks after Boxing Day, when they were visiting some of the friends Wade had promised to check up on: the Japanese golf pro who'd come down with malaria, the old Chinese lady who kept kicking his butt at gin rummy, and the young girl whose leg had to be amputated. "One leg is still better than none, sweetheart, and that won't stop you from goin' horseback riding up in Jasper. Trust me. Soon as we find your parents we'll be good to go."

How long could he keep spewing this BS? It was wearing him down. The heat, the long hours, the stench, the lack of sleep, the brightness and the energy-sucking heaviness of the sunlight, and especially all the lies he had to keep repeating to reassure the orphans that all hope was not lost.

Yves showed him into another room with four beds, all occupied and surrounded by bands of chattering friends and relatives. He explained a little about the art therapist. Sophia was working with three young Swedish sisters who were catatonic. The unconfirmed rumor was that their parents and siblings had died, but no one knew how or why because the girls were not able, or refused, to talk.

Sophia had set up a canvas and an easel by the window. In spite of the cast on her arm and the bandages around her knee, she was showing them how to mix colors and paint portraits. But the three blonde girls just sat there on the bed covered by the drab green sheet. They looked like dolls with blue eyes only half alive and half deadened by the terror of their ordeal.

With admirable patience, Sophia kept cajoling them, kept smiling at them and encouraging them to paint and draw. From time to time she would banter with Yves in French. Sophia's accent sounded French, but she did not look European. Her caramel skin and languid mannerisms gave Wade flashbacks of his holidays in the Caribbean, of beaches with black sand made of volcanic ash, of buying freshly caught lobster straight from the fishermen in their dugout canoes, of encounters with sable-skinned women who made love like they were dancing to salsa propelled by steel drums and who wore wildflowers in their hair. By dawn no traces of them remained in his bed save for some petals of red hibiscus and the faintest tang of the sea.

When the Thai doctor and a nurse came to check on the girls, Wade said to him, "Don't tell me. She's gotta be from one of those French colonies, like Martinique or St. Tropez."

"Not bad, man. Not bad at all. Her father is from Martinique but her mother comes from Paris, that Montmartre area, the Bohemian quarter where Toulouse-Lautrec and Henry Miller used to live. That's what we were just talking about. She's had a remarkable life as an actress, an artist's model, a TV presenter and now as an art therapist. Yes, a remarkable woman."

"With a remarkable rack. Look at the fun bags on her, would ya?" Wade kept his voice low so Sophia and the three sisters would not hear him.

"You are incorrigible, Wade."

"Since I don't know what that means, and frankly it sounds kinda gay, I'm gonna pretend you didn't say it and leave it at that. The way I see it, people get even hornier and have more sex after disasters like this. It's lust for life, just like that song by Iggy and Bowie goes."

"I thought you were a metal head."

"Not always. Far as I'm concerned there's only two kinds of music. There's good music and there's bad music. I like good music. Whether that's metal or punk or classical or country, my ears are wide open, bud. Bring it on, turn it the fuck up, and give 'er."

The middle sister went over to the easel and began sketching furiously with a black pen. Wade, Yves and Sophia were transfixed. The motions of her hand, combined with the movement of the lines, swirls and circles as the outline took shape, made it look like they were watching a comic turn into an animated cartoon. The boat was going up the wave like a surfer. The three girls were thrown off the side. A woman tried to grab them but the propeller cut off her arm.

The artist grabbed another paintbrush, dipped it in red, and started stabbing the sun and the sky with it until it broke in two.

The jolt of recognition snapped Wade out of his lethargy. He sat up in his chair. He gripped the arms. In his mind, he was going a thousand miles per hour, leaping days in seconds, to arrive back on that long-tail boat on Boxing Day. The little girl with the pink T-shirt that read "I'm Crabby" beside an illustration of a crab. The three sisters flying over his head. Their mother trying to catch them. The propeller. The sun spouting a geyser of blood. In the water trying to wrap his T-shirt around the woman's arm. His collarbone sticking out of his skin.

The artist put that sketch aside and started another one of two blond girls swimming for shore in a sea of blood where all the black waves looked like shark fins. Her hands were moving a mile a minute. Wade had never seen anything like this before, except maybe the little girl who became possessed by a demon in *The Exorcist*. But this kid was possessed by the tsunami, which was rushing and roiling through the rivers of her veins.

The other two sisters wept and hugged each other. Sophia sat down on the bed between them. She put her arms around them and clasped them to her bosom.

Wade watched the scene unfold, as any parent would, with an ache in his heart and arms that could only be relieved by hugging his own sons or at least hearing their voices on the phone.

The artist began another painting of a little girl sitting on top of a palm tree surrounded by water. Sinking beneath the waves beside the tree was an Asian man with a saint-like halo of sunlight around his head. Wade squinted at the painting. *It was Yai.* It had to be him.

In her next sketch, he was crucified on two palm trees surrounded by black sea.

The former snake-handler's disappearance and death had been much discussed among them, but no one had any proof of what had happened to him. Even after his body was found, nobody knew where he'd been when the tsunami struck. Was this what happened? Yai had come to their rescue and become a saint in the eyes of this girl? Yves was trying to talk to her, but she kept shaking her head and continued sketching.

Wade looked away. Then he noticed the altar in the corner of the room, the altar festooned with blinking fairy lights and bedecked with lotus blossoms, incense and yellow candles. Sitting atop it was the Buddha protected by the seven heads of the Serpent King. That was Yai's favorite Buddha image, the one he talked about the most.

By Wade's reckoning this was at least one coincidence too many. He had to be alone for a while to give this a long hard think. He told Sophia it was nice to meet her. He shook her hand. He wanted to say something to the girls, but he couldn't. The artist, it was like she'd been touched by the hand of God or the devil, Wade couldn't decide which.

Whenever he was drinking with Yves they would often circle back to that afternoon. Wade would mention his theory, but Yves would disagree. "No, she was touched by the hand of genius. Most people think watching a child being born is a miracle, right? I'm sure it is, but what we witnessed was an artist being born and that's equally miraculous."

Wade would not contradict him. He was not an expert on such

subjects. But there was more to it than that. Much much more.

For years he would puzzle over the events of that afternoon. To meet those angelic-looking girls again, all three of them, yes, a trinity, to discover they were still alive after he'd given them up for dead. To find out how Yai had saved one of them. To see how the artist had depicted him as a saint and a Christly figure. To look over and see Yai's favorite Buddha image with the Serpent King. And *then*, the kicker, to suddenly see Wade's father, plain as day, but just for a split second, standing under that Buddha image. His father who had taught him how to ski, skate, hunt and drive a snowmobile. The father who had been dead for more than twenty years.

And for all these things to happen within such a short space of time just when he'd reached a point of complete despair and utter exhaustion was a… *revelation*. That was the only word which fit and even that sounded inadequate.

After all these years and beset by so many doubts, God, the Creator, Whoever, Whatever, had visited them in that hospital room or at least made their presence felt. Wade was almost certain of that.

Growing up in the Bible belt felt more like a noose and straitjacket, because there were so many different rules to follow, the Lord's Prayer on the radio in the morning, saying grace every night at dinner and his prayers before bed, going to Sunday school every week and memorizing hymns to sing in the church choir. There was no escaping the word of God or his many laws. On Wade's way to school every morning on the black and yellow bus, looking out over the long flat prairies, desolate in winter, but abundant with sheaves of wheat and ears of corn during the summer, even the colossal grain elevators were etched with Biblical warnings: "What good for a man to win the world but lose his own soul?"

He did not want to look up at the night sky, vaulted like a cathedral and aglitter with thousands of stars, to see a moral written there about how cleanliness is next to Godliness, when he was awed by the boundless infinity of the universe and its millions of mysteries. That was the kind of religion he wanted—full of beauty, mystery, and eternity.

The tsunami and its aftermath had stirred up those old longings. As much as he'd lost, and as bad it was, and as fucked up as his collarbone would always be, for the rest of his days Wade remained grateful to the catastrophe for bringing him back to the Creator, who was maybe not a God at all, not even remotely human, probably more like an alien intelligence, he imagined, and a combination of architect, engineer, electrician, plumber, artist and astrophysicist.

Wade could not understand the workings of the universe anymore than he'd been able to understand the architect's blueprint for that new ski resort they were building. As a plumber who'd done an apprenticeship, and as an amateur electrician, he could work out where the shitters went and how the wiring worked, but the rest of the design was way beyond his meager capabilities. The same went for the universe.

Big tragedies ask huge questions. After 9/11 his American buddies from Montana and Minnesota, even the bikers, were more thoughtful than he'd ever seen them before. On their fishing and hunting trips, the small talk dried up pretty quick when they sat around the campfire at night, pounding back brewskis with twigs crackling and sparks impersonating fireflies, so they could talk of God and country, death, democracy and, in the end, what it all came back to was good friends, family loyalties, and the simple dignity of doing an honest day's work for an honest day's pay.

Wade would also never understand how Watermelon came to him in a dream, some four months after her disappearance, to show him where her body was hidden in the roots of a mangrove tree. She said it didn't matter what became of her physical form. In life it was only a bankable commodity. But in death it became a chrysalis for a spirit that was like a butterfly. After her body died, her spirit would use it as a runway to lift off into the sun, she said.

They found her body exactly where her dream ghost said it was. Just as Wade spotted it, a tiger butterfly circled around his head and flew up, up and up, until it disappeared into a shooting star of sunlight.

Wade did not know how to explain that either. His mind said it was a coincidence. His heart said it was love. His soul that it was a miracle.

Over the years, he did come to a few conclusions that he tinkered with and refined, like he'd tinker with his old motorcycles once in a while, changing the pistons and plugs, trying out different carburetors and valves. He did not need any religious groups or books on physics to confirm these convictions. He did not even think that any of them, save for an afterlife, were especially religious. All the same, he did not repeat them to anyone, just like he didn't talk about his love life with anyone except his partner. Some things are sacred and can only be conserved by silence. Out on the prairies, there were already enough preachers, televangelists, and Jehovah's witnesses going from door to door like traveling salesman. Nobody needed him to throw in his two cents on matters that he did not understand anyway. And he certainly wasn't going to etch any of his beliefs on the sides of no grain elevators.

But the gist of his experiences and imaginings boiled down into a few unshakable convictions:

There is a master-plan and a design to the earth,
the solar system, the universe, and the human race.
There is a higher power out there somewhere.
We are never alone and death is not the end.
In fact, it might only be the beginning.

WADE'S BACKGROUND IN ART appreciation had begun with barebreasted, sword-wielding Viking babes featured in airbrushed murals on the sides of the "boogie vans" that were popular back in the seventies, and ended with the drawings of timber wolves, beavers and polar bears on the walls of the resort where he worked.

He had never heard of "art therapy" before, but he watched Sophia perform a few minor miracles over the next few months. Through painting and drawing, she provided an outlet for those too traumatized to speak about their experiences. It proved to be especially effective with the many orphans.

Around the temple of Yanyao and the town of Takuapa, the tire-less Sophia was everywhere. Wade kept running into her as she escorted the families and friends of the missing through the temple, as she performed clerical tasks for Dr. Pornthip, as she helped the Buddhist nuns (dressed in puritanical white, their heads shaven in a rejection of vanity) to prepare food for the monks and the volun-teers, as she gave interviews on French TV: always with a smile on her face, always wearing these beautiful saris, bangles and scarves from India. The Thais adored her because she was so fun loving and down to earth, which was a lot more than you could say for many of the Westerners from the bigger aid organizations and DVI units, who were easy to anger, quick to judge and slow to adapt ("In the countries where I've worked we didn't do it like this.").

Her very French dedication to slapstick humor and comic prat-falls kept the Thai volunteers in a state of hysterics. One morning she showed up to work with her hair tinted red and gelled into punkish porcupine quills in the same style and shade as Dr. Pornthip. Thanks to her hairstyling, by noon, thirty different women were walking around the temple with the same hairdo as the forensics specialist.

During the nightly drinking sessions Sophia did not bitch like the other volunteers did. She didn't even complain about them put-ting ice in the beer—unusual for a woman with such refined tastes, Wade thought, who always brought a European literary novel to dinner every night and listened to Indian and Western classical music on her MP3 player. In English she was far from fluent, "I speak English… in a style very French," but she had enough brio to keep up her share of the conversation, even when she had to resort to body language punctuated by bursts of French, "*Mais oui. C'est sa.* In France, we are very enlightened and very liberal. We stopped using ze guillotine in 1981." Sophia seemed to have gone through life in a constant state of amusement or a state of reverence for all things artistic.

Wade was impressed by the fact that she was the only one of the volunteers who had ever been to Canada. (The Brits and Aussies kept mistaking or accusing him of being an American and asking, "What state are you from?") She was complimentary about the country and curious to learn more. "You have two national languages in Canada. You must speak French, uh?"

"Yeah, well, we had to study it when we were kids. I still remember a few phrases. *Ouvert la fenetre, Monsieur Thibault.*"

His deadpan rendering of French made her laugh so much that all the bangles on her arms jingle-jangled. "Open the window, Mr. Thibault. Yes, you speak French… in a style very English."

This became their in joke. Every morning when they saw each other, Wade would say, "Ouvert la fenetre, Monsieur Thibault," and Sophia would laugh and repeat the English equivalent.

By then Wade had decided that if, in the unlikely event that Watermelon turned up alive, she could go back to Yves. She didn't really love him anyway. All she wanted was a visa and for him to buy her parents a house. Wade would be better off pursuing Sophia. It would be nice to have someone to talk to for a change. As beautiful and feminine as some of these Thai women were, they made for dull conversationalists. Talking about food and prices all the time, or playing cards and making funny faces at each other, had its limitations. With Sophia he could talk about anything. She had few taboos. "When I was eighteen, because of my sexual life, I had to leave the Catholic church, uh?" Another bonus was that she was in her forties, he guessed, close to his own age.

Colin was the one who took him aside and said, as they stood beside a gilded statue of the abbot who had founded the temple and whose robes were graffitied in black and white with bird guano. "Between you and me and the gatepost, as it were, Sophia's husband and teenage daughter are both missing. The situation looks dire. So go easy or give her a miss."

Wade did not know how to broach this subject with her. The best thing to do, he figured, was to wait for her to bring it up first, which didn't work either because she refused to mention it.

He now saw her frenetic pace around the temple and town in a darker light. As long as she kept moving and talking and joking and cooking, as long as she did not allow herself the time to sit and contemplate the horrible truth, she would be fine.

At the party following the last night of work at Wat Yanyao, identifying more than five thousand bodies over almost six weeks, Wade got drunk and carelessly sentimental. He cornered her by the bar. "Ya know, Sophia, I just gotta take my baseball hat off to you. Considering what you been through and shit, you have put in one hell of an effort."

"What do you mean by zis?"

"I mean you've been through a lot… a lot of family troubles for sure."

She fixed him with a forty-five caliber glare that shot down all the fantasies he had concocted about seducing her in a matter of seconds. "My husband and my daughter are only missing and not dead. Do not ever speak to me again of zis." Her voice was so frosty that all he could do was stand there, frozen to the spot and feeling like a snowman in the glacial blast of air-conditioning, for twenty minutes.

Nothing messed with his self-confidence like getting rejected in such an icy and heartless way. Nothing made him question himself so ruthlessly either. The questioning led to doubting, the doubting led to drinking, and the drinking led to more questioning and doubting. His looks, his wit, his physique, his job prospects, his virility, his earning potential, his charm or lack thereof, all came into doubt and question.

The sum total was a feeling of gross inadequacy. No wonder she had given him the cold shoulder. She was too good for him anyway and he was a clown, a schmuck, an idiot. It was going to take weeks to dig himself out of this hole. He might never have another girlfriend or ever get laid again.

From what he heard on the grapevine, too devastated to leave his room, Sophia did not reappear the next day, nor the day after that or the following day either. A full week later, just as Wade was starting to come back to life again, he ran into one of the American volunteers in the lobby of the hotel, with its tacky Roman fountain full of golden cherubs and fancy carp. She was a Peace Corps volunteer who always wore what she thought were native clothes, like fisherman's pants, except none of the real Thai fishermen he had ever met wore those kinds of pants because they preferred blue jeans and T-shirts. Wade asked her what had happened to Sophia

"If you can believe it, like some creep suggested to her that her husband and daughter are dead, and the poor woman had a nervous breakdown. Yesterday her sister came to take her back to Paris."

Wade could not bring himself to admit that he was the creep in question.

What the hell happened? Sophia had seemed so tough and together. It was hard to believe that one conversation like that could push her over the edge. But she had been living in denial for weeks now and finally she could deny the truth no longer: her husband and her daughter, wherever their bodies lay, were dead.

Through some of the other volunteers, who formed an informal support group that lasted for years, Wade followed her decline: the slow descent into alcoholism, the premature retirement, the gradual seclusion until she became a total recluse, and finally, not four years after losing her husband and daughter, Sophia passed away too. The doctors said it was cirrhosis of the liver. Wade knew she'd died of a broken heart.

After the rejection and the news of her breakdown, he turned gloomy and introspective. Even the beer tasted bitter, as if it had been poisoned by all his regrets and inadequacies before it reached his taste buds. He would listen to Yves and Kendall, as they sat at the street-side bar, drinking, smoking and bitching about the media. By the time they were drunk the Aussie would be doing most of the ranting.

"When those media vultures piss off after two or three weeks in search of the next fucking disaster area or warzone, it leaves folks with the wrong impression. All they see on TV or in the paper is that the aid money poured in, the sick were taken to the hospital, the dead were honored, the authorities have the situation sorted, and everyone dealt with their grief and lives happily ever after. It's not on, is it? The biggest question goes unanswered. How the fuck does anyone live with a tragedy this big?"

Wade was still looking for that answer as the years drifted past like clouds slowly changing shape and, before he knew it, they'd already come and gone.

Whenever he thought that all those nightmares and experiences were gone for good, another wave of reminiscences washed over him, inspired by yet another earthquake or natural disaster, like the 2011 tsunami in Japan. He could not bring himself to follow that story, but he did send a thousand dollars to a small NGO working on environmental issues. Wade was surprised by how bitter he still felt towards all the bigger aid organizations and relief networks, which had turned down his numerous requests for grants ("We regret to inform you that your proposal does not meet our criteria for funding.") so that his dive shop and training center sank into a sea of red ink.

Fifteen years after that fateful Boxing Day, Wade was living on Barbados and managing another dive shop for an American owner. He had married a local woman and they had a young daughter together.

One of the volunteers whom he hadn't heard from for years sent him an email, along with an attachment for a feature story about the short life and sad death of a Swedish artist. At first Wade did not make the connection. It was only when he got to the paragraph where a gallery owner talked about the woman's strange beginnings as a painter after a few art therapy sessions in the wake of the tsunami that he understood who she was.

Astrid Eld had enjoyed a stratospheric rise in the art world of Europe, becoming the first artist to have solo shows at many prestigious galleries when she was still a teenager and already her paintings were selling for fifty thousand euros apiece. (Wade mumbled, "*Fifty k*? Wonder what that'd be after taxes? Man, I'm in the wrong line of work.") As her career rose, her mental health plummeted. She had several nervous breakdowns. She sought treatment for depression and substance abuse in exclusive clinics in the Swiss alps. At the age of twenty-three she died from an overdose of antidepressants, perhaps accidental, perhaps not, nobody knew for certain.

Wade opened the attachment of her last installation. He clicked on the image to enlarge it. Wait a second. He had seen this painting before. It was the one she had drawn in that hospital room all those years ago.

Except that sketch now filled the entire wall of a gallery. Amidst an ocean of towering black waves curved like shark fins, and dabs of rain shaped like teardrops, the only human figure in it was a girl, her head and blonde hair just visible above the waterline. The grey sky and the blue sun bled from multiple stab wounds.

Wade did not need to be an art critic to see that this was not only a reenactment of her and her sisters' ordeal, it was the state of her own mind, cast adrift in a sea of misery which had eventually drowned her. This was more of a suicide note, written in red, black, blonde and blue, than it was a painting.

Wade rubbed his forehead. Was there no end to this? Would he be laying on his deathbed remembering that hospital room in Takuapa and how he'd invited that little girl with the wounded leg to come trail riding in Jasper? "Don't worry about that little scratch. You're gonna grow up and still be a beautiful woman. When we find your parents we can all go horseback riding together." He still didn't know if that family had ever been reunited. After she got shipped back to the States, he never heard from her again.

On the other hand, if he had not taken a shine to Sophia and scuba-diving in Thailand, would he have ever wound up living and working in the Caribbean?

While they were standing next to each other in a supply line of people unloading foodstuffs from a truck, next to a Burmese fisherman, a Thai high-society lady with a shock of blue hair, a backpacker with dreadlocks and eyebrow piercings, a middle-aged couple from Scandinavia, and a volunteer doctor from Kenya, Wade told Yves, "I'm not sure if the tsunami is the worst thing that ever happened to me or the best."

"Exactly. My favorite opening lines to any book or column or article is still Dickens's *Tale of Two Cities*. 'It was the best of times. It was the worst of times.' Because you could say that about any era or time in your life and you'd always be right."

Wade's daughter with the mocha skin and mane of frizzy hair came barreling into the living room and launched herself into his arms. That was always the most gratifying part of raising his kids—the unconditional trust they placed in him. Because he had to live up to that trust, it made him a better and more reliable man.

He gave her a hug and tickled her ribs until she screamed and wriggled free.

She put her fingers on his cheek. "Daddy, why are you crying?"

"No big deal, got somethin' in my eye."

Sitting on his lap, she looked at the screen. "What's that?"

Sooner or later he'd have to tell her. The best and worst thing that had ever happened to him had to be passed down to the next generation. Now was as good a time as any to make a start. "Well, on the day after Christmas in the year 2004, your dear ol' dad was in southern Thailand. Little did he suspect…"

ONCE THE BODIES AND debris had been removed, the reconstruction of the Khao Lak beach community began in earnest. Wade set up his dive center in a Chinese-style shop-house down the road from a Royal Thai Navy gunboat. The three-ton vessel had been washed about a kilometer onshore and left at the bottom of a foot-hill as a memorial.

Yves said the boat was his boundary line. He would not live any closer to the ocean than that. When the next tidal waves came, he would be safe in his old house, next to an abandoned rubber tree plantation.

Wade saw little of him. He stopped answering phone calls and responding to emails. On those rare occasions when they met by accident at the supermarket in town and Wade asked what he was doing, he was elusive or mumbled something about "studying the black arts."

Under the circumstances and the horrible experiences he'd been through—the deaths of his dear friends, and his divorce-in-progress—

Wade cut him some slack. In time he would come around. He'd find some new buddies, rustle up a new gal. Wade still believed that time would heal those wounds, because memories dim, scars fade, and broken hearts mend eventually. That was the message Wade tried to ram home during their occasional phone conversations. But Yves defied him at every turn. "We're not talking about somebody chopping garlic, cutting their finger and going for four or five stitches. We're talking about the deaths of a quarter of a million people. We're talking about one of the worst natural disasters in the history of the planet. And who's to say that bones always mend the way they're supposed to? Have you seen Yai's thumb? He was bitten by a Siamese cobra ten years ago, and his thumb is still partially paralyzed and numb. It's never going to be like it was. He's damaged and the damage is permanent."

The most alarming thing about talking to him was the way he kept talking about the dead as if they were still alive.

Month after month, Wade looked for any sign of improvement on his part and a willingness to start socializing again. But he saw nothing on either score.

Just before the first anniversary, and the opening of the Tsunami Memorial Park and Museum in the village of Nam Khem (Salty Water), which had been pretty much obliterated, Wade jumped on his old dirt bike to drive over to his house. He doused the light and killed the engine before he got too close. If he didn't, Yves would have time to hide.

The decrepit, one-storey house sat in a dirt clearing in the middle of rows and rows of dead, tapped-out rubber trees. Every day around now, when the sky darkened and the insects ratcheted up their jamboree, Wade found himself remembering that this was Watermelon's favorite time of day. The indigo sky gave her childhood flashbacks of the natural dye her mother used to color the cotton shirts and pants she made by hand.

This was the curse, the worst curse of love, condemned to remember and unable to forget. Once, when they'd been sharing a post-sex cuddle and marinating in each other's sweat, Wade said, "The way

I see it, sweetie, after you fall in love with someone, it don't matter what happens or what they do, a part of you remains in love with them forever." On this point Wade wished he'd been wrong, but sure enough, whenever he thought he'd forgotten about her, some keepsake would turn up in the damnedest of places: an old photo of them smiling together in a field of Mexican sunflowers up in Mae Hong Son province, or a long-forgotten video from her in his inbox showing a cute kitty doing something silly. Healing this wound was going to take longer than he had expected. Yves was right; some injuries did not heal properly. Wade's collarbone still gave him grief once in a while. It was especially bad during the rainy season and when he went scuba-diving.

There were no lights on in Yves's house, but a faint glow came from the open windows. Wade crept up to the window, trying not to crunch any gravel or twigs. Squinting into the darkness, he could make out two people sitting on the floor beside an altar of wavering candles, smoking incense, and a severed pig's head. They spoke in low voices that underlined the seriousness of the conversation and the secrecy of their relationship. One of them was Yves. The other man appeared to be Thai. On his head sat a mask or crown. The room was too dim and shadowy to tell.

Yves said, "I need to speak to my departed friends. I have to know where they are now and find out what's on the other side."

"I can conjure them, but we need more herbs, more chanting. In certain places and at certain times, the membrane between our worlds is very thin."

"I hope so. This world is a wreck for me. Maybe there's something better on the other side."

"Maybe it's worse." He chuckled.

"What if there's nothing at all? Maybe death is The End in capital letters, like at the finale of a film, and what could be worse than that? Emptiness and black space for eternity… that's what scares me."

"I have been a ghost doctor for thirty years. Many of those in hell, many reborn as hungry ghosts, wish there was only emptiness and black space out there."

Wade figured a ghost doctor must be like a Thai version of a witch doctor or shaman, but this guy did not fit the stereotype he had in mind of a backwoods hillbilly with a string of bones or amulets around his neck. This man sounded eloquent. The way he spoke and the crown upon his head gave him a regal air.

He sparked up two more bowls of herbs. The smoke stung Wade's eyes. The smell was almost as pungent as marijuana and the taste was like puke. It made Wade's stomach try to turn itself inside out. He doubled over. He vomited.

When he straightened himself up and looked at his arm, the skin was giving off a fluorescent glow and slowly melting, to reveal the pink muscles and wriggling tendons beneath. The bones in his legs were melting too. Wade sank to his knees. His body dissolved into the earth, so all that remained was a dewdrop of consciousness that trembled on the edge of a leaf.

An ant the size of a dinosaur, its mandibles mashing, swallowed him. He fell into a dark cave, where he was no longer he but it, where he had no arms or legs or mouth. Everything he had ever been or done, every place he'd visited and every experience he'd had, was null and void. None of it mattered now.

The ant excreted him onto a rock where a sparrow stabbed him with its beak and picked him up, flying across the sky, to drop him on a green mango dangling from a tree where he was sucked up into the belly of a cloud that turned black and sent him hurtling back down to earth in a bullet of rainwater which landed on the head of a flying fish as it leapt from the ocean.

All these images flew past at the nauseating velocity of a carnival ride going around in circles. Life, death, rebirth. One cycle after another. It was nothing like his conception of life that revolved around the family, the job, the mortgage and car payments. All those cornerstones of his life had been swept away by this tsunami of brain chemicals. His old life was gone, his old self had died. In this new world he was but a tiny seed in a vast forest. If anything, it was more like Watermelon's conception of life. "There is no progress in Buddhism, only circles. We go around and around and around, but never go anywhere."

Standing above the engine of a whining jet-ski, Wade skimmed the waves of Khao Lak, flecks of salt coating his face and lips, as he searched for her. But she was not out on a jet-ski, as Yves had told him later, when the waves slam-dunked the coast. He was now in two places at once. Physically, he was back on Boxing Day 2004, but mentally it had to be some time later because he realized that bastard had lied to him.

Backing off on the throttle, he banked into a turn towards the ocean as the house-high waves came barreling towards the beach. Imprinted on the whitewater's surface were a thousand screaming faces, blood pouring from their eyes and mouths.

Wade woke up in a bed beside Watermelon, who was cold and dead and smelled like rotten fish. Wade bolted upright but she came with him. He looked down. Their torsos, hips and legs had been fused together. Between them they only had two arms.

Holding her up with an arm around her shoulder, Wade struggled to get to his feet. Walking anywhere was like running in the three-legged race back in junior high school, except now his running mate was a corpse.

They lurched into the bathroom and entered the reception area of the district hospital in Takupa. It was bedlam: bodies and stretchers everywhere, patients weeping and moaning, people shouting at each other in a dozen different languages, more of the injured being wheeled through the door in wheelchairs or hobbling past bandaged up like mummies.

Sophia, dressed in a white doctor's coat, approached. She did not seem to recognize him. "How may I help you, monsieur?"

"Sophia, it's me, Wade."

"Do I know you?"

"For sure. Listen, I'm real sorry I said that about your husband and daughter and stuff. I was hammered, eh? I sure as hell didn't mean to upset you like that."

"I do not know what you speak. Is zere a problem?"

"Uh yeah, you could say that. Check it out. I have a dead gal attached to me. Do you think you could separate us?"

"Not without killing you. You two are Siamese twins."

Watermelon screamed, "Why do you always flirt with other ladies? I cannot trust you never."

"Honey, you're alive."

"I don't love you now. I want to separate *na*."

Grunting and gritting her teeth, she pulled and pulled until she tore her leg free, then her hip and finally her torso. Wade fell flat on his face, snapping off a few of his teeth, but felt no pain. Without her he could no longer walk or even stand up. As she hobbled away on a crutch, Wade crawled behind her on his stomach, yelling and sobbing, while Sophia laughed and the Swedish girl painted a portrait of him.

Wade woke up on the floor of his bathroom, clad only in his boxer shorts and hung over as fuck. Groggily, he thought, this is some seriously bad shit, man. I ain't had a trip this bad since gobbling those five hits of acid at the Black Sabbath gig in Frisco.

By the time he finally got through to Yves's cell phone some three weeks later to tell him about the bad trip and ask him what was going on, Yves said, "That bit of secondhand smoke you had was mild. We've been doing doses five times that strong and blasting off into the next dimension. It's all part of my apprenticeship to the spirit medium and black magician. I want to be like Faust and cut a deal with the devil to find out the secrets of the universe."

"Okay, bud. Just make sure you keep paying those utility bills. Even Lucifer himself needs a hot shower sometimes."

Yves didn't get the joke. He went silent. Then he hung up.

It was useless trying to talk to him anymore. He had better get Zara on the horn. Wade needed a second opinion on whether it was time to get him to a shrink or have him shipped home in a straitjacket, before he did some serious damage to himself.

IN HIS YOUTH, YVES had once thought that "love at first sight" was among the corniest of romantic clichés. It never happened in real life. It was a cliché contrived by romance novelists looking for a shortcut between the ballroom and the bedroom, hacks who rhymed "love" with "dove" on Valentine's Day cards, and popular songwriters who had to condense an entire love saga into two verses, three choruses and four minutes.

Lust at first sight was common enough for most men, but love? That could not happen overnight, let alone in a stray glance or a drunken leer.

Love, in his youth and Bohemian circles, was a comparing and twinning of tastes in books, music, films, art, booze and narcotics that was forged in a blast furnace of sex, lit by candles in wine bottles hurling shadows across band photos, fine art prints and film posters that served as a theatrical backdrop. Over a few weeks or months, the affair played and guttered out amongst a rotating circle of parties, gallery openings, gigs in dive bars, plays in lofts, drugs in bathrooms, and art-house films in musty old repertory cinemas with moldering velvet curtains and chandeliers whose light had gone grey with dust spiders. By then, whatever passion had not been incinerated in bed or in a bong or both was funneled into arguments of increasing acrimony.

All his preconceived notions about love and sex were altered forever after on a Sunday afternoon in Barcelona. Still reeling from a smashing encounter with a bottle of absinthe the night before, he was walking the cobblestoned backstreets of the "Gothic District" in search of the best hangover cure and pick-me-up in Spain: the *carajillo*, a jolt of coffee strengthened by a shot of brandy. After two shots and a few cigarettes, the heavy gloom of the hangover had only begun to lift so he could raise his eyes from the wooden floor that served as an ashtray and a sleeping place for dogs, which wandered in off the street. He looked up as a woman who was part sculpture, part painting, strode into the bodega. As tall and thin as a model, she had a mane of scarlet hair that hung down to her hips. Her tight black jeans, the loose peasant's blouse and long black boots were streaked with different shades of paint.

She was not just an artist eager to promote herself as such, she was the personification of all the European artworks he had ever been enchanted by: Klimt's red-haired heroine covered in gold dust and kisses; Modigliani's muse Jeanne Hebuterne with her long face and lily-slender fingers; Raphael's pale and mournful Madonna; Max Ernst's surrealist vision of a woman with the plumage of an owl.

He was not the only one whose attention she had commanded. Almost every man in this basement wine cellar and café was staring at her through the curtains and tatters of cigarette smoke. She leaned over the bar to order something (what an ass), then turned around to return the stares of the dozen men, while wearing a Mona Lisa smile. She seemed amused by all the attention but a little smug too, as though she expected it and it didn't bother her; she could handle herself. Seeing that she was not intimidated by them, even though she was the only woman there, the men resumed their conversations and stopped staring, all their hastily erected fantasies reduced to rubble.

She looked at Yves for a few seconds. Her smile dropped and she walked straight over to sit next to him. He did not want her to see him from this close. He was hungover, his clothes were rumpled, his hair unwashed. He was not nearly handsome enough for a woman of her statuesque beauty. So he kept his head turned away from her and stared at a bull-fighting poster for an upcoming event (which would be reviewed in the art pages of the Spanish papers not the sports sections, he remembered) and kept smoking while his forehead and armpits oozed sweat.

She tapped on his shoulder and said something in Spanish. Slowly and fearfully, Yves turned to face her. Not many women he'd ever seen were blessed to have such a lithesome physique *and* such an exquisite face, pale and round as a pearl, with deep brown eyes that radiated curiosity and mischief in equal measures.

Her accent, once they worked out that neither of them was Spanish and settled on speaking English, provided a harsh counterpoint to those delicate features. It was a Germanic sledgehammer which squashed consonants flat and pulverized vowels; an accent which left no room for doubt or irony.

"You know who you sound like? Your accent reminds me of Marlene Dietrich or Nico from the Velvet Underground."

She did not smile at the compliment as he'd expected. "I am not from Germany. I am from Linz in Austria."

"Ah, yes—the birthplace of Adolph Hitler, the failed artist."

"Many people know this already. It is not so interesting. And I do not wish to have conversations about trivia and historical facts. I am trying to overthrow bourgeoisie conventions and the mundane in my art. So I disdain celebrity gossip and polite falsehoods spoken for the sake of filling the void that is modern living and hollow materialism. Silence is better than this emptiness." Almost apologetically, she allowed herself to smile. "If we are going to become lovers we must think of more interesting things to say that go straight to our hearts and discuss our real feelings."

If we are going to become lovers? The most beautiful woman he had ever met could not possibly be thinking about letting him share her bed after they had only spoken for five minutes. He didn't even know her name yet and now he was too agitated to ask. What was going on here? Was she a prostitute in artist's drag? Had she just escaped from a mental institution? Was she stoned out of her mind? But she didn't look stoned, and her breath did not smell of liquor.

Yves was pouring sweat and exhibiting all the tics and itches of a monkey with a bad case of lice.

"Am I making you nervous with my straight-forward talking?" Her laughter was a rich and throaty baritone, a few degrees warmer than her voice. So that was what lurked behind her enigmatic smile: a love of provocation and a passion for shocking people and trashing taboos.

It was one of her many traits that he sometimes admired but would never quite get used to. The other person's social standing did not matter. Neither did the situation. When one of the biggest European fashion photographers asked her opinion of his exhibition at the opening party, she said, "Technically it is very good, but none of these pictures make me feel anything. It is technique at the expense of emotion. None of them seem very original either. Excuse me, I need another glass of wine." The photographer looked crestfallen. Yves and everyone else within earshot cringed. Yet, she was not trying to be cruel or egotistical; she was simply stating her opinion. Behind the photographer's back, few would disagree with her assessment, and many were secretly glad that she'd stood up to this egomaniac and put him in his place.

Her outspokenness, combined with her height, her hip-length hair and her penchant for dressing like a Bohemian bazaar, would soon make her a very recognizable figure in the salons and galleries of Europe, after Yves helped her to discover a mode of expression bold enough to match her outsized personality.

She touched his hand, another bid for attention, for control. When no one was looking at her she seemed smaller, sadder. Her main vices, he quickly discovered, were an addiction to attention and a craving for control. "You are reminding me of someone… maybe an existential philosopher and novelist like Jean Paul Sartre."

He had never heard that before. Yves looked down at his rumpled black trench coat, his old black trousers spotted with cigarette ashes, and the unpolished shoes. "Thanks, I guess. Sartre was not a man known for his great looks, but under the shabbily dressed circumstances, that's very generous of you. I'd thought I was looking more like a down-and-out detective from an unpopular film noir set in Barcelona."

She laughed—charitably, he thought. "I think old noir novels are very funny." She did a passable impersonation of a male American voice, "That babe was a real looker who had two good reasons for wearing a tight sweater," and burst out laughing. Half the heads in the room swiveled in their direction.

Yves was relieved to discover that she did have a sense of humor after all, but the comic reprieve was short lived. "Tell me something interesting about yourself and why you are here in Spain."

"I'm trying to finish a novel and this is the most inspiring, artistic and magical city on earth to write in and about. For one thing the setting is almost perfect. You've got the beaches near here on the Mediterranean, and some are nudist. You've got the mountain in the middle of the city, which is Montjuic in Catalan, the mount of Jupiter, the God of War in Roman mythology. You've got the old Roman tombs and the Greek walls in this part of the city and the Gothic cathedral, which is one of only two churches that the anarchists did not burn down when they rounded up all the priests and nuns and shot them in the street in the nineteen thirties. The other one they spared was Gaudi's still unfinished La Sagrada Familia, because those two churches had outstanding artistic merit, or so they said. Every morning when I go to teach English at this real estate company where all the students smoke in the boardroom and the coffee machine has beer, I pass by the hotel that George Orwell guarded during the Spanish Civil War. You really have to read his book about those times called *Homage to Catalunia*, which spells out most of the ideas he later used in *Nineteen Eighty-Four*, particularly in regard to propaganda and how they edited and censored his articles about the war. The subway station where I get off is right beside the so-called street Calle de la Discordia with all those buildings by Muntaner and Gaudi's creations with the balconies like skulls, the mushroom-like turret and all those sculptures on the roof and wave-like lines, because Gaudi said nature has no straight lines so neither should architecture. On Sundays, when the museums are open to the public for free, I like to wander around them with all these Spanish families. Here, art is not elitist like it is back in North America. It's family entertainment for the masses. Over at the Palace of Music, designed by Muntaner with all these pillars featuring the winged horse sculptures, or Pegasus, of Greek mythology, there's a special rate for paupers and students on Sunday morning. Last week, we saw Mahler's *Symphony No. 1*. I'm not really a connoisseur of classical music, but this was an intense performance. At the end, the crowd threw roses on the stage for ten minutes and brought the orchestra back for three encores. Never seen that happen anywhere else. I mean, just look at the wine barrels in this bodega. People wander in here with their empty Pepsi bottles and get a refill of wonderful Rioja wine for a few dollars. No, this city has it all, the wine, the churches, music, history, art, public parks, nightlife, and you probably haven't even tried the grilled rabbit with this garlic sauce called *ali olli* yet or the fried octopus for tapas. Barcelona *es fantastico!*"

She began clapping loud enough to cause more stares. "That is the most beautiful summation of any city I have heard during all of my life. It is like you are knowing my mind. You must be a very good writer and you must give me some of your work to read."

Surprised by how complimentary and enthusiastic she was, he shrugged and looked away. "Thank you. I'm working on some travel stories too. That's some of my research and background details."

She took his hand in hers. "Come now. We must go and explore this fantastical city together."

They stood up and this was another point of convergence in their favor; they were almost exactly the same height. She said, "Height makes a big difference. Tall people always stand out. We cannot hide in the crowd and we can see things the shorter people cannot. Does it not seem to you that we walk faster too and are always waiting for other people to catch up?"

"Yeah, *exactamente.*"

She wanted to explore all the backstreets, landmarks and plazas of the Barrio Gotico. These streets were so narrow that the sunlight never scoured their gutters and every turn was another detour in the history of art and architecture: the street where Picasso painted his "The Whores of Avinyon" (the women long gone but the building and balcony where they used to sit to attract customers still there); Gaudi's first commission, the fountain in Plaza Real; the mosaic by Joan Miro on La Rambla, where hundreds of caged birds sang louder than the traffic and the buskers ranged from mimes and a juggler with chainsaws to flamenco dancers and a classical duo of violin and cello. Near Calle Escudellers stood an old wooden bar from the 1920s called Solo Quatro Gatos ("Only Four Cats") where Dali, Miro, Andre Breton and the other surrealists had once gathered. In there the waiters still conjured up the "green fairy" of absinthe in the traditional way by placing a cube of sugar on a special fork covering the glass before pouring water over it to dilute the licorice-tasting liquor.

Their walk through literary and art history was interrupted every time she saw a stray cat and knelt down to pet them. If they looked hungry she'd buy cans of tuna for them. Yves did not like cats yet. Every time she stopped to play with one, he'd curse them under his breath as "whiskered weasels" and "furry freeloaders."

Their happiest discovery of the night was La Paloma (The Dove), a dance hall from the nineteen twenties, which still had the same chandeliers, red velvet walls and candelabras on each table. Onstage stood an ensemble dressed in matching dinner jackets and ties playing big band hits ("In the Mood"), jazz standards by Ella Fitzgerald and Count Basie's Orchestra ("Dream a Little Dream of Me"), as well as bossa nova, flamenco, Elvis, and The Beatles.

In the only city on earth ever ruled by an anarchist government, which had prohibited the use of the formal word for "you" (*usted*), commandeered all motor vehicles to use as public transport, and attempted to level the class system so that everyone was equal and no one in their army had to take orders from anyone else, the atmosphere in those Barcelona nightspots back in the early nineties was friendly anarchy. As the gay painter from Valencia who lived with Yves said, "Franco the dictator died in 1975 and we're still celebrating in 1992." The only rules in effect seemed to be that everyone had to get euphorically drunk, everyone had to dance, and everyone had to be as gleeful and raucous as possible.

Yves had always been a reluctant and awkward dancer, but she grabbed his hand to pull him out on the dance floor. She had that rare ability, mostly seen in the very best teachers, to make everyone she came in contact with rise above their limitations. Because she was such a free spirit, it encouraged him to shed his inhibitions too. On the dance floor, teenagers were leaping around while old couples in evening attire, who had probably courted on this same dance floor, waltzed past doing the foxtrot, amid a sprinkling of expats and tourists trying to keep in step with the percolating Brazilian rhythms of "The Girl from Ipanema" by Astrud Gilberto and Stan Getz.

Dancing with her was a form of public foreplay. After brushing against each other a few times, after circling around each other and moving their hips in a pantomime of sex, she wrapped her arms around his waist and initiated the first kiss.

At midnight, the ritual was that the patrons would line up on either side of the stage. Then the club owner, nicknamed "El Tigre" for his alleged carnal prowess, and dressed flamenco style in red and black, strutted down the line as the crowd clapped and cheered to a Latin backbeat. Whenever he saw a woman he liked he would flick a belt around her hips to pull her out of the line so they could perform a mating dance together. As the belt went around her hips, Yves cringed. This was going to be ugly. She would slap his face, remind him that the word macho comes from Spanish, call him a sexist pig, maybe complain, as some Western women did, that Spanish men hissed at them like cats when they walked by.

On the contrary, she said something in his ear that made both of them grin. El Tigre pulled the belt away and held out his hand for Yves to shake. In Spanish, he told him, "You are a very lucky man."

As he danced away and the crowd resumed clapping, Yves yelled in her ear, "What did you say to him?"

Her mouth brushed against his ear and each word she spoke pulsated in his inner ear with her breath and the rhythm of the words. "I told him he is a wonderful dancer, and I would be honored to dance with him, but I am in love with another man. So I cannot dance with him."

Their eyes met. They did not look away. The patrons, the band, the club disappeared. Yves felt like he was standing beside the lip of a cliff, waiting to dive into the water below. It was a long way down. It could be dangerous. There could be rocks just beneath the surface. Still staring in her eyes and smiling a little, he said, "I want to say the same to you, if it's not a bourgeoisie convention that you are trying overthrow in your art, of course. But don't you think we should exchange names first?" She laughed and kissed him again.

Even if he had set out to write some erotic fiction set in Barcelona, he could never have come up with an outline like this. Meeting an artist from Hitler's birthplace in a basement wine cellar and, after a short chat and a long walk, two coffees, a few glasses of absinthe, some red wine, and a pack of Fortuna cigarettes, not five hours later they were confessing their love for each other and making out on the dance floor of a museum-like club to the tune of Latin jazz—and they still had not exchanged names yet!

Zara (she finally confessed before closing time, the name Slovenian), treated sex as another form of sculptural art, kneading his flesh like clay, melting his resistance and bones in the kiln of her sex and mouth, insisting on making eye contact in the midst of the deepest penetration and having the frankest discussions with his sweat dripping on her face. "You are making me so crazy right now. Don't cum yet. I want to reach my second climax. Here I will grab your balls." "You're the only woman who can keep me in a permanently erect state even after I cum. God, making love with you is like being a lightning rod in the middle of an electrical storm. It's scary and beautiful at the same time." "You are a poet of fucking." "Or just a fucking poet?" Zara laughed. "Do a sixty-nine now. I want to taste your cock and feel your tongue in my ass."

Barcelona became their alfresco bedroom and a series of stages and backdrops for their acts of lust. Stumbling out of bars at 3 a.m. in the Barrio Gotico, they had sex against the old city walls pockmarked with bullet holes from where revolutionaries had been executed by firing squad back in the eighteenth century, on the beach after a midnight screening of Ingmar Bergman's documentary about a performance of Mozart's *Magic Flute*, with the melodies still coursing through their veins, the sand still warm from the sunshine and the moonlight making the waves phosphorescent, on a bench in the cactus garden at the base of Mount Jupiter on a weekday afternoon, hidden by a blanket and surrounded by twenty-meter-tall cacti imported from Death Valley and, on the floor of her studio, their bodies covered in paint.

Afterwards, Yves pointed out the handprints, the curved lines of their buttocks, the dashes of hipbones and smears of nipples, the head of an uncircumcised cock that looked like a tulip bulb, all combined with the palate of mixed pigments they had left on the old canvas. He said, "This is a whole new genre, babe. I call it 'sexpressionism.' In fact, let's create a dozen more for your new solo show. And to think that all these artists moan and bitch about the agonies of the creative process when I've never had more fucking fun in my whole wretched and miserable life."

Zara was at her most beautiful and innocent looking when she tipped her head back and closed her eyes to laugh. "You are so funny. Every day I learn something new and fascinating about you that makes me love you more."

"I can't believe how sweet and warm-hearted you are. At first I thought you were just this ice queen and frigid intellectual."

"But I am an ice queen and frigid intellectual. You are the only man who can make me melted or warmed over. No, we say it in German like... oh fuck it."

"Wow. I never knew that expression was German. Yes, fuck it. Now you're talking my language."

They kissed again; they could not stop kissing.

Initially, the canvases were conceived as a joke between them, an artistic diary of their sex life. But Zara's agent thought they were saleable, so did the curators she knew and, much more significantly, so did the buyers, patrons and collectors who responded to her taste for provocation and her wild image, coupled with a frank approach to eroticism that guaranteed generous amounts of publicity.

"I don't believe in the bourgeoisie means of controlling women through marriage, making babies, and monogamy," she told one male art critic. "I've already had more than one hundred and fifty lovers. The top dozen were worth a painting or two each and all the others only a few dribbles of white." She laughed and the critic blushed. "This is a new genre I have created, which encourages women to open up and express themselves in different ways. I call it 'sexpressionism.'"

That interview, with all her thieving and ludicrous statements, would form the framework for many of their arguments over the next decade. He'd say, "I can't believe you'd lie like that just to sell some paintings. Counting me, you've only had ten lovers so far. And I also can't believe you'd take all the credit for my ideas and sell the imprints of our love life to the highest bidder. You are the worst sort of art whore there is."

Zara's counterpoints were just as malicious and precise. "You are jealous that I am more famous, rich, and successful than you are. You may pretend to be a feminist and female positive, but you are secretly embarrassed to have a woman who supports you and pays the rent and living expenses."

During his compulsive daydreams, while living in the old wooden house in the dead rubber tree plantation, Yves did not rerun many of their old fights, the endless splinters and reconciliations. He wanted to remain in Barcelona during the summer of 1992, in the run-up to the Olympic Games and the Cultural Olympics, so he would not have to return to southern Thailand during the post-tsunami cleanup operations of 2005 because, where others saw the ruins of a resort or a mattress torn and gutted, he saw the fallout of an eleven-year, on-and-off-again marriage.

But his most precious recollections of their early days together had now been invaded and contaminated by a phantom presence. Lurking in the corner, just off stage, stood that little Quebecois daredevil, poetry professor, and pathological exaggerator.

In directing and stage-managing his memories, Yves could never control the flash-forward to a scene which had not happened yet, where he was sitting on Stephan's chest with his hands around his throat, and Stephan was thrashing around like a hooked fish as Yves crushed his windpipe with his thumbs so he choked to death on his own blood, while Zara, gagged and tied to a chair, watched, her eyes almost a complete whiteout with fear. Then he went after her...

YVES HAD TOLD HIM that Zara was mean, petty, vain, that she talked about herself and her art all the time. But when they met at the resort, and now spoke regularly on the phone, Wade had found her both humble and approachable. She talked more about Yves and Stephan than herself, and when she did talk about the art world it was only to mocks its pretensions and the pretentiousness of her fellow artists.

"You sound to me very fortunate, Wade. You have spent your life around nice, normal people who behave in nice, normal ways, unless they get drunk and are bored of being so nice and normal all the time. But you have not been too much around artists, writers, musicians, photographers, film and theatre people, who are mostly egotistical jerks with an over-inflated sense of self-importance. I suppose the biggest difference between these two different mentalities is that a plumber or a cashier in a supermarket do not sit around talking about my work, my work, my work, all the time, and why the critics do not understand my work, and the public does not appreciate my work enough, and I do not make enough money from my work. So I must start rivalries with critics and other artists whose work is much worse than mine but they make so much more money, because I am great, I am a genius, I deserve to be treated very much more special than the plumber and cashier." As she spoke, Wade could picture her smiling snidely and brushing back her long red hair. He also heard the ripples of laughter bubbling up under the words. By the time she got to the punch line of her diatribe, "The sad truth is I am no better than any of the other artists," Wade's stomach was quivering with suppressed laughter that he had to spout.

"Always wondered what those weirdos are like. Thanks for the inside scoop, Zorro. Hope you don't mind the new nickname."

"Then I hope you don't mind if I call you Zoroaster."

"Who's that?"

"A Persian mystic who started his own religion."

"Oh Christ, not an A-rab."

"That is very sophisticated of you, Wade. I was quite sure you would call them 'sand niggers.'"

"Hearty har har. Ya know somethin', you're quite a bit funnier and more sarcastic than Yves had led me to believe."

"Why? What did he tell you?"

"Let's not get into that. I ain't no snitch or gossip, and I'm not taking sides, see? What you tell me is our business and what he tells me don't go no farther than my eardrums."

"Fair enough. I like a person with principles. You have integrity and that makes me know why Yves would trust you. He trusts very few people."

"Tell me about it. Was he always so suspicious and paranoid?"

"Hmmm…" more of a thinker than a talker, Zara would often pause for twenty or thirty seconds in their conversations. Wade used the lapses to continue cleaning the scuba tanks in the back of his dive shop. "Do you think he was seriously damaged in the tsunami? I am talking on the subject of psychological damage."

"For sure. He doesn't leave his house for days on end, doesn't answer the phone, doesn't respond to emails. Far as I can tell, the only one he hangs out with on a regular basis is this mangy cat with fucked up fangs. When he comes into the town of Khao Lak once or twice a month and we get shitfaced, he talks some crazy talk, like how him and the cat are practicing telepathy together. I was ribbin' him about it, eh? I said, what's he saying now?" Wade did a meowing cat voice: 'Gimme some tuna or I'll shit on the floor.'"

Zara laughed easily and often. She especially liked jokes about sex and scatology. Her warbling laugh reminded him of the cry of the loon, those lake-dwelling birds on the one-dollar coins known as "loonies."

Wade called out to one of the Thai dive-masters walking past in his wetsuit. "Did you check the BCDs yet? Remember, safety first. Let's get a move on. Chop chop. " Wade let out a long sigh. The heat was making him drowsy and grumpy. During the hot season, he was taking four showers a day but, ten minutes after toweling off, he was sweating like a pig again. "Sorry, Zorro, but my patience is growing mighty thin with some of my slack-ass employees in this forty-degree Celsis weather we been havin'. Many Thai women are good workers, but most of the men are lazy, useless fucks who won't exert much effort 'cept if they're in a bar or brothel. And, I hate to say it, but our grants are getting even thinner these days. Three years after the disaster and everyone has forgotten about us."

"I could do a benefit exhibition for your NGO. The last show we did, if I could find the spreadsheet on my computer, yes, I am seeing it now. We raised almost eighty thousand euros to build that school and orphanage for all the children who lost their parents. The construction costs are far above the three estimates I got, but Thailand is still a Third World country in many ways, at least in terms of corruption and injustice. If we must lose thirty percent to corruption I think this is acceptable."

"That's sweet of you, and I might take you up on it in the next six months or so, but let's see how we go."

"Are you sure, Zoroaster? You don't have to be so proud and manly all the time. Asking for help from a woman is not a sign of weakness."

"Yeah, it's cool. I'm not completely fuckin' incompetent, ya know." Zara knew when to back off. He could say that for her. It was a trait he wished more women possessed.

After she got pregnant, their conversations mostly revolved around that and family matters.

"I am almost forty now and I could not wait anymore for Yves to grow up and become stable and responsible. The chance of a miscarriage increases when a woman is in her forties and many other problems can happen, birth defects, etcetera. I am worried, still very worried, yes, but tell me about your boys and their mother."

Zara's command of English was strong but not when it came to the subtleties of politeness. Her requests came off as commands. Wade didn't mind. He was tickled pink that she even bothered to ask him about his family.

"I thought I told you about that. My wife was an ex-biker chick who did five years in the slammer for dealing drugs. But I didn't know any of that until quite a while after we met, back when I was the manager for this Canuck metal band called Satan's Sledgehammer, which was a good name for us 'cause we were heavy as fuck. The first few years I was with her were fine, even great. But when the boys were five and six my old lady relapsed into her old ways and left me for this other biker. So I had to stop working the oil rigs, which was fine by me. Being a rig pig is dirty, dangerous work, especially when those chains fly off. Christ, I seen guys lose fingers, arms, even a leg once. So I came back to Jasper, took the job in the ski resort and raised those boys up myself, with a lot of help from my mom and sister."

"Tell me something more about the boys and your relationship."

"I love kids and they're full-on energy. They're like chainsaws. Just before they run outta gas they get this last spurt of energy. But I'll level with you. Here's one of the things I love the most about having kids. When I'm dust, they're still gonna be walkin' around with my DNA, then passing it along to their kids. Before you know it it's the year 2300, the spaceships are taking people to live on Mars and there's a little piece of Wade Miranoski out there floatin' around the Milky Way Galaxy. Amen and hallelujah. Like the good book says, be fruitful and multiply."

"I did not know you are so religious."

Wade flinched. He had to lie. "I ain't really, but anything that justifies screwing a lot is fine by me, thank you very much." Wade caught himself laughing and smiling in the mirror. He had never been much of a handsome stud but he liked the way his face had aged. Many more signs of amusement bracketed his mouth than frown lines worried his forehead. And his laughter still came from that same boyish place, ringing down the years like the happiest sound of his childhood, the bell on the ice-cream vendor's bicycle that he rang as he pedaled down their block after school, not like some men of his age whose laughter got stuck in their bowels and came out of their mouths like they were passing gas.

"You must be very happy in Thailand with all those pretty young girls around."

"Oh god, that's what all the Western women say, with this real judgmental tone in their voices and a sour look on their faces, like they just got an enema with lime juice and vinegar. Scuse me, ladies, but you didn't pay no attention to me back in the West for the past ten years, now you're pissed 'cause I'm havin' some fun and don't need you anymore? How hypocritical is that, eh? On this one I'm gonna go with Yves from that book of his and say that Thailand is not the sex capital of the world, but it might be the bedroom farce capital. All is not as it seems."

Holding the cell phone to his ear, Wade walked out to the front of the dive shop to see if any customers needed help. Zara kept prattling on about sexism and exploitation, but he wasn't listening. Those were theories not real life. Electing herself to be the spokes-woman for all these other gals, who supposedly didn't know any better about their own country, was patronizing. Let them deal with their shit and let her deal with hers. That was his motto.

The foyer and front office resembled an aquarium in a state of suspended animation, with posters of whale sharks, scorpion fish, manta rays and psychedelic coral on the walls. His front-desk clerk was asleep in her chair. He suspected she'd been dipping her fingers in the cash box, too. This was quite the opposite of Zara's rant about Western men exploiting women from Third World countries. But he couldn't be bothered to bring it up. It sounded too petty and he was not going to play the blame-free saint card. "Tell you the truth, Zorro, all I been doin' lately on that front is going over to watch some peelers in the go-go bars on Phuket—"

"Peelers?"

"Yeah, that's what we call strippers back on the prairies, 'cause they peel off their clothes. Clever, eh? So I drain a few beers, pick up a peeler, and get the pipes cleaned once a month."

"Oh, you make it sound so romantic, much the same as a bowel movement." He could see her smiling again—see that mischievous streak in her deep brown eyes. Zara loved pushing his buttons.

"Now you're catchin' on. We're not talking morals or exploita-tion or feminism, we're talking about bodily functions, plain and simple. It's hard to legislate them, eh?"

"Yes, but how much does it cost to rent your mouth or asshole?"

"Now now. Let's put the brakes on and not get into a potty-mouth contest. Truth is, I'd like to find a relationship that was more long term, but I had a very special gal before. Watermelon was one in six billion, or whatever the population of the earth is now, and damn near impossible to replace."

Even across thousands of miles of fibreoptic cables, Zara's inten-sity could be felt as a low electrical hum. Talking to her was like standing outside a power plant, close enough to see the "Danger High Voltage" sign. One minute she was throwing off sparks of anger and the next she was all sweet and considerate again. When Yves told him that their marriage had been tempestuous and full of upheavals, Wade did not doubt that that was the truth.

Zara asked, "Do you still miss her very much?"

"Yeah, I do actually. That's one thing that keeps me here. See I set up the foundation for this training center in her name. She was really into making good karma and repenting for her sins. That's what this operation is all about. So failure is not an option. Bailing out ain't an option either. Come hell or high water, I'm anchored here for the time being, but if business doesn't improve and some more grants come through then we'll go belly up for sure."

"I admire your stubbornness. But I hope you can admire mine when I say the offer of the benefit exhibition is still—how is it? In the pipeline or on the table?"

"On the table is fine. All righty. I appreciate that and I admire your stubbornness too. Wherever the cash comes from, it's all for a good cause."

Every time they spoke, it always concluded on the same hopeless and hopeful note. "Do you think he will ever talk to me and Stephan again? We want to make amends and not hold any grudges. Life is too short for all of this bitterness and nonsense."

"I agree with you, but there's no telling with that guy. He's a stubborn, vindictive prick. Whenever I bring up your name, he still goes, 'Please don't talk about the dead. It's blasphemous. By that I mean they're dead to me.'"

"At least he stopped sending me death threats after the first two years. Stephan was very disturbed by his graphic description of how he was planning on breaking his windpipe so he would choke to death on his own blood."

"Him and his writing, you and your art. You two were the perfect shock rock couple."

Any references to them as a couple would choke her up. After that the conversation would falter and break down.

In the wake of Watermelon's disappearance and Sophia's snub, Wade was on familiar terms with that choking sensation, when the vocal cords get caught in a tug-of-war between the heart and the head.

BEFORE HE CLOSED DOWN the dive center and bailed out of Thailand for good, Wade thought he would stop by Yves's haunted house to say goodbye and see if he could get him to make an appointment with a doctor or psychiatrist.

Yves didn't look so bad, but he didn't look so good either: a tall, lean figure dressed entirely in black. He'd cut his hair as short as a monk's, but that was about the only difference Wade could see in his physical appearance.

His living room was a shambles. Stacks of books, newspapers and magazines dominated the debris. As the indigo twilight crept through the open windows, dousing a little of the tropical heat with a few hot breaths of wind, the only light came from a couple of candles on the coffee table and a lamp made out of coral on the Buddhist altar. The room smelled like a cat's litter box that needed emptying.

Clearing a place for himself to sit on the couch, Wade said, "Christ, this place is a pigsty. What do you say I send my maid over for an afternoon?"

"No, thanks. I find chaos quite conducive to the creative process."

Wade's opinions of him kept wavering. At times he seemed like he had his shit together. He had certainly retained his bookworm eloquence. But the worrying part was that he'd drift off into these long silences. Wade was not sure where he'd gone but he was not in that room anymore. His mind was elsewhere.

"Are you still studying with that spirit medium or ghost doctor?"

Yves, sitting with his legs crossed looking at the candles on the coffee table not Wade off to his left, said nothing.

Wade repeated the question. Yves said nothing.

After another long pause, Yves said, "No, I stopped those shamanistic and chemical explorations. They're too much like short cuts. The true adept in the mystical arts needs to generate more psychic power and have more discipline. So Yai recommended a really good temple and meditation master to me, and I'm practicing with him now."

"You still communicate a lot with the snake-handler, do ya?"

"In a manner of speaking, yes."

"Where is he?"

"In a different realm."

"Could I talk to him?"

"Depends… probably not. Takes a lot of spiritual power to punch through into that next dimension."

Wade had had enough. They had now been repeating variations on this conversation for the past two years. "Hey Yves, listen to me, okay?"

"What?"

"I want you to look at me and listen to me very closely. Okay, good. Yai and Watermelon and Kendall all died in the tsunami, okay?"

He considered this for a few seconds while continuing to stare at the candles. "Maybe to you they did. But I can still feel them all around us. Can't you?"

"No, not really. Sure I think about 'em sometimes, but those could be memories."

"No, that's them contacting you from the next world."

"Do you remember what everyone who was in the tsunami said? It was like being spun around in a gigantic washing machine. 'Cept there ain't no boulders or boat engines or refrigerators in a washing machine. Something like that could knock a few screws loose…" Wade waited for the realization to sink in. But Yves just sat there staring at the candles. "So all I'm saying, bud, is that you should think about going to a doctor and having a brain scan, EKG, the whole nine yards, and see if anything's wrong."

After a long pause, Yves said, "There are millions of other galaxies out there and universes and planets and alternate universes and wormholes and black holes. The last story I read, cosmologists have now said that our universe is 3.5 billion years old, but they still don't know what substance makes up about ninety percent of the universe. They call it 'dark matter.' And all of that applies to psychology and the human mind too. So it's difficult to come up with any hard and fast theories about what's real and what's not when all these other possibilities exist. I know you won't believe this, but I've become a kind of spirit medium. The dead can speak through me. In fact, the only reason I still exist is to tell their stories. That's my sole purpose. I am but an empty vessel for the gods, ghosts and demons to inhabit and speak through."

Wade grinned. "You got any room in that vessel for a cute gal who's hot to trot?"

Yves ignored him. "Look at White Fang crouched on top of the bookcase there. He's in the same pose as that famous statue of the Sphinx, which is appropriate because the ancient Egyptians first domesticated cats some three thousand years ago, which is still but a second in the history of the universe, estimated to be some 3.45 billion years old. But you look at him and all you see is a mangy cat with fucked up fangs. I look at him and see a living example of a mythical deity. It's all a matter of perspective, Wade. Your perspective is not mine, but it doesn't mean I'm right and you're wrong or that you're sane and I am not."

"I'm not makin' any accusations at all. But thanks for the lecture, per-fesser. Guess you must really miss teaching, eh?"

Yves lit another cigarette, ignoring the one in the ashtray. Back and forth he paced the room, obsessively combing his hair with his free hand.

Two or three minutes went by, but he kept pacing the room and smoking. Wade could not beat around the bush any longer. "No offense, bud, but I'm kinda getting the feeling here that you've, uh... lost it."

Yves laughed for about thirty seconds. "Yeah, that's good, man. It's straightforward, profound in its own simple brutish way. Let's see if I can repeat that again, 'No offense, bud, but I'm kinda getting the feeling that you've, uh... lost it.'" He was doubled over with laughter. The last time Wade had heard laughter like this it came from a homeless man talking to a telephone pole. "Lost it, *excellent*. That's really good. I should hire you to start ghostwriting my stories." He laughed again. "You think I've lost it? Of course I fucking lost it. I lost everything in the tsunami. I lost three of my closest friends, my wife and my marriage and my oldest friend in the tsunami."

"C'mon bud, you're only forty-five or so, around my age. Time to get back on the horse that threw ya."

"Yeah, I tried a few times but got trampled under the horse, and now I'm trying to drag myself out of the way of any another runaway mares or train wreck romances. The simple fact is that I don't have the heart to go through any more betrayals or divorces. And I was never very interested in those wretched, sordid, miserable, demeaning sessions with bargirls, or 'phantom fucks' as my old partner in crime called them."

"There's plenty more fish in the sea."

"Not for me there isn't. Zara is irreplaceable. No other woman could possibly possess her abundance and combination of cleverness, talent, artistry, ambition, humor, beauty and sex appeal. She's got it all."

"She's worried about you, eh? And she still wants to hear from you."

Yves yawned and stretched his arms. "Thanks for coming over, man. It was good to see you. But I'm tired now and need to rest."

Wade checked his watch. "It's not even eight pm, but never mind. Just thought I'd drop by and tell you that I'm winding things down at the dive shop and then heading for the Caribbean."

"Ahh yes, that was where Sophia was born. Martinique, if memory serves."

"Damn right. Your memory's still sharp as a tack."

"Yeah, not everything was destroyed. Soon as I finish my latest book I'm leaving too."

"Where ya headed?"

"Another plane of existence."

"Is that with Thai Airways or AirAsia?" The smile lines bracketing Wade's mouth branched out to his cheeks.

"Ha ha ha."

"Before we bail let's hook up for a final hurrah and pound back some brewskis."

"Definitely. Take care."

They shook hands. "Take 'er easy, bud, or take 'er any way you can get 'er."

Yves suddenly hugged him. "Thanks for everything, Wade. You're a good man and I appreciate everything you've done for me."

Wade was too startled by the sudden show of emotion to register its implications until he was driving down the highway on his dirt bike. He could not shake the impression, no matter how fast he drove, that Yves had bid him a final farewell.

IT WAS GOOD AND it was sad seeing Wade again. On the good side, it was not just people who were attracted to his kind and easy-going ways. As soon as he'd sat down, White Fang came right over and jumped up in his lap. Wade grinned and looked Yves straight in the eye. "I love cats." In spite of his losses during and after the tsunami, the failure of his business and NGO, he had not become a hater. Wade still used the word love more often and more openly than any man he had ever met.

On the sad side, he could never explain to Wade the real nature of his grief. Everything else he'd said tonight was beside the point. The real crux of the matter was that he'd lied about the events of that Boxing Day morning, and those falsehoods were at the epicenter of all his troubles ever since. From there and from then on, the lies had rippled across all their lives. Wade knew it was bullshit. Zara and Stephan would have figured it out at some point. But repeating the lie was easier than admitting to the truth.

Of all the personal demons that had ever bedeviled him—physically or mentally, in liquid, pill or powder form—his own conscience was the most persistent. It was a shape-shifter, assuming the form of snakes crawling across moonlit windowpanes and impersonating voices of the dead whispering on the wind.

The only thing that might lay all these demons to rest was if he set the record straight in his book.

On the morning of that Boxing Day, he had been sleeping off a hangover, after liquidating most of Christmas with Kendall, who was staying next door, when someone began tapping lightly but insistently on the door. At first he thought it was Zara. That she'd forgotten her key.

He threw on a T-shirt, inside out, and opened the door to knives of sunlight glancing off the waves and stabbing at his eyes. Standing there, clad in a baseball cap, sunglasses and a shawl around her shoulders, was Watermelon. What did he have to do to get rid of her once and for all? Year after year, she kept coming back like a chronic case of herpes. Just when he thought he was cured of her along came another rash of sentiments, another outbreak of longing, and there she was again.

He covered his eyes. "What is it now? What's up?"

"You look sick. No problem. I take care *na*." In an instant, she slipped back into her default roles as the dutiful wife and doting mother. She swept past him, poured him a glass of water and said, "You want aspirin?" He nodded. She got him one from the bathroom. Then she made him a cup of coffee, found his cigarettes and brought him the ashtray. "Yes, I remember your number one breakfast: water, aspirin, coffee, cigarette, *chai mai*?" She put on a brave and smiley face.

"Thanks, but make this quick. I don't want Wade or Zara to know you've come here." He sat down on the bed, sipping and smoking. She sat across from him, making a point of crossing her perfect legs very slowly. Over the years she had lost almost all her whorish affectations – the sparkly silver fingernails, the two-sizes-too-small "boob tubes," the hot pants in day-glo colors, and the rude pidgin English spoken at a volume appropriate for a noisy bar, but her sexual boldness and her ability to home in on a man's fetishes and use them against him was as sharp as ever.

"I told Wade we will not get married."

Yves sat up straight. "Why did you say that? He'll be a great husband, he'll get you a visa, you can live together in a nice home in the mountains. You'd love the mountains. Jasper is like Chiang Mai."

"But I don't love Wade. I love you *na*."

"Not this again. We've already talked about this a thousand times. Love is not important. I am Mr. Wrong and I'm already married. If Zara finds out about this she'll kill both of us."

"Zara doesn't love you anymore. She loves Stephan."

The caffeine and nicotine were igniting flares in his bloodstream that made muscles in his shoulders, toes and fingers flex and tense. "Huh? You've met them twice and spoken to them for like ten minutes and now you're saying you know them better than I do?"

Watermelon crossed her perfectly formed legs again. The denim shorts left most of her thighs exposed. But far more arousing to him than her legs or her Chinese-porcelain features was her near-perfect command of English. She had been studying and practicing for years now. She'd done that to impress him and because she didn't want to teach him any more Thai or he'd flirt with too many local women, she said. "When you stay together a long time with somebody they make you blind. She walks by, he doesn't see. She says something, he doesn't hear. After love disappears, people start to disappear from each other too. My mother and father lived together for a long time but they were not together. They were two ghosts in one house. Better to break up or get divorced before that happens."

"How did Wade take the news? Did he get angry or violent?"

"No, he was crying too much."

"Crying? God, if there's one thing that disturbs me more it's seeing another man cry." The caffeine and nicotine buzz was already wearing off, replaced by tingles of nervous exhaustion creeping up his back.

"When a man has a big heart like Wade, he suffers a very big pain *na*. I was crying too because I love him like an older brother. He taught me so much and he never treated me like a bargirl, you know, fuck and flee. He always treats me like a lady." She pressed her palms against her eyes to stem the tide of tears.

Yves had seen enough of her tearful displays; she was the most emotional person he had ever met. He looked out the window of the bungalow. Zara would be back soon. He did not want her to see this. She already suspected the worst.

"Can you go now please? My wife will be back soon."

"No, she's with Stephan now. So I should stay here." She smiled while repeating a couple of more expressions he'd taught her. "Fair is fair and what is good for the goose is good for the gander." With sweet sarcasm, she added, "Thank you, my teacher."

"Just forget all the sweet talk and all the little games you like to play to try and manipulate me, and please try to remember that we don't have, and never will have, anything in common. Our interests are completely different. That is why we broke up and stopped hanging around together."

"We have many things in common. We drink water, breathe oxygen, love sunshine, enjoy good food. We like to walk on the beach and see moonlight. We love music and scary ghost movies. We like to…" she looked away and smiled coyly… "make love and do *boom boom*."

How did she do it? This woman who had slept with five hundred men and still retained a sense of girlish innocence. This teen-aged bride and mother, who'd become a twenty-year-old widow, yet never turned nasty or self-pitying.

"We haven't even slept together in like what? Six months?"

"Four months, two weeks, five days and…" she glanced at her watch and smiled at him. "About forty-two minutes, more or less *na*."

"You counted?" What other woman had ever done that for him? Even Zara, sweet as she could be, was not *that* romantic. Nobody was. Not that he'd ever known.

He had been avoiding the truth for years now. Watermelon was more devoted to him than any other woman he had ever been emotionally entangled with. It was not an intellectual or artistic love like he'd shared with Zara. With her it was religious. Love was her religion, even more so than Buddhism, and she practiced it with a fanatical devotion. All she had ever wanted from life was to be happily in love with her husband, to be a mother, a housewife and lover.

But his religion was in books and writing. He was not capable of that degree of devotion to a spouse. "I can't believe you counted. It's like the end of that Marquez novel, *Love in the Time of Cholera*."

"You always say everything like book, movie, song, but I'm talking about life, real life, not some, I don't know in English, *maya*," she said, using the Thai slang for the entertainment world, which is based on the Sanskrit word for illusion. "But it's not."

From this close, it was not her youth and beauty (that flawless complexion, those chestnut eyes, the mane of thick glossy black hair) which touched him. It was her *sincerity*. It was the way she put her whole heart and all her feelings on the line in one glance. He had always been too timid and too wary to do that, except for one night in an old dance hall in Barcelona called the Dove.

Screams made his shoulders jump. He looked out the window. It was bedlam out there. Everyone was running and shouting or standing there pointing at the ocean. Yves went out on the verandah. He used his hand as a visor to squint into the sun. In the muddy shallows, locals were stuffing fish in their pockets and satchels, but he could not see anything farther out to sea.

He went back inside. "Come on. Let's go. People are running for higher ground."

"No, I stay here. You don't love me anymore." She put on that pouty teenager's face she used to hold him to emotional ransom. "Maybe if I die you happy *na*?"

"This is no time to be repeating lines from a Thai soap opera." He went back on the veranda. Someone yelled, "Tsunami," and he ran down the stairs and across the sand towards the restaurant and the front office of the resort, where a sandy lane led to the main road.

Whenever he had replayed that moment, examining it over and over again from every possible angle, he could not remember making a conscious decision. He had not decided to abandon her; he had not decided anything. He had not even acted; he had reacted, like an animal. Frightened by a sudden noise, he had bolted in sheer terror. It wasn't that he suddenly forgot about his wife and Stephan, or that Kendall was asleep next door, for that would also imply an element of choice. He had not forgotten them, because he was no longer capable of thought. As far as he could discern, an instinct for self-preservation had overpowered his reason and nullified all of his other mental processes. Was that it? Or was it more like, driven by fear, he had fled from that which frightened him the most? His own death. Was HP Lovecraft right? "Fear is the oldest and most powerful emotion of mankind." And death had to be the greatest of all fears.

Rerunning the events and quibbling over the details was pointless. Whichever way he examined them the conclusion was the same. If he had been more conscious, he could have saved three lives. Whether or not he'd seen Yai running towards the beach to help this little girl while he ran the other way was another point he had debated over and over again.

Of every dark, rotten thing he'd seen that was connected to the disaster—the looting of corpses, the necrophilia jokes, the media vultures circling and fighting over dead bodies—that moment when he'd lost his head was the worst. He could not live with it. So he'd concocted all these other fraudulent tales to cover up for what he could only conceive of as the most despicable act of cowardice imaginable.

But maybe he could not have saved Watermelon. She would have resisted him. That was certain. To her, nothing was more romantic than dying for love, like those tragic heroines in Thai pop songs. In a perverse way, she had finally attained her heart's desire.

The only thing of hers Yves had been able to find was a pink plastic hairclip with a single strand of her hair. He left it on his altar, sitting atop the bookcase, at the base of a Buddha image showing him protected by the seven hooded heads of the Serpent King.

Maybe he couldn't have saved Kendall either. By the time he had pounded and pounded on the door to wake him up the first wave would have engulfed the bungalow and drowned both of them.

Maybe he'd done the right thing by saving himself.

Had he really seen Yai in the distance? Or was that some other Asian guy wearing a baseball hat, sunglasses and a long-sleeved shirt?

In spite of the media playing up the story of how Yai had saved the Swedish girl, and she had depicted him as a saint and Christ-like figure in an art therapy session (an easy, heartwarming story that played very well in Christian countries) Yves knew it wasn't like that. It was not an act of heroism. It was a final act of self-destruction by a man whose sense of inferiority to the rich, white and attractive Westerners he had performed for at the Snake Farm and served in the bar had finally overwhelmed him. Yai was terrified that if he did not make some good karma he would be reincarnated as a snake, as he once feared he was after being bitten by a king cobra. "Imagine explaining the real story to a CNN or BBC producer with a two-minute slot to fill," Yves had told Wade over espressos at Col's Coffin Café, which was also not featured on any of the major news networks or in any wire-service stories. "It's ironic that you can only tell the truth about these extreme stories in fiction not journalism."

During the dozens of interviews Yves had done with survivors, their worst moment in the water came when, "I couldn't see where I was. The water was too cloudy. There was no visibility. I couldn't tell up from down or right from left. That's when I really started to panic."

Losing their bearings while spinning around in a whirlpool had left many survivors with skewed recollections or memories smudged with mud and blurred by dizziness. The first Thai paramedic Yves spoke to in the district hospital in Takuapa asked him had happened. "I don't know. It all happened so fast that… I'm not really sure."

The paramedic said, "That's the thing I hear the most after any accident. 'It all happened so fast.'"

All these years later and Yves was still grappling with a situation where acts of heroism could be suicide and attempts at self-preservation the only rational response.

But one thing was clear. Wade was correct when he said he had to get back on the horse that threw him, which meant going back into the ocean for the first time since that Boxing Day.

Yves put White Fang in the basket of his motorcycle. The vicious "little monk" had come to enjoy their midnight rides, mostly because it allowed him to pursue his favorite pastime other than sleeping: maiming and killing any and all creatures smaller than him. As he drove, the headlight attracted all sorts of insects. Fang reared up on his back legs to bat them out of the air, casting a panther-huge shadow across the road that clawed at the treetops.

On the way, Yves passed through the town where the Tsunami Victim Identification Center stood. It had closed down, but the graveyard attached to it, containing some three-hundred and eighty unidentified corpses, was still open. Down the highway, lit by orange sodium lights, past another intersection where gaudy billboards advertised temple fairs, pop concerts, and sales on cement, he turned into a two-lane road that wound past two fishing trawlers sitting in the middle of a dirt lot. Washed some two kilometers from shore, the several-ton vessels had been left high and dry as memorials. Past them, kissing the coastline, lay the park and museum dedicated to the dead. Relatives and friends had decorated the long, wave-shaped tunnel with photos of the deceased and floral tributes. Because of the sunlight, many of the photos and most of the epitaphs had faded. As with the bad photocopies of the missing Yves had seen in the Phuket airport, the effect was eerie (it made the victims look like decomposing ghosts) and because it mirrored a darker truth (they were fading from everyone's memories too).

The exhibits in the museum either showcased the scientific facts behinds the tsunami or paid homage to bluebloods, politicians, monks and high-society figures who, by all appearances in the press clippings, had done more than anyone to alleviate the suffering caused by the disaster. Not a single image showed Dr. Pornthip or her team of volunteers who had slaved away for forty-five days straight, and for free, at Wat Yanyao to identify more than five thousand bodies.

The last time he'd been in there, six months ago, Yves had signed the guestbook with a line from one of his favorite books, Malcolm Lowry's *Under the Volcano*: "It's amazing how the human spirit blossoms in the shadow of the abattoir." Then he added his own tagline: "Or in my case that spirit wilts and perishes."

Signs beside the road showing a stick figure running up a hill with a series of waves behind him read: "Tsunami Hazard Zone. In case of earthquake go to high ground or inland." These blue and white had become a common sight all over the Andaman coast of southern Thailand.

He carried Fang to the middle of the beach rutted with footprints, where he set him down on the sand. "Stick around here. Don't go wandering around the pine trees over there because there might be pythons around." Oblivious as usual to his pet's requests, the stubborn prick headed straight for the screw pines.

Yves had timed his visit well. High tide was churning the ocean, and the breeze was ruffling the water, as whitecaps rolled towards the shore like thousands of hungry mouths flecked with spittle. Tentatively at first, he waded in. The water was cold. His feet sunk into the mud and he walked in slow motion, up to his knees, his crotch, his navel, in water thick and heavy as black mercury.

He was shoulder deep when something grabbed his legs. He kicked out but nothing was there. Something pushed him from behind. He groped in the water but nothing was behind him either. He turned around and tried to swim back to shore, but something pushed him back. It was though an invisible barrier had sealed him off.

He paddled and paddled but could not make any progress. The phantom force field, as if mocking his pitiful efforts, now began pushing him out to sea. The more he struggled the more forcefully it shoved him. He would not be able to keep up this up for much longer. His muscles were on fire. His arms felt waterlogged, as if they weighed thirty kilos each. Now hundreds of meters from shore, he was choking on saltwater and panting for breath.

His mind swam with images: Yai's face a demoniac mask of blood and wounds, Watermelon dismembered by the roots of a mangrove tree, then a montage of all the photos he'd taken and given artsy names to protect him from the horrible truth that he was really shooting slices of forensic pornography: "The semiotics of the sandman"; "Deconstructionism is not humanism"; "Still life with coconut shells"; "Three limbs in search of a body."

From a place that seemed both within and outside him – the waves played havoc and billiards with all the hisses and whispers of the sea – Kendall shouted, "Never swim against a rip, mate. Let it pull you out, then swim back."

So that was it. A riptide.

Sure enough, it did pull him out several hundred more meters before he could begin making the long swim back to shore.

Strafed by moonlight, the pebbly sand on the beach looked like the cremated remains of millions of people, and a cemetery for mollusks and other sea creatures that was millions of years old. On his knees and elbows, he crawled out of the water and onto the sand, hallucinating about the first creature which had ever made this journey and a Rene Magritte painting of a creature that was half man from the waist down and half fish from the waist up.

Would the beach have looked any different when dinosaurs stomped the earth some one hundred million years ago? Out here little had changed. All the great civilizations of Rome and Greece had passed and this beachscape remained the same. The Italian Renaissance waxed and waned. The British Empire came and went. All the great advancements of medicine and technology had not altered it at all.

The tsunami had come as a reminder that human life, in a universe some 3.4 billion years old, is but a blink in eternity's eye. Doomed to extinction and much more fragile than these granite boulders and screw pines, the human being is cursed with a shorter lifespan than even the leatherback turtles nesting and mating farther down the beach.

Against these overwhelming odds and forces, the miniscule creature continued its pitiful and miraculous journey, crawling and crawling, elbows scraping the sand, gasping for breath.

No friends, family members or lovers awaited him to celebrate his survival. No gods or spirits appeared to proffer miracles and offer salvation. On this ancient beach, he was all alone, except for hermit crabs skittering to and fro, cicadas pulsating shrilly, sand flies alighting on his arms and, walking towards him, a white cat with crooked fangs and a bobtail, whose eyes flashed green in the moonlight.

AS A BOY, DURING a summer spent at the family cabin beside a lake north of Montreal, Yves had stumbled across the bones of a small animal scattered beside a silver birch tree. The tree's roots, as well as wild flowers and weeds, had grown through and around those lovely bones. In the beast's yellowing jaws was an old pinecone turned brittle and brown.

So it went with the lives and memories of all his lost lovers and late friends, which had become intertwined with his. He did not need to see or talk to Zara to hold a conversation with her in his mind. She would have found that line funny, "I am but an empty vessel for the gods, ghosts and demons to inhabit and speak through." Nothing amused her like artists behaving pompously. In truth, he'd had a hard time keeping a straight face when repeating it. Yet he was serious and he was skeptical and he was waxing satirical all at the same time. Zara understood that like no one else he'd ever met.

He would never talk to her or Stephan again, but he no longer despised them. To forgive was fine, but to forget would be folly of the stupidest kind, and only encourage the possibility of future treacheries.

He did not need to see Yai or Watermelon to hold them close in his memory. They would always be a part of him.

None of this was much solace, but under the circumstances it was the best he could do. There would never be any final sense of "closure" (the word most often repeated about the victims' loved ones in the wake of the tsunami and 9/11), because there would never be an end to the memories or the guilt. Time only heals physical injuries. It cannot do that much for emotional maladies, except bring a little distance, a little more perspective, and a sighing sense of resignation.

The only closure he could hope for was finishing the book and closing that chapter of his life.

His friends were dead. He was alive. What else could he do?

He'd done everything he could think of to communicate with them. He'd tried "automatic writing" to conjure up tales and legends about them, to contact them in the Great Beyond. He had tried to continue their lives in his book. He'd consulted a "ghost doctor" and smoked that wicked concoction. Finally, in desperation, he had tried to induce a near-death experience, like Kendall had once told him about after he was shot during a riot on the streets of Bangkok.

None of Yves's efforts had given him any tangible, unassailable proof of life after death. But there had been more than a few hints. Tonight, when he'd been floundering against that riptide, Kendall appeared to have shouted in his ear not spoken in his memory. He could not remember ever discussing riptides with him. Of course, it was possible that they had talked about them and he'd forgotten about it. Then, at the eleventh hour, when he needed it most, his brain had dredged up that scrap of information. It was possible, yes, but it was equally possible that the voice had come from somewhere else—where, he could not say. The Thai shaman had told him that the membrane between this world and other planes of existence was very thin. In a desperate situation like that, it may have been torn open for just long enough for Kendall to throw him that lifeline.

ON ANY LEVEL, personal or spiritual, scientific or philosophical, it's difficult, if not impossible, to sum up the complexity and far-reaching ramifications of a catastrophe that stole or damaged so many lives, and whose shocks were felt as far away as Somalia and Alaska.

Everyone who was involved with the tsunami and its aftermath had imposed some kind of "meaning" on it to advance their own agendas and state their priorities. The religious extremists saw it as a warning sign of an imminent apocalypse or a display of God's wrath. The hedonists twisted it to serve their party line: life is short so enjoy it while you can. The environmentalists used it as a platform to harp on about coastal erosion, coral bleaching and how the disappearing mangrove forests had served as breakwaters to protect some communities. Scientists produced graphs and charts to show the shifting tectonic plates in the earth's crust and spoke of the need to better educate the public. Wildlife conservationists pointed out that a herd of elephants working on the island of Koh Phi Phi had stampeded to higher ground, thereby saving dozens of tourists riding on their backs. Anthropologists made similar claims about the Moken, an indigenous tribe of sea gypsies, who knew the receding water foretold disaster and helped tourists to evacuate in the nick of time. Politicians and bureaucrats gave press conferences about disaster relief management and the plans they had drawn up to install early warning systems. Local and international celebrities, posing for photographs while handing out supplies and visiting patients in the hospital, used it to promote themselves and their humanitarian work. The members of the mass media interviewed and parroted all of the different parties, their pretenses of objectivity shattered by who got the most airtime or quotes in a particular story.

Everyone had a point, Yves conceded, that was also beside the point.

Late at night in the almost deserted airport on Phuket, staring at the faces of the missing, now presumed dead, who stared back at him from photocopies bleached by fluorescent light, the only "sense" he could ascribe to an otherwise senseless tragedy was this:

In the end, it wasn't all that important what any of the deceased did for a living, what kind of cars they drove or what grades they got in school. Whether they were accountants or police-women, travel agents or investment bankers, most were easily replaced in their workaday lives, as we all are when our time comes, which could not be said for the pivotal parts they played in any number of domestic scenarios as wives and sons, sisters, lovers, aunts, nephews, fathers. Their absences would be most sharply felt during family reunions on national holidays, at birthday parties in living rooms and at anniversary dinners in fancy restaurants lit by candles and smiles floating in the darkness, and during the photo sessions following graduation

ceremonies when the missing person popped up in everyone's
mind but not inside the frames of any photographs.

All the dead had been loved and that was their greatest
legacy. It was why their lives mattered and why their deaths
would be mourned by their loved ones for many years to come.

Long after the politicians and scientists, the hedonists and fun-
damentalists, the bureaucrats and scholars, the celebrities, environmentalists, and reporters, had all had their say, most of it forgotten.
And long after the ceremonies starring diplomats standing by coffins draped with flags while national anthems played, and monks
chanting on a beach as illuminated balloons were launched into the
night sky to give lost souls a Thai-Buddhist sendoff, had dimmed
in everyone's memory, the only epitaph he could come up with for
Watermelon, Yai, and Kendall, Astrid, Sophia, and many others,
was six words scrawled in black ink and desperation at the bottom
of a ghostly photocopy: "I love this person. Please help!"

END

The Tuttle Story
"Books to Span
the East and West"

Many people are surprised to learn that the world's largest publisher of books on Asia had its humble beginnings in the tiny American state of Vermont. The company's founder, Charles E. Tuttle, belonged to a New England family steeped in publishing.

Tuttle's father was a noted antiquarian dealer in Rutland, Vermont. Young Charles honed his knowledge of the trade working in the family bookstore, and later in the rare books section of Columbia University Library. His passion for beautiful books—old and new—never wavered throughout his long career as a bookseller and publisher.

After graduating from Harvard, Tuttle enlisted in the military and in 1945 was sent to Tokyo to work on General Douglas MacArthur's staff. He was tasked with helping to revive the Japanese publishing industry, which had been utterly devastated by the war. After his tour of duty was completed, he left the military, married a talented and beautiful singer, Reiko Chiba, and in 1948 began several successful business ventures.

To his astonishment, Tuttle discovered that postwar Tokyo was actually a book-lover's paradise. He befriended dealers in the Kanda district and began supplying rare Japanese editions to American libraries. He also imported American books to sell to the thousands of GIs stationed in Japan. By 1949, Tuttle's business was thriving, and he opened Tokyo's very first English-language bookstore in the Takashimaya Department Store in Ginza, to great success. Two years later, he began publishing books to fulfill the growing interest of foreigners in all things Asian.

Though a westerner, Tuttle was hugely instrumental in bringing a knowledge of Japan and Asia to a world hungry for information about the East. By the time of his death in 1993, he had published over 6,000 books on Asian culture, history and art—a legacy honored by Emperor Hirohito in 1983 with the "Order of the Sacred Treasure," the highest honor Japan can bestow upon a non-Japanese.

The Tuttle company today maintains an active backlist of some 1,500 titles, many of which have been continuously in print since the 1950s and 1960s—a great testament to Charles Tuttle's skill as a publisher. More than 60 years after its founding, Tuttle Publishing is more active today than at any time in its history, still inspired by Charles Tuttle's core mission—to publish fine books to span the East and West and provide a greater understanding of each.